INCANDESCENCE

Novels by Craig Nova

TURKEY HASH
THE GEEK
INCANDESCENCE
THE GOOD SON
THE CONGRESSMAN'S DAUGHTER
TORNADO ALLEY

INCANDESCENCE

CRAIG NOVA

DELTA
FICTION

A Delta Book
Published by
Dell Publishing
a division of
Bantam Doubleday Dell Publishing Group, Inc.
666 Fifth Avenue
New York, New York 10103

ISBN: 0-385-29720-3

Reprinted by arrangement with the author

Printed in the United States of America

Published simultaneously in Canada

May 1989

10 9 8 7 6 5 4 3 2 1

BG

To Christina

INCANDESCENCE

"**Y**ou had your chance," says Enid, "and you blew it." Enid means the job in the think tank. We did some great stuff when I was there: waffles that jump out of toasters, an insecticide that makes cockroaches fuck themselves to death, luminescent smoke for nighttime skywriting, plans to stick it to the Arabs so bad they'd stand out by the camels and cry, a computer model of the universe (empty and cold: one atom per cubic meter), bacteria that eat plastic and shit honey, nasty bombs, the Stargell. If I had kept my nose clean, I'd have a helicopter to fly me down to the World Trade Center. Enid thinks I quit, which isn't true: I got fired, primarily because of the moths (Stargell, can you feel the tender, slight rustling of their wings?) and because I used the computer to play the horses. My boss, the Slasher, a whiz kid in his own right, bald at twenty-one (a man with a mind like a tennis racket: taut), looked through the universe and found, in the crab nebula, where I thought no one would find it, the day's daily double: Smiling Harry and Barbara Come One. It paid $38.40 and Enid and I spent the night at the St. Regis. It gives me the willies just thinking about it.

Enid is my wife and she knows the King of Lampur. Lampur is a small country in the Himalayas, someplace between Sikkim and Kashmir. Enid comes from the Mediterranean and her father met the king at the war college in Georgia.

Lampur publishes a paper once a month and Enid gets twenty-five copies of it by way of surface mail. The *Gazette* is meant to drum up a little tourism for Lampur, and Enid reads it religiously, even the front-page stories, which are usually something like: "Finance Minister and Chevrolet Repaired . . . New Sparkers and Plenty of Pointers. Reports of Typhoid Not True." The paper looks like the kind of thing you find in the remains of exploded firecrackers.

My name is Stargell.

The Barber runs numbers. His real name is Sal, but people only use it to his face. The Barber's store is on the corner, at the intersection of two streets that are partly residential and partly lined with warehouses. Kids have written a lot of filthy things on the walls. Some old people are standing in the cold, staring into the sky. Empty pints in brown sacks, sneaky petes, are everywhere. It's a cheerful neighborhood. Most of the cars on the street are new, but here and there you can see a Berliner, a burned-out and stripped hulk: the most pleasant thing about them is their broken glass.

I used to think the Barber just had policy, but last week I found out he was selling guns to the kids in the neighborhood. The Rimbaud of Little Italy. The Barber gives solid value for the money: M-16s.

I go into the Barber's store. He's about fifty, has a face that looks like an ax used to break up cobblestones, and his eyes are slow, the color of greasy licorice. He's drinking liquor so raw it would take your skin off.

"How you doing?" says the Barber.

"Couldn't be better," I say.

"I'm glad to hear that," says the Barber. "How about the ten bucks you owe me?"

The Barber has a pa and mistress grocery. I call her Smiling Mary. She stands behind the Barber, next to the freezer case. She's about thirty-five, has a pasty voluptuousness, Day-Glo orange hair, a face caressed by a bruise. The M-16s are in the case. Smiling Mary is the powder-house sentry. The bruise is the color of weak tea.

"What's ten bucks between friends?" I say.

"We ain't friends," says the Barber.

He looks at me and sighs. I sigh back. Sometimes we do this for five minutes at a stretch. The Barber knows I haven't got it, so why bother? That's his credo: Get what you can and fuck the rest.

"Let the ten bucks ride," says the Barber.

"You're a great man," I say.

"Go on," he says, but he's pleased. He thinks he isn't someone who beats the woman with whom he lives and who sells guns to kids.

"We'll make it fifteen," he says.

"Good," I say.

We sigh. Smiling Mary sighs.

"How about three in trade and two in cash?" I say. "I'd like a little coin of the realm."

"Ha," says the Barber. He inflates his jowls: this is the way he thinks and it makes him look as though he should be locked up, or wear one of those hats with flaps for ears. I blow my cheeks up, too. Smiling Mary glowers. For a moment I wonder whether she keeps one of the M-16s loaded. She'd go through the neighborhood like wildfire, Stargell, she'd show people what she thinks, all right.

"Four in trade and one in cash," says the Barber. "You're going to start paying juice at twenty."

This isn't idle talk: I've seen old women in the neighborhood, walking horror shows of themselves, drawn, dry, just back from scrubbing floors or picking rags. They're still paying juice on the twenty dollars they borrowed from the Barber when they were young and foolish.

"All right," I say, "O.K."

Smiling Mary touches her bruise, cradles her breasts in her folded arms.

"I'll put in your number," says the Barber.

"Good," I say.

The store itself is a space about ten feet on a side and it is in front of the counter, a plank covered with linoleum: it looks the way it should considering the deals that have been closed over it. The linoleum is turning up and is worn away in places and there are cigarette burns, as regular as the marks on Robinson Crusoe's calendar, along three sides. I take a loaf of bread from the shelf, ask for some salami and American cheese. Smiling Mary gives me three quarts of beer, too. I watch her working at the machine, moving it quickly back and forth, the blade turning with the ease of a flying saucer.

I want to tell Smiling Mary about a salami slicer I worked on in the think tank, but she'd just look as though her kidneys hurt. The cutter was built right over the scales. No more walking half the day to weigh things. My boss, the Slasher, looked at the drawings and said, I don't like Wops. Think about oil. It wasn't long before the moths took me. I think for a moment of their dry, fluttering wings, the stark kaleidoscope markings on them.

"That's four dollars," says the Barber. "Your number is fifty cents."

I look at the sad brown paper, the sack the Barber pushes at me.

"Here's four bits," he says.

Smiling Mary watches as he pushes the quarters across the counter: she looks like a submariner who's just seen a leak.

The Barber is also the local distributor for clothes that have been (let's call a spade a spade, Stargell) hijacked off trucks. The Barber is suspicious of his share of the inventory. On his left there is a Seventh Avenue rack stuffed with red-and-white plastic raincoats which have been cut to look like western shirts. The Barber says, "They ain't got no legs. They ain't moving." The rack is shoved against the refrigerator for the M-16s. At the Barber's feet are boxes of shirts in cellophane pouches: the shirts are purple and green and they remind me of Nogales, Mexicali, Tijuana, border-town madness. Once I heard the Barber say to one of his salesmen, a man who smoked a cigar and chewed gum at the same time, and who wore the Barber's clothes as a walking advertisement, "It's pure profit for you after you sell the first ten coats."

The salesman was wearing one and he looked like he had the malaria sweats.

"Yeah, sure," he said, "only they don't breathe so good."

I stare at the shirts, the fabric that looks as if it had been dyed by a color television set, and the Barber says, "Cheer up, Stargell. Have a shirt."

He picks up a green one in its cellophane sack, holds it up to me, and says, "Yeah. That looks pretty good, don't you think?"

Smiling Mary nods, even though the Barber hasn't looked at her.

"Enjoy, enjoy," says the Barber, giving me the shirt.

"Thanks," I say, thinking, Tonight I'll wear the shirt, drink a half gallon of Thunderbird, and break all the furniture. The Barber pours himself another shot of porcelain remover. I can hear glassy thunder as I open the door.

It's February and there's still snow on the ground, but I can feel the first stirrings of spring, the tick in the roots, their squirmy anticipation of light, warmth, clear water. There are four or five dogs on the street, lean, alert, and they stalk old men, wait to pull one down. The old men usually carry something from a packing crate, heavy canes, a piece of pipe. You can see them saying, Just try it, you mangy curs, just give me the chance. Women stand in the doorways and smoke cigarettes.

I check the mail, find bills for me, a letter for Enid, then climb the slate stairs, the four flights. Our apartment is not beautiful: three rooms, one of them a kitchen with a shower in it, a bedroom behind a glass door, a living room. We have some ugly furniture I bought on a heritage binge: chairs, sofa, tables, and lamps that came out of a Holiday Inn, class of '62.

"Hello!" I say.

My darling is in bed and she is asleep.

"Time to get up," I say.

I rattle the beer bottles in the sack. Darling wife hears them. She stirs. It's four o'clock in the afternoon.

The living room is filled with books and papers, a half-finished glider I've been working on, dirty plates, glasses, paper napkins, piles of dirty clothes. This is the beginning of our third year on the nuptial job. I clear a space on the table, make a plow of my forearm, then open a bottle. The carbonated hiss reminds me of my childhood and youth, days on the beach, the pale sunshine. I was born in California, almost thirty years ago. Here I sit in the dark furrows of New York, drinking a quart of Rheingold.

The bedroom is dim, shielded from the dead-man's light of the air shaft. There are stirrings within. I hear the rustle of sheets, a grunt, the squeak of a spring. Enid emerges.

"What's in the bag?" she says. Only she says "bug."

"Victuals," I say.

"What's that?" she says. English is Enid's fifth language. In the middle of a great fight, a real scar-maker, I'll scream, Stop acting like you shit ice cream cones! and she'll look puzzled, so I'll say, You are behaving with a certain amount of pretension. That may well be, she'll say. Arch as a cat.

"Salami and cheese."

Enid sits opposite me, opens a bottle of beer, drinks. There are long bubbles in the bottle's neck.

"Ah," says Enid. "Ah."

We sit opposite each other. Enid is short and dark, and her skin is the color of ripe wheat, her eyes a black that verges on purple. She has a crooked smile, which she says gives her "charm."

"Good morning," I say.

I toast her, gently clink bottles. Enid wears a long gray wrapper and it makes her look like a bird with its gray wings folded. Enid's eyes are puffy with sleep, watery with carbonation.

"I had a strange dream," says Enid. She stares at the wall beyond my shoulder where she sees some nocturnal rerun. I set myself like any pagan priest, prepare to divine, to search for headline omens.

"Yes, my dear," I say, all fifty-buck-an-hour sympathy.

"I was chewing gum and my teeth got stuck in it and then there was a big ball of teeth and gum in my mouth. My teeth came out and they were in the gum. It was terrible."

I have my suspicions about this, but I keep them to myself. Enid has enough to deny as things stand now. I make some sandwiches and we eat in silence. Enid's cheeks are full, moving. She licks her fingers.

"Yum," she says.

I can see Enid eying the third quart of beer. Always buy things in even numbers, Stargell, I think, it makes matters easier. I want the beer, too, but I'm not above sharing. Enid has stricter views of property.

"How much money do we have?" says Enid.

"Fifty cents," I say.

"We're poor," says Enid.

She looks sad, almost on the verge of tears.

"We're not alone," I say.

But Enid's not convinced. She looks at the wall, thinks about chewing a wad of gum and teeth.

Enid has delusions of European grandeur. Her father was an officer in the Greek army. Enid tells me she's short because she didn't get enough milk after the war, and she gently chastises me about the stuff America sent for Greek kids to drink. Her family (her mother's side anyway) think they can sell their blood by the ounce, as a souvenir. The old man, the ex-army officer (who took Enid to the front during the civil war, where there wasn't even any powdered milk), now has a shop in Athens. He has dreams of bringing to Greece the first flying machines for one man, those Buck Rogers jets with a harness. Until they're perfected he's contented himself with less fantastic inventions: some junk he gets from France, machines that reduce thighs and enlarge breasts. The family lost its money when a patriarch with the jack got caught by a religious high roller in Alexandria. The great-grandfather put the money into war bonds and a map to paradise. They never caught the priest. I keep asking to see the map, but no one's showing it. You can buy Egyptian bonds from the First World War by the bale.

Enid was sent to school in New York.

It's a stand-off now: the odd quart sits on the table between us.

"You want another sandwich?" I say.

"No," says Enid.

It's almost bedtime for Enid: a couple of hours of waking agony is about all she can stand. We stare at one another.

"I didn't think we'd be poor," says Enid.

"I've got a job," I say.

"Yes, dear, you do," she says.

She means that's the problem: I've been driving a cab recently.

"I know," says Enid, "I deserve as much."

This is heavy artillery, and I know Enid's serious about that last quart. She'll have a good day, you know, if she can just get that beer and climb into bed. She points at the bottle on the table and says, the way an anarchist lights a fuse, "Can I have a little more?"

"Of course," I say. "I think I'll have a glass, too."

She sours. It's not even hers yet and she's already unhappy to lose a glass. I fill a dirty tumbler, one with some whitish scum around the top. Enid stares: if a look could break glass, the tumbler would have shattered.

"There," I say.

I put the bottle down and Enid wraps her small hand around its neck, pulls the quart to her side of the table, cradles it. She takes a sip, then looks over my shoulder to the wall, where there is the afterimage of the gum and teeth.

"When I get straightened out," she says, "I'm going to dance like a black."

There are rats in the apartment and I have told Enid to think of them as pets, since they won't go away. She started laughing, and in her case, that's a bad sign.

I'm almost done with my tumbler.

"What day is it?" says Enid.

"Tuesday," I say.

I slowly reach for the bottle and Enid's face is stricken with displeasure, anger. My hand is spread out in the middle of the table. Enid picks up the bottle and brings it down on my fingers with a practiced, roach-killing motion.

"Ow," I say.

I shake my hand as though it were wet.

"That's mine," she says.

I admire the action of her wrist, the quick movement of the bottle.

"I think I'll have a sip more," I say.

She sees my eyes, recoils: she knows I'm cooking now. Enid, my darling, I'm not as safe as you think. But she has spine, the courage of her greed.

"I need the beer," she says.

"I want a sip," I say.

"No," she says. "I'm depressed."

She's going psychological on me. I can see her sink. Explanations, explanations. She'll explain her life away.

"Well, well," I say.

I drum my fingers on the table.

"I'll get better," she says.

I stare out the window, at the dead-man's light, the clothes hung across the air shaft.

"You are my own true love," she says. "You know that."

She stands, nods, bows as though accepting applause, makes a Garbo exit. I can hear her getting comfortable in bed. She sighs. I follow her into the bedroom, but she doesn't like that at all.

"There's a letter for you," I say.

I drop the envelope on the counterpane. By the handwriting I can see it's from her father: all the letters are standing at attention. Enid snaps on a light as though she were taking medicine, reads. I'm all ears. Stargell, I think, maybe the old boy will spring for a few drachmas and Enid can get her legs waxed: it's as good as a shot of dope. Enid folds the letter.

"What's up?" I say.

"My father's coming to visit," she says.

She turns out the light.

"Maybe you could drive longer hours," says Enid. "That way we could have a little more money."

This doesn't sound half bad. I enjoy the devotional, fast-like quality of a sixteen-hour shift.

"He's coming to look for a product," says Enid. "You know, to make money."

Still scheming, I think, Stargell, still on the scent. It may be a little cold, but the old hound is still quivering, has still got his nose in the wind.

"Maybe we could borrow an apartment," says Enid.

"What's wrong with this?" I say.

"Nothing," says Enid, but you can see she thinks it's not what suits quality. Let's face it, I think, the place is a dump. But as far as they go, it's not bad. Cozy. Romantic, in fact. One day we'll laugh about this so hard we'll cry.

"When's Aristotle going to arrive?" I say.

Enid looks toward the air shaft: I think she sees a big ball of gum and teeth and it's rolling right out of Macedonia.

"Next week," says Enid.

She lets me sit on the bed, but she bristles when I reach for the bottle.

"I miss my father," says Enid.

"I don't want any gun play in the apartment," I say.

"He doesn't carry a gun anymore," says Enid.

She looks at me and blinks.

"I think," she says.

The old boy used to pack one, though, a forty-five, and he menaced the happy souls around him. He'd say, You. You there. Waiter. Bring me a whiskey soda and make it snappy. He'd wave the forty-five under the waiter's nose. When he took Enid to the front, she got frostbitten feet. It always excites me when she tells it: she was left with the radio operator when the action started, and I see her in a tent in Macedonia, laughing and crawling around on a sleeping bag while the mortar shells burst in the air. The old man is all right by me. Maybe he should bring a gun, I think, and a forty-five is just the thing for nice, tight work, the kind you have to do in New York.

"He says he's got to have a product," says Enid.

I give her a chamber of commerce grin: it makes me feel fat to smile like that. I feel the old surge, too. What if the old boy makes a killing? Easy street for the kids, I'd say.

Enid pulls the covers to her chin, nestles back into the pillow, sips the beer. She squeezes my arm.

"Goodbye, my darling," she says.

I go into the living room and find my cigar box, the money coffin. Inside there's the driver's regalia, pen, watch, and clip. There's my license, too: a picture of me looking as sincere as death. It's not a bad face, really, I think, if you're in the market for one that's kind of handsome and belongs to someone who's probably looked into one secret too many.

"Comfy?" I say through the bedroom door.

"Ummmmm," says Enid.

I'd like to pop you one, I think, I'd like to give you a lick that would make the genes hum.

"Bring home some beer," says Enid.

She whispers in the dark, pulls the pillow against her cheek. My anger passes and I'm left holding the cigar box, standing before the apartment door.

"I love you," says Enid.

I take my jacket from its hook and go.

"Sweet dreams," I say.

The first time I saw Enid she was standing in the living room of an apartment that had a view of the East River. A Magritte on the wall, cut flowers, furniture that had been comfortable two hundred years ago. A man was pursuing her so eagerly I thought he was going to say, Can't you see I'm somebody? For Christ's sake, I've got a seat on the Exchange, and I've put money into a movie. Enid was sipping a drink, looking out the window, watching the silken, foam-webbed rises on the river.

"Do you play tennis?" said Exchange.

"No," said Enid.

She looked over his shoulder.

"I have a court at my place," said Exchange. "I'll teach you."

"No," said Enid.

Exchange liked her accent, and he said, "I go to foreign films."

He put his hand gently on her forearm. It was a slimy, vulgar gesture.

"Do you know what's wrong with you?" said Enid.

"No," said Exchange.

"You've been through analysis," said Enid, "and it worked."

That a girl, I thought. You're the one for me. Exchange drifted away. Later, in the bathroom, I saw him take a pill from a small silver box. Take a shower, too, Jack, I thought. Welcome back to dread. Punched out again, hmmm? Well, someone's got to wear out the couch, and it might as well be you.

"Hello," said Enid, as bright as platinum, when I stood next to her.

"You want to talk to me?" I said.

"Yes," said Enid. "You."

Later, when we were taking a shower together, she put both hands to her hair, tried to keep it dry.

"You can wash me if you want to," she said.

The Star Garage is cavernous, cold: it makes me think of potato cellars. I walk through the cold streets, over the gray leavings of winter, the drifts covered with soot: it looks more like they're decomposing than melting. I pass beautiful women. They can sense it, too. Winter dies. The wake is coming. The beautiful women smile at me, dip their heads, blush slightly. I can feel that helium rise, a lighter-than-air tug. Stargell, I think, what you need is an insured automobile, a taxi.

The day boys are breaking, and there's a line of cabs up the avenue, all flying flags of defeat, the lighted off-duty signs on every roof. The taxis come into the garage one at a time, stop at the gas pumps. Their drivers seem to have a just-back-from-the-front weariness.

Munson's the night dispatcher, a tall man, six four anyway, who has a large belly, a long face, a grin that's compounded of ulcers and dirty jokes. The night men stand behind him, just waiting for a car, each with that quality of looking away from something unpleasant. The smell of exhaust fills the cement vault: it's like living in a cool engine.

"Hey, Stargell," says Munson. "How you doing?"

"I'm feeling so good," I say, "they shouldn't let me walk the streets without a leash."

"Ha," says Munson.

He keeps his distance, though. I bob and weave, throw combinations, dwell for a moment on the mongoose, the incomparable Archie Moore.

"You going to bust chops?" says Munson.

"Yeah," I say. "Yeah. It's time to bust chops."

I'm a driving man: California was my Yale and my Harvard. The night boys seem a little grim, Stargell, everyone's got their smoke screen out. You can smell the sooty odor, the fear.

"What's up?" I say.

Munson avoids my eyes, calls a name, sends one of the boys on his way.

"They're just a little edgy," says Munson.

It's as though he were speaking of massuh-men, dumb beasts who are so low as to be running on lizards' brains: smell and light more than numbers and words. I want to kick Munson in the balls, just to remind him of the Declaration of Independence.

"No kidding," I say.

Another cab comes in and Louis the Scum, the garageman, gasses it up. I smell the execution odor.

"No kidding," I say.

Munson looks at me and says, "One of the boys got shot today."

"How's he doing?" I say.

"Fine," says Munson. "His worries are over."

I look at the gas and oil mixed with water on the floor: the spectral colors are the only lively things in the garage. The men along the wall are gray imitations of themselves. The Cowboy is there, too, and he waves. We started work together, just four months ago. We stood around, ignoring each other, the fact that we had both come to the same end of the line. A tired little alarm clock of a man made us get into the front seat of a taxi. He said, Turn on the ignition. There are your turn signals. That switch makes the meter go. The Cowboy has brown hair, a thin, hard West Virginia face, lousy teeth. He sat quietly while the instructions were hissed at us from the back seat. The Cowboy had a clipboard and he wrote everything down. The little slime who broke us in said, Remember, gas and tires are expensive. Cowboy wrote this down, too. Afterwards Cowboy and I had a cup of coffee. Jesus, he said, in his voice that sounded like a talking banjo, I just want to do something right. Every now and then I'll see him moving across town, determined, aloof, correct as newly creased pants.

I wave back to him.

Another cab pulls in.

"I'll take it," I say to Munson.

"Sure," says Munson.

I climb into the driver's seat, wait for Louis the Scum to fill the tank.

"Have fun," says Munson.

I start the engine, slap it into gear, push through the garage's blue smoke: Munson, the anxious men, the dark cavern, are gone.

Rush hour opens: short rides and low tips. Everyone's sighing, settling, letting the old paunch show. The smell of martinis fills the car. Grand Central, Penn Station, Port Authority: dread leaves the city, allows the evening to begin. The cab is filled with the scent of perfume, beautiful women. They go to dinner, the theater, parties, movies. Stargell, I think, life is grand. I listen to the nylons swish together, the sound of a firm ass on the seat. A beauty thanks me as I give her some change and I can feel her warm, damp breath on my fingers.

There's no doubt about it, Stargell, I think, you've suffered a little setback: this death-drone patrol has got to stop. It wasn't so long ago that I had prospects, expectations. Enid and I were invited to black-tie dinner parties, Fifth Avenue affairs where the butlers moved with a quiet, oiled grace. What times, Stargell. I remember the lingering perfume, the taste of dry champagne, the slick ease of an oyster. I was a freak for these people, and when I told Enid about it, she got mad. There is only one immortal, and that is snobbery. I'm not invited to lunch, or dinner, my abilities are no longer praised. But I'm not old enough to know better (that's just too fucking old), so maybe I'll kick the city in the slats, just to see it jump, just to taste champagne again, to look everyone in the eye and say, How nice to see you.

I met Barbeau at a dinner party given by a great old cripple: she had a motorized tricycle and a horn with a rubber bulb. The cripple loved to use the horn, to come up behind someone and sound off: everyone looked as though his ass had just been grabbed. Barbeau and I were seated at the same table.

"I understand you've invented some things," said Barbeau.

Barbeau was about twenty-eight. Her eyes were green and her hair had a special color. It's not blond, not silver, sometimes dark, always touched by bright specks: it's the color of deer in November.

"What things?" she said.

I knew she'd been looking for a husband, a man who had a fortune equal to her own, and who wasn't queer or dull as wet bread. She hadn't been successful. I could smell the strange whiff of desperation, her dry-ice odor. I told her about a street with hinges at the gutter (you lift up small sections with a crane: no more jackhammers), space industry (perfect ball bearings made in free fall), a recording of a tortured, teased mouse (you play it and all the mice run out of your house).

"I'm wearing silk underwear," she said, "with a slit in the crotch."

Stargell, I thought, what is this?

Our legs touched under the table. I stuttered. She spilled her wine.

"They're very comfortable," she said.

The old cripple on the tricycle had an expression on her face that said (as loud as a bullhorn), The freaks, the cowboys and astronauts are not supposed to tamper with rich and beautiful young women.

Those were the times, Stargell. They should have charged you an hourly rate for being alive.

"Is there any insanity in your family?" said Barbeau.

Yes, yes, I thought, we're all as crazy as coots. We throttled the last straight one a year before I came to New York. He's in a shallow grave, in Ventura, just over the Los Angeles county line.

Barbeau finished her glass of wine and looked at me with the eyes of a horse in a stable fire: I could see the reflection of the candle's flames.

"I want you to make me a baby."

For a moment (and longer than that) I was sure she was absolutely serious. The old bat on the tricycle came crashing through the room, almost pushing the tables and guests aside: she knew we couldn't possibly be discreet, and the crip wasn't going to have any part of that.

Barbeau was taken home by a tall, thin man. He was bald. His name was Jimmy.

She married him in about six months.

Once, after the engagement was announced, I went to visit her with one of her friends. In those days, Barbeau was big-time shrink fodder: every morning. Her fortune came from bandages. Her friend and I found her, just up from a nap, looking out the window, her face a little red. The sun was low, and I could smell that dry-ice odor, could feel her distance. She looked up and smiled, and said, "I'm sorry about the underwear."

"Do you really have them?" I said.

"Yes," she says, "but I can't show them to you."

I've kept track of Barbeau, and every night, when I start my downtown cruising, I hesitate in front of her building. I haven't seen her yet.

The end came at the think tank because of the moths: I had been reading about them, and noticed in a paper prepared by the Department of Entomology, University of California, Berkeley, that moths spend a moment or two shivering before taking off. This shivering is necessary to warm up the wing joints, which *are filled with oil.* I was sitting on the twenty-eighth floor, looking out the window, watching the sluggish beauty of the river, the white puffs of silk from the top of the generating plants. Stargell, I thought, this is it.

I had certain discretionary powers (what words: I could spend almost whatever I wanted) because of the success of the Stargell, and some other gadgets. So I ordered a hundred thousand moths, a hydraulic press, a centrifuge, rented a warehouse to put everything in, ordered, too, some stuff to refine what I had begun to think of as "moth crude." I spent about half a million, which, all things considered, is a drop in the bucket, but the Slasher didn't see it that way. I tried to explain that under ideal conditions, every six months we could have a mountain of moths, millions of barrels of oil. Two moths (under ideal conditions) can produce two trillion (of the lovely creatures) in just six generations.

"You're through in this shop," said the Slasher.

Jolting Joe, from security research, came to say goodbye when I was cleaning out my desk.

The doorman whistles: I stop the cab. Barbeau gets inside.

In a tired voice she gives me the address she wants. I drive across town, staring into the rear-view mirror. She looks a little older (it's been three years), and I can still smell the dry-ice odor. She watches the trees in the park, the snow there. I want to scream, How's the underwear? I think of you all the time, my darling. I've been lurking around your house for months, just to get a peek. My wife is crazy. Barbeau lets me see the lines of her face, her long neck. She smiles once about something, then shakes her head, lapses into the tired, drawn look of a woman who is just itching to have a good time. Do you recognize me? I think. Can you see who's driving you now?

Barbeau gets out of the taxi and walks up the steps of a brownstone. I watch her hips, their cool tug and drop in the cloth of her dress.

I'm glad to see her.

Stargell, I think, you lucky dog.

I don't even bother to think about it: I pick up a man in a flasher's raincoat. He's got his hand in his pocket.

"West Ninety-eighth," he says. "I'll tell you where to stop."

His coat is greasy, stained, and he has a hat pulled over his face, but you can still see he's as cheerful as death row.

"Step on it," he says.

The cab sounds like a trash can that's filled with pieces of glass and nuts and bolts and the trash can is about to break the sound barrier. I don't like that hand in the pocket. That looks bad. It's his right hand.

"Nice night," I say.

"Yeah," he says.

I drive on, try to forget about Death Row, calculate the length of the sine curve that moves along the computer lights: three hundred and twenty yards at the base. I try to do the summation for the curve. If he'd just take his hand out of his pocket, I think, if he'd just let me see what he's got in there.

"I'm finishing up for the night," I say.

Stargell, I think, sometimes you even amaze me: this is advertising yourself as a bank. Shit.

"Shut up and drive," says Death Row.

The atmosphere builds. I cross at Ninety-sixth Street. The intersection is filled with purple light and the corners are crowded with men who are drinking wine. The atmosphere isn't bad, even though a man is on the sidewalk, bleeding onto the concrete. You can see the holy slickness, his life reflected in it. A friend is still giving him an occasional sip. Others watch, gossip: you can see their breath, the white and floating words.

We go up Riverside Drive. The Hudson looks like dark oil and the lights from New Jersey are smeared over it. I think of seaports, harbors, the scent of diesel oil, the sound of bilge being pumped at the slip, the yellow light of a dive. The deadbeat just sits behind me, looking as happy as a man who's got mousetraps hanging from every finger.

I turn into the street he wants, climb the slight hill. There are rows of brownstones, no street lamps. The taxi idles. There are some trees on the street and they are as leafless as roots.

"Stop here," he says.

I stop the car, the meter, wait. Death Row gets out of the back seat and stands next to my window. His door slams. Stargell, I think, take a good look, make the postcard, since you may not be by this way again. I turn toward Death Row and there it is, a thirty-eight, long barrel, full belly. He taps the gun against the window and I roll it down quickly.

"Give," he says.

The light on the gun is strangely silver, hard as ice. He puts the nickel-plated barrel against my head.

"Here," I say.

I give him the box and my wallet. Death Row seems hesitant. You don't have to shoot. You really don't.

My expression says, I don't see shit, boss, and if I do, I don't remember too good. Death Row seems unsure. All right, I think, all right. Shoot then. Even murder wouldn't help scum like you. But he takes off, running, his dirty coat flopping from side to side. I watch as he disappears down the avenue.

I have a sprinter's heart, the rising sensation that comes from speed: I put the cab into gear and when I come to the intersection I'm doing sixty miles an hour. The taxi drifts into the oncoming traffic as I make the turn. Horns honk. My smile deepens. Stargell, I think, most things are great, as long as you live through them. I pass Death Row. He sees me wave as I go by, since I'm feeling as generous as an Eskimo who's just filled himself with caribou and rotting salmon. It doesn't last, though. The incandescence dies and I'm left with the certain knowledge that after ten hours behind the wheel I've only got the Barber's fifty cents. I can smell Death Row's fragrance, the stench of terror, so I pull over, open the doors, give the taxi a nice airing. On the floor, in the back seat, there are a wallet and a notebook. The notebook is the kind of thing you'd expect to find in the hands of someone who went screwy on haiku and rice: trim, neat, covered with plastic leather. The wallet has no money in it, but there's a complete set of identification. I look at a picture on one of the cards and remember the man, who was as grim as surgical clamps. He said, "Do you know of a woman who . . . you know . . . doesn't mind taking a few bucks to be slapped around? . . ."

I open the notebook and see there is only one entry. It has today's date.

Barbeau's name, telephone number, and address are written on the flyleaf.

J immy (reads Barbeau's one entry) is afraid of burglars. There have been a couple of houses broken into recently in our neighborhood. Jimmy has bought what the detective books call a "sap," and this evening when I was preparing a rib roast, Jimmy brought the sap into the kitchen and said he wanted to try it out. He hit the roast so hard he broke the ribs. We ate it later.

His problems persist.

I pull into the Star. I've got Barbeau's small notebook in one pocket, the wallet in another. The night boys are leaving their cabs and Louis the Scum is gassing them up. Louis the Scum has an assistant who takes the cabs and parks them someplace.

Munson is standing at the counter, but he sees me, comes my way.

"How's my favorite?" he says. "How's the inventor?"

I have a wounded expression, empty hands.

"What happened to your box?" says Munson.

The night boys are working on the counter, figuring their bank, their tips. They look like accountants doing the books for a Hooverville.

"I got jacked up," I say.

"That's a shame," says Munson.

His face is set with veteran concern: he's used it before.

The exhaust is at high tide. Everyone in the garage has red eyes.

"You hurt?" says Munson.

"No," I say.

"That's good," says Munson. He slaps me on the back. "That's really good."

The night men drop their cash envelopes into the safe and then they take their boxes (Don Diego, Producto, Garcia y Vega, El Primador) and leave. Each drops a shoulder and plunges into the darkness as though trying to break down a door.

"That's tough, kid," says Munson. "That's really . . . you know, awful."

"Yeah," I say.

The garage is cool as low-tide sand.

"You know what I got for ten hours work?" I say.

"Look," says Munson. He begins to turn away, looks at the

office as though it were a lifeboat. I feel like a shark. "I know how
you feel. . . ."

"I haven't got a fucking thing!"

Munson eyes expand. It looks like he's going to take my picture. Even I'm surprised, but I'm still tempted to let go completely, to take a tire iron and break the windows out of every taxi
in the garage. Munson's scared. That feels good, too. Everything
feels fucking great!

"Look," I say, "if I don't get something I'm going to pop you
one. And you aren't going to forget it."

"Sure," says Munson.

"Yeah," I say.

There are still a couple of night boys standing at the counter.
They're making small piles of bills, counting on their fingers since
they can't add. They look at Munson, and he doesn't want trouble with them, so he glances back with a face that's as good as
saying, I've got Stargell under my thumb. Everything's under
control. Tidy. I know what Munson's made of, though: sponges
and dried chicken bones.

"Shhh," says Munson. "Stop screaming."

"I'm not screaming," I say.

"These things happen," says Munson.

Holy shit, I think, he's getting philosophical. The payoff can't
be far away now.

Munson reaches into his pocket and fishes out a twenty he
keeps there for these occasions. He sticks it into my shirt pocket,
does it with a spirited paternalism, an easy concern, a slap on the
back. Munson takes care of the boys: that's what he wants us to
think. He just sends us to the front every night.

I take the twenty and my anger breaks up, dissolves, leaves me
standing in the cold, damp garage. Stargell, I think, it was a
twenty-dollar rage, one that wasn't worth breaking all the windows for.

"Get smashed," says Munson. "That's what I'd do."

I shrug. The illiterates are still struggling. I smell the air, the
exhaust: it's enough to make an oilman happy. Louis the Scum
stands near the pumps. There are no cabs there now and he
doesn't know what to do with himself. He looks like a man guard-

ing a border with a nozzle from a gasoline pump: crazy enough to
be serious but too nuts to be effective.

"It was great," I say to Munson. "The cars, the city, the
women . . ."

"Come into the office," says Munson.

We walk across the floor, the rainbow oil, up two steps, and
into the office. There are two wooden chairs (oak with slats: early
FBI), a desk that's notched with cigarette burns, an ashtray from
a tire company, a calendar with an Oriental woman on it. She's
discreetly nude, coquettish.

"Here," says Munson.

He takes a shot glass from the desk and fills it. There's an
inscription on the glass that says, "Just a swallow away," and the
picture of a bird with a tail like partly opened scissors. The liquor
is familiar, raw.

"I saw an accident," I say. "On Seventh Avenue. Pow."

I slam my hand onto the desk.

I can still hear it: the tinny, bass-drum thump, the Oriental
tinkle of glass, a moment of silence. Everyone on the street turned
toward the cars, which were locked in a steamy, leaking embrace.
Then there were screams, shouts, two drivers (great counter-
punchers when it came to insults) giving each other what for.

"Pow," I say.

Munson raises an eyebrow, pours me another shot. He has a
water tumbler and he fills that with liquor, too, then opens a little
packet that has two Alka-Seltzers inside. He drops them into the
glass. We listen to the slight oceany buzz.

"It helps," he says. "You'd be surprised."

I put the swallow glass next to the ashtray that sits on a small
tire.

"I could get a McDonald's franchise," says Munson. "What do
you think of that?"

"Lots of burgers," I say.

Munson laughs.

"You don't take me seriously," he says.

He has a hound's expression: sad, sad. I don't think a million
hamburgers would help. Munson looks at the garage the way a

horse looks at a dog food factory: with more resignation than hope.

I can feel the liquor move, it's I-love-you warmth.

Louis the Scum is standing uneasily, staring into the street. He's about forty-five, small as a jockey, quick, dirty enough to live in a gutter. I heard a rumor that his skin was growing over his shirt. He carries a briefcase to the garage and at lunchtime (about 2 A.M.) he goes into the office to eat. He opens the leather box, takes out a small cloth, some china and silver, lays the table. He has a small bottle of Pouilly-Fuissé, pâté foie, cold suprêmes champignons, broccoli vinaigrette, a small roll. Afterwards he has a cup of coffee from a Thermos. Louis the Scum looks pleased, sitting under the Oriental woman, smoking his cigarette. He closes up his meal and goes back to work. It is a way of praying.

Now he stands, still holding the nozzle, waiting for a cab.

"Well," says Munson.

"Let's open the safe," I say. "We'll take the money and go to the track."

Munson pours me another, caps the bottle with a that's-the-last-one-you'll-get twist. My difficulties tonight were three shots' worth: not bad, not good. We celebrate irritation more than tragedy.

"Seriously," says Munson, "didn't that place you worked for have any ideas?"

"You're asking me?" I say.

"You're just fucked up," says Munson. "That doesn't mean you can't remember something you might have heard."

Stargell, I think, it's nice to be asked. As a matter of fact, I'm flattered. I remember the old days, when I could pick up the paper, read the listings in the futures market, the price of Egyptian cotton, and tell you who in the Middle East had just had a hemorrhoid removed. I'm a little out of touch now. Just before the moths (*Lepidoptera heterocera,* my darlings, with their fluttered bump), everyone at the office was staring out the window and dreaming up ways to get more money into frozen French fry futures. Even the Slasher was hot and greedy.

I moon off a little. Munson sighs.

From the office you can see both the entrance and the exit of the garage. The floor is below the level of the street, so there's a descending ramp that runs from a hump at the sidewalk to the pumps, where Louis the Scum is king. Beyond the pumps there's another ramp, which leads back to the street.

"I'm feeling better," I say.

"Good," says Munson.

He sighs again. Stargell, I think, he's even beyond your help. We stare into the garage, as quietly ill at ease as two old geezers who can hear a ticking clock. A cab is in the street, idling along, straining at the bump near the entrance ramp. It looks like a large yellow bird, a fantastic creature: both doors are open. The taxi hesitates, seems to rock back and forth at the bump, then strains again and rolls forward, descends. The doors open and close a little, flap like stiff wings. Munson's face says, Something isn't right. The cab seems to be empty. It rolls slowly across the garage and up to the pumps. Louis the Scum puts the nozzle in the tank, lets the gas run.

Munson and I walk out of the office.

Louis the Scum looks inside the taxi, then jerks his head aside, as though someone were pulling his hair.

"He don't need gas," says Louis the Scum. "He's dead."

The taxi's still idling. The blue smoke rises, fills the cavernous space. I reach into the car and turn off the ignition. There's a mess on the front seat that used to be Cowboy. His life is everywhere, smeared, dripping, misting a little. Munson watches me gag.

"He's dead," I say.

Munson goes to the office to call the police. Another cab pulls into the garage, stops behind the Cowboy's. The driver is squirming at the wheel, listening to the radio. He honks the horn.

Louis the Scum says, "Shut the fuck up, you miserable scum bag."

"Yeah?" says the driver.

The driver's got the Broadway heebie-jeebies. Moving, moving, moving: he's held together with coffee and Tums, wine and aspirin.

"Yeah," says Louis the Scum. "We got a dead guy here."

"Oh," says the driver.

It must have happened close by. The Cowboy was just trying to make it home, smelling the vinyl seat, feeling the reducing-machine throb of the engine. I remember the first date with that girl, he was thinking. When we stood on the porch. I remember, but why don't I feel good at my stomach? The last thing the Cowboy saw was the neon sign outside that says "Star."

"Who is it?" says the driver.

"Cowboy," says Louis the Scum.

I go into the office. Munson is sitting at his desk, staring at the Oriental nude. I can hear the driver in the garage say, "Jesus, there's a grease job every night now."

I stand before Munson.

"That's, you know, . . ." says Munson. "Awful."

"He was a good kid," I say, "that Cowboy."

Munson stares into the garage.

"He didn't bank much," says Munson.

The police cars look like helicopters with red rotors. I can't face a cop. I can't even face Munson anymore. The red lights on the police cars are fantastic, intense: I can feel them on my face. Red seems to be a weighty light. Cowboy's lying out there in his cab, his hat full of some slime.

"I'm through," I say.

The office is filled with pulsing light: it's as insistent as a sign that says "Eats, Eats, Eats." The ambulance arrives, too. Everything is shrieking. A cop who came in from the beat is wearing a slicker and he looks like a big bird, dark wings folded. His bill, the visor of his cap, reflects the sanguine light.

"We still got to talk to the cops," says Munson.

"Not me," I say. "I'm through with this shit. I'll be around for my check."

It feels like there's a butterfly under the skin, near the eye. I shake Munson's sweaty hand.

"What are you going to do?" says Munson.

He has a jailer's knowledge. The Star has a monastic, withdrawn quality. Everybody who drives has been defeated. Munson doesn't trust the outside world too much because that's where he gets his drivers and they are a scary lot. They're all religious.

There's a shrine in every taxi, a private collection of relics. I'd like to ride along, to attend each small service.

"Ah," I say, "that's the question. That's it, all right."

I walk through the garage, past the police, the gray bird, the stuff they're taking from the front of the taxi. I admire the skill of the ambulance men, their just-another-stiff detachment.

The air outside is cool but tainted: it smells as though it had come out of an aerosol can.

Well, Stargell, I think, you're unemployed again.

I'm going to miss it, though: the rush, the speed, the lights, perfume, the jumble of addresses, chance encounters. I wouldn't even mind driving a drunk around: you know, the kind you take from girlfriend to girlfriend, from ex-wife to ex-wife. They end up crying in the back seat because no one will let them in. And there's thirty-five dollars on the meter. One said to me, Boohoo. Boohoo. I've made another mess.

It's 3 A.M. I kick a can, sing "Hail Britannia," find myself standing in front of a bakery, inhaling the fragrant odor. I can see the wheat fields in August, blond and undulant, can smell the dust at the grindstone, can hear the machinery's creaking gears. The back door of the bakery is open and there is a man dressed in white who is loading sacks of bread into a van. I find myself in something like a trance, standing on the sidewalk, smelling bread in the oven.

"Hey, bub," says the man in white, "you can't stand there all night. You O.K.?"

I smile.

"Look," I say, "that bread smells good."

"You want a loaf?" he says.

"Yeah," I say.

He gives me a loaf that's as warm as a baby. I hold it under my arm, feel the crust, as delicate as an eggshell, the springy and moist interior. The heat from the bread feels good.

"I've got some money," I say.

"I don't want no money," says the man in white. "Take the bread and beat it. Get out of here."

The delicatessen is up the street and I buy quarts of beer and a quarter pound of butter. There are women in the store, hothouse beauties, dressed with spangles and shawls: they only pause in front of mirrors, where they have no shame. They're thinking, How do I look? Am I beautiful? The deli has the odor of incense and cocaine.

I knock the snow off a low wall on Seventh Avenue, sit down there, spread the butter on the bread with my pocket knife. The bread is still warm and the butter melts. Stargell, I think, this is the place for a picnic. I watch the hothouse beauties, eat the bread. It's so good I could scream.

In the hall of my building there are small tiles with six sides. The walls are two-tone, half green, half something else. The place has the atmosphere of a hospital in southern Italy. There's one bulb burning at the end, near the staircase.

The television is on, so I know Enid is still awake. I open the door, walk through the kitchen. Enid is in the living room, before the TV. It faces her and she is sitting in the gray comet glow of its light.

"Hello!" I say.

"Shhhh," she says. "There's a movie on."

It's a love story: I can hear the people crying. The music reminds me of something I heard in an elevator. Some years ago, to be sure. Stargell, you've got to go and ride the elevators, just to see how it feels.

Enid smiles for a moment, looks up and says, "Did you bring *podikimo* a present?"

This means did I bring my mouse a slug of booze. I nod, give her a bottle from the bag. Enid has a long drink, goes back to the movie. I take off my jacket, have another piece of bread and butter, sit next to her. I touch her hand. She pulls away.

"There's a movie on," she says.

It's a sad movie and by the end Enid is crying to beat the band.
The music comes up.

"I love you," she says, "I love you."

This doesn't mean anything, though. It's just that the movie
has gotten to her. If I weren't around she would say the same
thing to the mirror. Her eyes are red.

"I'm tired," I say.

"So am I," says Enid.

I turn off the TV after we stare at a test pattern for a while. The
set is a fifteen-dollar miracle, a three-time loser at the junkshop. I
expect an engineer to show up now any day to find out why the
goddamn thing is still working. It is the perfect blend of geriatrics
and electronics: the television reminds me of an old genius. His
signal isn't strong, but it's as clear as a trout stream in July.

"Hard day?" I say.

Enid nods, pulls her gray bathrobe to her neck. She still has
some movie tears on her cheek, and I can see that she's savoring
them, clinging to a definite emotion, safe tragedy.

"Don't you be bad to me," says Enid.

We march into the bedroom. The walls are cracked and the
dark lines look like the map of some long and complicated river:
the Amazon, the Nile. I smell muddy water, hear the parrots
shriek. It's been so long I've forgotten what it's like. I try not to
touch Enid, to control myself, but I still have desires that would
make an Eighth Avenue hooker tired just thinking about them.
Maybe, Stargell, I think, you should put an ad in the newspaper,
you know, spelling everything out, a blow-by-blow description of
exactly what you want to do. There'd be a line downstairs a mile
long. Oh, yes, I think, and I'd get to start at the beginning: young,
old, fat, thin.

"Why are your teeth chattering?" says Enid. "Stop that."

I think of the early days (just over three years ago) when Enid
and I were courting. I had an apartment with a skylight and Enid
came to see me one night when it was raining. She climbed the
stairs in her wet trench coat, spoke to me in her accented, spy-
movie English. We made love beneath the lights of the city.

"Don't look at me," says Enid.

All right, I think, all right, my darling. I love you and I don't need any movie to tell me so. I turn toward the wall, leave a space between it and me so that Enid can climb in. She wants to be on the inside in case Jack the Ripper should come through the door with his chopper. He'd get me first and then Enid would have a chance of getting out alive: that's the way she tells it anyway.

I feel like I've been at sea for a year. There is glory in Enid: she has a small Attic figure, dark hair. I can smell her. I put my arm across her side, snuggle next to her, put my nose against the nape of her neck.

"No," says Enid. "I'm depressed."

It's as final as a tombstone, but the urge lingers. It makes me feel as though I've been handed a fire-and-brimstone rap. I'm squirmy, all right, and Enid knows it.

"What's wrong?" she says. "Can't you stop moving?"

"Sure," I say.

I nod my head in the dark. Life is grand, thinks Enid, I'm going to sleep. There's plenty of Bud in the icebox. She drifts, twitches. I stare into the darkness, see the cracky map on the ceiling, hear the sounds of the waking tenement, the footsteps on the stairs. Alarm clocks are going off everywhere: the building sounds like a test market for two-dollar timepieces. Enid breathes as softly as a child.

Then I'm gone, too, drifting into a high-priced horror show. Boy, I think (even when I'm having them), these are terrible dreams, Stargell, you better have your head examined. But they're pleasing in a way: the dreams are Technicolor and filled with stinging landscapes, waves as large as the swells from the Pacific in typhoon. A plucked chicken flies by. Stargell, I think, that's the moths, my darling creatures. There are other things, too, even more fantastic: lizards whisper secrets from preglacial times. Finally I end up in a house outside Paris. It's two-storied, sun-washed, has oxidized paint, a veranda, a wrought-iron balcony, shutters. The door downstairs is hung on handmade hinges. It's shady in the garden, but the house is filled with light and there, on a brown settee, I see a woman. She's about thirty and she has reddish hair that's cut short and eyes that are a reddish brown and she has long legs. We've known each other for years. The color of the cognac she drinks is the same as that of her eyes

and hair and nipples. We care for one another, are gentle, watch-
ful, considerate. We share a drink and get into bed. This isn't any
tedious affair, any shoddy business: we've been meeting for years
and know how to play each other like flutes, or tubas, or maybe a
whole marching band, but (in any case) well. The best thing is I
know what's going to happen. There is a strange light to her, an
odd glow that you can't see but is nevertheless there, as bright as
Christmas candles. We get down to business and I can see her
strain. Her head is thrown back and I can see her swallow, her
neck moving. I begin to come and I wake up and it doesn't stop
anything.

There I am, squirting all over Enid's legs.

"What," says Enid with a jump, "are you doing?"

"Nothing," I say.

Stargell, I think, this is not the kind of thing you can lie about.

"Oh, oh, oh," says Enid.

Enid stares at me, turns over, puts her hand on the back of her
leg, then jerks it away as though she'd touched a frog. She feels
sullied. Raped. You're nothing but a dirty pervert, Stargell, and
don't you forget it. The woman outside Paris dwindles, evapo-
rates. The fact of the matter is I really miss her.

"I'm going to take a shower," says Enid.

"That'll help," I say.

Enid backs away from me, then turns on her heel with a matador's flourish: Gore me if you will, she's thinking. I look at the
clock and see that it's 8 A.M. The sheets are cold and sticky. I sit
up and listen to the sound of water in the metal shower, but it
doesn't run for long, since Enid knows where to wash.

"I'm sorry," I say.

Enid is wearing a child's pink nightgown, one that covers her
to her ankles. She looks as sour as morning-after wine.

"You should control yourself," says Enid.

The room has a cold humming quality, as though the whole
place were a funny bone and somebody had just slammed a door
against it. I'm ready to start raving about the Parisian, but Enid
doesn't like it when other women are praised. Sometimes when
Enid makes a rare appearance on the street, when we go out to

the movies, I'll say, Look, there's a pretty woman. And Enid will say, Her? Why, she's just a filthy slut.

The light that comes from the air shaft looks like it has been filtered through yellow fingernails. Enid sits next to me, takes my forearm, and gives it a squeeze. We sit quietly for a moment or two, holding hands like any innocents.

"I understand," says Enid.

She squeezes my hand again, gives me a small kiss on the cheek, and climbs into my side of the bed.

"I'll sleep in the living room," I say.

Enid snuggles in the pillow.

"Yes," she says, "that will be better."

When I unfold the beartrap bed, the convertible sofa, I find it's already been made. Stargell, I think, at least she's considerate. I slip into it, feel the cold, lonely caress of the sheets. The tenement is filled with the sounds of footsteps on the slate stairs, the odor of strong coffee. The mornings are ceremonial here. I'd like a cup of that coffee, the dark liquid with the scent of Turkey and Rio. I like mine with milk that is swollen with heat, just about to bubble. I drift off, thinking of dark women, their faces halved by a veil.

I wake at an implosive pop: someone on the top floor has thrown a light bulb into the air shaft. Thank God, Stargell, you've been dealt another. I see casino hands cutting the deck, snapping up a day that's as sharp as a new card. Enid is still asleep. Our shower is made of tin, and I stand under the stream of water, hearing the Niagara splash. I'm tempted to sing, but there's enough trouble with the neighbors as it is.

Jack the Ripper, who lives downstairs, is a fan of mine. Enid has a pair of shoes that are made out of hornbeam or hickory. She says she has to wear them because her feet hurt. So she passes back and forth in a Sing Sing gait, the exercise yard half-step. When Enid's not sleeping she's walking or trying to clean the oven with a toothbrush or sticking a Q-tip soaked with Windex into the corners of our rooms. These occurrences are rare, but definite. One day there was a timid knock at the door and I answered it.

A man of about my height and weight (five eleven, one hundred and sixty-five pounds) was standing in the hall.

"I'm from downstairs," he said, pointing in that direction.

He had the face of a man who cannot understand why anyone in the world would argue.

"Look," he said, "you've got to stop walking around like that. It sounds like you're walking on my head. Please don't do it anymore."

"Sure," I said, "sure."

"My brother sent me up here," he said apologetically.

"Don't mention it," I said.

The man left and I said to Enid, "Knock it off. You're driving that guy crazy with your shoes."

Enid was pursuing the lint on the sofa with a pair of tweezers, using her pickings to make a ball of fluff that was as big as a grapefruit. "Fuck him," she said. "I'm talented, I'm beautiful. Everyone says so. When I get straightened out I'm going to dance like a black. So I can wear what I want. Don't *you* tell *me* what to do. You are a hopeless failure and I don't have to listen to anything I don't want to."

She's turned her siren on: I listen until the words run together, until there is only noise and moving lips. She glares at me and then it's back to the Q-tips and the toothbrush, the tweezers and the magnifying glass. These episodes of Enid's are a little frenzied, but at least she's moving around.

A few days after the first complaint, the urge took Enid in earnest. I came home from work and there she was, as bright as a new car. There was an eviction pile of furniture in the middle of the room, our table, both chairs, sofa (the beartrap), a desk, lamps. I stood at the door and watched her drag some of our other sad sticks from the bedroom. The floorboards are loose and every one vibrated. Usually Enid hates our furniture, our pieces of junk, but then she knew the pride of the secondhand store could be beautiful if arranged properly. She had tears of gratitude in her eyes, an expression of beatific thanks. I smoked a cigarette and was as careful as a bird watcher.

"It's three o'clock in the morning," I said.

"I had an idea," said Enid. "It couldn't wait."

I touched her trembling hands, felt the tendons as taut as cello strings. Her eyes were dark, wide, and they reflected light in a way that reminded me of broken glass.

"Let's wait until the morning," I said.

"You're being bad to me," she said.

"No," I said. "I'll help you in the morning."

"I can see through you," said Enid. "You're being bad."

Enid was winding her spring, but I was saved: someone began beating on the door so hard it was going to come right off the hinges. And if it weren't going to come off the hinges, then the frame would be knocked out of the wall. My darling thought it was Jack the Ripper and a mess of choppers, so she hid in the bedroom.

"My God, my God," said Enid.

She held two pillows to her head, bit her lip.

"Who is it?" I said.

The pounding stopped. The tin door vibrated, made a humming sound.

"Make him go away," said Enid.

I was tired, groggy: it all seemed to be happening under a strange fluorescence.

"Open the fucking door!" said Jack the Ripper.

Stargell, I thought, maybe the beast will listen to reason.

Usually through the open door you can see the light bulb that hangs from the ceiling of the hall, but I didn't see anything, aside from Jack the Ripper: he filled the entire frame, and his face looked like it had gone through a windshield. The bones in his cheeks were covered with a tender web of scar tissue. His brother, the one who first asked me to stop Enid's hard-soled walking, stood behind him. Occasionally the brother jumped up to look over Jack the Ripper's shoulder.

"He's the diplomat," said Jack.

He pointed a thumb the size of a Mason jar over his shoulder. The shorter brother had, when I could see him, an avenger's smile, and I couldn't blame him one bit. Enid had been making a hell of a noise. Stargell, I thought, just look at Jack. Just think what you could do with an army of Rippers. No problems then, my boy. Jack's shoes were large. All you needed to go with them is a pair of oars.

"He asked you to be quiet," said Jack, "didn't he?"

I squinted at the brother for a moment, then nodded, revealed some distant recognition. This didn't sit well with Jack: I could see he was a direct sort of fellow.

"Yes," I said.

"You call this being quiet?"

I shook my head. Jack looked me in the eyes.

"How come you moving the fucking furniture?" he said. "You behind on the rent?"

"No," I said, but I was thinking, Not yet.

Jack the Ripper's skin looked as though it had been made out of greasy burlap. There is an expression of simplicity in his eyes, the kind you see in the faces of lifelong model builders: everything is done by numbers, instructions.

"I ain't a diplomat," said Jack. "So this is what I'm telling you. If it ain't quiet, we're going to fight."

I nod.

"O.K.," I said.

"My brother has to move out," said Jack, "my own flesh and blood can't stay under my roof. You think I like that?"

I shake my head. Maybe Jack would like to borrow Enid. She's not flesh and blood, but she still packs a wallop.

"You listen to me," he said. "I don't make, you know, just threats."

Jack the Ripper and his brother walked away, descended. I closed the door, while thinking, Stargell, he didn't say he'd rip your arms off, didn't say he'd throw you down the air shaft. He said we'd fight, which meant he thought there'd be some resistance. That was good news.

"Is he gone?" said Enid.

"Yes," I said.

I tried to hide my feelings, but I broke into a smile that was as broad as a beach.

Enid looked suspiciously at me for a moment (smiles make her nervous) and then said, "Good. Now I can finish."

I shook my head.

"In the morning," I said.

Enid stood there, looking at me as though I'd thrown a drink in her face: proud, enraged, mythically offended. That a girl, I thought. An ounce of that will buy you a pound of ice-pick murder.

"O.K.," she said, "but I'll remember this."

We searched for the TV in the pile she'd made, moved the furniture quietly, found the Old Genius under a chair. The case was cracked and Enid had tried to fix it with glue, so everything was a little sticky. We watched a movie and Enid told me she loved me when I was changing the channels to avoid an old or unpleasant commercial.

Jack the Ripper and I became friends. I greeted him in the hall, smiled: it took a while but he began to smile back. Soon he started slapping me on the back and invited me for a beer at Scooter's, a bar next to the Barber's. Jack the Ripper turned out to be a truckdriver and a deeply religious man. He showed me the bills for his electronic equipment—a tape recorder, amplifiers, tuners, speakers, and some other stuff that was all chrome and majestic dials. His apartment looked like you could fly it to the moon. Jack only uses the equipment on Christmas, Easter, and his birthday, when he plays the Longines Symphonette Society's great moments in music album and goes into a monkish swoon. On his birthday, two weeks ago, Jack invited me to listen to the music and share a bottle of sparkling Burgundy. The wine was so sweet you could make a sandwich out of it and we drank it out of crystal glasses. When the music was over, Jack came out of the swoon, blinking away the tears.

"That's fucking beautiful," he said, "that's the real thing. Not like that crap you get on the radio."

Jack the Ripper saw me to the door.

"Thanks, Stargell," said Jack. "For sharing this with me."

I shook his hand. When he smiled you could see the creases in his scars.

"Will you listen at Easter?" said Jack.

"If you'll let me," I said.

Jack filled up his glass with sparkling Burgundy, closed the door, left me in the hall. As I climbed the stairs I could hear what was Jack's favorite, the "1812 Overture." He explained to me that his version had real cannons in it, and I heard them banging away. I knew he sat in his chair that looks like it had been upholstered with opera robes, that he swooned, felt himself drawn into the music's slug-of-booze warmth. His scarred face smiled at the cannons. Happy birthday, Jack. Say hello to Chopin when you see him.

The next morning I saw carpenters putting plywood into the frame of one of the windows at Scooter's. On the sidewalk there were the dark stains of dried blood, long triangles of glass, pieces that looked like cross sections of icicles. Scooter was watching the carpenters, and he told me that Jack the Ripper had thrown a tourist, a man from East Eighty-first Street, through the window.

Scooter is about five ten, a man who wears "snappy" clothes and stylish glasses. He wants to join a country club and then he'll think he has it made. He looks like a bug with a layer cut.

Jack the Ripper had been sitting at the bar, saying over and over to Scooter, How come I'm getting old? How come? I don't feel no older. And everything seems so cheap these days. Good hi-fi equipment costs a fortune. A fucking fortune. Jack sat there, brooding, and the tourist from East Eighty-first Street came in, cheerful as a sunrise, and Jack reached out and squeezed the guy's shoulder.

"I heard the collarbone snap like a broomstick," said Scooter. "Then the next thing I know it's raining glass. Some people from out of the neighborhood should watch where they drink."

I looked at the broken glass, the ink-blot stains on the sidewalk, and thought, True, true.

"Remember, Stargell," said Scooter. "I didn't say anything bad about him." Scooter meant Jack the Ripper. "When you see him you tell him he can do anything he wants in my place. Anything at all. Usually he isn't, you know, so vociferous."

Scooter smiled when he said this: he'd been doing some word-power building on the sly. Stargell, I thought, this is a good sign. Soon we'll be having spelling bees, and the winner will drink on the house.

I stand in the shower, listening to the artificial thunder, the rumble of the tin stall. Enid is still asleep.

Well, well, I think, unemployed again.

I have a sandwich with hot mustard for breakfast, read yesterday's paper, get my mail, bills marked "Final Notice." Soon, Stargell, I think, they'll be beating on the door. How will that make Enid feel?

Hours pass. Enid hangs on to sleep with a pipe-wrench grip. At four-thirty I become alarmed, begin to think that Enid might do herself some harm. Brain damage seems to be a possibility. Stargell, I think, maybe Enid was bitten by a tsetse fly. She shakes her head when I try to wake her, but then submits when I promise her beer. Enid walks through the living room and sits down at the table. She looks like she's been shooting smack.

"I had a strange dream," says Enid.

I open a quart of beer and drink.

"Hey," says Enid. "That's mine."

I pour her some beer, too, into a tumbler with a foamy residue on it.

"Did you ask last night about driving extra hours?" says Enid.

"No," I say.

Enid flares, drinks her beer. I can see the coals were just smoldering under the ashes, the gray dust of sleep.

"Were tips good last night?" says Enid.

"No," I say.

"Why didn't you ask?" says Enid.

"I didn't get the chance," I say.

Enid fills her glass, smolders, drinks.

"I'll bet that's not true," says Enid. "I know how you are."

"How am I?" I say.

"Bad," says Enid.

Stargell, I think, you've played right into her hands. Both of us smile.

"I got jacked up last night," I say.

"You what?" says Enid.

"I got robbed," I say. "They took my money."

"Oh," says Enid. "That's too bad."

It's all for the best, since I was just begging for a piece of the ranch. Someone was going to give it to me, too. I think for a moment of Cowboy.

"Maybe they'll feel sorry for you," says Enid. "Maybe they'll let you drive extra hours."

I look at the floor.

"I quit," I say.

"What?" says Enid. "What about the rent? What about my father?"

Enid breaks into the old boohoo. I touch her but she recoils as though I had dropped something slimy on her. This big-league crying cheers me up, because I didn't think Enid still had it in her. Things can't be so bad after all. If it had been me they'd shot, she would have said, "That bastard. I always knew he'd do something like this. What am I going to do now?"

"Look," I say.

Enid closes her eyes, boohoos, only stops to hiccup and sip beer.

"They shot some guys at the garage," I say.

"They didn't shoot you," she says, "did they?"

She's my wonder: mind like a steel trap.

"No," I say.

"Well?" says Enid.

"You know what I made last night?" I say.

Enid shakes her head. Her tears are as thick as baby oil.

"I didn't make one fucking cent!"

She looks like she caught her finger in a rattrap: hurt, surprised. Enid trembles, recoils. My hands are waving around in the air, picking at one another, jumping on the table. This is it, Stargell, I think, we'll stay right here, Enid crying, me raving, until an emergency squad arrives with blue pills and kind words. I wouldn't mind a little advice from the rescue handbook, the sound of a gravelly voice, the look of a sniper's sure gaze.

"You're being bad to me," says Enid.

I nod my head.

"We're poor," says Enid.

"That's right," I say, "we haven't got bean one."

I subscribe to the car crash theory of life: take as much as you can head on and pray you walk away from it. When I started to drive a cab, Enid wanted to know if she could be sued for any damages I did.

"You didn't tell me we'd be poor," says Enid.

"It's just as big a surprise to me as it is to you," I say.

"What about my father?" says Enid.

"He'll see us for what we are," I say.

"But I don't want that," she says.

"I see," I say.

Enid wants to rub the old country's face in it. She wants to say, You see, I'm beautiful, we live on heavy cream and caviar. Her father's eyes will be as big as bowling balls, and he will treat her with respect.

"I'll get some money," I say.

Enid takes a handkerchief from her sleeve and gives her nose a nice blow.

"How much?" she says.

"Five hundred," I say. "We'll be able to show Ari a pretty good time on that."

Enid fingers her handkerchief.

"My mother didn't want to have me," she says, as mournful as a student of philosophy. "When her time came she wouldn't even lie in bed. She had me squatting in the middle of the room."

All right, Stargell, you pinchpenny.

"How about seven fifty?" I say.

"That's better," says Enid.

"A thousand," I say.

"Yes," says Enid, breaking into a heartfelt smile. "That would be best."

She dries her eyes, puts the handkerchief back into the sleeve of her robe. Enid pulls back the curtain, looks at the jaundiced light of the air shaft, smiles. Her eyes fill with tears again and she says, "That would be wonderful."

As I walk down the stairs I listen to the arguing of the unemployed. The tenement is like a shelf, or a library, of useless people. They don't know it yet and they're mad. I like the rising sound of their voices, the thundering of men with deep chests, the quick words of women with beautiful mouths. Maybe, Stargell, I think, today's the day the social worker is going to take it on the ear. Maybe they'll paste the bastard right on the kisser.

"Sal," I say to the Barber, "you're going to be feeling great after I'm done with you."

The Barber sits on his stool, sips his coffee. He looks strangely Arabic today, as though he were sitting in the center of a shop the size of a telephone booth. He's drinking his coffee from a demitasse and his finger is curled so perfectly that I would like to hang a coat on it. Smiling Mary looks like she's just swallowed a cockroach. Her bruise is wearing out, although the Barber wouldn't need much encouragement to improve on his handiwork.

"I ain't feeling so good this afternoon," says the Barber.

Stargell, I think, death will never take the Barber by surprise, since he's always looking for it. This hypochondria allows him moral lapses that are forbidden to other people. The Barber thinks, I'm dying, so fuck you.

"Look, Sal," I say to the Barber, "I need money."

The Barber raises an eyebrow with a flourish.

"Ah," says the Barber. "Stargell needs money."

Smiling Mary nods at her station next to the freezer filled with M-16s. I notice the Barber works with his right hand. Smiling Mary only has a bruise on the left side.

"Yeah," I say.

The Barber wheezes, sits as though he were in some languid trance, sniffles. The pink-and-white neon sign in the front window

makes a buzzing sound: the Barber keeps it for sentimental rea-
sons since the beer it advertises has gone out of business.

"How much do you want?" says the Barber.

I take the stool on the customer's side of the counter. The
Barber's still in a half trance, his eyes still as dull as dusty marble.
He speaks sloppily, and his voice sounds like someone walking
with a boot filled up with water.

"A thousand dollars," I say.

"Stargell, Stargell," says the Barber. "You ought to be
ashamed."

Smiling Mary swallows, almost chokes. You can see she wants
to throw herself down on the floor and slobber. I'm already paying the price. I have to listen to the Barber in the pulpit.

"A thousand dollars," says the Barber, "a thousand."

"That's right," I say.

I feel myself perk up: it's like the old days, Stargell, when you
thought you could tell the Shah to eat shit.

The Barber rises, too. For a moment he lets the mask drop, lets
me see what his friendship is. When he smiles I can hear thumbs
snapping all over town.

"How long do you want it for?" says the Barber.

"A month," I say.

The Barber nods.

"Look," he says, "I'll sell you a carbine. You can go up to the
bank."

The Barber chuckles and Smiling Mary puts her hand on her
sore kidney. I shake my head. It would be great, though, to take
some hostages and issue demands. Maybe I could trade Enid for a
Parisian beauty. Enid would probably like France, too, where she
could sit around and talk about Pascal.

"No," I say.

"What do you want it for?" says the Barber.

"It has to do," I say, "with international trade."

I feel like the pharmacist is explaining to me in front of a bunch
of teen-agers how to use an ointment for an itch. I blush.

"International trade," says the Barber.

"Yeah," I say, "like between here and Greece."

"In-laws," says the Barber. "Stargell, my heart goes out to you."

In the cooler behind the Barber's head I can see the cheerful cans of soft drinks. There was a soda pop company that hired the think tank to promote the recycling of cans. I tried to convince them to build a plane out of old beer and soda containers. I see it as a bi-plane, its skin made from a quilt of Coke and Seven-Up and Budweiser labels: Tuborg, Miller, Hawaiian Punch logos flash in the smoky air. I'm at the controls and the plane flies through the reddish air over Pittsburgh. I can feel the awkward shudder, the nauseating vibrations of the flattened cans.

"You're a great man, Sal," I say.

"Sure," says the Barber. "Everyone's a great man when you want to borrow a thousand dollars."

"Wise, too," I say.

The Barber rises to this like a cat that wants to be petted.

"It's going to be five for six. Two pops a month."

Gad, I think. The Barber isn't kidding. I think how wonderful Enid will feel. Maybe she'll get out of bed and we'll go for a walk the way we did before we were married.

"That's four hundred a month," I say, "just in interest."

The Barber turns into an Arab again. Smiling Mary has an auto-da-fé sincerity.

"Take it or leave it," says the Barber.

I can see Enid's trembling fingers, her glad smile.

"We're in business, Sal," I say.

I slap him on the back and he spills some of his coffee.

"What do you think this is," says the Barber, "the stinking Kiwanis?"

Smiling Mary glides through the room as if she were filled with greasy ball bearings, picks up the cup, and disappears. I hope Smiling Mary has an M-16 of her own, just to keep the Barber on the up and up. She brings the demitasse back with a little bit of coffee in it, just a touch, but the coffee is strong enough to dissolve rubber.

"Here," says the Barber.

There's a contraption of some kind under the counter and the

Barber works it with both hands. He pushes toward me a dusty, heavy pile of money.

"You're thirty short," I say, after leafing through it. This surprises me, since the Barber seems above short change. I give him my most severe expression, the look of a hypocrite who, for once, is firmly in the right.

"Your number," says the Barber. "I put in your number for the next month."

Prospects, too, Stargell, I think. Things are really moving now.

"God go with you," says the Barber. "I'll see you in a month. With the fucking money."

I take the date of the day of judgment without batting an eye, to show I'm as responsible as anybody else. Enid will get out of bed and we'll eat fried squid and stand in Grand Central, just to feel the space. Enid will giggle, hold my arm, and say, You're a treasure, Stargell, that's what you are.

"You know Torre?" says the Barber.

He means Jack the Ripper.

"We're the best of friends," I say.

"You know how he got that electronic equipment?" says the Barber.

"No," I say, but I'm beginning to have my suspicions.

"He got that electronic equipment by collecting for me from deadbeats who owe me money," says the Barber. "See you in a month."

Smiling Mary lets her face twitch happily for a while. The Barber looks like he's going to sell some rugs today. All he needs is a turban and a long clay pipe.

Once in the think tank I had to meet the assistant director of the CIA, a man who looked like the picture on the label of a bottle of Old Grand-Dad. He was in charge of "dark work" and I could feel the dead souls rustling around him.

"You be polite to him," said the Slasher. The Slasher's idea of a good time was a light show and an enema. He had discipline and a high IQ.

Old Grand-Dad had come to the think tank because he was selling timber off some land he owned and wanted to be sure the logger wasn't cheating him. The think tank came up with a double marking arrangement (each tree marked twice, once with blue paint, once with some stuff that was only visible under ultraviolet light). If Old Grand-Dad found a stump that didn't have both marks, he'd know he'd been cheated.

I explained this to him in a restaurant.

"Yes," he said, "oh, yes."

He laughed. We drank a lot.

"You're a nice young man," he said, "and here's my advice. Wear a Brooks suit and do whatever the hell you want."

I climb the stairs to our apartment.

"Here," I say to Enid.

The money is spread on the table before her. Enid looks at me as though I had just escaped from a polio poster, begins to cry.

"What's wrong?" I say.

Stargell, I think, it's a happy end.

"It's just dirty loan shark money," says Enid.

"It buys beer like any other kind," I say.

"Thank God," says Enid.

She continues crying warm tears which drop onto the bills.

"You do your best," says Enid with a kind of noblesse oblige. She thinks she's in a movie, but I don't mind.

Enid, of course, decides to spend the money. If she had thrown it away I would have been insulted and probably would have smacked her so hard it would have sounded like the Ringmaster cracking the black whip.

Enid sits at the table, staring at the bookshelves, picks at some balsa wood from the glider I'm building: it looks like the skeleton of a large bird. I like to put the Japanese silk on the frame, to feel it become taut as a drum. I know what Enid is thinking of our prospects, of the time when she was filled with hope. She still remembers the day a Nobel Prize winner called to speak to me.

"What's happened to you, Stargell?" she says.

"I don't know," I say, kissing her hands, the tears on them. "I really don't know."

Not that I care. Things are looking up, Stargell, I think, and don't you forget it.

We prepare for Aristotle's arrival. Enid gets out of bed at noon, which is an improvement. We open windows, clean house, wash the clothes. They were getting a little rank, but now sheets and towels, shirts and trousers, smell of Clorox and soap. The house smells of ozone from the vacuum cleaner. I think we should leave the dump alone, though: polishing it up somehow makes it worse. It has the feeling of a man combing the last of his hair over his bald spot.

A week passes. I buy cut flowers. We go to the supermarket, where Enid gets frightened, but we make it through the shopping list. Greek specialities are in the oven, being baked for Aristotle.

"Do you think it looks O.K.?" says Enid, pointing to the living room.

"Fit for a king," I say.

Enid has made some cushions: she does this with the same enthusiasm she gives to her toothbrush and Q-tip work. When her difficulties first began, the apartment looked like a warehouse of gaudy pillows. Sometimes I think there's some connection between Greece and Fourteenth Street. The new cushions could have been cut from a bullfighter's vest. Enid blinks at them, gives them a satisfied motherly pat.

"Maybe it'll be O.K.," says Enid.

She's not seeing the place clearly, and that's for the best. A jolt of insane crying now and Aristotle might get violent. I polish up the TV. The living room has a cheerful countdown atmosphere, since Aristotle should be arriving any second.

"How about a little beer?" says Enid.

She's wearing a silk dress which has been scorched by the iron, and her fingers are stained with nicotine, but her hair is clean and brushed. I know she sees herself in a sunroom, with servants, Queen Anne chairs among the plants.

"No," I say.

"There's some in the icebox," says Enid. "Yum."

"Aristotle's going to come," I say.

"He wouldn't mind," says Enid. "I really love him."

She stares at me with her half-smile, speaks with an accent, but I gave up being charmed when I couldn't get her out of bed.

"I know," I say.

"Then let's have a little something."

She goes to the icebox, pours out two glassfuls. This gentility is a sign of her love for her father. Once I came home from driving the hack and Enid was tipping a bottle of liquor straight up. "At least," I said, "you could put it in a glass." "No," said Enid. "This way you get as much as you want."

"You remember when we were first together?" says Enid.

She savors the memory: it's as though she had something tasty in her mouth. She flinches when I take her hand.

"What plans we had," says Enid.

I was going to be a film director, a politician, a mogul, a circus clown: just thinking about it gives me the kind of chills you get when someone steps across your grave. Stargell, I think, the city hasn't seen the last of you yet.

Enid closes her eyes.

"Oh," she says. "Oh."

She starts on the ouzo.

"That's for Aristotle," I say.

"I really miss him," she says.

We sit quietly for a moment, listening to the sound of the lamb in the oven.

"You and I were nice to one another," says Enid. "We made love under the skylight. You remember?"

Enid acted like she'd escaped from a nunnery, and I'm still pretty sure that we were the only ones to have done such things. The city protected us. Even the bums were fantastic. I saw one digging in a trash can, where he found a bunch of rotten bananas. He was drinking a diet soda. He held the bananas and looked up at me and said, "Look. A whole bunch of bananas. I need bananas because I haven't got any teeth." He started to cry tears of joy. Once, late at night, we were the only passengers on a bus, and we sat in the back, huddled together, watching Central Park slide by. The driver could feel it, too, our youth, dreams, visions. He let us off on the West Side.

Enid takes her ouzo in small, quick jolts, then drifts for a while, closes her eyes, smells the spinach pies and lamb in the oven.

"Baby, baby, I love you," sings Enid.

It's a wonder what a little cash will do, I think. Enid's voice is jagged: if it were a bottle it would have been thrown out the window of a car moving at seventy miles an hour. She breaks off, stumbles over the words, then rights herself and comes out of the tunnel of confusion singing a bouzouki song in Greek. I don't know the words, but it doesn't sound happy. I can see Turkey shimmering in the heat, can smell the harsh hashish. Veiled women beckon. Enid takes another slug.

"We were all right then," says Enid.

Enid is sending signs, personal smoke signals, and I know she's getting ready to blow her top, just like Krakatoa. She weaves a little, stares at me with a wavering, inconsistent expression.

"It's just dirty loan shark money," she says, "from that terrible man in the grocery."

"The Barber's not so bad," I say.

"Yes he is," says Enid. "And my God. The slut he lives with."

The food in the oven smells good. I want to defend Smiling Mary, but Aristotle's going to arrive soon. Let's keep everything mellow for Aristotle.

"What are we going to do for money?" says Enid.

"I'll get a job," I say.

"What can you do?" says Enid. "You're just worthless."

"I'll get a job," I say.

I relish the prospect, the outcast feeling, pounding the pavement in my gray suit, the one in which I was married. I'll hold a copy of the paper, folded to the classified ad section.

"I'll look in the paper," I say.

"The paper," says Enid, as though she were a champion who had been offered a match with a bum, a real plodder. She turns up her nose.

"If that doesn't work," I say, "there are my inventions."

I tell her about my salami slicer, make drawings, do quick calculations (man-years saved), show profits.

Enid sighs into her glass.

"You do your best," she says.

I take the lamb and the spinach pies out of the oven, and Enid sails along, drinking and humming. She stands and dances, then strolls around the apartment, straightening things, looking at me with the same expression she'd have if she were trying to find my picture in a pile of mug shots. Our rooms have that baking, warm, just-from-the-oven odor. The paint on the ceiling is curled, chipped, delicate as an ancient scroll. Enid turns on the radio, pokes at our furniture.

"I should have been an acrobat," she says.

I agree.

"You don't believe me," she says.

"I do," I say.

"I'll do a flip," she says. "I'll do it like they do in the circus."

"I believe you," I say.

Enid wants to prove her theories, her smoldering explanations for the way things are.

"Don't you be bad to me," she says.

"Sit down," I say, "sit down over here."

"Don't you touch me," says Enid.

She lets out a scream that makes me squint. I think she's been bitten by a snake, that Jack the Ripper has come through the door, that her underwear is filled with leeches. There is the faint ghost of her voice in the tinny hum of the shower. Enid stops screaming and begins to leak tears that are as clear as ouzo.

"You've got to be good to me," says Enid. "I'm depressed."

She says "depressed" as though it were a brand name or a nationality.

"You've got to take care of me," says Enid. "Will you take care of me?"

Enid breaks out the old boohoo and gives it a run for the money. She's cried so hard that it looks for a moment as though she were dissolving inside and leaking out of her eyes, so hard that I find myself thinking of the corner of a windshield in a cloudburst. Enid is small (actually, she's a little stunted: maybe

she's right to accuse me about the milk), but she makes up for it
with noise and movement. She cries so hard that she gets the
hiccups. I try to reach out to her, to comfort her, but through the
hiccups and tears she says, "Don't touch . . . me, *me* . . . you
. . . you . . . scum . . . scum *bug.*"

Enid sits in her chair for a while, leaking like a broken pipe,
and then she gets up and goes into the kitchen, where she has
another slug. Her dress is a little wrinkled, but she doesn't mind,
since we only have a small mirror that acts as a kind of porthole
on your face. There is, however, the smell of scorched silk about
her. Enid stands in the kitchen, hiccuping in a prayful frenzy,
walks back to the living room, sits down opposite me. I can see
that she wants to look dignified, and she pulls it off in a drugged
sort of way.

The hiccups stop.

"I feel wonderful," says Enid.

There is a hammering on the door, not as loud as Jack the
Ripper's pounding, but one that still sounds like someone in the
hall means business. When Enid stands up she doesn't realize that
she's falling over, and her ramrod posture makes her fall like an
ironing board. I catch her before she does herself an injury.

The pounding continues.

Enid turns to me and is about to say something, but then decides against it. She looks as though there were a mouse in her
mouth, running back and forth, from one cheek to another. Enid
opens the door. Aristotle stands in the hall.

He's about forty-eight, stocky, broad, and he looks grim. Aristotle has a hound's-tooth coat, a pair of purple pants, a shirt that
is strangely luminescent. He's balding, and what's left of his hair
has been dyed red.

Enid and Aristotle jabber at one another in their language and
it sounds to me like a parrot in a garbage disposal.

"Father," says Enid in English, with her onstage voice, "what's
happened to your hair?"

"A friend," says Aristotle, "gave me a potion to stop baldness. It turned my hair red."

He smiles as though he had grown a tomato and it had won a prize.

"So this is your husband," says Aristotle.

I give him a firm handshake, the I'll-storm-the-machine-gun-nest grip, and I stare into his (regrettably) recognizable gaze. He takes my measure twice, his eyes moving up and down as regularly as a railroad signal. I'm braced, just like a cadet. He has a military bearing, a pleasant smile, fatherly concern for Enid. I seem to pass muster, but not by much. Aristotle has manners, too: he takes the dump in with one look and doesn't even flinch. I like the old fart. Stargell, I think, maybe we'll get smashed together and go to look at the belly dancers.

Enid closes the door and erupts, turns into a human Roman candle, makes liquid fireworks: she vomits all over the kitchen. Aristotle and I make a move toward her but she turns to face us, still squirting, in convulsive throbs, still shooting a warm, acidic fluid. We jump back. Enid tries to say something, but it sounds like she's under water. Aristotle and I stare at her in amazement, since we've never seen such vomiting before. I'm tempted to sit and watch, but Enid looks like she's going to break something. I grab her, hold her, stroke her hair. She stops, but she's trembling and gasping for air. I wash her face in the kitchen sink, gently dry it with a towel.

"Oh," says Enid. "Oh."

Aristotle sits in the living room.

"How dare you," says Enid, just before falling asleep.

I have her in a groom's lift and I carry her past Aristotle and into the bedroom, where I make her comfortable. She's already snoring the hinges out of the door. Stargell, I think, at least the booze swept her through the whole performance before she had a chance to boohoo for Aristotle: she looked just like someone getting sick. I didn't get a chance to see if Aristotle had his forty-five.

I go back to the living room.

Ari has found the Barber's present, the green shirt.

"This is a nice shirt," says Ari, holding it up to the light. I can hear his fingers crinkling the cellophane, trying to feel the fabric.

"Would you like it?" I say.

"Me?" says Ari.

I rip open the cellophane, hold it up to him.

"It's perfect," I say.

Ari puts it on: I notice a little spring in his step, as though he were a peacock trying to balance himself with his tail feathers spread.

He glances at the bedroom.

"Is she all right?" says Aristotle.

"Sure," I say. "Couldn't be better."

Aristotle looks suspiciously at me.

"It was the excitement," I say. "She gets excited."

Aristotle glances at the bedroom and then at me. Stargell, I think, the man's as lucid as crystal. His red hair looks like the dye for it had come on a flying saucer: it's an unearthly, metallic color. Vanity, vanity, I think. The man wants to be young. He wants to have hair on his head. I want to shake his hand: at least he isn't taking the kick in the chops without putting a little lotion on his head.

"Would you like some lamb?" I say.

"You have a lamb?" he says.

His eyebrows shoot up as though they're on strings.

"Just out of the oven," I say. "And spinach pies, too."

"I have a bottle of retsina," says Aristotle.

He takes the bottle from the bag and gives it to me. I carve the lamb quickly, and with a flourish. Aristotle nods, approves. There are roast potatoes in the pan and I put them into one of the ugliest dishes in the world. It's made out of green glass and whatever's inside looks like it has spoiled in a jungle. The table is set, but I spend a moment or two cleaning up after darling wife.

"This is good lamb," says Ari.

He's right, too. We eat with survivors' appetites. As a matter of fact, it's so delicious that I think about waking Enid, but then decide against it since she'd just be insulted. Nothing like a little home-cooked food, Stargell, to set the compass. Ari doesn't say a word, but I know he agrees: his cheeks are full, moving. He smacks his lips and has more wine.

"Ah," says Ari.

He smiles at the joint. I carve more meat, and we eat again, finish the last of the potatoes, the juices in the pan, the last spinach pie. Ari gnaws a bone, the leg of the lamb, while I bring out the ouzo. The wine is gone. The ouzo was in the freezer and it's so cold it makes my nose ache.

We toast one another's health. I toast Enid. Ari toasts her mother. We toast the lamb.

"I have come," says Ari, "for a product."

This is the way it begins, I think, all the greats started this way. John D., Howard H., all the money heavies. Here we sit in a Portuguese tenement and Aristotle is looking for a product.

"I'll help you," I say.

We toast my assistance.

"Look," I say, "how about some belly dancers?"

"Belly dancers?" says Ari. "You have them in the city?"

Ari's already standing up, looking for his coat.

"Belly dancers," he says. "Yes."

"Are you tired?" I say.

Ari gives me a look that would wilt a cactus. Stargell, I think, you should remember that he has dyed his hair red because he was getting old and going bald.

"I slept on the plane," says Ari.

I check on Enid and find that she's snoring, happy, calm. I leave a note for her in case she should wake and I give her a kiss, too. It's best to do it when she can't complain.

Stargell, I think, there it is. There's the relic. I see Ari sticking the forty-five into his coat pocket.

"For the thieves," says Ari with the natural air of a man who is always armed.

They usually want cash, I think, but maybe they'll settle for a gun. Who knows? I put on a coat, gently close the door. Ari and I stand in the hall, under the dim light bulb there. We descend and I see our shadows collecting in fuzzy pools at our feet.

I hail a taxi, pray the driver doesn't recognize me, since I don't think Ari would understand. The driver has the look of a double-shift zombie and he doesn't care about anything. He drives so fast the hack trembles. It reminds me of my best times, when the city was greased, slick, open, when the lights beckoned, when a hack was running so well I could feel the pistons tingling in my fingertips. Ari is bouncing from side to side, holding his hair over his bald spot. I'm so excited I want to climb into the front seat and take the wheel. My foot is on the floor.

"Do you think he'll kill us?" says Ari.

Ari looks a little stricken, but not much: he's a veteran of hand-to-hand combat, the death willies, his own crackpot enthusiasms.

"No," I say. "Everything's all right."

"They're worse here than in Athens," says Ari.

I bite my tongue, but I was about to scream, Athens! What the hell do they know about driving a hack in Athens? The old fart might be hurt by this, so I keep my mouth shut. Especially since he's carrying the forty-five.

We move west on Fourteenth Street, pass the closed stores, the goods (actually, the products) that are imprisoned, held behind bars and harsh metallic nets. The avenues tick off: Fifth, Sixth, Seventh. When we come to Eighth, the driver crosses to the south side of the street, into the oncoming traffic, so that he can make the turn. The hack seems to shudder, quake: it makes a sliding motion that takes us from side to side as though we were on skis. You can see the sine curve in the lights, the easy wave as the signals change ahead of us.

"Do you mind if I take a few of these lights?" says the driver.

He means the lights that are turning red.

Take them, I think, take them!

"He should slow down," says Ari.

I look concerned, bounce from side to side, but I'm just trying to see the street ahead. It's as deserted as a shopping center's parking lot on New Year's Day. Shit, I think, let him go for it.

"You go slow," says Ari.

I think Ari's screaming, but I can't tell, because the cab sounds like a trash compactor. My foot pushes against the floor, and I'm thinking, Give it the gas.

My admiration for Ari has soared. I knew he wasn't going to take this lying down: he's got the forty-five out and he is aiming it at the back of the driver's head. The cab is still shuddering, trembling, making a chirping sound as it flies over the potholes. I don't think the driver got near eighty. Well, Stargell, maybe this man shouldn't be on the streets. Ari doesn't look like a shooter, but it's better not to take any chances.

"Slow down," I say, "for the love of God! Slow down."

Even I am impressed by my voice, its urgency, the sound of blind panic. The driver turns his zombie eyes toward me and they are as flat and the same color as a pewter plate. But there's something in them, a bright scratch of recognition: they settle on Ari's forty-five.

"I always thought I was going to die like this," says the driver.

He puts it to the floor.

"Don't shoot," I say to Ari.

Ari and I feel the car speed ahead, its strange lifting quality. There can't be that much left in this heap, I think. I am impressed when I see the speedometer slapped all the way over to the right.

"Eighth Avenue and Thirty-eighth Street," I scream.

I can see the driver's hands tighten on the wheel, the Grand Prix straightness of his arms. The lights rush toward us, spread to both sides, become long streamers in the night before they disappear.

"We want to go to Thirty-eighth Street," I say.

"I'll kill him," says Ari.

The engines misses, and I can see the driver shake his head, can see his lips mouthing the words "fouled plugs." Just to save face, something I understand, the driver puts the hack into a four-wheel stop: we slide up to the intersection of Eighth Avenue and Thirty-eighth Street like an elephant on ice skates. I put some money in the cup, grab Ari by the arm, pull him out of the taxi.

"Come on," I say.

The sirens start their wailing down the avenue where there are pulsing lights: the police cars are small but quickly moving cele-

brations of the Fourth of July. The lights are red, white, and blue.
The hack driver wakes, tears away the zombie's veil. You can see
he doesn't know where he is or how he got there, but he's sure
that the police are after him. The cab takes off and I can feel the
wind as the police pass by.

Ari puts the gun away.

"I am a guest in this country," says Ari.

I nod, but I'm still trembling.

"If I weren't," says Ari, "I would have behaved differently."

The distant sound of bouzouki music fills the empty street. Ari
and I stand underneath an awning that has on both sides palm
tree letters and they spell out "Club Nile." Ari is already swaying
gently from side to side, smiling like the old hound he is. The
bouzouki music is a little mournful, and it's cold in the street.
Everything is forgiven now: Ari is thinking of the belly dancers of
his youth.

We go through a door upholstered in green Naugahyde,
and climb the stairs. Ari goes ahead of me, stalks the music, and I
can see his purple pants and brown shoes. Ah, Stargell, the old
boy's still got some fight left in him, I think, he's not played out
yet. The stairwell is filled with smoke and the odor of damp skin,
talcum powder. The bouzouki music is electrified, as soothing as
a tin drum: it's just what we need. At the top of the stairs there is
a large room, its ceiling supported by pillars or beams that have
been dressed up to look like palm trees. There are tables among
the pillars, and there are women with lots of hair and bright
dresses sitting with men who look like they've got the world's
lard market cornered. The men are large and bald and alert. In
the middle of the tables and before the bandstand there is a dance
floor. The bandstand is decorated with palm trees, too, and the
musicians are playing their odd-looking instruments. The belly
dancer is in the center of the floor, and she shimmies from table
to table. Ari is transfixed.

The belly dancer is about thirty-five, voluptuous, dressed in a
spangly costume. The room has the strange sense of loneliness

that exotica brings. I can see her undulant skin, the fantastic movement of her body. Ari shouts, screams, is getting ready to stand on the table and applaud. The bouncer, a young man who leans against an imitation palm tree, puts his hand into his pocket. The belly dancer recognizes the shout of a true believer, of one who appreciates her skill, her perfect contractions. She stands before Ari, shimmying, bringing us into her faint odor, her presence.

"This is the seduction," says Ari.

We drink ouzo, watch the dancer. Ari takes a bill from his wallet, licks it, and sticks it to the dancer's skin. Ah, Stargell, I think, it's not many who can handle a belly dancer. She stands next to me, and before I have a chance to look into her remote eyes, Ari pulls a bill from his pocket and shoves it at me.

"Stick it on," says Ari, making a quick, encouraging motion with his hand. "Stick it on!"

I lick the bill, push it against the woman's cool skin, feel the hum of the music in her flesh. The band seems to strain and then she is gone, and I am left with outstretched fingers. Ari is laughing. He slaps me on the back. The dancer kneels, but the back of her head is on the floor and she stares into the fronds of the plastic palm trees. Her stomach makes an odd lapping motion. She stares again, shimmies once around the room, and then the music stops. Ari is throwing money at her, at the musicians, shouting and applauding. The bouncer is just waiting for inspiration, but before it strikes, Ari is behaving himself. The lights come up and the fat men and their women with acrylic wigs sit quietly under the imitation fronds. The musicians pack up and leave, too, and we are left in the forlorn and almost empty room. The fat men and their bought women withdraw as regularly as the tide. I enjoy the rank atmosphere, the smoky, tired air.

"Do you have a job?" says Ari.

I shake my head. My fingers are buzzing where they touched the belly dancer's skin.

"No," I say. "I haven't got one."

"Enid wrote to me about some . . ."

Ari searches for a word, digs through dictionaries, tries to be delicate, then says, "Expectations."

He smiles because he's found the right word.

"All bust," I say.

"Oh," says Ari.

We finger our glasses. Ari gives me a sly smile, then looks at me from under his brows.

"You are a shrewd one," says Ari. "You are biding your time and thinking of a product."

"Yes," I say. Stargell, I think, the old jackass is a mind reader.

"I knew it!" says Ari.

The waiters are making small stacks of quarters at the table next to ours. When I turn back to Ari, I see that he is looking at me from under his brows and that he has that same sly smile.

"Such shrewdness," says Ari.

I sip the last of my drink, smell the air, the stale perfume and sweat. Ari still has his I've-found-a-diamond-in-the-rough smile.

"My wife had a large dowry," says Ari, "and when I was finished with the army I went into business. I was not shrewd. There are thieves in the world."

Ari says this with such personal regret and outrage that I want to tell him I'm sorry.

"Thieves!" says Ari.

I want to ask about the map to paradise, but this doesn't seem to be the time.

"I can see we've both had experience," says Ari, "that we are shrewd men. There's no reason to worry."

Stargell, I think, there's no need to be a wet blanket. I slap him on the shoulder.

"Yes," says Ari. "My wife was upset. I have mortgaged the house, the last of her dowry. Now she will see."

This sounds like sound policy: after a certain point, a thing is worth having only if you can fit it into a suitcase. Or a shopping bag.

Eighth Avenue has an after-the-fair quality: it's quiet, deserted, damp. Ari and I walk north and I can feel the street as it rests, as it becomes ready for the day's trucks, cars and buses, hand dollies, the angry voices and red exhaust.

Ari is exultant, as incandescent as someone who's come up with a system to break the bank at Mount Parnassus. He smiles and sways in time to the memory of a bouzouki song. We pass a woman in a blue wig and Ari turns and speaks to her. She is wearing a short black skirt and ripped stockings. Ari has a horrified expression on his face, but then Blue Wig shrugs and says something and Ari looks relieved.

"I've got a deal here," says Blue Wig, pointing to a door beneath the stoop. "We don't have to go to a hotel."

Blue Wig is wearing a short skirt even though there is still snow on the ground. She has high cheekbones, a beautiful nose, eyes through which you can see a coal mine. Ari and Blue Wig go into the door beneath the stop and before it closes I can see a bare bulb and a cot. There's a bunch of junk beneath the stoop, beer bottles and candy bar wrappers, but Blue Wig has swept them to one side of her door. I know she pushes the trash away, that she shouts at someone who's thrown a bottle there, that she says to herself, The place got to look nice a little. People like that.

The sky is overcast but beginning to lighten: it looks like gray cat fur. I think about Ari, Blue Wig, Enid sleeping in our bed, about the days when she was full of spit.

Ari and Blue Wig climb the stairs (after about five minutes: Stargell, the woman is a pro), and linger for a moment at the sidewalk. Blue Wig looks about twenty dollars happier. Stargell, I think, it would take about five hundred to make her smile and I'd give it to her if I had it, just to see her face. I'd like to do it at about this hour, or maybe a little later, at dawn, when the sky is a gold band shell in the east, when the sun has risen. She'd think I was crazy, but it would be worth it: Blue Wig smiling and the sun rising and both of us thinking the other was crazy. Maybe a big truck would come by, too, and the pavement would tremble: the light would break on the bleak walls.

"So long," says Blue Wig.

Ari waves as we get into a cab: we move downtown as smoothly as though we were traveling on silk.

"I'll find a product," says Ari, as he gets out of the taxi in front of our building.

He is still smiling: he remembers Blue Wig, the belly dancer, the flight across the Atlantic. Maybe it was the jet engines, the sense of speed, the humming push of flight, or the music, but for whatever reason, Ari pulls out his forty-five and starts shooting into the air. The slap and whoosh of the gun makes me think the street has exploded, that we've stumbled into a private assassination. It sounds like someone beating an airplane hangar with a baseball bat: *Bam. Bam. Bam.* The muzzle flash is as bright as Fourth of July gold. The sky is still purple, the color of dark squid, and Ari is emptying his forty-five into it. For a moment it seems that someone is returning the fire, but it's just a distant echo. I grab Ari's arm and pull him inside the building. He is laughing and trying to reload. I can't explain that the neighborhood is filled with lunatics and that they are armed. The Barber's sold over a hundred M-16s and everyone keeps his handy. What would be better, I think, for one of the neighbors than popping off an early-morning Greek?

"Where have you been?" says Enid sleepily.

"Having a good time," I say.

I give her a kiss.

"Did my father enjoy himself?" says Enid.

"Yes," I say.

"That's nice," says Enid. She rolls over and goes back to sleep.

Ari and I drink beer at the dining table. The beer is cold and refreshing. Ari tells me war stories. He was captured by the Germans, by some of the think tank boys. Jolting Joe would have approved. There'd be a place for them at our shop. Ari sees the Genius and turns it on. I leave him before the ashy light where he worships his past. There's a movie on, a Richard Widmark marine epic. The men speak too fast for Ari to understand, but he attended the war college in Georgia, so he gets most of the tactics right.

I undress in the bedroom and climb under the covers.

"Don't touch me," says Enid.

I listen to the Genius, hear Ari reload his forty-five. I think of the woman in Paris, of Barbeau, and begin to drift: the night wraps around me, pulls me into its warm and tender embrace.

The women with fat arms work the winches in the air shaft, put out their clothes to dry. It gives the building a nautical aspect, as though we were at sea and the crew was comprised of heavy women: the course is set, all the sails are trimmed. It's above freezing today and I can feel the streams and rivers, the oceans gladden at the warmth, can feel them swell before it. Enid rises, looks at me, and falls back to the pillow.

"I don't feel well," she says.

"I'll bet you don't," I say. "You are my darling, my booze swiller."

"Oh," says Enid. "Oh."

I find Ari sprawled on the beartrap bed, dressed in his underwear, his hand on his forty-five. The bedclothes look like he dreamed of dinosaurs and rabid hounds. His strange hair is in disarray and you can see his bald spot. The Genius is off, looking (I suppose) with a gentle understanding at Ari, and the forty-five. I'm just glad Ari didn't plug a TV Jap. Ari wakes with a start, then slowly closes his eyes, lets me know that his nerves are humming, too. This is one of the best hangovers I've ever had: everything is alive, twitchy. I give Ari some cold juice and I bring some into the bedroom.

"Oh," says Enid, "that's too cold."

She puts it on the floor and holds her head.

There's no need for pretense now that Ari and I are friends: I shove the dishes from last night's meal against the wall and give him his coffee cup in the cleared space. He's still a little shy or ashamed, so he pats his Martian hair, holds it over his bald spot, refuses to look at me. All gloom, Stargell, sinner's morning. Underneath it all the old goat is proud of himself. In a few moments he is savoring his coffee, pursing his lips, squinting in fantastic memory. He sees me smiling, chuckles with a quiet self-incrimination.

"I'll find a product," says Ari.

No, no, I think, let's spend the last of the dowry on hookers and belly dancers, liquor and dissipation. Just think, Ari, what memories you'll have when they put you out by the ocean, dry as a raisin, to die in the sun.

Enid comes into the room, braced and rigid: she's got a grip on herself that's going to leave bruises.

"Good morning, Father," says Enid.

"Good morning, Enid," says her father.

They give each other a peck and Enid collapses, falls into her chair and sits with her legs spread a little. I give her some coffee, and then the two of them savor the brown muck, each lost in spotty memory, alcoholic residue. Enid sees that the kitchen's clean, and this confuses her a little, since she's half convinced she made her splashy departure there. But she bucks up, pushes on like any would-be aristocrat.

"Where did you go last night?" says Enid.

"To see the belly dancers," says Ari.

Enid gives me her most severe expression: she doesn't like it when I am entranced by women. Once I went to a showing of photographs of nudes and Enid tried to make me sleep in a plastic garbage bag.

"They're so vulgar," says Enid.

Thank God, Stargell, I think. I remember the sweat, the rank music.

We drink our coffee.

"Do you know anything," says Ari to me, "about a machine for one man that flies?"

I describe the think tank version, an engineering failure that's crippled half a dozen men. So far the only good that's come out of them is that one was used in a cigarette advertisement for a magazine, in which a test pilot, dressed in functional clothes (all silver and buckles, zippers and hooks), a helmet, and weird-looking boots, is relaxing after a jump across a rice paddy. He has the cracked smile of the stylishly insane.

"Yes," says Ari, "that's it. That's what I would like to bring to my country."

He's as solemn as the Pope. I can see it, too, his vision of Athens, of the Acropolis, the musky olive trees, the dust of the cement city. Over it are men in small back harnesses that have two little arms with which to steer, and coming down from each aluminum rucksack is a flame as blue as the Aegean and yellow as gold. The men are floating over the city as though it were covered with a large transparent trampoline. Everyone going to work or play. At rush hour the city is domed with people, jammed shoulder to shoulder, each with a flame coming from his back. The people who walk carry umbrellas made out of tin foil.

The strong women make the winches screech.

"It's in the experimental phase," I say.

Ari looks a little disappointed, but his eyes are still glazed at the prospect.

"I'll keep you posted," I say.

"Please," says Ari.

The women have begun to sing in the air shaft as they work the winches: their songs are in Portuguese and they are laments. Enid hears them, looks relieved, smiles.

Ari and I go over the subway maps and I show him where the department stores are, explain about express trains, the buses, taxis.

"Macy's," says Ari, "Korvettes, Bloomingdale's."

Ari climbs into the shower, hums, then dresses in the green shirt to go with his purple pants. He puts on his hound's-tooth coat, takes maps and instructions, his briefcase that's the size of a suitcase and filled with pieces of paper he's ripped out of old copies of *Mechanix Illustrated* and catalogues from Frederick's of Hollywood.

"I'll see you later," he says.

He waves, smiles, closes the door. Enid gets back into bed, sighs with an almost beatific satisfaction, pulls the pillow over her head, and falls asleep.

I do a little shopping at the Barber's. Smiling Mary looks sour today.

"How's the import-export business between here and Greece?" says the Barber.

"It's beginning," I say. "It's beginning."

"Glad to hear that," says the Barber.

I stop at the mailbox: there are some notes from bill collectors, each one as shrill as a sawmill. There is a letter, too. I throw the notes away and think, Stargell, you are big game for the bill hounds, or like some rare and almost extinct butterfly that can only be found in Central Africa: they'll need a safari to get you. I can see the topees and bush jackets, the shiny bearers carrying boxes, the delicate nets. I carry the letter upstairs, into the quiet apartment.

The envelope is addressed in a handwriting that I know better than my own. Each letter looks like it had come out of a copybook, a grammar school pamphlet where there are neat rows: *Aa Aa Aa Aa.*

It's from my mother.

Things are hard here, the letter says, things are hard now. Your father is not doing so well. He was mad a lot of the time. I would try to find nice things for him to eat but he wouldn't eat them. He would get angry and say it doesn't taste good. I looked for lamb chops. He always liked lamb chops but when I cooked them he wouldn't eat them. I made some soup, finally, some vegetable soup like I used to make when you were a child. You remember? He ate that. He ate bowl after bowl and then I figured out why he wouldn't eat the lamb chops. He couldn't swallow. Do you see? I looked all over town but it was just that he couldn't swallow it. I think you should come to see us soon.

I sit in the gray light of the air shaft and look at the letter. The women sing, pull the winches. Stargell, I think, she loves him and wants him to live for a while. He's as stubborn as gravity. Cancer's dragging him right into the ground. Carrots, celery, white onions, potatoes, beans, a tomato, a bay leaf, broth: soup. Stargell, he can still feel the hot juices, can taste the vegetables. He eats it with a spoon from a cup. Perhaps he has a slice of toast with the crusts cut off.

I walk to the subway station and take the A train, get into a car that is filled with newspaper people (each carrying a copy of the *Times,* the *News,* or *El Diario*), students, a girl with beautiful legs, a man with a bamboo cane. I work my way to the front of the train, where I can look through the porthole and see the cool, expectant tracks. We make local stops until Fifty-ninth Street: short runs, subway lethargy. Newspaper people get on, sit down, keep the print so close to their noses they seem to be smelling the accounts of disaster, bank robbery, and divorce rather than reading them. After Fifty-ninth Street the train makes a straight run to 125th Street, and I stand with my face against the glass and feel the car slamming from side to side, its highballing coal-tender smash and thump. It seems that the train rises as it makes its extended rush into the tunnel: the minelike supports move quickly, jump at the sides of the car, and disappear. I push my face against the porthole, watch the light on the shiny rails (clear and cold: untroubled), feel the passing of the underground forest, the regularly spaced timbers. The driver is in his booth and he has the same view I have: he must be thinking, I'll give it a little more. Give it a little more, I think. A little more. The cars are banging from side to side with such cheerful ferocity that I can feel my bones. I want the driver to open it all the way up, to hold the throttle against its last stop. I slap the metal at the side of the porthole, hammer on it with a fist, get ready to scream, Give it the gas, Jack. Let the tin can rip. But I can feel the speed die, the gentle drifting away from the sense of the crest, the driving force, the train's shot weight. The passengers are relieved that the train has stopped and they fold their newspapers. I cross to the other side of the station and wait for the downtown train.

The tunnel is cold as an icebox: winter lingers here, makes its arctic presence felt. There is metallic dust in the air. After a moment I can feel the station tremble, and then the light is smeared across the rails. When the front car stops I go inside and stand at the porthole. A woman comes into the train and takes a seat. She has curled platinum-colored hair, a short skirt, high-heeled shoes, lovely legs. She is wearing a short imitation-leather coat. Her lips are red and her nails are painted purple and she is reading a magazine with insane headlines. The train starts and this time the door of the driver's cab is open and I can see the driver as he sits before the throttle. We move into the lighted space, pass the timers, gain speed. I push my forehead against the glass and feel the slamming of the cars. We move through the tunnel, jerking from side to side. There are lights on the timbers and they blink from yellow to green. The door of the driver's cab swings open and I can see his hand on the throttle.

"Give it a little more," I say.

He looks at me, closes the door, but the train jumps. I can no longer hear anything aside from the sound of my thoughts, which meshes perfectly with the banging and trembling of the train, since it seems to me that my thinking is now done with words that are being ripped, one at a time, from sheets of tin. The subway is moving so fast that it turns into a streamer, a train made of smoke. It is blown away from the driver, me, the one round light. For a moment I look at the young woman, at her squirmy beauty, the almost mathematically perfect curve of her legs, her insolent, garish lips which are pursed in concentration as she reads an article entitled "Phrenology and Sex: What Your Head Lumps Tell You." I can feel her presence, her vulgar health, as the entire train becomes as ethereal as a comet's tail, luminescent, ghostlike, dissolving. I can feel the pressure of the speed and then even the banging and slamming seem remote, only remembered.

The train pulls into the station.

Lamb chops, I think, lamb chops.

At an underground stand I eat a stale doughnut with a jelly center and sip a cup of coffee. The crowds have rehearsed for years: not one person bumps into another. On the street there are fantastic women, beauties who have come out for the brief sunlight. They walk slowly, turn toward the warmth. Their fragrance, their lips and hands, the curve of a breast, a hip, blend into the false spring, the thaw, the blinding speed of the train.

In the sealed atmosphere of the apartment, I sit at the table and look at my mother's letter, then tear it up and throw it away.

Enid is still asleep. I stand at the side of the bed and watch her twitch.

"Time to wake up," I say.

I whisper against Enid's ear, her soft hair, and she recoils as though I had slapped her.

"You leave me alone," she says.

"You can't be sleeping when Ari comes home," I say.

Enid stirs, rustles in the sheets, shakes her head beneath the pillow.

"You are a brute," she says.

I make some coffee and sit in the living room. Soon Enid rises and drifts, in her pink, childish nightgown, through the door and to the table. She supports her head with one hand, turns up her nose at the coffee, shields her eyes from the air shaft's dead-man's light.

"What strange dreams," she says.

I reach out to her and she lets me take her hand. Stargell, I think, what's this? I can feel a blood rush, lightning desire. I try to keep the lechery out of my smile, try to show my concern for her. There's hope for us, my boy, I think.

"Germs are getting in my underwear," says Enid.

Enid has a severe expression and she is staring at the icebox, thinking about the beer bottles inside.

"We can't have that," I say.

"No," says Enid. "We can't."

I go into the bedroom and open a drawer in her bureau. Her underwear is lined up, neatly spaced and folded. Stargell, I think, let's face it: this folding and storing job is the work of an organi-

zational genius. Enid is standing next to me, looking into the
drawer as though there were a child inside who had just had
open-heart surgery. I've already done a nice, tidy job: the drawer
is lined with plastic.

"Don't touch them with your hands," says Enid.

"O.K., my darling," I say. "Don't you worry about it."

I reach for the laundry bag, but she shakes her head.

"That's dirty," she says. "There are germs on it."

"I've got what we need," I say.

I bring a new garbage bag into the room. Enid approves of its
slick sterility, puts her underwear inside, watches as I close the
sack with a piece of papered wire, the kind of thing you use to
stake a tomato plant. Enid gets dressed and we walk downstairs
and up the street to the laundromat. I put the underwear in a
washer and add enough bleach to make it disappear. The machine
starts with a comforting sloshing sound. There is a bench in the
laundromat for people to sit on, a comfortable one with slats, but
Enid won't sit on it because she's afraid something will climb up
her pants. Aside from us, the place is deserted, and we walk up
and down before the gently swaying machine. There is the reassuring odor of soap and bleach. Enid takes my hand, squeezes it,
gives me a peck on the cheek, and says, "You won't tell anyone
about this, will you?" After the underwear has spun, I take it to
the drier and give it enough heat to kill anything that Enid knows
about. I haven't got the heart to tell her there are bacteria that
live in boiling water. While the drier turns over and over, like
some amusement park ride for midgets, Enid paces, holds her
hands behind her back, breathes deeply in the laundromat's air. I
take the underwear out of the drier and we go home with the big
hump, the black bag of underwear, on my back. We spread another garbage bag on the bed and Enid folds her underclothes and
stacks them neatly in her drawer.

"There," she says.

She smiles as if the drawer were a flower bed in early spring
and the daffodils and crocuses had just come up. Enid wears big
underwear. I think of small trumpets, the yellow petals, trembling
in April's wind.

"I love you," says Enid.

We go back to the living room and have a couple of quarts.

"I have to go to California," I say.

"Of course you do," says Enid.

She smiles, looks as happy as when she is wrapped in a warm towel, one right out of the drier.

"I'm beautiful," she says. "Everyone says so. I'm intelligent."

Enid and I sit quietly together. She smiles, holds my hands. For a while it is like the old times. I reach across the table, caress her face, kiss her fingers. She laughs, tells me secret fantasies, plans. I have an easy touch, a sureness that any lecher would give a leg for. Enid responds, becomes coquettish, looks at me through her lashes, makes me a fan of her Parisian-fog act, her I've-got-nothing-on-under-my-trench-coat sensuality. I can see the ancient itch in her glance. We go into the bedroom and sit, side by side.

Be gentle, Stargell, I think, don't scare the poor woman.

I slowly rub her hands and arms, caress her cheek, kiss her along her hairline. Enid breaks into tears.

"Oh," she says. "Oh. I don't know what I'm going to do."

I'm getting twitchy now, I think, no doubt about that.

"You'll be O.K.," I say.

"I'll try some other time," she says. "You should wash your hands. They should be clean when you touch me."

We go back to the living room and sit at the table.

"I love you," says Enid, as though she has won a beauty contest in a cow county: she wants to make sure all the hicks know how graceful she is in accepting their cheap trophy.

A little later she bites her lip, looks at me, and says, "I really do, Stargell. That's the problem."

There is a distant crashing and banging and then a strange rustling outside the door. Enid looks to me for a sign, since she wants to know whether she should hide in the bedroom. It sounds like someone wrapped up in newspaper and tape is thrashing around in the hall and thumping against our door.

"It's Father," says Enid.

I open the door and there are two piles of packages, one carried

by Ari, the other by a man who looks like a taxi driver. No two of
the packages are the same size, but all of them are wrapped in
brown paper and tied with the string you get in department
stores. Ari throws his on the floor and shouts. The driver is a
little less exuberant, but he gets rid of his packages, too. Even he
seems amazed, infected with Ari's overheated enthusiasm. The
driver takes his money and clears out after shaking Ari's hand.
Ari looks as though he saw Jesus at Macy's. His red hair is
pushed away from his bald spot and his clothes are wrinkled.
There is a button missing from his hound's-tooth coat. Stargell, I
think, the old boy's seen it all. His mind is as stuffed as a ballot
box in a crooked election. The packages are everywhere, on the
floor, table, sofa. They make me feel like a color-blind man at
Christmas.

"What things I've got," says Ari.

He pats his hair and blinks for a moment. I pour him some
beer, which he drinks in one draught.

"Ah," says Ari. He wipes his lips with the back of his hand.
"Look at this."

He takes a package from the floor, rips through the wrapping
paper, and holds up a pogo stick. It has cream-colored handles
and a cream-colored tip.

"What is this pogo stick?" says Ari. "Is it a medical appli-
ance?"

It does have a certain prosthetic quality, the hint of what's to
come: the geriatric walker, the aluminum cane. Stargell, I think,
maybe they should throw out all that junk in the old people's
home. These will do. Everyone will hop to the stewed prunes and
the Jacuzzi bath.

"No," I say.

I take the pogo stick into the hall, since I don't want to rub
Jack the Ripper's fur the wrong way, and begin to hop. Enid and
Ari stand at the door, watching, critical, each trying to judge the
Mediterranean temperament, the depth of the future market. The
pogo stick makes a satisfying sound, a steady spring and thump.
Ari is thinking, and I know he sees Old Los Angeles (Athens),
where there are thousands of people and everyone is on a pogo

stick, hopping like mad. People sit at cafés, and everyone has a pogo stick, parked like a crutch, next to his chair.

Enid and Ari have only their noses stuck out the green door of our apartment: altogether I can see two noses and two eyes. In case of trouble they want to be able to disappear. I bring the pogo stick back to the apartment.

"Not bad," I say.

Ari throws the pogo stick aside, mutters in his language. I turn to Enid with a questioning glance.

"That'll fetch the little beggars," says Enid. "He means the children."

Ari rips into the packages, tears brown paper: he produces a face steamer, a lawn trimmer that cuts with a plastic whip, an electric carving knife, some Astroturf, a Veg-O-Matic.

"A Veg-O-Matic," says Enid.

She takes from the kitchen a bunch of carrots and begins. The table looks like it is covered with chips from a sawmill that cuts up carrots the size of redwoods. Enid has an earnest expression, the kind of squinting you see in the face of someone who is trying to read the Ten Commandments off a peanut shell. Ari attacks his packages, exposes knife sharpeners, a pen set, the sound track from a pornographic movie. He has a tape recorder and he slips the cassette in. Ari stands in a stormy sea of paper and listens as a man's voice says, "Sit on top of me, baby, and talk dirty. . . ." A woman obliges, and Ari smiles, thinks of Blue Wig, waits for the cassette to end. Enid is chopping.

"Well?" says Ari.

"I like the pogo stick," I say.

"It costs too much to make," says Ari.

"That's true," I say.

"That's the problem with all this junk," says Ari. "It costs too much to make."

He kicks the paper, smashes the electric carving knife, throws the lawn trimmer against the wall, tears at the Astroturf. That's it, I think. Who needs this shit? I kick the face steamer, finish off the lawn trimmer.

We sit together at the table and Ari broods. He sips ouzo and looks at Enid.

"Stop that chopping," he says.

Enid stops, looks at the ouzo, pours herself a shot. We sit around like Indians at a council of war. What do we do, I think, when the settlers form a ring with their carts? Drag burning mesquite bushes? I have not forgotten their gift: the blankets that gave us the pock disease. Ari takes his head in his hands, squeezes it until the tips of his fingers turn white, sighs. What Ari needs is Jack the Ripper chasing him for loan shark juice. That'll put a little snap in the old boy's disposition.

"I knew it would come to this," says Ari.

He smooths his hair over his head, fixes his eyes upon me.

"Burglar alarms," says Ari.

He takes from his pocket a pamphlet that has been read many times. I open the wrinkled front page, which is so fragile that I feel I am about to turn the leaves of a holograph version of the Tibetan Book of the Dead. Burglar alarms are described in the pamphlet.

"I want to bring those to Greece," says Ari.

"But we have no burglars there," says Enid.

Ari's a counterpuncher. Just a moment ago he was stomping the electric carving knife, but he's back on the track. Enid thinks he's making reservations for the booby hatch, but I know better.

"Yes we do," says Ari.

His eyes are large and blurry: they look like he is examining us through a magnifying glass. He slams his hand on the table. I don't think he's slept more than four hours in the last forty-eight: jet lag, Blue Wig, a day of hunting the tiger in Macy's jungle. Enid jumps back, sips her ouzo.

"I will wait for a big crime," says Ari. His voice rises. "A big one. When a whole family is murdered for revenge. Everyone will be terrified. Everyone will jump when they hear a mouse. Then I will advertise in the newspaper and everyone will beg for my alarms."

We sit quietly and contemplate murderers and sneak thieves, prison-break bells, Ari's firm belief in banking on cruelty. Better cruelty than love, I think, at least as far as coin of the realm is concerned. Ask any dollar apostle, any big-time God man: nothing makes the jack jump like dread.

The burglar alarm factory is in an industrial park which is in a town with an Indian name. It's on Long Island.

"Do you know where it is?" says Ari.

He points a trembling finger at the address. I can see the millions of small windows, the bright cyclone fences, the flat roofs and undistinguished brick walls, the parking lots.

"Yes," I say.

"When can we go to this village?" says Ari.

"We need a car," I say.

"We'll rent one," says Ari.

Stargell, I think, you could use a little machinery, a few hundred horses.

"Sure," I say, "we'll rent the car."

"Tomorrow morning," says Ari.

"Yes," I say, "in the morning. Crack of dawn."

"Crack?" says Ari, with his military, eve-of-the-assault diction. He takes the magazine from his pistol, checks it, shoves it back into the butt. No belly dancers tonight, Stargell, I think. Ari opens the beartrap bed, strips to his underwear, and climbs under the covers. I turn on the Genius, search for a war movie, one from Ari's theater of operations. Enid picks up the products, stacks them neatly against the wall, even the broken bits from the lawn trimmer and carving knife, and then folds the brown paper into neat squares and makes a ball of the twine.

Enid's lip trembles and she says, when smoothing out the brown paper, "Dowry. Poor dowry."

Enid sits at the table. Ari seems restless, unsatisfied by the Genius, tonight's jolt of the South Pacific, the palm-tree marines. He tells me that he had a friend who was terrified of heights, and that he and his friend were being trained to be parachuted behind German lines. They went up in a plane with some other men to make their first jump, and Ari saw his friend foaming at the mouth, shaking his head, screaming. The friend took off his parachute and refused to jump. The other men gave him a raft of shit. Ari frowns at one of his own unkind remarks. Ari was the last to jump, and he looked over his shoulder and saw the friend sitting on the slatted bench, alone, holding his head in the wind. As Ari was floating down, swaying from side to side, under the perfectly creased canopy, he heard a *whooosh!* which was made by his friend, who had jumped without his parachute. I can see the moving arms, the aerial terror, can hear the scream mixed with the wind, can feel the puffed, gusty acceleration. Everyone's falling and then, bang: you hit the bench in the park where you gum your sandwich, just another old fart waiting to have a black umbrella popped in the sun. Ari waves the gun around, watches the movie, eats a lamb sandwich, falls asleep at the credits. I turn off the Genius, have a slug of ouzo, and gather up Enid, who's asleep on the table. I carry her into the bedroom.

"I never wanted to get married," says Enid.

I undress her and she turns toward the wall. I take off my clothes and lie in the darkness of the room, imagine the rush, the pure sensation of falling. Tomorrow I'll find an old woman in the park or an old man in a greasy spoon and I'll bask in their presence, in the glory of a withered bag of bones.

Enid and I are snug under the covers and I try to put my leg against hers, to touch her a little, since it makes it easier for me to sleep. My foot touches her calf, but she pulls away. I stare into the dark, at the ceiling, the cracks that make it seem as though I'm covered by one large and white leaf. I can feel myself being absorbed by the mattress. Enid moans in the night.

The dreams come off Bellevue's walls for a while, those visions the painters cover up with latex every couple of years: dancing lamb chops, blunderbusses that shoot slaughterhouse leavings, airplane-crash forests, twisted metal edged with flesh. Those are bad, all right. But then Paris rises and I meet her again, the woman with the eyes that are the color of cognac. I taste her mouth, touch her side, and that's it: I wake to gray blur, morning TV, a staccato sound track. Ari's up and ready to go.

Enid starts, flinches.

"Is the building on fire?" she says. "Do I have to run?"

"No," I say.

She looks at me with an anger that snaps like a turtle.

"You're bothering me," she says.

"Go back to sleep," I say.

I kiss her, squeeze her arm, tell her that I love her.

Ari's chain-smoking cigarettes. I take a shower, listen to the splashy thunder and think, Ari, I'm going to make you rich. I'm going to take you to the burglar alarm factory.

I dress, drink a cup of coffee. Ari is still brooding.

"I retired from the army," he says, "and I sell some shit to make tits big."

The coffee is rich, so strong I almost feel enlightened. I understand about Ari's present business. There are beautiful women in Athens and they are buxom, robust, and not one of them comes near Ari or his stinking machines. Enid told me that Ari's shop has eaten up everything, aside from the house (which is now mortgaged) and Ari's pension from the army.

"Let's go look at the alarms," I say.

Ari smiles, lets his sun rise. He sees his fortune and it can't come a moment too soon. Ari grabs his briefcase and we descend, pass through the layers of morning odors, strong coffee and cigarettes laid above and below stale beer and wine. It's cold outside and Ari smiles when his teeth chatter: he's glad they're not going the same way as his hair. Stargell, I think, this is handy. After a few more disappointments the old goat will start to bite.

The car-rental agency has a fly-by-night façade, architecture vague enough to be adapted to any need, from pizza stand to massage parlor. The office itself is a cramped room with a counter. The walls are covered with quarter-inch veneer: it's imitation imitation schmaltz. This is the place for us, I think. They won't send dunning letters for long, and the massage parlor won't have to redecorate. The man behind the counter has a foreclosure expression, a quiet desperation: I have the feeling he wants to ask everyone who comes in if he's interested in a car-rental agency. His wig doesn't fit.

"Compact?" says the man behind the counter.

Anything, anything, I think. Just give me the keys. But I consider the budget, Ari's well-being for the next week or so.

"Well," I say. "Whatever's most reasonable."

Ari stiffens.

"I am going to ask to be the European representative," he says.

I approve: seize the opportunity, I think, take the plunge. Who gives a shit if the brochure looks as if it were printed in Hong Kong. There are Christians in the world.

"Great," I say.

"Of the burglar alarm factory."

Only a retired colonel who has killed men with his bare hands can look as proud as Ari. My sun rises, too. Ari, I think, you are a wonder.

The rental agent is working on an ulcer the size of a bathtub drain, but he's dreaming: his plastic pouch is filled with pens.

"What kind of big car have you got?" I say.

Ari is improved, although still a little wooden. He gently taps the back of my heel with the toe of his shoe.

"Black," says Ari. "I want a black one."

"Black," I say to the rental agent.

"Cadillac?" says the agent.

He's smiling now, too. It looks like the poor bastard's going to be able to buy his lunch today: American cheese on balloon bread, cup of instant coffee.

"Limousine," I say.

Ari gurgles with delight, blinks his approval at me, pushes his Martian hair over his bald spot. He's still as rigid as a stump.

"I've got a new one," says the agent a little sadly, "and it's only been rented once."

Ari gently taps my heel again, blinks.

"That would be fine," I say.

"Insurance?" says the rental man.

There must be four hundred horses under the hood. Stargell, I think, can you feel the long black machine, its geared power, its aloofness? It's like having a thoroughbred gently reined in, feathered, although ready to break into those long, cool strides.

"Stick it on," I say.

Ari stands behind me, now aloof from this tacky business of arranging for our transportation: he seems to contemplate Byzantium, the shape of an urn, the distance of a star, a woman's quiet orgasmic sigh. I sign the forms, initial the boxes for insurance. I want to read the fine print closely so I know exactly what havoc I can wreak (the damage figures), but I know it would ruin the rental agent's day.

"We start you with a full tank," says the agent.

That's what I want to have: a full tank and four good tires. Good rubber. The rental agent disappears through a door that's as substantial as cardboard.

"Pssst!" says Ari.

He is lounging on the plastic sofa next to a potted plant that is wilting (*Tuberculariaceae fursarium*, I'd say), his legs crossed at the knees, his socks collapsed at his ankles.

"How do I look?" he says.

Desperate, I think, but nothing a little drive won't straighten out.

"Great," I say.

The Cadillac doesn't arrive so much as it is unveiled: the atmosphere is one that surrounds a rifle being removed from its carrier. Four doors, bright chrome, black lacquer.

"It's all yours," says the agent.

He watches us as we walk into the street, where Ari stands before the car. I think he is admiring it, and this creates an awkward moment, a slight misunderstanding. Ari sniffs. I kick the tires. Ari clears his throat. Steel-belted radials, good tread. Ari is in a cadet brace. Ah, Stargell, I think, an embarrassment. The gloomy face of the agent is at his window.

"I'm sorry," I say to Ari.

He accepts this apology with a slight dip of his head, then gets into the Cadillac through the rear door I hold open for him. So there, Jack, I think, looking at the flat-tire face of the rental agent, I know what to do.

I drive directly to our apartment building.

"What's wrong?" says Ari. "Is there something wrong? We are where we began."

"Wait here," I say.

I park in front of a fireplug and run upstairs, taking them two at a time, thinking, Stargell, be quick. You don't want to see the headlines that read "Greek Mafioso Shot in Little Italy." Enid turns over when I come into the bedroom.

"I have to get up," she says.

"No you don't," I say. "We've only been gone a half hour."

"That's nice," says Enid.

She burrows into her pillow.

I change into my gray suit and put on a dark-blue tie: it makes me feel as though I were in my prime, young, graceful, brilliant as an arc lamp. When I come downstairs and get into the car, Ari gurgles and smiles, taps the back of my seat with the toe of his shoe. I haven't got a cap, but that's no matter: a cap is just some nouveau trash. There's nothing better than having a sandy-haired young chauffeur. Ari understands this, settles back, relaxes. He has a little fan, a reading light, an armrest. The ceiling is made out of some acoustical material that looks like the raw sheet from which Band-Aids are cut. I have dials, gauges, swinging needles.

The industrial park has an Indian name, a phrase from a dead language, but I can hear it whispered in the tires' hiss, the escaping exhaust. I go through the tunnel, where the fluorescent lights are ghastly: we seem to be driving through one long tumor. We break into sunlight, onto the open road. After the toll booths, I open it up. At eighty-five the Cadillac shudders. I can feel (in my fingertips, in my low lizard brain) a turn's course: it is a parabola as pure as a mathematician's dream of the secret of the universe. I slap the Cadillac into it, turn on the radio, listen to the traffic reports, the psychotic chopping of the helicopter blades. All clear for us. The Cadillac lifts, becomes ethereal. Ah, Stargell, I think, blue sky, sunshine as white as a silver screen.

"Hey," says Ari. "Hey. You are going too fast."

I touch a chrome switch and a piece of black glass rises between us: it is like tying a rag around a horse's head in a fire. The old boy can't see where he's going and that's a good thing.

Ari hammers on the partition.

The landscape seems greased with speed, slick. I am a danger-ous man, I think, and there's nothing better. I touch the switch again and put the black glass down.

"The roads are great here," I say. "Better than Greece, I'll bet."

I can feel the smashed, incandescent heat of the engine, the forced exhaust. Ari is hanging over the front seat, waving his arms. His face looks like he's just seen a bunch of spiders, mil-lions of them, each the size of an Alaskan king crab, running at us with their pincers snapping.

Stargell, I think, he's still got the army issue, the forty-five.

"I am the European representative of the burglar alarm fac-tory," says Ari. "We must be careful."

This seems a little premature to me, but I see his stricken face, his bulging eyes.

"O.K., Ari," I say. "O.K., I'm sorry."

I slow down, behave myself: the Cadillac moves along at a demure, almost funereal rate. Ari becomes stern again, rigid as a silver-mine Calvinist. I meditate on the beauty of the machine, but it's not up to snuff: Stargell, I think, speed is the best. Leave Eastern religion to the incense-and-rice drones.

"We are men of the world," says Ari.

That's it, Stargell. That's what we are. The question is: where do we go from here?

Beyond the sign on which there is an Indian name (green background, white letters and border) there is the industrial park: all red brick and sheet-metal work, chain link fences, panes of glass with chicken wire inside. Yes, I think, this looks like the eye of the storm: low costs and steady profits. Ari gurgles, combs his hair, straightens his coat with the missing button. I can see the Mediterranean burglars sitting in the sun, their bellies full of mac-aroni and retsina: they sleep, have visions of colder climes, and when they wake, one says to another, I saw sick snow and a fence and a place that looks like an American motel and a big bell. What do you think it means?

In front of the building there is a covered walk, a cement path that leads up to a double glass-and-aluminum door. Through the windows I can see that men in white shirts and ties are looking out at us and that they are slipping into jackets, some yellow, some green, all looking like something the Barber might sell. I stop the Cadillac, jump out, and open the back door for Ari, who stands in his hound's-tooth coat with his ramrod posture and sniffs the air: it smells like burning plastic. I get rid of the car and then run back to open the doors of the burglar alarm factory for Ari.

The receptionist is about forty-five and she's got what I call bobsled looks: going downhill fast. She has on some costume (or charade) jewelry, a dress that's too tight, inspired make-up. She doesn't like the fluorescent light. Oh, I think, oh, she's kicking, too. I want to give the old bat a squeeze, want to say, You've still got some juice left, some of the old troublemaker. Maybe we could get together and drink gin and tell amazing lies.

"Yes?" she says to Ari.

"I would like to speak to the sales manager," says Ari with a formal, rehearsed air.

"Who shall I say is here to see him?" she says.

The receptionist gives Ari her limousine smile, and Ari lets her have it with both barrels. He rattles off his name. There's one thing you can say for Ari: it's no slouch of a name. But the receptionist doesn't bat an eye.

"The man in the Cadillac is here to see you," she says into the box on her desk.

It's all I can do to keep from grabbing her right there and giving her a hug: everyone is as flattered as a small-town prom queen. Ari smiles, shows the receptionist that he still has his own teeth. Oh, I think, oh, she must have been hell in a house trailer. I can see her lecherous smile, her old squirmy gift. She's good for a while yet, and she knows it: convincing the people around her is the problem.

To the right of the receptionist's desk there is a waiting room in which there are two sofas and an end table and a lamp. The lamp is made out of a big bell. There are Venetian blinds over the window and I open them a little with my fingers to look at the

Cadillac. I'm doing this when the salesman comes into the room. He's wearing a maroon suit and he's made a quick stop at the washroom, where he gave his rug a little dusting, a shot of aerosol freshener. He doesn't look bad, really, I think. You could say he was the Valentino of the burglar alarm. His stock falls, however, when he ignores the receptionist's searching glance. I want to grab him by the neck and say, What's wrong, Jack, are you a zombie? I give her a nice smile myself, and she's flattered, but I'm too young (to acknowledge in public anyway).

"Hello," says the salesman. "My name is Rivers."

Ari introduces himself. They shake hands. Rivers turns toward me with a slightly raised brow.

"This is my driver," says Ari.

Rivers dips his wig at me, then turns back to Ari.

"What can I do for you?" says Rivers.

"We have come," says Ari with that same rehearsed and formal tone, "to look at your alarms. Do you have a European representative?"

"No," says Rivers.

"Ah," says Ari.

Smiles everywhere. Rivers extends his arm, directs us to the showroom, and his stance, the way he holds his arm, reminds me of a bullfighter's cape work. The showroom has religious acoustics, silence, the kind of quietness you would expect down in the silos where they keep the rockets and the H-bombs. There are alarms everywhere, mounted on the walls, sitting on tables: gray boxes, silver tape, bells. Ari, I think, old boy, you've hit the jackpot this time.

Rivers shows us his alarms as though he were a gardener and these were his favorite flowers. There are alarms for safes, doors, windows. There are electric eyes, heat sensors, detectors of voltage irregularities. My favorite is one called a "capacitance alarm" and it is for a safe: all you have to do is to try to pat the till and the whistles blow. (The static electricity of your hand trips the bell.) Ari smiles. I grab all the paper I can, the technical specifications. Ari sees this as assistance, but I'm thinking, Shit, Stargell, you never can tell when this stuff will come in handy. Same cheap printing everywhere. Logo with small lightning bolts coming out of a rabid dog's mouth. Rivers brings us up to a row of bells and he points out the twelve-, fourteen-, sixteen-, and eighteen-inch disks. They all look like plaques in the burglar alarm hall of fame. Rivers pauses before one that is almost twice as large as the biggest one we've seen so far.

"This," says Rivers as though he were about to announce the results of a grudge wrestling match held on chicken wire, "is one we sell to the government. They use it at the missile bases."

Rivers touches a button on the wall. The bell goes off. It sounds like all the riveters who worked on those buildings in Manhattan had been put together in one room, something like an auditorium, I guess, and they have all been given large trash cans to rivet and they all go to work at one time. I am stunned. It is impossible to think, even to hear, since the ears become oddly numb. Ari's eyes start out of his head. It is so loud, so physical, that neither of us can do a thing. I feel as if I were standing in subzero weather, my skin anesthetized by the cold. Ari is trembling. Rivers lets us have the full treatment. We stand this way for a minute or so and then he touches the button. The bell dies.

Let's buy some bells, I think, some of these big ones.

"What do you think of that?" says Rivers.

"What," says Ari, cupping a hand to his ear.

"What do you think of the bell!"

"I think that's a good bell," says Ari.

Ari and Rivers go into a conference room with a window in one wall: they look like fathers inspecting babies in the nursery. I am left with the alarms. Ari and Rivers yammer back and forth. Ari rubs his Martian hair, stares for a moment at Rivers' rug, the hair weave, reaches out and touches it. Rivers looks offended. Ari points at his own bald spot, his hair, shrugs. Rivers seems to warm up and he lets Ari have a gentle tug on the acrylic strands. Ari thanks him, but then he is drawn toward the showroom again. They talk for a while, and Ari nods his head as if to say, Of course. Of course. But I think he's selling everyone down the river. I feel the lush warmth of the delta, the lash of the overseer's whip, hear the chains rattle, the insistent buzz of the Mississippi mosquito. Rivers gets up and leaves Ari alone and Ari pales, so I know they've come to terms, but even in this serious brush with reality, he is still hypnotically affected by the Minuteman bell. I touch its carefully machined surface, feel the lingering vibration there. It's clear that the old fool wants to take out his forty-five and celebrate, but even he knows they won't stand for that kind of thing in a factory. I move from alarm to alarm and finally get a glance at the receptionist. She looks into her compact, touches her spun-glass hair. What would you give, my darling, I think, to stop the clock?

I turn to the alarms.

Rivers comes back into the isolation booth with some papers and a small steamer trunk or large suitcase. It's covered with plastic alligator skin and has taps on the corners. Gad, I think, Ari's put himself on the door-to-door squad. He looks a little crestfallen, but not for long. Rivers opens up the steamer trunk and inside there's a demonstration kit, a small window, a small door (cozy miniatures), and they are covered with the silver tape and the necessary switches. There is a small gray box and a small bell, too. Rivers turns a key on the gray box and opens the miniature door (from which I expect a small man to emerge with a lawn mower) and the alarm goes off. Ari nods, but he's not happy with the sound of the six-inch bell, since, in comparison with the Minuteman, it doesn't make much more noise than an egg timer. Rivers closes up the case and Ari points out in the showroom what he wants: the safe alarm, the electric eye (which, with mirrors, can see around corners), the quiet police alarm, the smoke alarm, and, with his finger trembling, the Minuteman bell. Rivers works an adding machine for a while, hums, and fills out the official contractual papers he had brought with him. Ari watches with a certain doomed fascination. He signs his name and takes a roll of fifties from his pocket, counts the bills off, slaps each one down with a so-long-pal thump. That's the end of the dowry, Stargell, I think. All that's left is the map to paradise.

Ari comes out of the isolation booth, begins to sweat in the air-conditioned showroom.

"I've got a product," he says.

He shows me the agreements, a letter with the company's rabid-dog logo.

"Look," he says.

The agreement makes him the sole licensee for his homeland. It's written with a lot of lawyer drivel (the linguistic correlative of barbed wire), but it boils down to this: Ari agrees to sell twenty-five alarms or "generate" fifteen thousand a month or the deal is off and Ari forfeits his deposit. Ari is carrying his demonstration kit.

"That's a lot of alarms," I say.

"A big crime," says Ari, "and they will come to me."

He has already forgiven the errant flock, those people who first refused his attentions, and I am proud of his generosity. Stargell, I think, Ari will go down swinging. Twenty-five alarms a month. I feel a castaway glow, real camaraderie: I'd like to say, Welcome to the leaky dinghy, you old jackass. The water's warm as soup. Here's the plastic pouch, some sticky shark repellent. Can you hear the sprinkler hiss of fins, the quiet rush of papers in the bankrupts' court? We'll scream and shout, moan into the last and empty can of C rations, and the sharks will sicken on the lingering eddy of memory, satin thighs, pursed red lips, a beautiful woman. Ari stands in the cool air of the showroom, and he's got the third-degree sweats.

"Axes and knives," says Ari. "I will give my help to the frightened city."

He pats his bald spot and ogles the receptionist.

"Ha," says Ari, dismissing a phantom adversary.

Ari makes crazy motions with his free hand as we go out the door, a dying-chicken-wing kind of stabbing motion. The receptionist is talking on the phone, caressing the mouthpiece, touching her hair. Good for you, I think, a personal call. Have a good time, my darling. Don't be afraid to ask for what you want.

Ari sits in the Cadillac, in the front seat. The demonstration kit is in the back. I bring the car around to the shipping department, where the anonymous but strangely powerful boxes are stacked next to the demonstration kit.

"I have purchased the big bell," says Ari, "the Minuteman."

I chauffeur the alarms, the bell: they ride along as dignified as a Russian prince.

"I also know where to get," says Ari, making a combing gesture with his fingers, "some new hair."

It is noon and the city rises out of its golden haze. It looks like a fortress emerging from the Middle Ages and the twenty-first century: sharp spires, sheets of glass, church towers, the harp strings of the bridges.

"Slow down," says Ari. "We have the alarms."

He relaxes, settles into the seat next to me, becomes as certain as a brick.

W e enter the tunnel, the ghastly light, and drive under the moat, the East River.

"Well, Ari," I say, "what now?"

Ari looks at the alarms, and then at me. A smile takes his face and he squints as though smoke had got into his eyes.

"I don't know," Ari says with a little shyness. He lights another cigarette.

"We've got the car," I say. "We don't have to take it back."

Ari squints at me and smiles again.

"You want some hair?" I say. "A nice new rug?"

Ari shakes his head.

"Not now," he says.

He's still squinting at me, though, shyly smoking his cigarette.

It goes through my mind like the lightning bolt in the mad-dog logo: I know what he wants.

"Maybe we should drive to the other side of town," I say.

"Where is that?" says Ari.

"By the belly-dancing place," I say.

"Yes," says Ari, smiling shyly. "Maybe we could find the woman with the blue wig."

I cross over to Eighth Avenue. Ari starts jumping up and down in his seat, points her out. She's standing in front of her stoop, smoking a cigarette and looking impatient as hell. She has on her short black skirt and her blue wig.

"Pull over," says Ari.

He jumps out on the traffic side. A truck stops short, squeals: the driver blows the horn, says something unflattering about Ari's mind. Ari dismisses him and crosses over to the stoop. The horns

are honking, shrieking: it sounds like a slaughterhouse for machines. Hand trucks move in the traffic. The colors on the walls,
the signs, are weathered, tinted by the acidic rain, the sun. The
avenue has the atmosphere of a panicky evacuation.

Blue Wig's recognition of Ari makes her smile sourly. She
points at the basement stoop, but Ari shakes his head, gestures
toward the Cadillac. Blue Wig is impressed. Stargell, I think, the
woman is flattered. She walks toward the car with a healthy,
insolent shake of her ass. Before they get in, Ari spends a few
moments piling the packages, the bells and alarms, on one side of
the back seat. As they begin to get reacquainted, I discreetly put
up the partition, but I can hear them back there, grunting and
thrashing around. The avenue is filled with cars, trucks, buses,
vans, and everyone is screaming. Blue haze rises. Damn, I think,
there's not even enough room for an accident, but then one of the
screamers might have a heart attack. The exhaust is everywhere,
and the gutters are filled with sooty snow, but I can feel the
undeniable tick of spring. I stop when I see a delicatessen, go
inside, buy some beer. Yes, Stargell, I think, this is it: here we are
in a rented Cadillac filled with a bunch of burglar alarms and an
Eighth Avenue whore.

Ari and Blue Wig rustle in the back: I can hear the rhythmic
movement of the burglar alarm boxes. Blue Wig says something.
Ari lets out a deep, satisfied groan. The back seat is quiet for a
while and then there is talking, the circular rising voices. If you
could see the sound it would look like a hypnotist's turning spiral.
Stargell, I think, they're having a lovers' spat.

"I want what you owe me," says Blue Wig.

"No," says Ari, "don't do that."

I slide down the partition. Blue Wig has a box and is hitting
Ari on his face and shoulder. Ari isn't trying to protect himself so
much as to lessen the impact on the boxes.

"Please," says Ari.

Stargell, I think, just look at her: mad as hell, her hands grip-
ping the box. She pops the old goat another.

"Please," says Ari. "Here."

He reaches for his wallet, gives her something, and she tosses the box aside. Ari carefully picks it up, shakes it, tries to guess what it contains.

"You got to treat me right," says Blue Wig.

"They are well packed," says Ari, putting his box down, patting the others.

Blue Wig is sitting in the back with a victorious expression, one that says, See? The new roach powder really works.

"You shouldn't cheat people," says Blue Wig.

"I am not a citizen," says Ari. "I didn't understand."

Blue Wig sniffs, lights a cigarette. I can smell her odor, the acrid whiff of someone who has been both cold and scared. I stop the Cadillac and Blue Wig and Ari get out and climb into the front seat.

"How are you?" says Blue Wig to me.

"Couldn't be better," I say.

"You are married to my daughter," says Ari, stiffening.

He opens two bottles of beer and hands one to Blue Wig, and she takes it with a daintiness that is surprising, her I'm-with-the-quality grip. She puts the mouth to her lips, kisses it while she drinks.

"Are you still mad?" says Ari.

"No," says Blue Wig. "I'm O.K. now."

When she wants to she can be as mean as a stick with a nail in it. But things are cheery again: smooth sailing for a while. We ride through Central Park and I point out to Blue Wig the trees, give her Latin names *(Quercus alba),* tell her about xylem, phloem, cambium, the tender membrane where the new cells pop up like soap bubbles.

"Phloem," she says, as though she had milk chocolate in her mouth.

We take the turns, look at the buildings on Fifth Avenue, those apartment houses that seem as safe as Boulder Dam. No one says a word. The twitch of spring, the smoky air, Blue Wig, Ari, the alarms, are bound together. Blue Wig closes her eyes. Ari arranges his hair. I hold the bottle next to my ear, listen to the shell roar, and then we leave the park. I stop in front of Blue Wig's stoop.

"Anytime," says Blue Wig, "you want something regular, you know where I am."

The traffic pushes against us. For a moment it sounds like we're driving through a horn-blowing and shouting contest. The garbage trucks moan in some mechanical ecstasy. Blue Wig is left behind, drawn into the receding buildings, obscured by the trucks, the hand carts, the pedestrians who never make a false step.

Ari waves and smiles, grins, smokes a cigarette.

"We were passionate," he says.

The Cadillac has a certain after-the-party atmosphere. We drive downtown.

"Enid doesn't seem well," says Ari.

Ha, ha, I think. If you only knew.

"She's going to get better," I say.

Ari glances at the boxes of burglar alarms, then back at me.

"You must face reality," he says, tapping each word into my shoulder.

That's it, Stargell, let's take the bull by the horns.

"I think," says Ari, "that Enid should have been an acrobat. Her feet were a little frostbitten at the front. Did she tell you?"

"Yes," I say.

He looks at the boxes again as though they were the secret weapon. I stop in front of our building, help Ari unload, then take the Cadillac back to the rental agent, who removes the keys from my hand and gives me a brochure. Stargell, I think, the man's fading fast, but they're going to have to take him out with a net: the number on the brochure has been censored and a new one has been written in with a ballpoint pen. Auto-da-fé, Stargell, the man's a believer. I want to tell him about burglar alarms, but he'll run across them soon enough, probably on his own, after his course in motel management.

Motels, motels, Stargell, I think, do you remember the first? It was in California and I must have been seventeen and the girl couldn't have been more than sixteen. She was short, blond, full of that itchy desire. The motel was one of those that have a sign saying, "$8.50 per couple, free ice, coffee, TV," and it was tucked in a small canyon, back from the freeway, and everyone had a little bungalow, a shack with a screen door. We were embarrassed about our clothes, the big double bed. Orange lampshades, curtains that looked as though they'd been smeared with eye shadow, statues of horses. We got down to business. She had never been in a motel before, either, but she said, For a moment it was like there was only the bed and you and me. I want to go to a telephone booth and call the girl, find her fat and married (or tennis thin, hungry, and divorced) and fly to her and give her a great fuck (I'll bet we've both learned some things) just for the pure wonder of it. Then I could say, Do you remember that motel?

Jack the Ripper hears me pass his landing.

"Stargell," he says with a dirty-postcard hiss.

The door of Jack the Ripper's apartment is open only an inch or so and there doesn't seem to be much light inside.

"What can I do for you?" I say.

"Come on in," says Jack.

His resonant voice comes out of the dark crack, but even from a distance it sounds as though he were speaking out of the bottom of an oil drum. I push the door open. Jack is sitting in his chair, staring at the equipment that surrounds him, the chrome, functional-looking amplifiers, tuners, an aluminum mixing console (with at least twenty plastic levers), the green screen of an oscilloscope.

"You know I'm not a diplomat," says Jack.

"I'll bet you get what you want, all right," I say.

"Yeah," says Jack.

He shrugs, gestures toward the equipment, the cathedral: it's the cool presence he loves, the ready power, the finished surfaces.

"You borrowed from the grocery?" says Jack.

"What the hell," I say.

"Yeah," says Jack.

I look through the window, see on the glass the silver tape, the burglar alarm delineation. Jack's not taking any chances with his equipment.

"I'll get the money," I say.

"Yeah," says Jack, still staring at the dials and knobs. "I don't want to have to hurt you, especially after, you know, we listened to the music together."

Jack puts his fist next to the scars on his cheekbones, those silken webs of flesh. Jack says "music" the way a nun says "vows."

"Don't worry," I say.

Jack makes a surprised, grunting noise that sounds like someone had jumped on a large bellows. He shakes his head.

"That wasn't smart," says Jack the Ripper.

"I know," I say.

Stargell, I think, why not admit the truth?

"Do you?" says Jack the Ripper. "Do you? Sometimes I think you aren't as smart as I think you are."

"Don't worry," I say.

Jack makes that same snorting sound, and I know I've heard it before, at the zoo, in the sound track of a documentary film about hippopotamuses: you know, when they come up from the bottom of a river, opening their mouths, showing their peg teeth.

"I want to be friends," says Jack, "but you got to get things settled with the Barber."

"We're friends," I say, "you and I."

"Stargell," says Jack as he stares at his NASA oscilloscope, "if you think that's going to help you when it comes to, you know, what I do for the Barber, I want to tell you something."

"What's that?" I say.

Jack speaks as though he'd just sprung the hangman's trap.

"You're wrong," he says.

I stand for a moment in the cool silence of his apartment: it's as

quiet as a stone cellar. There's a new carpet on the floor and paths
are marked on it with sheets of clear plastic. It makes me think
I'm in the garden of a chemical factory, where the attendants say,
Look at this, will you? The fucking grass is growing up through
the Astroturf. Jack the Ripper's rug is orange.

"That's a nice suit," says Jack.

"I was married in it," I say. "It makes me feel good just to put
it on."

It does, too. We drank cool, perfect champagne. It made the
hands steady, the head clear. It was a celebration and Enid
looked lovely, and she was filled with a quiet joy, a touching, shy
reserve. Nothing happened, really. There were no earthquakes or
floods, no natural disasters of the mind. Enid just turned into
Edith Piaf, only Enid's more maudlin.

"You still going to be around at Easter?" says Jack.

"Yes," I say.

"Are you still coming down," he says, "to listen to the music?"

"If you'll still let me," I say.

"Wear the suit," says Jack.

"Sure," I say. "Don't worry."

"I'm not worried," says Jack. "I'm just a little sorry in advance."

Our living room looks like a small warehouse for burglar
alarms and Ari is sitting in the middle of the boxes. I can smell
the cardboard and the gluey tape. Ari is quiet, in Pall Mall meditation. Enid is still in the bedroom, and when I touch her she
flinches and says, from beneath the pillow (so that it's a little
muffled, but still distinct), "No." She shakes her foot, and I realize that if she were standing up she'd be stomping the floor.

I stand before Ari again.

"How about a war movie?" I say.

"Later," says Ari.

He looks at me suspiciously through the smoke. He's using a
mixing bowl for an ashtray and I empty it, and when I come back
he looks at me with that same suspicious expression. Stargell, I

think, he looks like a conspiracy of one. The steamer trunk with the alligator skin and the metal taps on the corners sits next to him.

"Hungry?" I say.

"No," says Ari.

Actually, Stargell, I think, the old skunk looks like he is about to make his first jump.

"Look," I say, "I'll be a customer."

"What?" says Ari out of his smoky presence.

"You can try the case on me. You can demonstrate the alarms."

"Would you?" says Ari, coming out of the smoke like a bull out of the fog. He straightens his hair, drops his suspicion, smiles.

"Be glad to," I say.

"I have been thinking," says Ari, "how I would convince people of the value of the alarms."

Ari straightens his coat, gives his case the once-over, touches it carefully. Stargell, I think, you can't say Ari is just another asshole who's substituted ambition for character: he really believes in these screwy schemes, in alarms and pogo sticks. This hits me hard, as though someone had slapped me in the face with a frypan, but I come out of it all right.

"How shall we do it?" says Ari.

"I'll go into the hall and knock on the door," I say.

Ari busies himself with his kit and I go into the hall and stand beneath the fuse box. I mess up my hair, loosen my tie, indulge myself in a little mean, junkyard dread, find myself pounding on the green door of the apartment. Ari opens up.

"Yes?" says Ari.

He speaks as though he's been soaking in warm oil overnight. I shake his hand.

"Mr. Ari," I say. "I saw the news in the papers. Horrible. What a crime. Chopped up the whole family. Chop, chop, chop."

I make the appropriate motions.

"Grandmother, babies. The mutt."

"Yes," says Ari, as though he had been there or (at worst) had seen the official police photographs. What a cool leech he is, what a conniver. He's all right in my book.

"My wife, my dear wife is so upset," I say. "She can't even *get out of bed*."

Ari touches my arm, gives me a reassuring pat, nods, looks like an Aegean Freud.

"I understand," he says, trying to draw my attention to the kit. "We have . . ."

He turns toward the alligator case, the small steamer trunk. Stargell, I think, he's not going to get away with that trick.

"No, you don't," I scream. "She thinks the end is near. *What the hell am I going to do!*"

Ari flinches.

"Now wait a moment," he says.

Actually, he's not bad at this: he shows some commercial cape work. I find myself staring at the case.

"Things have gotten pretty fucking screwy," I say.

Ari makes a kind of yogi hum, a strangely reassuring sound which he probably picked up from the King of Lampur, or the resident Dali Lama, the Himalayan rice man.

"You have nothing to worry about," says Ari.

He opens the kit.

"All you need is an alarm," he says.

"Yeah," I say. "That's it. What have you got?"

He describes (in garbled terms) the essence of the alarms, tells me about tape that goes over glass, switches that are installed on doors and windows.

"Now," says Ari. "We will make a test."

He reaches into his kit, turns a switch. He reminds me of someone who's just discovered alchemy, a pig-shit-into-gold heavy.

"Open that door," he says.

He points to the dollhouse door.

"If a burglar should try to open it . . . ." he says. "Well. See for yourself."

I grab the small doorknob, open the door, and the alarm goes off. It isn't very loud, really, not when you consider the Minuteman.

"Turn it off," I say.

Ari hesitates for a moment, twists a switch first one way and then another, and finally turns off the alarm.

"That's great," I say. "You'd have to be crazy to go into a house that's making a noise like that."

"Yes," says Ari.

Enid rises, opens the bedroom door a little, peers out at us.

"More boxes," she says.

"I have been busy," says Ari.

Enid seems to run on wires: she drifts through the living room (looking once at Ari's alligator skin suitcase), through the kitchen, and into the bathroom, where she spends a moment or two (probably hovering over the toilet) before drifting through the kitchen, the living room, and into the warmth and reassuring odor of the bed. We wait for her to pass as though she were a subway.

"And if you have a safe," says Ari, warming to the pitch like a snake-oil man, "we have an alarm built for it."

I wouldn't mind having a little money oven, I think. Enid could keep her underwear inside.

Ari uses his hand like a hatchet, chops into a brown box. The safe alarm emerges.

"Here," says Ari after cracking open another seal, "is an electric eye."

He laughs, tears into other boxes, shows me the alarms.

"You don't have to worry," he says.

"I feel better," I say.

I can smell the industrial odor of the alarms, the faint scent of milling oil, the musk of styrofoam packaging. Ari has the kind of smile that usually goes with driving nails into the coffin of one's bitterest enemy: it seems to say, Here I am, Jack, sealing you up. A tidy job, Jack.

"Sold," I say.

"But wait," says Ari.

He looks through the opened boxes, the styrofoam balls, sees that there is still a sealed package.

"We have another bell," says Ari.

Ari smashes through the cardboard, throws stuff that looks like gray waffles from the box, and holds (for me to admire) the Minuteman bell. It is smoother than a discus, three times as large: it makes me think Ari should have a license for it, a kind of gun permit or top security clearance. Ari holds the Minuteman like a trophy, a prize taken in the industrial wilds. His hands are trembling.

"That's some bell," I say.

"Wait until you hear it," says Ari.

Before I can say a word, he's undone the wires from the demonstration kit. That a boy, I think. Five will get you ten, you'll never be able to put it back together. No walking from door to door for you, Frog Prince. But Ari surprises me. He works with a quick dexterity, mumbles about using explosives during the war, slips two wires into the Minuteman bell, then pushes a button, and the wires are mounted. Ari throws the main switch and opens the dollhouse door.

If sound were an object, this one would be Grand Central Station. The floor is vibrating. The skin on my face feels as if it were asleep.

"Turn it off! Turn it off!" I scream.

The bell has blown Ari back into the beartrap bed, where he squints and grits his teeth: he looks like someone on a rocket sled, taking at least ten G's. His face sags and his eyes pop with wonder: he's cracked the sound barrier.

"Turn it off!" I scream, but I have that helpless underwater feeling, a dreamy, slow-moving horror.

I see Enid rise and come from the bedroom. She stands at the door, puts her hands over her ears, stomps up and down. The vibration is as distinct as that from a reducing machine: I can feel my chair hum. Enid stands in front of me with her hands at the sides of her head and she is screaming. I can't hear her, but I know she's saying, "You're being bad to me!" I notice the apartment door is bouncing on its hinges and plaster is dropping in earthquake puffs from the top and sides of the frame. Stargell, I think, there's only one man who could hit the door that hard. Ari notices my stricken face and decides he's had enough of the Minuteman. Enid sits down on the beartrap bed and stomps her feet, and she lets me know (by her puffed-up cheeks) that she's holding her breath. Ari pushes a small red button, one that works a mechanism for holding the wires to the bell. Nothing happens. Ari gives the wires a gentle tug. Nothing. Or more pounding, vibrating, numbing sound. Enid gets mad, stops holding her breath, and stands before me, and when she opens her mouth I can only hear the bell, but I know she's saying, "Why are you being bad to me? Why are you being bad to me?" Ari tugs, frowns. Enid starts crying, throws herself on the sofa, covers her head with pillows, makes swimming movements with her legs. The door jumps on its hinges and its frame is surrounded by the smoky falling plaster. Enid can't stand it anymore: she jumps from the sofa, stands before me, slaps my face. "Why are you being bad!" she says.

I go into the kitchen and open the door for Jack the Ripper. He throws me against the shower, walks slowly into the living room, reaches over Ari's shoulder and into the kit, turns a key there. The alarm stops.

The quietness is as smooth as soft water, refreshing. I wonder how many people in the building are perched by a window, holding the family goods (wrapped in a sheet), ready to jump. Ari looks up, sees Jack, the veiny, large, scarred face. Enid is still crying.

"That's a big bell," says Jack the Ripper.

"Yes," says Ari.

Jack looks at Ari's red hair.

"You seem to know about alarms," says Ari. But this is just a dodge. Ari really wants to get his hands on the forty-five.

"I got an alarm," says Jack with a modest shrug of his shoulders. "But I ain't got a bell like that."

Enid sobs on the sofa.

"You sell this stuff?" says Jack.

"Yes," says Ari.

"He sells it overseas," I say.

"I am the European representative of the company," says Ari. "I will begin in the Mediterranean."

Jack nods, frowns because his worst suspicions have been confirmed.

"Yeah," says Jack, "they sell all the good stuff to the Arabs and leave us the shit."

Jack stares at Enid for a moment, and under his heavy glance Enid cries all the harder. Jack walks to the door.

"Stargell," he says.

I walk into the kitchen. We stand at the door, where the dust from the plaster looks like someone has spilled a pound of flour.

"I know you got problems," says Jack, "but you got to stop the fucking noise."

The scars on his cheekbones are silky and white.

"You understand?" says Jack.

"Sure," I say to him. "I'll do better."

As he turns to go, he looks over his shoulder at the Minuteman bell.

"It's a great bell," he says.

"It's called a Minuteman," I say.

"Yeah?" he says. "Like Paul Revere?"

"Yes," I say.

"Fucking Arabs," he says.

Our shoes leave neat patterns in the dust and there are flecks of plaster in Jack's eyebrows.

"You heard me, Stargell," he says, tapping me in the center of the chest with a baseball bat finger. "Keep your relatives quiet."

He says "relatives" with the same tone he would use for "iguanas." I close the door behind him.

Ari is a little trembly, more impressed than ever with his equipment. The bell sounded louder (if that really is possible) in a small space than at the industrial park. It is an awe-inspiring sound. I can see the end of the world, the sky scratched by long, perfect cylinders: they look like windblown rain on a window and they are moving fast (so goddamn fast I get the willies just thinking about it) toward the flatlands, Kansas and Nebraska, where the spring corn rustles in the wind. Sleek and green stuff. Then the bells ring. The insects stop their quiet nibbling, turn and listen. Ari's bells are going as the heat and light bloom over the fields.

"Come on," I say to Enid.

She lets me put my hand on her heaving back.

"Is he gone?" says Enid.

"Yes," I say.

I give her a little kiss. I've got some nice turkey in the icebox, so I say, "How about a nice turkey sandwich? With butter and lettuce."

"Yes," says Enid. "I'm a little hungry."

"I'll cut the crusts off," I say.

"Are there any chips?" says Enid.

Things are looking up, Stargell, I think. The woman wants chips.

"Yes," I say.

I make the sandwiches, cut off the crusts, make small triangles, and arrange them on the plate: it looks like we're going to eat a geometry lesson. I put out chips, too.

"I've got to wash my face," says Enid.

Ari and I sit at the table and wait for her. Ari's still a little shaky, but he's getting over the effect of the bell. My ears are ringing, and I sit there, contemplating the sandwiches and listening to the high-pitched hiss.

"Ah," says Enid, after coming back to the table and tasting a turkey sandwich, "that's good."

"Yes," says Ari. "Refreshing."

We eat in silence and then Enid and I leave Ari with his boxes and styrofoam. I follow her into the bedroom, where she sits down on the bed and squeezes my hand.

"I love you," she says.

I sit down next to her.

"I'm going to California," I say.

"Of course you are," says Enid.

She smiles, and for a moment she is as pretty and healthy as she was in the old days: faintly crooked smile, wet, pink lips, dark eyes, a musky presence that is as exotic as Istanbul.

"It'll be best," says Enid.

"Yes," I say.

"When you come back you can find a place of your own," she says, "and then I could come and visit you."

Yes, that's it. I'll find a place with a skylight and a fireplace and it will have a view of some trees, a garden. A child and mother will spend an afternoon there. Maybe there will be tulips in the garden and in the spring they'll pop up, as bright as a cartoon. Enid could ring my bell and climb the stairs in her raincoat with nothing on beneath it.

Enid gives me a real hug.

"I'll be gone a couple of weeks," I say.

"Good," says Enid.

She stares into the air shaft, sees the dirty brick, the black streaks in it, hears the winches squeak. Women are taking in their frozen clothes. The black markings on the stone make the air shaft seem oddly precious: it is as though the women have come into a church to hang their clothes. Enid watches as the frozen long johns, stiff as ironing boards, are dragged over a window sill.

Having Ari around upsets Enid, because it means she has to get out of bed before nine o'clock in the morning. Maybe it's the memory of Macedonia, the lingering sensation of the air blast of an exploding mortar shell, but for whatever reason, Enid does it. She drags herself out of bed as though she had a tail.

"God," says Enid, when she hears the morning television shows. "Oh, God."

She stands in her pink nightgown. My darling is right: morning television just makes me feel like I'm in a nut house.

Enid whispers as I stumble in the dark, trying to find a pair of shoes.

"I had a pet deer and I didn't feed it once and Father called me into the yard. This was in northern Greece. Look, he said, the deer is hungry. The deer is thirsty. Who has let the deer become this way? I had, and I told him so. This will teach you, he said. He took out the pistol, the same one he has in the other room, and he shot the deer's head off. What a mess."

Enid scowls at her father through the glass door, into the video light of the living room.

"He did other things, too," says Enid.

Enid takes a cold shower, begins to do sit-ups in the bedroom. Soon she's running around the block. We eat oatmeal with cream, nuts, brown sugar, and raisins. Enid and I go to the movies. She grumbles at night.

"Good morning, Father," she says.

"Good morning," says the old goat.

We drink coffee together, just like people. I can tell that something is gnawing at Enid. I get her to take a walk with me and she insists on going down to the West Side Highway, where she can watch the cars pass by.

In the evening I see her lighting a cigarette with a match from a book that has an advertisement for a driving school on it.

"Father," says Enid.

"Yes, my dear?" says Ari.

"I want something," she says.

"Tell me what it is," says Ari.

They sound like they have escaped from a language laboratory.

"I want to learn how to drive a car," says Enid.

She holds up the matchbook.

Stargell, my boy, she'll become an American yet. I think Enid needs a big Oldsmobile, a Rocket Eighty-Eight. She'll escape to California and live in a condominium and go to surfing parties and swap meets.

Ari reads the matchbook carefully.

"Do you think they are safe?" he says to me.

I look at the matchbook. There's a list of features the school offers, and each one has a dot, a bullet, next to it: dual controls (that will cause some fun, Stargell; wait until the teacher tells Enid to slow down: he'll get an earful then), state certification (this will come in handy, too), full insurance, experienced teachers, new cars.

"Sure," I say.

"I want to drive the car," says Enid.

She puts her arms out in front of herself, as though she were holding the steering wheel of a car, turns it back and forth the way old ladies do when they're nervous. They don't think they're driving unless they're doing something, stepping on the brake or turning the wheel. Stargell, I think, just be glad you're not going along for this particular ride.

"Then we will get lessons," says Ari.

"Thank you, Father," says Enid.

She gives him a peck on the cheek.

"Thank you, Stargell," she says.

She squeezes my hand and looks into my eyes and I can see she's on the verge of crying. She's thinking, I've got a second chance. Maybe I'll get a Plymouth.

"Voom," says Enid.

The old goat smiles at her.

"Which do you think is the superior automobile," says Enid, "Oldsmobile or Buick?"

She is still sitting at one of the chairs next to the dining table. One foot is up against what she imagines is an accelerator, the other is flat on the floor. One hand holds the wheel, the other toys (in a professional manner) with a gear shift knob.

"My preference is the Studebaker," says Ari. He has a serious slash of an expression. "I had a fifty-one, after the war, a white convertible. It had a radio and whitewalls."

Enid giggles.

"Of course," says Ari, as though he were explaining something of great importance, "I had more hair then. Enid was just a little girl. Her mother was still young."

Enid drives for a while.

"So it's decided," I say.

"Yes," says Ari. "Would you call the school?"

"You call them, Stargell," says Enid. "You speak so well on the phone."

Oh, I think, you little charmer, you. No wonder I married you three years ago.

"Ace," says a man with a brisk voice. Listening to him is like taking a whiff of ammonia. We have a quick, refreshing talk.

"He'll be right over," I say to Enid and Ari. "His name is Frank McGraw."

Enid makes Ari and me wait in the bedroom while she takes a shower. Ari and I sit on the unmade bed and stare into the light of the air shaft, and Ari says to me, "What do you think of this?"

"It's good," I say.

"Yes," says Ari. "We should have thought of it ourselves."

Ari smokes cigarettes while Enid takes the longest shower of her life.

"I must prepare," she says.

When she's done with herself, she's slinking around the apartment, swinging her shoulders from side to side. She takes quick puffs from her cigarette.

"Once I thought I would be a *femme fatale*," she says, looking at me over her shoulder.

"I must take a picture," says Ari.

He digs through his weird-looking luggage, picks out a camera, bangs it on his knee, then pries it open. The camera is covered with imitation skin, so it looks like a small alligator that's having an autopsy. Ari pokes at it with his finger. Enid is still posing, moving her shoulders from side to side.

Someone knocks at the door.

"Stargell," she says, blowing out a quick puff of smoke, "could you get that?"

I let McGraw in. He's wearing dark glasses and a uniform of some sort. He smiles at me, at Ari, and daintily shakes Enid's hand. McGraw is about forty-five, short. He has a vaguely aeronautical quality, and I expect him to say "negative" for "no." He also has a gold tooth and big ears.

"Have you ever driven a car?" he says to Enid.

Ari and I sit on the beartrap. Ari is still playing with his camera, slamming the lid against its latch, gnawing at the plastic alligator skin. McGraw and Enid ignore us.

"No," says Enid. "But my father is a wonderful driver."

Ari grunts.

"Good, good," says McGraw, but you can see he doesn't believe it for a minute.

He explains about a learner's permit, gives Enid a booklet entitled "The Rules Of The Road." Enid frowns. The booklet has already made her feel excluded.

"Study that," says McGraw. "Then we will take the written test. I'll pick you up. The down payment for the lessons is a hundred dollars and it is nonrefundable."

Ari is still chomping on the camera, trying to get the latch to work, but he mumbles at McGraw.

"Excuse me?" says McGraw.

"How much altogether?" says Ari.

McGraw twists around in his chair and looks at the two of us as though we were two fops in the Bellevue waiting room, the Mutt and Jeff of Thorazine.

"For everything?" says McGraw.

"The works," I say.

McGraw cocks an ear and says, "Didn't I speak to you on the phone?"

"That's right," I say.

"Well," says McGraw, "the whole package comes to four hundred dollars."

Ari bites through the plastic alligator skin, looks at McGraw with the eyes of a retired and angry colonel, spits out the brown hunk of plastic.

"You," says Ari, "are a thief."

McGraw bristles, but then he's in business, so it just puts another drop in the bucket of his ulcer. Scream, I think, show the colonel what you're made of.

"That's not true," says McGraw.

"Ha!" says Ari. "Stargell, what do you think?"

"It's a bargain," I say. "What the hell. Pay him."

"He is a thief," says Ari.

"Father, Father," says Enid. She's moving her shoulders from side to side, trying to light a cigarette. She strikes match after match, but the blue sulfur just crumbles at the tips of her sweaty fingers. Always spend top dollar on promotion, I think. Look at that lousy matchbook for the driving school.

"Three hundred and fifty," says Ari.

"Four," says McGraw, stiffening a little. He pushes his dark glasses against the bridge of his nose.

"Father, Father," says Enid. Her lips begin to tremble.

"Three seventy-five," says Ari.

"Sold," says McGraw.

Stargell, I think, that's the boy for me. He's already got his hand out. Ari looks like a lizard has run up the sleeve of his shirt, but he counts out the money, the first payment.

"How about a little practice?" I say.

I can see Enid doesn't want to mess around with the learner's permit. She can't even stand the checker at the A & P, so how the hell can she wait in line at the Department of Motor Vehicles.

"She doesn't have her license," says McGraw. "It's not legal."

"Legal, legal," says Ari. "You're the thief."

"Now wait just a darn minute," says McGraw.

"Stop, stop, stop," says Enid.

I light her cigarette.

"Thank you," she says.

McGraw sits on his chair, looking at Enid, at the pile of burglar alarm boxes.

"O.K.," he says. "A couple of times around the block."

"That will be wonderful," says Enid.

I can see her getting her first ticket for doing 110 in a school zone. She'll say to the cop, Who are you to tell me what to do? I know of what my machine is capable.

We go downstairs. Enid and Ari and McGraw go outside and look at the school's car. The postman comes in and I stop to say hello. He's a country-and-western-buff postman and he usually sings something for me. He gives me my mail.

"How are things?" I say.

"I'm as happy as a pig in shit," he says.

He gives me "On the Wings of a Snow White Dove," listens to the hard acoustics of the stairwell. After he's done, a woman who is upstairs on a landing says, "What are you wasting time for? I want my mail. You lazy, singing bastard!"

The postman looks at me and says, "I've got to go back to work."

The car is a Duster, and Enid is already behind the wheel. Ari kicks the tires. It's painted a daffodil yellow. McGraw gets in, behind the second steering wheel, and the car goes down the street, its turn signals blinking.

"It's not a bad-looking car," says Ari. "There are many people in Athens now who have the money for a Toyota. But they don't know how to drive."

He rubs his head.

We wait. I can hear the postman opening the mailboxes, the *clop, clop, clop* of his sorting.

The woman from upstairs says, through the stairwell, "I want my mail, you slimy bastard. You're putting on airs, aren't you, talking to that man from the next landing. He's crazy. I want my mail."

Ari and I stand in the street and I can hear the distant but moving sound of a honking horn. There is the roar of an engine, the pale, weak roar (to be sure), but a roar nevertheless, of a Duster. It comes down the street with its headlights on and its horn honking. It's stopping and starting, swinging from side to side. I can see McGraw gesticulating and arguing, and Enid's giving him what for: the lower part of her face is one quick shudder. The machine lurches, and then I can see Enid spitting on McGraw. He puts his hand on his face, and then the Duster races down the street and smashes through the telephone booth in front of the building and continues right along, taking out the fireplug. Ha! Stargell, I think, look at the water. McGraw is screaming. The car's blinkers are still going. Ari and I run up to it and open a door, which takes a little doing, since the fireplug was hit on Enid's side, and it creased the door. Ari and I give it a yank, and Enid steps out as regal as can be. McGraw is still shouting. Enid walks right around the remains of the telephone booth and the fireplug.

"That man insulted me," she says.

She goes into the building.

McGraw gets out of the car and says, "Who the hell is she?"

"My daughter," says Ari, bracing a little in the misty breeze.

"You can have her," says McGraw. "What about my car?"

"You are insured," says Ari.

"But she didn't have a license," says McGraw. "My insurance isn't any good unless the driver has a license."

Ari shrugs. I shrug. McGraw stands in his wet uniform.

"Hell," says McGraw.

The trunk of the Duster is half open and McGraw reaches inside and takes out a tire iron and stands in front of Ari.

"You're going to pay for this Duster," he says.

"I am not," says Ari.

"You made me give her a lesson," says McGraw. "I didn't want to."

"Go away," says Ari.

"I'll sue you," says McGraw.

There's a little blood on his forehead from the broken glass on his side of the car. He menaces Ari with the tire iron. Jack the Ripper comes out of Scooter's, walks across the intersection, and says to me, "Stargell, is this man bothering you or your relatives?"

"Who are you?" says McGraw.

"Is this your car?" says Jack the Ripper.

"Yes," says McGraw.

"I don't want it in front of my building. And look at the fire hydrant."

McGraw is a little dizzy: just a moment ago he had a tidy business, a Duster. Now he's just another sap who's fallen into the greedy hands of the insurance company. McGraw hits Jack with the tire iron. Jack slaps him down as though he were a bug, right into the broken fire hydrant. I can see a rainbow in the misty air.

"Some people have all the nerve," says Jack.

By the time the police arrive we're all inside the building. McGraw is taken off in an ambulance. As I pass the mailman he touches my arm, then finishes closing up the boxes.

"You know what?" he says.

"What?" I say.

"The old woman didn't get a goddamned thing."

He sings "Silver Threads and Golden Needles Cannot Mend This Broken Heart of Mine" as he goes down the hall.

When Ari and I get upstairs we find that Enid is preparing for bed.

"That man was not a nice man," she says. "He tried to tell me what to do."

Ari and I stand side by side. I realize that both of us are shrugging the same way.

"I'm going to bed," says Enid.

She closes the bedroom door. Ari looks at his burglar alarms. Stargell, I think, you've got to get the woman downstairs on a mailing list: tools, down clothes, auctions, antiques. It will snap her light, my boy. She'll bring the postman a cup of tea and say, Is that bundle there, the one bound with twine, is that one for me, my darling?

The days pass. Ari waits for his exile to end, for the return date on his airline ticket to arrive. One morning I find a letter from my father. His handwriting is functional, precise: every letter looks like a design for a building.

I want to see you here soon boy and I don't mean maybe, the letter says. Was there anything in your work for the pain?

My father means the work in the think tank. The Stargell was more medical than anything else: my successes came on hospital jobs. After these I hit the moths at full throttle (bump and wing, the almond heads). Jolting Joe knew about pain, but his work would only give me the best way to bomb Los Angeles.

Heat kills, says Jolting Joe, L.A. is perfect for it. Nice megaton clusters, well spaced. Nothing left but the paper work.

Ari comes into the apartment, carrying two shopping bags and a small bottle of ouzo.

"Stargell," he says.

I go over to the door and see that the bags have come from a secondhand-china store on Sixth Avenue: the place has a dusty odor, the smell of bankrupt hotels and restaurants. Ari has his head bent to one side, his cracked expression. His Martian hair is messed up.

"What's in the bags?" I say.

"Plates," says Ari. "Come down to the courtyard with me."

Stargell, I think, Ari's getting more gentle every day. He means the air shaft. We go downstairs, come to the door which leads into the bottom of Ari's courtyard. I push it open and we stand in a gray luminescence. Ari stares at things with his mouth open, then puts down the bag and opens the small bottle of ouzo. We share it, standing in that TV light, and Ari goes through his plans now (it's become a litany), and I nod, while thinking, Yes, yes, yes.

"Here," says Ari, reaching into one of the sacks and handing me a plate. It's a white piece of china, cafeteria heavy.

"Like this," says Ari, taking a plate from one of his sacks. He

throws it across the air shaft. Stargell, I think, that's the ticket. I
throw mine, too. And there we are, throwing plates as fast as we
can get them out of the sacks, not laughing, not grim, just throwing those plates against the wall.

The Portuguese have their noses stuck over their window sills
and Enid does, too. From the bottom of the air shaft it looks like
a pink mole (or family of moles) is living in every apartment and
they are now peering down at us.

"Father, Father," she says, "this is America."

"Huh," says Ari, reaching into a sack, holding his head to one
side and breathing through his mouth. He looks at me with such
great surprise that it almost verges on suspicion.

"You don't break plates here?" he says.

He wrinkles his nose and squints at me. I'm still thinking of the
wrecking-ball crash the plates make against stone.

"We do now," I say, picking up a navy platter and sailing it
(Frisbee style) against the streaked wall. The noses stay on their
sills until we're done.

"Ha," says Ari.

We finish the bottle and smash that, too.

"Now," says Ari, with a certain diplomatic ceremony, "it's
time for a nap."

As he climbs the stairs to the apartment, I see that Ari has
made another purchase while killing time: he's wearing a pair of
black high-top tennis shoes, and he jumps a little from step to
step, as if he could feel the new springiness.

I give Enid some "household" money and this leaves enough
to buy a bus ticket to California. I'll get two loaves of white bread
and a big piece of cheese, some Colman's mustard, and I'll sit in
the back of the bus, eating sandwiches and watching the country
roll by. That mustard will be so strong my eyes will water. The
black fields will slip around us as smoothly as a turning record.
The dark land will be ready for planting, and I'll taste the mustard and smell the rich, fertile odor, see machines moving across
the fields, dropping seeds the way a turtle lays its eggs. I'll get an

onion, too, and slice it and put it on the cheese sandwiches.
There'll be enough cash left over for a pint, and I'll drink it as we
cross the Mississippi, as we push into land so flat you can feel the
pressure of the sky. I've got a barlow knife to cut the onion and
the cheese. My cheeks will be full and moving as I look out the
window of the bus.

Ari is reading his technical papers, tracing, with a finger, the
lines of electricity through the printed schematic. He looks up
suddenly, as though he'd felt a sharp and sudden pain.

"What's up?" I say.

"Nothing," he says, although I can see he's blushing so hard he
must be as warm as a wood stove. Occasionally he pats his weird-
looking hair and chuckles.

I drop downstairs, already feeling the sea-tide swaying of the
bus, the prairie-schooner rocking. Might as well buy the bread
now, I think. I'll go to the cheese store for the rest. The Barber's
sitting behind the counter, smoking cigarettes, and challenging
his raw liquor to do its worst. Smiling Mary has a beauty. My
advice would be to have it made permanent at a tattoo parlor.
Enough experimenting.

"How are you, Sal?" I say.

I squeeze the long loaves of bread. Sal looks a little sour.

"Where you been?" says the Barber.

Smiling Mary gives me a look that could skin a cat.

"I was at an industrial park," I say. "What do you think of
that?"

"Nothing," says the Barber.

Smiling Mary gives me another one of those looks. The Barber
toys with his glass, has a little nip, but he still looks sour. Smiling
Mary has on a pants suit.

"I'd of thought you'd been here sooner," says the Barber.

"I think you're a great man, Sal," I say, "but these days I'm
keeping my visits to a minimum."

"Ah," says the Barber, "I'm just a grocer."

He loves it, though. The Barber needs his stroking. Maybe one
night Smiling Mary will give it to him, too, with a baseball bat.
She can tell what I'm thinking and her face twitches once in
acknowledgment.

"Here's what you came for," says the Barber. "Leave the bread alone. People don't want squashed bread."

He pushes an envelope across the counter. Smiling Mary nods.

"What's that?" I say.

"Your number," says the Barber. "Your number hit."

He sighs. Smiling Mary sighs. And in a fit of idiotic politeness, I sigh, too. It's as though we were looking at a dead canary.

"You could pay me half what you owe," says the Barber.

"We made a deal," I say, putting the envelope in my pocket.

"That's right," says the Barber with a click in his voice that sounds like someone shoving a full magazine into a pistol and working a cartridge into the chamber. "I'll see you in two weeks."

Smiling Mary blinks, touches the cool blue bruise. The Barber's liquor gurgles into his glass.

"Two weeks," he says.

The street is cool and the snow is almost gone.

Well, Stargell, I think, you can get a jet. Beautiful women walk up and down the aisles and the whole business moves at six hundred miles an hour. There's strange food and you can look into the wing and see the mechanical works, the slick hydraulic pistons.

Fucking money, I think, filthy trash. I want to throw the scummy slop in the street. Stargell, I think, you're getting rabid. And it's about time, too, thank God.

I come into the apartment. Ari is still sitting at the table, tracing the flow of electricity.

"Things are looking up," I say.

"Yes," says Ari. But he doesn't seem interested. He's still blushing and patting his head, running a finger around in his bald spot.

"You're going to make a pile selling these things," I say. "Just think of the lonely women you'll meet if you start working door to door."

Ari groans.

"What's wrong?" I say. "Is there something wrong with the burglar alarm? We'll take it back and shove it down their throats if they sold you shoddy goods."

That's the way to deal with an industrial park.

"No," says Ari. "The burglar alarms are beautiful. Look."

He gestures to the sofa and floor, where the alarms sit as if they were eggs laid by a flying saucer.

"What's the problem?" I say.

Ari blushes again, blinks, squints, and looks up at me. He makes a polishing motion with one hand at the side of his head.

"I've got a low disease," he says.

"How low?" I say.

"I have a drip," he says.

"You got the clap," I say.

"Yes," he says. "That's what I think they call it in your country."

Enid comes into the living room, stands at the door, looks at her father. He is still making that motion with his hand: it seems that he's trying to adjust an invisible watch cap. Enid has wide, backward eyes.

"What is wrong here?" she says.

I shrug, gesture to Ari, who is now smiling, humming a bouzouki song, smoking a cigarette: the cat's out of the bag, so he dwells on his enjoyment, the sub-stoop lust and satisfaction.

"Can you believe it?" I say. "The old goat's got the clap."

"Clap?" says Enid.

Ari looks up at her with the most childlike sense of ignorance and says something in Greek: his hands are held palms up as though he were carrying a large platter.

"Oh, my God, oh, my God," says Enid. "Have you touched anything in the bathroom?"

"Of course," says Ari.

Enid jumps back. Ari reaches out for her.

"We've got to clean the bathroom," says Enid. "We've got to boil the sheets. All the towels."

I write the address and telephone number of a doctor on a slip of paper and give it to Ari.

"He'll fix you up," I say.

Ari goes on humming, staring at his alarms and his high-top tennis shoes, which are sitting next to the beartrap and which I think he likes almost as much as the Minuteman bell.

"Thank you, Stargell," he says.

"Don't mention it," I say.

He sees me following his gaze to the high-tops.

"It's funny," says Ari, "but those shoes make me feel like hopping."

He holds up two fingers, makes a small rabbit with his hand.

Enid has thrown her heart into it. There are large kettles on the stove and there are bubbles along the bottom of the pots where the water is almost ready to boil. Enid stands before them, wringing her hands and waiting. At best she seems skittish, as if she were standing in a flooded room where there was also a live wire. The water boils. Enid pours some of it into a bucket, mixes in Lysol, detergent, bleach, Drano, Comet, and then charges the bathroom. I look in after a moment and see that she's hard at work with a toothbrush.

I make my reservation, speak to a woman who has a lascivious voice that's as cool as silk stockings.

I pack a small bag and put it in the living room.

"I'm going to California," I say to Ari.

"Yes," he says. "I know."

"It's been great," I say.

Ari blushes, looks at his alarms, his high-top tennis shoes.

"We are friends now," says Ari.

He stands up and shakes my hand with his most severe military crispness.

"Thank you," he says.

I go into the bathroom and find Enid on the floor, scrubbing and muttering. She keeps her nose over the pail as though the cleaner's odor were oxygen and she had emphysema.

"I'll be back," I say.

Enid is wearing rubber gloves. She dips the toothbrush into her bucket and begins working on the white bolts that hold the toilet over the drain.

"Here's a little more money," I say.

She takes the money from my hand and I can tell that if she had to take it with her fingers she'd shove it into the Lysol and hang it out to dry, but the rubber gloves protect her. Enid is wearing a pair of blue jeans, a blue cotton top, a pair of tennis shoes. One hand in a rubber glove rests on the top of the bucket and the other is now moving the brush over the porcelain tank. The tank is clean, white, and shiny: it looks like a big tooth.

"How did he get that goddamned disease?" says Enid.

She is shaking now, crying into the Lysol, still scrubbing the big tooth.

"How did he?" she says.

I reach out to her, but she squirms away.

"How do I know you haven't got it, too?" she says.

"I haven't done anything," I say.

She turns, shows me her face that's now as red as a radish, her amazing anger.

"But you wanted to, didn't you?" she says.

It would be great. I think of Barbeau, of women I have known.

"I didn't do anything," I say.

"Filthy, filthy," she says.

She starts working with the brush again.

"You are a freak," she says. "They should put you in a side show."

"I'd like that," I say.

I would, too: the smell of sawdust, the tent, a big fat woman, an alligator man, the people, the faces going by. Everyone trying to explain miracles.

Enid works her way around the lip of the bowl.

"Did it feel good?" says Enid.

"What?" I say.

"Wanting to," she says.

Thank God for the old troublemaker: at least I know I'm still alive.

"Yes," I say.

Enid throws the toothbrush into the bucket and I can see the crown-shaped splash it makes. Enid starts the old boohoo and gives it a good workout.

"Oh, what am I going to do?" she says.

I squat next to her, look at her swollen eyelids, her red face. She doesn't seem to mind when I touch her hair. She gently leans against me and I can feel her breathing, her small gasps for air.

"Do you remember," I say, "the old days, the first winter we spent, when it was so cold you could hear the rats creak in the wall? Do you remember?"

I squeeze her hand. We get comfortable next to the bucket of brew, the cleaner that would make a subway bathroom sparkle.

"I had never seen it snow," I say, "and there was a blizzard. I thought it was the second coming. Flakes like big pieces of soapy foam."

I start squirming just thinking about it.

"We were all right," I say. "Everything was all right."

"It was a fraud," says Enid, looking right at me. "I didn't know what else to do."

She sees me recoil, as though she had spit in my face. Her hand goes back to the bucket like a trained seal and brings up the foamy brush. She makes a gesture that includes herself, me, the toilet.

"It's just a problem," says Enid. "That's all."

Those times linger. I think of the nights, the blizzard, the air that was so crisp it was like biting off a piece of fresh carrot. It's not turning out the way I had imagined: we're getting old, all right, but not together.

"What wonders," I say.

There we sit, holding each other, trembling like a couple of dogs that have been dosed with a fire hose in January. I leave her there with her rubber gloves and her toothbrush.

"Have a good time," says Enid through the bathroom door. I can tell by the jerky quality of her voice that she has gone back to work with the fervor of a convict filing at his leg irons.

Ari is sitting before the television and looks a little ill in the gangrenous light. The Genius has a war movie going, and for a moment Ari has forgotten the alarms, the clap, his daughter crying on the bathroom floor. His eyes follow some action I can't see.

"They're above you," he says. "Above. The swine. Shoot them. Shoot them."

A quick burst of automatic-rifle fire fills the room. Ari seems relieved. He is sitting in his undershirt (the kind that looks like the upper part of a basketball uniform) and I see him reach underneath it and stroke the smooth, slick tissue of his wounds.

He sees me at the door with my bag and says, "We are friends now. I will not forget. I will keep you apprised of the developments."

I wave goodbye and then find myself standing in the hall, hearing the snap and pop of the television, the whine and explosion of a mortar, the shout of the enemy. Downstairs the Barber and Smiling Mary sit beyond the neon advertisement for a beer that doesn't exist. They seem caught in the bluish matrix of fluorescent light, like prehistoric insects preserved in amber. The Barber is staring through his window, at the writing on the wall, the garbage cans, a woman who has stopped for a moment and rested her shopping bags (from a supermarket) on the sidewalk. The only movement in the street is her white breath. The Barber sees me and my suitcase, but he doesn't care: he's a believer, an apostle of himself. The Barber knows I'm not going so far or so long that he won't be able to find me. Ah, Sal, I think, you're a great man.

From the air Los Angeles looks like a nerve cell under tremendous magnification: it's gray and slickly speckled. There are houses in the grain, squares off the fibers, the web of roads. The wing rises and falls as we make a turn over the Pacific, which is misty, as haunting as a recurrent dream. Then I can see the city, the stretching, reaching cell, its color of gray lichen on brown rock. There are small chips of light (sun-struck swimming pools and automobiles), subcellular movement: RNA cars, trucks, buses, motorcycles. I can hear the quick screech of the tires. Reverse the engines, I think, reverse them! The plane trembles, shimmies, and stops. Through the window I can see the white concrete form of the terminal.

My luggage emerges from a machine that looks as though you could use it to leave the solar system, to travel at unbelievable speeds beyond the galaxy. Through the window I can see the African hills, the brownish growth on them, the first hint of spring. Women are watching the airplanes, the large aluminum creatures that labor in the air. For a moment I stand with them, hearing the shriek, the sawmill whine of the engines. A woman smiles at me and I am flattered by the healthy invitation in her glance to go with her to a bathroom stall and fuck.

From the taxi I can see the wide streets, the glorious neon, the mutant beauty of the repetition of shoe stores, gas stations, restaurants. The air has a tropical odor, the stench of hydrocarbons, and I can feel the lush growth, the berserk vitality. I know that behind every sign, under every roof, creatures are touching one another and trembling. The city's jungle texture makes me quiet, curious: I've been away for years.

It won't be long now, my mother's letter says, It won't be long. They are trying new drugs on your father. They think he will be allergic to them so they put spots of the drugs on his forearms, you know, so they can see right away if it's going to do anything to him. They put the drugs on his forearms. One spot on each. Only goats and baboons have taken these chemicals. Then they give your father the drug and they increase the dosage. More and more until he gets a little tremulous and then they try something new. He still likes the soup, but he doesn't take as much as he used to. I'm glad you are coming.

The house is more dated than I remember, so much so that it looks like a movie set. It is beneath the level of the street, surrounded by acacia, eucalyptus, and elm trees. There are banana plants, too, and beyond them, in the valley, there is the grid of streets. In the distance there are the foothills.

My father opens the door.

"So," he says, "you have come to see me."

He's shorter than he used to be. It's as though he were in a frypan, cooking down. I can see the sharp bones in his face.

"Come in," he says.

He has a blanket over his shoulders and he moves with a cautious gait. I put down my bag and reach out for him. Our awkwardness is something to behold, perfect. I take his forearms and squeeze them. He looks at me, trembles, flinches.

"I love . . ."

"So what?" he says.

He waits for a moment (trembling all the while), and I realize I'm pushing my thumbs into his forearms, into the spots for the drugs.

"I'm still living," he says.

The house has a sickroom quality: there's a medicinal odor, a faint coolness, a smeared, greasy quality. The old man looks like an Indian under his blanket. His cheekbones are high and his nose is curved and pointed.

"I got you some beer," he says. "I can't drink it anymore. Come into the kitchen."

He has a bowed posture: the strings that are pulling him down seem to be strung from his head and shoulders to his feet and the strings are being twisted each day, tightened: I can see him strain against them, tremble with the effort. He puts a can and a glass on the table.

"Thanks," I say.

It's cold and good and it cuts the airplane's unctuous atmosphere, the city's hydrocarbon air. My father swallows and licks his lips. His blue eyes are drawn to the glass, and I can see that they are paler than before: it looks like they are giving him bleach with his drugs.

"Is that good?" he says.

"Yes," I say.

"It looks good," says my father. "Drink another."

He pours out another can, watches as I drink. He purses his lips, has the savoring, remembering expression of one who has been dismissed. He closes his eyes.

"Ah," he says, smiling for a moment, thinking of an instant, the heat of a day, the drawn, puffy feeling of muscles, tight skin, the damp touch of a shirt, the taste of beer from a bottle. He reaches under the blanket, rubs his side, then looks at me.

"Come outside," he says.

My father gathers his blanket together with one hand and we walk through the yard. Beyond him, over the valley, I can see the red-brown stratification of smoke. My father has grown things in the yard, and as he steps over each plant, he points at a bud, a new leaf, the clinging tendril of a vine. He stops at his orchids, the delicate blooms, flowers he was never able to grow before: only recently has he discovered the gift, the patience to make them respond. He points at the delicate flesh, the petals that are pink and white, speckled with rust, others that are a reddish purple, labial and slick, and I can see the trembling in his arms: he lets me see the shaking, the tears in his eyes.

"It's hard to grow them," he says. "There was nothing here at all. Nothing." He points at the land that runs to the abrupt drop-off, the end of his small plateau. "Now there's Chinese elm, hibiscus, bananas, eucalyptus."

"Yes," I say.

He touches my hand with the same gentleness he has reserved for the flowers, leads me through the garden. He stands for a moment, looking at me, then puts his hand under the blanket and walks into the house, where he dozes in the pale sunlight on the sofa.

In the evening my mother comes home.

"Oh, oh," she says, jumping up and down a little. "It's been so long. So long since we've seen you."

In ten minutes my mother and father are arguing. I listen to the harsh sounds, the vital, angry words. They're still at it, Stargell, I think, still snapping like crocodiles. If the house were an instrument it would be a violin, strung with angry gut: the walls are vibrant. When my father sees me smile, he says, "Are you looking for trouble?"

"No," I say.

"That's good," he says.

At night we watch the news, the daily death count. There is a piece of film which shows black cars in a cemetery, a tent, flowers, mourning clothes, a veil.

"None of that shit for me," says my father, "if I should die."

"I've taken care of it," says my mother.

"Is that clear?" says my father, turning to me.

"Yes," I say.

"Good," says my father, staring again at the black cars.

My mother goes to her job in the morning.

My father and I walk in the yard, look at the plants. My father can see almost microscopic differences, a slight tropism of a leaf, the presence of one insect's egg. There's a light breeze and the smell of oil is in the air.

"Look at the flowers I've grown," says my father. "Aren't they something?"

He pulls the blanket over his shoulder and goes into the house. In the afternoon we take a drive downtown, get on the freeway. The air is reddish, dusty: it looks like tons of rusted cars have been ground up and then sprayed over the city. I drive. It hurts the old man to sit up, so he slouches in the corner, his shoulder against the door, his feet on the transmission's hump, but he keeps his eyes above the level of the windshield. I can see his pointed nose, the bones in his face against the passing gas stations, palm trees, houses, parked cars. There is a huge sign which shows a man dressed in spats and a cutaway (with striped pants) and a top hat. The man is bent at the waist, pointing a finger at and talking to a rat. The rat has a dark rubber-ball nose, whiskers, a nasty smile. The man in the cutaway has a large mallet behind his back and he's getting ready to give it to the rat, although it seems to me he's been taking a long time about it, since I remember him having the same conversation and pointing the same finger at the same whiskered rat twenty-five years ago. In the distance there is a cluster of buildings rising out of the flat land and air that's slick and warm. The city hall stands like a monument to the movies. I expect at any minute the police cars to come dashing out like long black dogs, whining and howling, pursuing space monsters or bank robbers.

My father's silhouette is sharp against the landscape. He watches the oncoming concrete, the flashing white lines, and says, "Give it the gas."

He puts his hand under his coat and touches something there. I get off the freeway downtown and stop in front of the train station. It's a Spanish building, covered with pink stucco, surrounded by palm trees, and it has, in the center of its Romanesque façade, a large clock. Our favorite restaurant (which may as well be a shrine) is across the street. The old man puts his nose into the air, sniffs, gently shakes his head.

The restaurant has a high ceiling, green-and-white walls (two tone, hospital style), sawdust on the floor, long tables at which customers sit on stools. Overhead there are fans with wooden blades (almost as wide as airplane propellers) and they are turning in air that's fragrant, filled with the odors of freshly baked bread, crisp celery, potato salad, onion soup, roasted meats. The counter is made of marble and people wait in line before it. I buy a sandwich on a small roll and a bottle of beer, and my father and I sit down. Each table has two or three pots of mustard, and each has a tongue depressor to spread it. The mustard is the hottest in the world. I spread some on my sandwich, have a bite, feel my eyes immediately begin to water, a wonderful stinging in my nose. There is a jukebox in the restaurant, although I've never heard it played: the machine looks like the front end of a Southern Pacific train. My father doesn't stare at the people who are around us, but he's watching. There is a man in a long black coat. His gray hair, which has never been cut, hangs down his back: it looks like a gray rope (something from an abandoned sailing ship) that's slowly unraveling. His fingernails have never been cut either, and they coil at the end of each finger. He doesn't want to break them so he eats carefully, with as much ceremony as a queen. There are women who have their entire history, household and all, in a Safeway shopping cart, and they stop for a sandwich, too. I see a woman spreading mustard with a tongue depressor.

"I remember," says my father.

He nods, sniffs the air, the vegetables, the rolls, the sweet scent of butter, the odor of freshly chopped parsley.

A blond woman, who is tall and who is dressed in clinging white silk, comes through the door and takes a place in the line before the marble counter. She fits perfectly, since the place is so crazy it didn't seem complete until she arrived. A breeze follows her through the door, pushes the silk of her dress against her legs, hips: she doesn't wear underclothes. The old man watches her.

"I don't get out that much," he says.

The woman moves away from the counter and sees the old man watching her. She stands with a sandwich on the heavy plate and holds a beer bottle with a glass upside down over its neck, and looks at the old bastard for a moment and smiles. It snaps his light. She is still standing there, looking at him. He puts his hand under his coat and strains, tries to pull his face into a smile, but all he can do is grimace. He sniffs the air and trembles. The woman in white silk, who's cool and spirited, is still watching him, curious about what kind of crazy old man he is. She shakes her hair out a little, is still smiling. The old man has a guy wire trembling, but you can see he's working on it. The smile rises, fills his face. The woman in silk smiles again, nods, walks away so that we can see her move. The old man sighs, relaxes, rubs his side. Stargell, I think, put some more mustard on the sandwich. It's so hot it clears my head. The old man is taken with the woman in silk and I know he's thinking, That's it, boy, that's enough (just looking) to keep me going for another week. He sees me watching him.

"Finish your food," he says.

I finish the crust, a sharp-tasting bit of parsley, and then we go outside: the sunlight is as heavy as a glass door. The old man staggers a little, turns and glances once at the restaurant, savors the odors, the people, the slowly turning fans, the pots of mustard, the woman who smiled at him. I think of the way the silk clung to her, the sound her bare legs made when one brushed against another. You can feel the warmth of the beach beneath her dress. It hurts the old man when he gets into the car. He looks at the downtown buildings, the bullet-shaped arches, the Mediterranean train station, the Byzantine library, a natural-gas tank that looks like an accordion the size of a blimp, and as we drive on the freeway, he smells the ashy odor, feels the slight (regularly spaced) bumps in the road, the cold and vibrant tug, the cancer's tendrils.

We drive quietly for a while.

"I can't, you know," says the old man, "do anything with a woman anymore. It's the disease."

He stares at the road ahead of us, touches his side, and I can see his face against the drive-ins, an artificial lake filled with ducks, lots filled with motorcycles, mobile homes, used cars. There are apartment houses that look like Christmas ornaments: they've been sprayed with gold flecks.

"She was beautiful, though," says the old man about no one in particular. He used to get around plenty, and now he's missing it.

He smiles for a minute, remembers some heat, a lovely groan and jump, awe-filled eyes, the smell of cunt. He watches the houses, the gas stations and taco stands, the gritty glitter, billboards that are the size of drive-in movie screens.

In the morning I go to the garage with him to look at a car he can no longer drive, a royal-blue 1956 Thunderbird. He used to put on his yachting cap, a blue shirt, and drive around town, ogling the women, racing young men. I've seen him perched at the limit line of a signal trying to peek into the stovepipe light, the yellow one, to get a jump on the other cars. There's a musty smell in the garage, dust on the car. My father puts his finger on a dent in the chrome Continental kit.

"A two-by-four fell on it in the last earthquake," he says.

We stand before the car. My father has the blanket over his shoulder, Indian style. I put my hand on the chrome Continental kit, and my father looks at the fingers and nails, the veins and knuckles, and realizes that our hands are identical. We have a mole in the same place.

"I never noticed that," he says.

He puts his hand next to mine.

"Look at that," he says, shaking his head in wonder.

The days come and go. I walk in the yard with him, look at the orchids, the trees. The smoky air changes color, from blue to brown, and back again.

"The engineering of a tree is remarkable," says my father. "It is thickest at the stump because that is the site of the most stress. From the wind."

My mother comes home and cooks, but the old man doesn't eat. They stop arguing. The old man stops eating.

"Why the hell should it be me?" he says. "I never had a fucking chance!"

He looks at my mother, at me, and then I see him screw down to watch a game show. Later, when I'm sitting next to him, he pulls the blanket to his chest and says, "Don't get me wrong, Stargell. I wouldn't have missed it for the world."

We look at one another. I can see the diaphragm in his eyes, the iris, open like blue peacock tails. He acts like one of those circus performers who put a couple of boards over their chest and then have a garbage truck run over them. I can see him grimace. He lifts against it, sets his shoulders, and strains. The television blats.

"You'll come to see me again?" he says.

"Yes," I say.

"You promise me?" he says.

I've never heard him plead before.

"Yes," I say.

"That's good," he says. "We'll go downtown and eat a sandwich."

He's still straining, still letting me see what's in his eyes. He puts his hand next to mine.

"The doctor says I should tell him when my ankles swell," he says.

I nod.

"Well," says my father, "fuck him. They aren't swelling."

He turns back to the television, the otherworldly colors, the beauty of high voltage, of x-rays: he seems already to be moving through the galaxies, the phosphorescent clouds.

My father eats slowly now with his spoon. I see him flinch when he swallows. He continues. Before he goes to bed he shows me his ankles.

"See?" he says.

They are the ankles of a long-distance runner, a little swollen, but not much. He pulls down his other sock, and then stands before me, his blanket over his shoulder, still looking like an Indian with his socks sagging beneath his ankles. He puts his hand against his side.

"What are you doing in that city now?" he says.

He looks like some alkie Indian who just escaped from a booby hatch, a mad old man, touching his side and staring at me.

"Trying to keep body and soul together," I say.

He sees me blush.

"You can do that anywhere," he says.

He stands there for me to see, his socks still bunched at his heels.

"You can do that right here," he says.

He shakes my hand, gives it a farewell squeeze, then goes to bed. He knows I'll be gone in the morning, that I'm catching an early plane. I pack my clothes.

My mother comes into my room. I look at her face and think, Stargell, now you know what hard work dying is.

"Thanks for coming," she says.

"You tell him I'll be back," I say.

"Of course," she says.

I've been away so long she doesn't know how to say goodbye, so I give her a hug.

I sit by the window of the airplane, feel myself being sucked into my seat, the now-we're-serious surge: the rumble and bounce are gone and we are airborne.

My father was proud of me when I worked in the think tank. He got me started. On Saturday mornings he'd say, If you were in the desert and had a piece of plastic and a cup, how would you get water? Remember, no rain. Or, Why can you see your reflection in a window at night?

We ate toasty English muffins, lightly scrambled eggs, cherry tomatoes, cantaloupes, slices of ham, potatoes. The butter melted quickly on the muffins and I put strawberry preserves on them. I can still taste it, can feel the crunch.

Well, said my father, well?

I'll think about it, I said.

Good, said the old man. And while you're thinking you can buck and split those railroad ties I bought. It'll make you strong. We'll burn the wood next winter.

This is how you get water if you're in the middle of a desert and you have a piece of plastic and a cup. You dig a hole and put the cup inside. Then you spread the plastic over the hole. You put stones around the edges of the plastic and one small stone in the middle: this makes an inverted cone, with its peak over the cup. During the day, the air under the plastic gets very hot, so hot that it draws the little bit of moisture there is out of the ground. The plastic cools quickly at night. Water condenses on it and runs to the peak, the top of the cone, and from there it drops into the cup.

A five-by-four piece of plastic will produce a pint of water every twenty-four hours.

Windows become mirrors at night because they are opaque on one side, sealed by darkness.

I get into a taxi, look at the hack license, recognize a man from Star: Shoeless Joe. He weighs three hundred pounds on a good day, a little less when tips are low. He hits the meter and we pull into traffic, although the car is tipped to one side. It reminds me of a small sailboat in a wind. The hack is from the Star, all right: it sounds like a robot coughing up dry washers.

"Hey, Joe," I say.

He looks around, lets me see a jowl the size of a bowling ball bag.

"Stargell," he says. "What the hell!"

His voice is muffled in himself: it comes out as a heavy slur.

"Where you been?" he says.

"California," I say.

"Ain't that something," he says.

He reaches onto the seat next to him, takes a doughnut from a box that looks like a small barn (with a cow sticking its head out a window), and puts it into his mouth.

"Is it warm there? Is there lots of pussy running around in the sun, you know, like they say?"

"Yeah," I say.

"That's good," he says.

"How are things?" I say.

Shoeless Joe's face is so wide it is as if he had stepped out of a billboard poster. I can only see a patch of jowl in the rear-view mirror.

"There was another grease job last week," he says, reaching for a doughnut.

"Who?" I say.

"I don't know," he says. "Some green hand, a new guy."

We drive for a while and I see the city rise, the lattice-like arrangement of the lights, buildings that seem to be large crystals.

"I ain't making any money either," says Shoeless Joe. "Look at me. I lost fifteen pounds."

He grabs a hunk of his stomach.

"That's too bad," I say.

Shoeless Joe is a monument, a rolling, miraculous creature.

"When somebody's been in my hack," he says, "they've had an experience."

"I've never seen anyone like you," I say.

"You think so?" he says.

I nod. His eyes watch me in the rear-view.

"What about the fifteen pounds?" he says.

"It doesn't show," I say.

He continues eating the doughnuts, pulls up in front of my building.

"Take it easy," I say.

"Sure," he says.

"Say hello to the Scum and Munson for me," I say.

"Sure," says Shoeless Joe. "It'll be a surprise. They can't remember if you quit or if you're dead."

I watch the hack's dome light disappear.

No two televisions are tuned to the same program: climbing the stairs is like walking through *TV Guide*. I knock on the green door, then use my key. Enid is sitting before the Genius, intent on a movie. The furniture has been rearranged and looks now like Enid is ready to paint the floor. There is a large pile in one corner, and Enid sits before it, staring at the Genius's snug perch.

"Oh," she says, "you're back."

"What's on the late show?" I say.

"A terrible film," she says. "I'm just watching it for the commercials. There's a wonderful one with enzymes. They go chew, chew, chew."

She holds her hands up, makes them snap like small Doberman pinschers.

"The enzymes are eating the stains out of clothes."

She smiles.

"How is your father?" she says.

"Dying," I say. But not dead, I think. Still ready to say, Fuck off, Jack. I know about my ankles. And do you see these onions, their skins breaking like old silk? Can you see the ridges in the orchids?

"There it is," she says. "Look."

I give her a kiss, take her shoulders in my hands, but she is staring at the television. There are small circles moving across the screen, and they are split down the middle so they look like they have mouths and they are chewing, snapping, eating some kind of stain.

"I'm sorry, Stargell," says Enid.

I sit down next to her after pulling a chair from the pile.

"You can sleep on the couch for a few days," she says.

I want to touch her, just to sleep with her.

"Don't make it any worse, Stargell," she says, when I sit down and gently put my leg against hers.

In the old days she used to read ancient Greek aloud, explain the words, made me tremble with the grand old stories. We watch the movie together, and it's not so bad, really. It's about huge snails that eat people. Somebody kills one with a fire extinguisher, freezes it. Well, I think, no one cares about snails anyway; it's probably what a big snail deserves. But underneath it all I'm thinking, What great snails, what great snails. Everyone hates them and wants to spray them with a fire extinguisher, but that doesn't stop them. These snails just want a little peace and quiet and they wouldn't eat anybody if everyone would just mind his own fucking business. The vegetable choppers come on.

"My father went home," says Enid.

We're trapped in a TV tide, that quiet trough between the Sermonette and the Blue Birds (who fly while The Star-Spangled Banner plays). There are four planes, and they rise in a diamond pattern, all streaming smoke, flying directly into the sky. When they reach a certain altitude the diamond breaks and the planes stream away from one another. The jets are flying close to or above the speed of sound. There is one shot from a wing camera and you can see that the wing is buffeting, pounding in the wind. All the pilots have their visors down.

"He went to the doctor," says Enid.

"Is he all right?" I say.

"It was a new strain," says Enid, gathering her bathrobe around her neck, as though the disease were a draft.

The Blue Birds come on! The Genius is bringing them in like memories of his youth. They rise, streaming smoke, dissolve into Old Glory. A test pattern hums at us.

"I think my father was proud of it," says Enid suspiciously.

I shrug it off, since I'm willing to give the old goat a break.

"I boiled the sheets," says Enid. "And the towels. I stirred them in a pot with a wooden spoon I bought."

I see the spoon (the kind usually displayed on a wall with a fork of equal size) leaning against the stove in the kitchen.

"That should do it," I say.

"Do you think so?" says Enid. "Do you?"

I turn off the test pattern, the inane humming.

"Yes," I say.

"Are you sure?" she says.

"Absolutely," I say, making my voice sound as solid as a steel ingot.

Enid gathers her bathrobe around her neck and I can see that she'd wear a surgeon's mask if she thought she could get away with it. She stands up and says, "Good night, Stargell."

She drifts into the bedroom, closes the door. There's a little lock on the inside and I can hear her throw the small bolt. I carefully take the furniture off the sofa (this is no time to aggravate Jack the Ripper) and open the beartrap, stretch out on the clean sheets. They seem more cooked than boiled, old, as though a lifetime of nights spent on them, the squirming and restlessness, the silent rigidity, had been smoothed into comfort.

"Stargell," says my Parisian.

"Stargell."

"What?" I say.

"Stargell," says Jack the Ripper, "I know you're in there. I heard you come in last night."

I wake, turn toward the door, see it tremble, the puffs of plaster falling from the frame. I pull on a pair of pants, look at the clock: it's 7 A.M. Jack is standing in the hall.

"Good morning," says Jack the Ripper.

One of his hands leans on the upper part of the doorframe. His fingers are as big as hot dogs.

"I've still got a week," I say. "A little more, if you want the truth."

"I know you do," says Jack. "But I don't want to do anything. I just want to make sure you got the money."

"No problem there," I say.

Jack looks at me with a pained disbelief.

"This comes by way of a friendly warning," says Jack. "You just make sure you do what you're supposed to."

"Don't worry," I say.

"Don't worry!" he says, slapping the doorframe and making a little more plaster fall. "You should worry! And what did I tell you about the furniture? What did I tell you about the relatives?"

I begin to close the door.

"I'll see you at Easter," I say.

"You just get the money," says Jack. "Leave Easter out of it."

Jack looks a little sad, but he doesn't say anything else. He turns and walks down the stairs.

"Easter," he says.

I close my eyes, but the Parisian is gone, so I have a strong cup of coffee, then take a shower. I give the tin stall a couple of kicks: it's like being in a thunderstorm, right in the clouds where the sound is so loud it makes you feel like you're inside an aluminum garbage can that someone is beating with a tire iron.

I go out for a paper, find myself walking with the employed, those people who have the luxury of being late. I match their strides, put my nose into the air, add mysterious figures in my head. I stop at the subway entrance, although I'm tempted to hit Wall Street for a few hours: I could sit in the Exchange, watch the moving ticker, enjoy being in the center, the medulla oblongata of cash and power.

I go into the newspaper store, a nice neighborhood place (all the pornography is covered up so the kids can't see it). The woman who owns it lost the family nut at a Miami dog track: lousy face-lift, cheap permanent, a tan that came out of a bottle. She has a sullen, fast-food beauty.

"Hey," she says. "Stargell. Where you been?"

"The usual," I say.

I can't say Los Angeles. The words makes me feel the cold hum of cancer.

"Is that right?" she says.

I pick up a copy of the *Times*.

"I hear you owe the Barber money," she says.

"It's a crime, isn't it?" I say.

"Not yet," she says.

I walk on the avenue. The sun is out and there is a peaceful quality in the air. An old woman is being taken out to enjoy it. She is in a wheelchair and her head is on a pillow. A nurse is pushing the chair. When they pass I can see the old woman as she nuzzles the sunlight: she blinks her eyes, turns her head, sighs. She doesn't smile, since she's beyond that, but there is something in her pale skin, something in that wrinkled flinch, that acknowledges the season's tick, the push in the earth. That's the way I want to be when I've turned into a big pink prune: wheel me around where I can feel the sun, hear an argument, feel the cars crashing into one another.

What jobs there are in the newspaper: it seems that everyone has a long nose, no chin, and shits ice cream cones. Accountants, advertising executives, data processors, bankers. I'd like to sit in a bank, you know, in a nice suit. I just sit there, peaceful as a jar of Vaseline, so the people could look at me and hear the Zen hum of the air conditioner. Field representatives, insurance, systems analysis. I put the paper down. When push comes to shove, the want ads make me feel as useless as one sock.

I sit in the living room, drink coffee, wait.

Enid rises, goes into the bathroom. When she comes out she stops before me.

"Have you paid that dirty loan shark?" she says.

"Not yet," I say.

Sleep has mauled her: puffy face, swollen lips, welts.

"You should pay him," says Enid.

"I've been looking for a job," I say.

"Who would want to hire you?" she says.

She's got me there. Once she said, Stargell, you can do any-thing. Do you know that, my darling? So this little pique, this ill humor, makes me think of other times.

Enid sits opposite me, puts on her magistrate's expression.

"It makes me depressed," says Enid, "to have you sleeping out here."

It's like watching a train on flat land: you can see it coming for miles.

"We can't have that," I say.

"That's right," says Enid.

We sit for a moment. Enid holds my hand.

"You've got to find someplace to stay," she says, "until I get better."

We spend the afternoon together. I watch a baseball game from spring training. One day your curve ball is breaking like a win-dow in a riot, your fastball is hopping, and the majors call.

"When are you going to leave?" says Enid.

"Soon as I can," I say.

"When will that be?" she says.

As soon as I pay the loan shark, I think.

"I love you, Stargell," says Enid, gesturing with a quart of beer, "but I'm intelligent. I'm beautiful. Everyone says so. I should have married a rich man."

The building has its evening atmosphere. The Portuguese are yelling, cooking goat. It sounds like everyone is going to get a good spanking. Enid hums, sways back and forth, has her eyes set on some personal vision: Mr. Right, a tap-dancing stockbroker. I'm pacing around a little, getting into a sorry mood, one that produces inventions and religious schemes. Ari left us a package that looks as though you should use it to blow up a bridge, but there's just freeze-dried chocolate ice cream inside. Not half bad, really.

"What's wrong with you?" says Enid.

"I'm waiting for the *Times*," I say.

Enid shrugs.

"You would," she says.

That a girl, I think. Pretty soon you'll be cleaning the oven with a Q-tip dipped in Windex.

I walk up Sixth Avenue. The street is filled with people who are too medicated to talk so they wave at one another, look like big birds that are using the avenue as a runway. I wait in line at the newsstand, leaf through slick pornography, show no shame at all.

The *Times* truck seems like an airplane that's dropping supplies to the troops. I buy my paper and walk home, smelling a little bit of New Jersey in the air: the odor has a saw-blade edge. My favorite is the stench from the tranquilizer factory, just across the river. It smells like shit and rotting sharks, all the dreams that crazy people have: they've been aired out to dry so everyone can be reasonable at the office.

"Well?" says Enid.

"Lots of jobs," I say.

I skim along, looking for something suitable.

"Gorilla impersonator," I say. " 'Wanted. Person to work in gorilla costume.' "

There's a telephone number. The ad wasn't in the paper yesterday. Enid flips on the late show, is oblivious, remembers the days when I was going to be somebody. The ad has appeared tonight for the first time. Stargell, I think, you're saved.

"I'm going to bed," I say.

Enid grunts. I remember when we watched *How Green Was My Valley* and cried until we had the hiccups. I move Enid into the bedroom with the TV, climb into the beartrap. During a commercial break Enid comes through the door and kisses my cheek, just holds me for a moment and squeezes me and then closes the door.

Gorilla, I think. Gorilla.

The Portuguese quiet down. Hollywood has taken care of Enid. I sit under the covers and think of every zoo I've been to, of the orangutans hanging from the tires and hunks of drift they put in the cages, of the shaggy beasts swinging from branch to branch in the jungles, moving with fluid, pendulum-like alacrity, making the foliage quake. I can see the red eyes, the face that looks like a flat football, the dread-lock, zombie hair. At the think tank we did some gorilla work: some asshole wanted to know how the chimps got along, you know, which chimp was grabbing another's wife, and I talked to a real gorilla man, a guy who had spent years in the jungles. One day he took off his clothes and walked into a band of monkeys and he lived with them for a year and a half. They accepted him as a member of the band, as one of their own. I talked to him on the twenty-eighth floor. He was wearing a three-piece suit and you'd never know he was as crazy as a whore with one leg. He knew plenty about apes. We talked about "band dynamics" and then he shook my hand and got into the elevator. Stargell, you've got the jump on the other stiffs, since you already have the inside track on the chimp act.

The whore with one leg was in Saigon and everyone thought it was good luck to fuck her: now she dances with a crutch in a bar on Fourteenth Street. She was from the superstition study. I still go up to Fourteenth Street, walk through the market, the open-air stalls where the wind-up toys and aluminum pots sit. The bar is near the meat-packing district and butchers stand in bloody aprons, eating a roast beef sandwich, drinking a shot and a beer, and watching the old girl shaking the stump, knocking the platform with her crutch, upstaging the jukebox music, the Supremes. She's thinking, Do you like that? Do you? I applaud, stomp, whistle, but everyone in the bar is as lively as a potato, except for my darling, who gives me a grimace that's as hard as vice, who lets me see the beauty of her eyes.

I fall asleep thinking of the light moving in the leaves, of the lips and flat noses of gorillas, of the scent of their hide, the odor of bananas, of cool mornings when the band is sluggish and when the days are spent with one ape grooming another.

I'm clean, waiting, dressed in a gray suit, filled with coffee, expectations. The paper sits before me. I don't want to appear overanxious, but then I don't want to be late.

"Hello," says a woman, whose voice scares me. I had expected a carny screech, a barker or hustler, but this comes right out of the air conditioner, the electric typewriter, and chrome-and-leather furniture.

"I think I have the wrong number," I say.

"I don't think so," she says.

"Did you advertise for a gorilla?" I say.

"Yes," she says.

"That's good," I say.

"Have you had amusement park experience?" she says.

"Yes," I say.

I think of the parks in California, of the sailors and their girl-friends (chewing gum and drinking out of a pint), the cotton candy, the smell of popcorn, the reek of ozone from the rides, the buzz that made you think of the death house dim, the Rosenberg hum.

"There's a tryout," says the woman, "in Queens this afternoon. At the park."

She tells me to go to the Trip to Mars ride, to meet the manager there. The Trip to Mars, I think, Stargell, just think what good times have been had there.

"Four o'clock," she says.

"Four," I say.

"Have you got a car?" she says.

"No," I say, a little sadly. But I've been in the showrooms, have smelled the leather, touched the wheel, kicked the rubber.

"It would be easier if you had a car," she says.

She gives me directions: a little subway, a little bus, a little walk. It's convoluted, but I get the most mileage this way.

"No problem," I say.

"We'll provide the suit," says the woman.

She hangs up, leaves me alone in the apartment again, but I'm thinking, Stargell, old boy, you've got an appointment. And that's not all. I've got to prepare, got to clean up my act. It's ten o'clock, so I've got a couple of hours.

The table where I sit is next to the window. I have a view of the air shaft, the windows on the other side. There is an electric guitar repair shop downstairs, and the people who own the shop take the guitars into the bottom of the air shaft to test them. This makes Enid mad, but she's learned to sleep through it. What terrible people, says Enid, putting her head between two pillows. Through a window on the other side of the air shaft I can see a woman, my favorite neighbor: this morning she is making herself a cup of tea. She has no clothes on, and I can see the movement of her breasts as she moves from the stove to the table. She puts the tea into the pot. I can see her eyes, her body that is never exposed to light. She must be twenty-two or -three. The water boils and she pours it into the pot. I can see her buttocks, the perfect crease in her back. She sits and waits, then pours herself a cup, and holds it gently with her fingers, lets the mist come off its surface. I can see her ribs, the slope and curve of her breasts, her bed-ruffled hair. She puts her lips against the cup, then jumps back: the tea's too hot. The electric guitar man plays a few bars. It sounds like he's beating a gong under water. My neighbor has the paper before her, but I don't think she's reading it.

I take off my jacket, loosen my tie, and think, Stargell, gorillas are the ticket. I dwell upon them: I want to scare the shit out of the people who surround my tree, who stand there with their topees and their tranquilizer guns. I grunt. It doesn't sound quite right, though. It sounds more like a pig whistling through his snout. I make the sound come from further in my throat, deeper in my chest: pow. I can see the zoo keeper bringing the bananas. Nothing to it, my boy, you're a natural. But the stance, the gait, is another matter. I stoop, let my arms dangle before me. Jungle, tundra, time: I'm thinking back to the beginning, the flash of lightning in the first big soup. My arms swing, head moves lazily from side to side. I take what I want. That's mine. Give. Stargell, it wouldn't be a bad life, you know, fresh fruit, a lovely bride, swinging through the trees: people love gorillas. They want to put them in the zoo. My neck feels like rubber and my arms are coming along, too. I pucker my lips, wrinkle my nose, then take a step, roll to one side, as though I were carrying a tub filled with water on my shoulder. I feel drunker than hell. I can smell the mulchy floor of the jungle, the sharp succulence of the vegetation, can see a flower that's as bright as red lipstick. The grunt comes on now in dead earnest. Stargell, that's it. Shoulders and legs are working, too. The boys in the amusement park better look out, because they've got somebody to contend with. They'd be stupid not to give me the job. As a matter of fact, it would be their loss. Stargell, you don't look half bad, but it's not enough. I know this to be true. It's not the walk, the lumber, but the jump, the quick maneuver, that counts, what the gorilla man called "delineal stances," the I'll-fight-to-the-death-for-this-miserable-patch-of-swamp quality. Yes. Hmm. I turn my wrists so the backs of them face forward, rub my eyes, then hop, swing my arms, even give myself a nice little swat on the chest. More heart, Stargell, more anger. Someone's been playing around with my woman. That's not it. I take a jump, a weak thump on the chest. All right. More heart. Stargell, what do you think about this: your father's sitting out there in that greasy sunlight and something's eating him up, something's taking another bite out of him every fucking second, something is sinking its tendrils in there, into the organs, and sucking his life away, and your wife's in there on her back trying to kill herself with sleep. What do you think about that, Stargell? I'm hopping around the room now, grunting and thrashing my chest, making a deep satisfying thump that should scare everyone. I knock a chair out of the way, am still hopping and grunting, now almost screaming, becoming the perfect side-show attraction. The door opens and Enid looks at me.

"Stargell," she says.

She doesn't want to be bothered right now: she just closes the door. Maybe she'll end up pissing in a coffee can, I think. I'm moving in earnest now. Fuck the amusement park. I'll get on TV or maybe I'll just stop traffic on Fifth Avenue. I look up, out the window, across the air shaft, and there is my neighbor, holding her tea, looking across the cooling surface. She is nude, pale, fertile. The tea has gone cold. She smiles.

I stop and go to the window. My bubble's popped, all right, but there she is, still waving and smiling. Her flesh trembles.

I stand before the glass, panting, hot, hearing the radiators banging themselves into a hard frenzy. The electric guitar man plays a chord. I study the directions to the amusement park.

A cup of tea would have been nice, I think.

My neighbor pours herself another cup, stares at me, pushes her lips against the porcelain. I'm still a little stooped, can still hear the slithering of the leaves in the savanna air. She lets me look at her, lets me see her perfect shoulders, the fine bones there. We are both exposed for a moment, her small pleasures and my insistence, nude tea and gorillas.

I travel for a couple of hours, north to Times Square, then the Flushing Line, a bus. The woman on the phone was right: a car would have made things a little easier. The bus is filled with shoppers, retirees, housewives, lower-echelon salesmen, the unemployed and desperate. We all wait for it to come along, standing on the corner, at the stop near the elevated train tracks. The landscape is grubby-L.A.: muffler shops, liquor stores, used-car lots, banks that have nothing to do with weather. I'd like to go in and look at all the mufflers, at the rows of tires, the shiny sets of tools. When the bus stops I'm ready, thinking, Tundra, savanna, gorilla. Stargell, there's no way they can stop you. I wait in line to get on the bus.

I climb aboard with my carfare, my bag of sandwiches, file ahead like the rest. The bus is crowded, the aisles filled. Damp wool, cozy atmosphere. Some shouting is coming from the rear of the bus, some good-time raving. I can feel my spirits lift. Everyone seems a little uncomfortable. The change meter keeps on turning. From the rear comes a young woman, nineteen or so, and she's carrying a copy of a book written by a nationally known existentialist. She has a face like a rattrap: ready to snap. She knows all the concentration camp details and she's as earnest as a pair of pliers.

"There's a man on the floor," she says to the busdriver.

The raving continues. I can't make out the text, but some points are being scored. The busdriver looks ripe for one of those schools you see advertised on the back of match packages: Draw Me. Rattrap insists. The driver closes the door, puts on the brake, climbs under the bar that separates him from the passengers. I follow in his wake, behind the girl. The people in the aisle are turning their heads. Near the back a man is on the floor, a regular muscatel advertisement: piss-stained pants, flushed face, long, gray hair. He's leaning against the seat, has his elbows on it. Rattrap continues to the back of the bus, feels that her job's been done. The busdriver looks at Muscatel, bends over, picks him up, and throws him into the seat. The man stinks a little, so there's a place opposite him. I sit down. The solid citizens are smiling to one another. Bouffant hairdos everywhere. I'm with them, all right, I'm trying to get a job. They know best. You're nothing but a bum. My shit smells like roses. The bus moves along, sloshes down the boulevard.

The man opposite me lets the whole bus have it. Look, he says, at these gray hairs, caused by worry. No one cares about me, no one. He points out the spots along the way where there used to be barbershops, the places he went to for a shave and a haircut when he was sparking some woman. Most of the places have been torn down. The man raves, mumbles, becomes poetic. But the atmosphere is there: pure backward. I ain't got nothing, he says. I ain't got a pot to piss in. He's almost at the God stage when someone in the back of the bus catches fire: a hairdo, a beehive, who's wearing a pink shirt and jacket, comes out of her seat, hot as a toaster filament. I don't like what you're doing to me, she says, I don't like what your drugs are doing to my mind. She pushes her way toward the door, the bum, me. She has bandages on her knees and on the top of her feet. It looks like she's been falling down recently.

"I don't like it at all," she says. "I can't stand it anymore."

That's right, I think. Let them have it.

"No more," she says, "or I'm going to do something."

She sits next to the bum. He's quieted down a little. As a matter of fact, he's just watching the woman with the Band-Aids. She's still going pretty good, mumbling and shaking her head, a little twitchy, feeling her wheel spin. He watches her a little longer. The other bouffants just look the other way, every one of them a little less smug than before, but they're still hanging on. I have my hopes: maybe they'll all catch it, maybe they'll all take off and the bus will be filled with the screeches and ravings of a whole generation. Every disappointment, every squint, every limp, every weak kidney, every hysterectomy will be dealt with at one time: you'll be able to hear us coming down the street, past the muffler shops and gas stations and hamburger stands, like a fire engine, like an air raid siren. We'll go until we can only croak at one another, like a bunch of sorry frogs, and the bus will run out of gas in front of a foundry: we'll all get out and watch the sparks, the firework gold, the huge pots of boiling metal.

The bum looks at his pink-haired friend, the middle-aged woman with the skinned knees, and bursts into tears. His chin looks like a peach pit. I hold my sandwiches and think, What can you do, Stargell, ask them to the Trip to Mars ride to watch you eat a banana? The singed smell of electric shock comes off the woman. The bum has had enough, has met his match. He hits the bell: the bus stops and he runs out. When it starts again I can hear him swear as he gives the rear door a good kick.

"That's right," says the woman.

I walk toward the amusement park. The streets are laden with afternoon traffic, trucks and station wagons: everyone means business. Occasionally I see a woman looking out the window of her apartment, watching the snow melt in the empty lots, the slowly emerging grass, quick frozen and preserved from last fall, enriched with cans and broken glass. I walk along, humming, thinking of a job. There is one woman who is looking out her window at a large billboard on which there is a picture of a beautiful woman who is sitting on a beach. There is a palm tree and the woman is in a bathing suit and it makes me want to climb right up there with her to get the full drive-in-movie effect. The woman on the billboard is smoking a cigarette. The woman in the apartment is smoking the same kind, pulling away on it for dear life, fixed on the billboard. I think of the apartment, filled with cases of cigarettes, brought up cheaply from Georgia: the day is spent in rapture, in smoking cigarettes and gazing at the billboard.

The amusement park rises, makes itself apparent. There is a fence around it that's covered with rockets and stars and half-moons: from a distance it looks like the fence has been made out of a wizard's cape. Beyond it I can see the usual amusements, a Ferris wheel and a rocket ride, its two bomb-shaped capsules going around and around, always rotating so that the rider stays straight up.

"I've got to meet the manager at the Trip to Mars ride," I say. "At four. The tryout."

I look at the man who's selling tickets. He glances at me, takes a quick inventory: two arms, one nose, two eyes, two ears. He lets me pass, points toward the center of the park, but he needn't bother. There, in the middle of the smaller rides, the Ferris wheel, the bumper cars and merry-go-round, rising out of the center of the park the way Manhattan's buildings rise into the air, is the Trip to Mars. It's a building that's at least three stories high and is covered with outer-space designs, all Day-Glo and clashing, Saturn's rings, the moon, rockets, stars. You can hear its track running. It's something like an enclosed roller coaster, and at one edge, on the left-hand side when you're facing it, the cars jut quickly out over the amusement park, as though they were going to fly right into the shooting gallery and the hot dog stand. Stargell, I think, can you imagine getting a couple of pints and riding it all day long, listening to the shrieks, the clinking chains? That's the place to have an argument, all right.

There's a bench in front of it, right by the ticket office for the ride. The bench is beneath a sign that says "The World's Only Trip to Mars."

It's about a quarter to four, but some of my colleagues are already waiting. I sit down on the bench and watch the strollers, the people coming out of the Trip to Mars ride, off the Ferris wheel and the rocket ride.

"Has the manager come yet?" I say to a man who seems to be waiting for the tryout.

"No," he says. "No, the manager hasn't come yet."

He's about twenty-eight, has lips as purple as a grape popsicle. His skin's a little yellow, as though he'd gone a few rounds with some liver heavyweight, hepatitis, jaundice.

"I need a job," he says.

"Me, too," I say.

I open my sack and take out a sandwich. I offer it to him, but he's too suspicious to take it, even though he's hungry. I put it back in the sack. Farther down the bench, at the end, there's a man who's about fifty. He sits quietly, without blinking an eye. He doesn't even flinch when the cars of the Trip to Mars ride pop out over our heads. It sounds like two trucks colliding at unbelievable speeds, but it's a little repetitive and that takes some of the snap away: the sound has the aspect of those slow-motion car crashes with the dummies inside. No spontaneity.

Other applicants drift in, but not one seems to have the proper attitude. Purple Lips has started shaking a little. Stage fright, I guess.

"You all right?" I say.

"I need a job," he says.

I think for a moment of telling him about gorillas. They eat a lot of green fruit and that makes them a little gassy. They make a grumbling, bubbling sound and this means they're content, filled up and sleepy.

"It's a beautiful day," he says.

The sky is clear as glass, and it's brisk. The afternoon is gaining, but there's still some light in front of the Trip to Mars ride, and we sit in it like old people in the park. Just give me the obituaries and a One A Day vitamin and I'll go through this like wildfire.

"A little cool," I say.

"It's a beautiful day," he says.

He's started shaking again, but he's got his teeth set, is letting the sun hit his face. I open my bag and take out the sandwich again.

"Why don't you eat it?" I say.

He swallows, looks at me.

"There's nothing wrong with it," I say.

I offer the sandwich. It's wrapped perfectly, as though done in Japan for a Samurai rite. In the think tank we worked on Baggies and I still play with the plastic, with the right designs.

"Look," I say, "I'll eat one, too. There's nothing wrong."

He takes it, unwraps it, holds it in his hand. I unwrap mine, too.

"You like hot mustard?" I say.

"Yes," he says.

There's the hottest mustard in the world on the sandwich. I make it myself to put on the Barber's cheese. The secret is to put a little beer in it. The mustard clears the head, mind, is a kind of culinary incense: all the spooks are chased away.

"That's hot," says Purple Lips.

We sit next to one another, eating the sandwiches. The Trip to Mars ride clinks and booms overhead, its cars periodically jumping once into the air overhead before turning back into the dark recess of the building. The place is something like a car wash that's gone haywire.

"How about a Coke?" I say.

Purple Lips nods.

"Yes," he says, "a Coke."

I buy one and come back to the bench.

"Thanks," he says.

More people drift over to the Trip to Mars ride, men who seem to be a little suspicious of one another. I realize I have stopped thinking of us as applicants: we've moved more into the realm of contestants. There's a nice queen-for-a-day atmosphere.

"I got to have a job," says Purple Lips, "because I just got out of the nut house."

Ah, I think, so that explains it. I'm ready to coach the miserable wretch. I know how apes behave. Purple Lips looks at me when he lets the cat out of the bag: his eyes are a couple of Thorazine beauties. He could have won them in a marbles game. I'm tempted to say, Look, Jack, this isn't your style. You better try a shoe store. But then he's spent time in a cell with a drain: maybe he knows what he's about.

There are about twenty-five of us now. Short, tall, fat, thin: everyone wants to be a gorilla. The man who sat quietly at the end of the bench stands up and looks at a house trailer that's opposite the Trip to Mars ride. The manager approaches. He's about forty-five, has dark hair, a correspondence school smile. He wears a turtleneck sweater and a sport coat. There's a woman with him. She's carrying the personnel shotgun: a clipboard. I'd love to feel her cool skin. She's blond, at that ageless thirty, has beautiful legs, lips, eyes that are as cutting as scissors.

The manager recognizes the man who had been sitting quietly at the end of the bench.

"Hello, John Wesley," says the manager.

"Hello, Ellis," says John Wesley.

Ellis is still smiling by the book. It looks like he's getting ready to tell a joke. I expect him to say, Look at my false teeth. Better than the real thing. Feel my bite. I can eat corn. I can eat apples. They wear like iron.

"Sorry to hear about Palisades Park," says Ellis, the manager.

"Yes," says John Wesley. "I worked there twenty-five years. I've been out of a job since it closed."

Ellis smiles.

"Now you'll work for us," says Ellis. He's still at it: his smile says, What do you think of these swizzle sticks?

"I come for the tryout," says John Wesley.

This looks bad for the rest of us, but I've got the theoretical edge. Purple Lips is staring at the skyline.

"Beautiful day," he says.

We are interviewed, one at a time, by the woman with the clipboard. Her name is Bev. I look into her eyes, into the arctic waters there, tell her everything. Age, education, even the think tank. I tell her about the patent that has my name on it. At the think tank we had a small job. They sent us out to a hospital to watch the cerebral palsy boys eat. They can grab the spoon but they can't turn it, so their dinner falls in their lap, a spoonful at a time. My light started to glow. I thought a mule had kicked me. I said to the engineer, A weighted spoon and a swivel. Let me tell you, he felt pretty good, too. They made a spoon with a swivel right where the bowl part is attached to the handle. It keeps the spoon level so everyone could get something to eat. Everyone's getting plump and cozy there now. They call it the Stargell.

Sometimes at night I can hear the slurping and clinking, the sound of everyone having a little supper.

"What are you doing here?" she says.

"Waiting for the tryout," I say.

She nods, moves on to Purple Lips. I know what she means, but the fact of the matter is that I've started to scare people. My genius days are done. All my screws are loose: I can hear them rattle on the subway. No, Stargell, I think, you've got to make a place for yourself. I can feel the city's tight-cunt feeling, its glorious tug.

The manager brings out the gorilla suit.

Bev finishes with Purple Lips. It looks like he leveled, too. Bev moves down the line, from man to man. Twice she stops and looks at me and I give her a smile which, even though I can't see it, makes me feel like I have a winning ticket for the daily double. Bev listens to itemized failure, nods, notches her gun, the clipboard: I see it moving down legions of unemployed. Life is sad, she thinks, just look at all these drones. A man near the end of the line lifts up his trousers to show her that his socks are held up with thumbtacks. She gently shakes her head. Gimps, too, she thinks.

It looks like someone has shot a gorilla. The suit sits in a hump on the asphalt. Ellis tells us that we can change in the house trailer, that we are to run out into the space in front of it, and that we will display our abilities there. The suit is used: its feet are almost worn out. The hair looks like it had been taken from a shaggy black carpet. The face has a zombie quality. Not a bad suit, take it all around. The feet are rubber, the color of pumice stone. It has rubber hands, too. Ellis sprays the suit with Lysol. He says he'll spray it between tryouts. He's still smiling.

"No one said anything about TV," says Purple Lips.

Ellis tells us that there is also a ladder on the Trip to Mars ride. If any gorilla would like to give it a try, that would be fine.

"TV?" I say. I'm looking at the suit, already feeling a little twitchy, the pendulum swing, the heat of the suit, its odor of sweat and Lysol. The cars on the Trip to Mars ride carry the funlovers into the recesses of the building: factory sounds, smashing metal, conveyor-belt clink.

"See?" says Purple Lips.

A station wagon is parked next to the gate and some people are unloading neat aluminum cases from the back. Bev gives the crew a look. Every gesture, each movement, is swift, unerring: it is as though everything around her is sharp and she doesn't want to get cut. That's some suit, I think, that's just the thing.

"I'm not going on TV," says Purple Lips.

I make a quiet, tentative snort. The leaves are so soothing in the afternoon, in the warm breeze. Bev gives us the order in which we're to try out: John Wesley, me, Purple Lips, and then the rest of the boys, pretty much in the order of the bench.

There is a PA system for the amusement park, and it's been playing Elvis Presley music. I'm humming "Viva Las Vegas," thinking about the suit, watching as the TV crew approaches. The cameraman's headline should read "Cameraman Strangles Hell's Angel on a Ten-Cent Bet." The music is interrupted and Ellis's voice comes on. He tells the park, the people there, that the try-outs for the gorilla job are about to begin. He comes out of the house trailer, smiling: these teeth are better than the real thing. My wife loves her vibrator.

John Wesley has been sitting at the end of the bench, but now he pushes himself up and goes over to the suit, grabs it and takes it into the trailer. He lifts it in the same way an old-time catcher picks up his mask. The people from the amusement park begin to assemble at the Trip to Mars. The cameraman stands before the building, the stars and rockets, the clanging, garbage truck rumble. He nods, recognizes an old adversary.

Ellis goes into the trailer to zip up John Wesley.

"I'm not going on TV," says Purple Lips.

The lighting man hits his sun gun. John Wesley comes out of the house trailer. Bev is standing next to me and she says, "Holy shit." Purple Lips flinches and the rest of the boys look a little limp. The gorilla is moving across the blacktop with long, easy strides. He stops and gives himself a thump on the chest. One hand is on the ground. If I didn't know better I'd call the zoo keeper. Stargell, my boy, this is the competition. The kids applaud him. John Wesley moves all the way over to the Trip to Mars, takes a step or two on the ladder, jumps at a child. He walks on all fours, putting his wrist toward the direction he walks. The film crew is following him around, moving with a perfect choreography, never tripping: it looks like all of them have just come back from working in Africa or New Guinea. John Wesley comes by the rest of us, stops in front of Bev, makes a shaggy twitch for her, then chases after the kids, who are laughing and eating cotton candy. Applause. Ellis shows some teeth, pats his hair weave. He stands by Bev for a moment so she can see the porcelain, too. John Wesley is a man of economy: once more around the crowd and then into the trailer.

"Stargell," she says.

It's as though Bev's cut the word out of paper and hung it on a hook. She touches my hand: her finger is as cool as a pair of scissors.

"Good luck," she says.

I thank her, and walk through the crowd and then into the house trailer. Low ceilings. Masonite everywhere. Nice kitchen. John Wesley is pulling on his shoes. The gorilla is collapsed on the floor: shot again. It sits in the corner, waiting for some juice, the spark of the living. More than anything else the gorilla looks blankly confused: everything's slipping away, boys, how come the sun is such a strange color, the earth so near? Ellis comes into the trailer, tells John Wesley he was great, then sprays out the suit. He gives it a jolt under each arm and in each foot, just the way he does himself in the morning. He looks at me and realizes we're smiling at one another in exactly the same way, as though we were both staring into a mirror. I turn toward the gorilla. Ellis goes out the door.

"Watch the feet," says John Wesley. "They bend. You got to walk with your toes up."

I step into the suit, slip my hands into the sleeves, my feet into the legs. Everything's a little damp. Bev comes in the door to zip me. The zipper runs all the way up my back. Her long, strong fingers run it right up to my neck. I grunt, look around the house trailer, see the bed there, unmade. Good atmosphere. I put the head on and Bev fastens it at the back. I can hear myself breathing against a rubber nostril. Bev stands before me, cool and delicate as shaved ice. When she smiles you can see her shrink squirm. That a girl, I think, keep them guessing: you'll get to Southampton yet.

She gives me a pop on the head, as though I were a deep-sea diver.

"John Wesley's got the job," she says.

"You want to bet?" I say.

I can feel the jungle rise, the push of new growth, can smell the danger on the wind: the men with the tranquilizer guns.

"What have you got?" she says.

I stare at her through the eye holes: she gets the message. I want to go home with her, to her apartment that's all chrome and glass, cheap Parisian despair. What things we'll do there, nude and cool, with the city light coming in the window.

She laughs.

"Of course," she says, "we'll have that bet."

The crowd is getting a little restless. I can see Ellis is still smiling, but the TV crew seems impatient. Stargell, I think, this is it. I look at Bev and crash out, hopping and moving, swinging my arms: the crowd roars. It sounds like I'm trapped in a big sea shell, since everything has the distant sound of the ocean behind it. I race across the asphalt. The children follow, whooping and yelling. The old man's being pulled down, I think, it's just killing him, at its own sweet time. Enid's worrying about her underwear. I can see the savanna, the approach of the zoo buyers, the living-meat boys. I'm snorting and hopping, smashing the back of my wrist against my chest, making a good deep sound. The children follow, some of them clapping. I see the cameraman, backing away, backing away: I make a good charge at him, at the sun gun. They retreat. Everyone's having a hell of a time. I'm moving through the undergrowth at startling speeds. I stop for a moment to catch my breath, stand on all fours near the edge of the crowd. I can see Ellis and Bev, Purple Lips, the other boys. The camera crew looks like something escaped from an industrial Mardi Gras: four people seem to be in a jackass suit, the kind beneath which you can see only the legs, but this suit seems to be made out of lenses, lights, wire, headphones, magazines of film. It dances around, comes my way.

A child kicks me. I turn toward it, slowly revolving, seeing the

house trailer, the crowds, the bench pass by. The little monster is
looking up at me, smiling, faintly unsure of himself. His friends
are there, too. I lean slowly forward. The child is freckled, blue-
eyed. I put my nose right against his head.

"How would you like to get fucked?" I say.

His face falls. Stargell, I think, that's the way to deal with the
little fiends. Before he has a chance to kick me again, I move
across the asphalt, beating my chest: I make tremendous noise as
I go and my throat feels as though I were gargling kerosene. The
sun gun is before me again. I hit the ladder for the Trip to Mars
ride on the run, take the rungs two at a time. The crowd roars.
The sun gun follows me. There is a balcony, an open space with a
railing where the cars pass by, and I swing up to it, hand over
hand, thinking, Stargell, listen to them. I grab a rail at the side of
the opening and shake it, jump up and down, screech as though
someone had filled my banana with red pepper. Ellis is still smiling, but he wants to take a quick peek into his insurance policy.
The cameraman is right below me, never stopping for a moment,
but I can see him pull his head back from the eyepiece and look
up at me: he nods slightly, and gives me his hard-ass grimace. I
shake the railing, reach up to the one above me, get both hands
on it and give the bar such a shaking that the kids start screaming. I can feel the whole Trip to Mars ride tremble. Look at that, I
say, look. I shake the railing, then swing out over the heads of the
spectators and hang by one arm. The cameraman keeps his finger
on the button, but I can see he's smiling. John Wesley is sitting on
the bench, as circumspect as a diplomat who knows big secrets. I
swing back and forth, smell the odor of distant water, of the tree's
sweet fruits. Stargell, I think, this is all right, but how the hell are
you going to pull yourself up? The crowd becomes anxious. I
swing back and forth, feeling the muscles in my arm heat up. It's
only fifteen feet or so, straight down. What the hell, I think. I can
see Bev looking at me, a smile cracking the ice. I switch hands,
swing out once over the screaming, shouting children, then put
both hands on the bar and swing back to the platform. Even I am
impressed. It looks as though I've been doing it for years. The
spectators break into frenzied applause, are convinced it was all
part of the show. I give the Trip to Mars ride an affectionate

shake, a home-tree pat, and then a good rip: I roar down the ladder, scare the crap out of everyone, and tear across the blacktop and go into the house trailer. Everyone is laughing. The cameraman looks toward the house trailer and nods, says something to the sun gun man, who nods, Yes, yes, yes. I take my head off, and sit on a lawn chair, breathe hard, think, Did you hear the applause?

Bev comes in the door, unzips my suit. I put on my shoes.

"Ellis is thinking about it," she says.

"Good," I say.

Purple Lips is scheduled next, but the man who was sitting next to him comes into the house trailer.

"Where's my friend?" I say.

Bev shrugs. The next man is good-looking and stupid: an actor.

"You done with the suit?" he says.

I'm breathing hard, feeling everything work, heart and lungs. I step out of the suit, give it to Ellis, who's come in the door with the can of Lysol. He sprays, smiles.

"You were great, great," he says.

I look at Bev. She's running her strong, cool fingers up the gorilla suit's back.

"Wonderful," says Ellis.

"Have you decided?" I say.

"No," says Ellis. "We have other contestants."

He smiles. I walk out the door, wondering where Bev lives. From the step of the house trailer I can see that the child who gave me a kick is making himself scarce. I sit down next to Purple Lips. He's shaking and trembling, rocking back and forth on the edge of the bench.

"I'm not going on TV," he says.

"I understand," I say.

John Wesley turns, looks at me, and says, "Did you ever work California, Pacific Ocean Park?"

"I been here and there," I say.

"Yeah," says John Wesley.

Purple Lips stares at the house trailer door.

"I just can't believe I came all the way out here and I'm not going to try it." He starts rocking in earnest. I can see the nut house rise, can see it's netlike shape taking form.

"Did Ellis tell you I'd be here?" says John Wesley.

"No," I say.

John Wesley looks toward the trailer. His face is white, and his head is so bald it looks like there had never been hair on it at all.

"He didn't tell me about you," he says. "Ellis is a little prick."

The camera crew sets itself, waits for the door to open.

"He better look out," says John Wesley, "or I'm going to break his teeth."

Purple Lips is staring at the palms of his hands as though the answers to the quiz were written there. The crowd babbles, closes in on the house trailer. Bev and Ellis come out, and then the gorilla. It looks like the ne'er-do-well brother of the previous two. The crowd boos a little. John Wesley stares at it for a while, then turns to me and blinks, as if to say, Look at that. You and I understand the mysteries of the gorilla. These people are just a bunch of pissants. The gorilla performs only for the TV camera: the crowd resents it, boos louder. The actor knows the jig is up. He walks back to the house trailer with his ordinary stride.

The gorillas come and go, none particularly better or worse than another. John Wesley sits as quietly as a monk, taking one quick glance at each new gorilla, then lapses, is drawn into the silence of a formal Oriental garden. Purple Lips rocks and wrings his hands.

"I just can't believe this," he says.

Another gorilla comes flying out of the house trailer, its arms raised above its head: no juice, no spark, just another guy in a hairy suit. The television crew has had enough. They shoot the last one, go over to the car, pack their stuff in: everything fits. The cameraman gives me a look that would kill kittens, then gets into the front seat. The car pulls away from the curb.

Bev comes out of the trailer. Another gorilla plays before a smaller though still enthusiastic audience. Ellis comes out, too, and stands on the steps of the house trailer with his can of Lysol.

"They make the suit clean," I say to Purple Lips. "Smells just like a new car."

Purple Lips nods.

"It is a beautiful day," he says.

We look at the sun setting behind the Trip to Mars ride.

"Yes," I say.

It feels good to watch it: the clouds look like the edges of smoldering newspaper. I can feel something in my arm that's not quite right, but I can remember the applause, the feeling when I thought the whole Trip to Mars ride was going to crash down around my ears, when there was a noise that sounded like jet planes crashing. It's getting cooler. Bev hugs herself and smokes a cigarette.

"The TV crew is gone," I say.

Ellis stands on the step with the aerosol can. He speaks to someone, an assistant, who walks to the Trip to Mars ride.

"O.K.," says Purple Lips.

There is still a crowd left. They look a little ragged, like the people who are left an hour after the parade's gone by. The kid who gave me a kick is back, looking as endearing as a scorpion. The little bastard just loves to see someone squirm. He'll get over it, if someone doesn't throw him out a window first. Ellis crosses the blacktop, moves through the crowd. He talks to Bev, and then to John Wesley, who points once at me and once at Ellis's teeth. Bev listens to what they say, stares at me, and I can tell she's thinking, Why not invite him home, why not? Ellis is smiling, smiling, nodding, selling me and my darling Bev down the river. Stargell, I think, maybe you should bust his teeth. Purple Lips pulls my sleeve.

"I want to get in the suit," he says.

"Sure," I say, "don't worry."

I feel the cool wind as I walk across the blacktop and I can smell the odor of cotton candy, peanuts, stale vomit, sweet wine.

"John Wesley's got the job," says Ellis when I come up to them.

Wesley nods, turns on his heel, and walks back to the bench. Ellis sees me looking at Bev.

"Here," he says, taking twenty bucks from his wallet and sticking it in my coat pocket. "Buy yourself a beer. You were great. But we need John Wesley."

I can hear the Trip to Mars ride start up, the chains clinking.

"I'm going to announce it," says Ellis.

"Wait," I say.

Ellis holds the aerosol can. Bev shivers, embraces herself. From the Trip to Mars ride I could see the flat rows of houses, the gas stations, muffler shops, hamburger places, shoe stores, a neon totem pole. Stargell, I think, Bev's got birth control pill despair, estrogen willies. I'll take her out to the oil refineries so she can see what she feels like.

"He wants to try it," I say.

They look at Purple Lips, who's still sitting on the bench, rocking a little, but not so much as before. He looks embarrassed when we turn toward him, but he manages a smile.

"It's been decided," says Ellis.

He gestures with the aerosol can at the Trip to Mars ride, the sky beyond it, the stars: the TV crew has made him a little giddy. Bev is shaking her head, looking at me.

I walk across the blacktop. The colored lights go on above the Trip to Mars ride, illuminate the gaudy heavens there: it's as though the amusement park had captured light-years, outer space, Orion, Cygnus, Centaurus, glowing gases, all purple and gold. Yellow bulbs go on above the concession stands and around the fence. There's a sign near the entrance, in red neon, which flashes on and off: "Amusements, Amusements."

"It's been decided," I say to Purple Lips.

"I don't care," he says. "I want to try out."

Ellis and Bev are standing next to one another.

"He wants to do it anyway," I say.

Ellis shows me his porcelain, clicks uppers and lowers, then looks at the thirty or so people who are still lingering before the house trailer.

"It's no skin off my nose," he says.

Purple Lips is rocking back and forth on the bench.

"It's all set," I say.

"Thanks," he says.

I sit down next to him. John Wesley is still at the other end of the bench, not moving. He's basking in the light of the Trip to Mars ride. Purple Lips is cooking.

"My father shot himself," says Purple Lips. "He came back

from the track one day and shot himself. So I found myself think-ing, 'My father shot himself, my father shot himself, my father shot himself.' You should have seen what it did to my tennis game. No one had a chance with me. Then they locked me up."

He's working himself up to it, all right: maybe Ellis spoke too soon. Purple Lips walks across the lot, goes into the trailer with Ellis. Bev stands in the cool air for a moment and then comes through the small crowd and sits down next to me.

"Ellis and I are going to the Pow Wah Lounge," she says.

Bev and I sit together, feeling the breeze.

"It's important," she says.

Yes, I think, if you play your cards right you'll hit the brand-name big time.

"I'm sorry," she says.

But I'm thinking about the Trip to Mars, the view from it, the city in the distance, the lights, the sprawling beauty.

"It's O.K.," I say.

"I didn't think you'd take it seriously," she says.

"I wanted the job," I say.

It's just cold now and we sit together. The crowd is a little restless. The door of the trailer opens and the gorilla comes out. It runs a couple of yards. The crowd cheers. You can see that the applause does something for the gorilla, because it runs with a little more heart. The feet, which are half broken, bend, fold double, and the gorilla goes down, as though the gorilla had slammed into a neck-high wire. The crowd laughs. The gorilla gets up, kneels, turns his head from side to side. The crowd knows they're on top, all right. The last applicant doesn't have a chance. They can smell something, the whiff of things they'd rather not have themselves. A child gives the gorilla a kick. The gorilla turns, says something that makes the children jeer. In the air I can hear the sound of the Trip to Mars ride, now running again, the cars rattling on their tracks. The gorilla beats its chest, hops up and down. There is a little applause, but most of the people in the crowd have seen the show before: they turn and begin to walk away. A few children chase after the gorilla, and perhaps ten people are still watching. The gorilla puts his heart into it, shrieks once, and then again. It sounds like the thing he's always feared has got hold of him and is doing its worst. The kids chase him some more. He turns, stops, kneels again, makes Al Jolson gestures, as though he were singing "Mammy." Above and behind him is the Trip to Mars: I can hear the dungeon rattling of its chains, the roller-coaster count as the cars are lifted to the top. The gorilla trips over the broken feet.

"They gotta fix those feet," says John Wesley.

The crowd stands around him. It's time to quit, I think. One of the kids gives him another pop in the ribs. The gorilla gets up. You can see right through the mask that he's pleading. They can smell it, too: the awkwardness, the desperation. I'm thinking, Show it to them. Let them see it. The gorilla jumps up and begins to run, and the crowd follows a step or two behind him. Bev is sitting next to me, still shivering, watching. Stargell, I think, the boy's come unglued, right there in the suit. The crowd can feel it, too, and leaves off, lets the gorilla run around, shaking his fists above his head, blowing white mist out of his nostrils. Quitting time, I think. The crowd begins to applaud, to whistle: he's so far away from them now that they can afford it. It picks him up, though, and he streaks across the blacktop, taking a steady fix on the Trip to Mars ride, on the ladder that leans against it. The crowd applauds.

"He shouldn't go up there," says John Wesley.

The gorilla has already hit the ladder and is making long, apy strides, hand over hand. He flies up the ladder to the platform where the cars jut once into the air and then turn back into the flashing recesses of the ride. It's dark enough now to see that there are the glowing reaches of outer space inside, figures that jump from the darkness, illuminated by short, thick beams. The crowd applauds him. He steps on the track of the cars, then jumps onto the railing, hangs there, then jumps up and down on the balcony. He's shrieking, screaming, shaking the beams near the balcony.

Ellis comes out of the house trailer, still smiling, still carrying the can of Lysol. Bev hugs herself. The crowd is slowly winding down, slowly letting their irregular applause slip away. It just makes the ride seem louder, more insistent. You can hear the factory smashing, the foundry screech. The crowd is now completely quiet, and I can hear the PA system: it's still Elvis, a movie theme now, "Spinout." Ellis looks at the gorilla from the steps of the trailer.

"Turn off the ride," I say.

Ellis puts down the can of Lysol.

"Oh, my God," he says.

The gorilla is shaking and trembling, shrieking. The crowd stands before the balcony and stares. Ellis walks across the blacktop, makes for the entrance of the Trip to Mars. The door is locked and he runs to the ticket booth.

I stand beneath the balcony.

"Come down," I say. "You were great. Great."

The gorilla continues. The crowd watches.

"Come down," I say again.

The gorilla shrieks. I see Bev standing by the bench. John Wesley shakes his head once. That's right, I think, we can hear you. Just come down. You can tell me all about it: I'll listen. You can tell me all about the Bellevue lights, the cloud monsters. Just come down. The Trip to Mars is still running.

"Come down," I say.

The crowd stands behind me. The gorilla is still shaking the railing.

"Come down, come down," says the crowd.

The gorilla thinks they're not satisfied, that they're condescending. He shrieks, beats his chest, runs around on all fours, then stands and looks down at his audience. He puts his hand over his head, begins to wave, makes half a shriek, and is cut down by one of the Trip to Mars cars. There are two people in it and they are having a good time. The car catches the gorilla in the belly: it lifts him up and, after making him waggle once over the balcony, over the surprised and now awed crowd, carries him, without twitching, into the depths of the Trip to Mars, of outer space.

"Maybe that prick Ellis," says John Wesley, "will buy a new suit."

The ride stops as though the afternoon whistle had been blown: I expect to see hundreds of workers carrying their lunch pails as they file out of the exit. I'm thinking, The kid didn't look that bad up there, shaking it for the world to see, giving the customers their money's worth. He's O.K., I think. I've known someone who was run over by a street sweeper. Limps a little. Everything O.K. Interesting scars.

Ellis comes out on the balcony, smiling, smiling: what great teeth these are.

"Bev," he says, "there are some smelling salts in the trailer."

Bev glances at me: she wants to go to the Pow Wah Lounge and brood over vodka and Frank Sinatra.

"Sorry about the bet," she says.

She shakes my hand, walks into the trailer, gets the first-aid kit, and climbs into the Trip to Mars. After a while they bring out Purple Lips. He's a little woozy and he's holding his side. They bring him out to the bench. I don't think he's clear enough to start raving again. Ellis just wants to get him off the amusement park grounds.

"You were great," says Ellis.

"Was I?" says Purple Lips. "You thought it was O.K.?"

"Yeah," says Ellis, "you were wonderful."

Purple Lips is a little suspicious. Bev tells him he was good.

"You were good," says John Wesley.

You can see this means a lot to Purple Lips. He smiles, then walks out of the compound, past the Trip to Mars ride, the Ferris wheel and merry-go-round. Just outside the gate I see him kneel and vomit. He hangs on to the hurricane fence there, has his fingers pushed through the diamond pattern, and he gives it a gorilla shake, a small one while he retches again. He looks back at us once, and then walks quickly away from the park.

"What about a new suit?" says John Wesley.

"Sure, sure," says Ellis.

The Trip to Mars starts up again.

"You want to come to the Pow Wah for a Mai-Tai?" says Ellis.

"Yeah," says John Wesley.

Bev waves goodbye. They walk to the gate and get into a car. I sit before the Trip to Mars ride for a while, thinking of the savanna grass, the clear, warm evening breeze, the taste of fruit.

It would have been nice, I think, to have won the bet.

The couples on the Trip to Mars ride shriek and laugh.

It's rush hour: everyone's grim. I take the train to Times Square, climb the steps, watch the buildings against the sky that's now the color of eggplant skin, read the news as it's flashed up by amusement park lights: Arabia, Italy, India, all the old places are mentioned, the parts of the world that fill my head with the scent of spices, the sight of sand dunes and camels, white slavers, dark women, opium, chests filled with precious oils. I stand on the street, watch the locals: everyone walks with a sandwich-board gait. I go into Grant's and order some clams and sit with a plateful in front of the window. Next to me is an old man who is eating soft-shell crabs. We both have a glass of beer. The crowds seem to slither along, but the people are surprising, infinitely fascinating, outrageous, startling. The clams are cold. I can taste the ocean, feel the sharp recognition of it hit me in the roaring cafeteria. The light is yellowish and everyone is eating and drinking. The old man tenderly lifts each of his crabs to his lips and bites. I sip beer, savor the clams, watch the foreign names: Hamburg, Kuwait, São Paulo.

"Those were good crabs," says the old man when he's done.

I want to tell him that eating a good meal is spitting in the face of death, but probably it would just frighten him. There are a lot of vegetable people around these days.

The downtown subway moves across the rails, approaches me as smoothly as a sunrise. The train is an express and it slams from side to side. I'd like to ride all the way to Brooklyn, but I only made $18.50 (when you deduct the carfare). The train is filled with Friday-night couples, holding hands and mooning a little even though they're being tossed around and the car sounds like a transmission that's having its gears stripped. They want to mate so bad you can hear the glands squeak like a squeegee on a window. It makes them a little more polite than usual. I blend in with them when they get off at my stop, then wait until they have climbed the stairs. I'm alone on the platform, feeling the rank, used air rush by as the trains enter the station. I climb to the street, thinking, Stargell, what a day. Tomorrow I'll send bricks of ice to the Eskimos. I walk along, thinking of seals in cold water, of fish drying in the wind, the perfect architecture (that has everything to do with the weather) of igloos, of caribou and polar bears, of oiling down a woman with walrus fat and inhaling the odor. In the nutrition department of the think tank there were some people who dealt with the Eskimos. A woman went up there and found that when there was a famine, when the caribou had some disease, the Eskimos starved before eating Campbell's pork and beans. I can't stand that shit myself. The woman organized a small cannery on wheels to put up the things that Eskimos liked: tripe, walrus puffs, blubber in black sauce, great delicacies. The Eskimos loved them. Someone decided to import Eskimo food to the lower 48. At least, Stargell, I think, some people are keeping the faith.

Enid has taken her battle station in front of the TV: she's armed with a cheese sandwich and the page of listings she's cut from the *Times*. On Sunday she buys the paper and sits with a pencil, marking off the week's viewing. Oh, oh, oh, she says, I've got to see that. She uses both checks and crosses and sometimes an X, if it's something like *It Came from Beneath the Sea*.

"Where have you been?" she says.

This takes place during a commercial. Enid doesn't usually like to miss them, but she's watching a local station and they tend to have a B quality: exercisers and vegetable choppers, Great Moments in Music and machines that sew on buttons. The actresses in the exercise commercials are so lascivious I can hardly keep my hands off the Genius. They're in the same league as the intellectual's tit show: *Yoga for Health*.

"What were you doing?" says Enid.

She looks at my hands, sees that they've got some strange-looking stuff on them, putty-colored dirt from the hands of the gorilla suit.

"I tried out for a job," I say. "Look. I made eighteen dollars."

I take the money out of my pocket.

"Eighteen dollars," she says.

She says it like, The Queen of England will see you now.

"And fifty cents," I say.

I start to count out the change, but Enid gives me a look that would wilt a parking meter.

"How dare you?" she says.

I put the change back in my pocket. Enid gives the commercial a once-over, dismisses a man who is demonstrating a sharpener, putting an edge on a pair of scissors, a pair of garden shears.

"I don't want you to be bad to me," says Enid, "but I must say this. You have turned into a failure. Soon you will be a bum."

I want to tell her there's still hope. I may make a million and wear three-piece suits and act like a cocaine nouveau from Long Island: the waiters better look out then. What the fuck, I think. Enid will get drunk on Shalimar and wear shoes made out of filet mignon. That would fix her up.

Enid and I watch the movie.

"I'll be gone soon," I say.

"Yes," says Enid.

Enid's eyes are dry at the end of the film.

"It wasn't good," she says. "Now we will watch the news."

We wait for the news as though it were a train and we were standing on a deserted platform. Every second has staying power.

"Your hands smell," says Enid. "Why don't you wash them?"

My hands smell like the gorilla suit's sweaty rubber. I climb into the Niagara shower, stand under the running water.

The think tank had the reputation of being "rehabilitatively acute" after the Stargell, the spoon with the swivel. Jolting Joe said to me, "Stargell, I'll take them apart and you put them together. Ying and Yang."

Jolting Joe was working on a clear, odorless gas that was explosive. You let someone inhale it and then you set it off. Jolting Joe played squash, collected ivory miniatures (elephants and intricate castles, nudes and *ben hua* balls) and pornographic films of twelve-year-old girls, drank mint juleps, enjoyed the opera, kept up his correspondence. Jolting Joe had run an advertisement in a magazine called *Hunk,* a clearing house for would-be pen pals.

His ad read, "Red Hot Mamma in Jersey Looking for Big Man for Correspondence." Soon Joe was writing (as the "Red Hot Mamma in Jersey") to a merchant seaman, who sent silks and perfume, photographs of himself in a watch cap. On slow days I used to sit around and think, Stargell, there's going to be some fun when the sailor shows up here.

The Slasher came into my office and told me I was in demand, sent me to a VA hospital, where I watched the quads (men paralyzed from the neck down), spent time in the wards, nights in the strangely unmoving darkness: no one turned over. The men wanted to call a nurse, but they couldn't. I felt my lamp begin to glow. Switches, I thought, switches. . . . I used pneumatic ones, the kind you work when you drive over a rubber hose in a gas station. We pinned the end of a tube to a pillow and when someone wanted to call a nurse, all he had to do was to blow into the tube. The switch turned on a light in the hall. When I got back to the office the Slasher was smiling, as happy as a baseball scout who's found a Hall of Famer in the minor leagues.

"This will mean big funding," he said.

"Switches," said Jolting Joe, a little later, when he stopped me in the hall, "Shit, man, come in here."

He showed me a slow-motion film that was horrifying and beautiful. It looked like a sausage factory had gone haywire, a lazy dance of intestines and gray-blue tripe.

"I've got the carburetion time, after the gas is released," said Jolting Joe, "down to ten seconds."

We watch another movie and I don't blink.

"And getting quicker every day," said Jolting Joe. "You can't see it, but those are sheep we're using to test it on. Down in Florida."

I worked in other places, applied the switches, which weren't in the same league as the Stargell, but I was still proud of them. The Slasher called me into his office, a room with a sofa and a coffee table, gaudy as hell, but then the Slasher thought of himself as Mr. Big. He gave me a folder and told me to take a look. It contained a medical description and some photographs. I read for a while. Jolting Joe came in, looked over my shoulder, and said, "That's the paper work I'm always talking about."

The description and the photographs were of a forty-five-year-old man. Both arms amputated, face scarred, hooks on each stump, blind. Airplane trauma. I could hardly look at the photographs without gagging. The man's name was Robert Bolinski.

"There's pilot funding," said the Slasher. "Go out there and see this guy. Maybe you can do something."

I shook my head.

"He's idiosyncratic," I said.

"So?" said the Slasher.

"If," I said, "I can do something for him, it wouldn't do anybody else any good. It would only work for him."

"Suit yourself," said the Slasher.

This was always a bad sign, but I walked down the hall anyway, where Jolting Joe was waiting.

"Look," he said. "Just look."

We watched some more movies. The sheep took a sniff, looked alarmed for one brief moment, and popped like soap bubbles.

"What are you working on?" said Jolting Joe.

I walked back down the hall.

"I'll go," I said to the Slasher. "Give me the folder."

Fuck it, I thought, when I was sitting in my office. I'll have this guy playing a banjo.

Robert Bolinski lived in San Francisco, and I took the plane out to see him, spent days with him, walking through the city, stopping in parks, trying to see where he hesitated. One day Bolinski hit the post of a No Parking sign so hard it was still vibrating five minutes later. In San Francisco they put the No Parking signs on four-by-fours.

"It doesn't hurt," said Bolinski, taking his stick in his hook. The tears ran over the scar tissue. We stopped before an open-air market and Robert could smell the fruit. We went inside and Robert pulled up his sleeve, gently touched the peaches and pears, the oranges, grapefruits, new potatoes, and apples, all of which were as bright and shiny as a color photograph printed on slick paper. The manager took a run at Bolinski and saw me standing there, ready to pop him a good one, so he stopped and glared and wiped his hands on his apron. I bought some raspberries. They were a little dusty but they looked good. We went down to the beach. It was one of those California days in September when the sky is distant, clear, as blue as the ocean. I fed Robert raspberries one at a time.

"My God," said Robert, "raspberries. I haven't tasted raspberries in years."

He stood out on the hard sand where he could feel the Pacific wash around his feet and smelled the spray while the taste of the berries lingered. I put Sea & Ski on his face and he liked that, too. At night he liked to listen to old songs like "Earth Angel" and "Smoke Gets in Your Eyes."

After a couple of days he told me there was a problem, and I thought, Stargell, what the fuck is wrong with you?

I read Robert the ads in the local skin sheets, checked with the local hookers, but Robert didn't want to feel like he was disgusting anyone. He enjoyed listening to me read the ads, though: "Blond, nineteen, on call, half and half, twenty dollars." We talked over the other advertisements in the back of the paper and then I made the purchase.

I went back to the office and after a couple of days a card came to me.

"Thanks," it said. "Robert Bolinski."

The Slasher saw it and said, "What did you do?"

"Look in the expense reports," I said.

By this time I was reading about the moths, the shivering, clinging darlings.

"What's an Acu-Jac?" said the Slasher, holding the file.

"A rubber cunt with a vibrator," I said.

The Slasher stepped into the hall so that everyone could hear him scream, "You mean to tell me you spent federal money on an Acu-Jac?"

The Slasher went down the hall, and Jolting Joe came in. His solution would have been, Here. Smell this. Light your cigarette. Nothing left but the paper work.

"What are you working on?" he said.

"Oil," I said.

Oil is to the think tank what God is to religion. It shut up Jolting Joe, because oil is even more important than death.

I think of Robert listening in the dark to "Earth Angel," the

Acu-Jac humming, his head filled with the scent and touch of fresh fruit, Sea & Ski, his mouth with the taste of raspberries. The neighbors downstairs start banging on their ceiling with a broomstick. Jolting Joe found out, and after the Crab Nebula Daily Double, after the moths, he was still saying, even as I cleaned out my desk, Ying and Yang, Stargell, you got to do better than an Acu-Jac.

I get dressed and sit on the arm of Enid's chair.

The news is almost over, but I get there in time to see a gorilla hanging from the balcony of the Trip to Mars ride, shaking it for the whole world to see, as insistent as an alarm clock. You can hear, over the applause of the crowd and the sound of Elvis Presley singing "Viva Las Vegas," a definite shriek. The kids are going wild for the gorilla. Enid looks at me suspiciously, especially when I begin to hop around, to applaud and whistle. Look at him, I think. That's a gorilla. Better than the trash you get at Palisades Park. I see Enid looking at me: She remembers this morning when she caught me rehearsing in the living room. I sit down again.

"That was you," says Enid, "wasn't it?"

"Yes," I say.

"What's happened to your self-respect?" she says.

I just want her to care for me again. I tell her so.

"But you won't take care of me," she says. "I can tell."

She goes into the bedroom, closes the door, gets into bed, begins to cry herself to sleep. I can hear the sea-shell applause, think of bananas, the wonderful smell of new grass.

A few days go by: it's as though they've escaped. I can hear their ball and chain dragging. Enid sleeps, is surprised when she finds me at the table in the living room, reading the want ads, drinking coffee, and staring into the air shaft. I go to the mailbox and find a letter.

Your father is not much better, the letter says. He trembles.

The doctors are giving him new drugs and they make him tremble. He doesn't complain. He never complains about anything. He doesn't eat as much soup as he used to. The doctor says he can call at any time because he is taking more drugs than anyone ever took before. They can not believe it. It hurts more now. He won't let anyone come into the house to fix anything. He says he will do it after he rests a little. This spring, he says. There is a terrible leak in the bathroom, but I don't mind. Sometimes he gets mad again and he won't give me any money. You see? It comes from being sick and why should someone spend it? It's good I have my own job. Will you come to see us again when I ask? I'll call if the time is short.

The next morning, after coffee, I meet Jack in the hall.

"Stargell," he says, "you got four days. I'm telling you our friendship isn't going to do you any good. Strictly speaking, this is business. Do you understand?"

There's the stale, dirty-underclothing smell in the hall. Jack puts a hand that's as big as a baseball glove on the wall. A woman carries a piece of salted fish upstairs. It's stiff and white, about three feet long: the woman carries it by the tail.

"Four days," says Jack the Ripper.

"I know," I say.

"Do you want me to tell you what I have to do?" he says.

"No," I say.

"Good," says Jack. "It makes me ashamed."

We stand together for a moment, and Jack looks at me sourly because he's afraid I'm going to disappoint him. Stargell, my boy, I think, this is what it's like to have a fan. Jack has a drooping eyelid, a face that looks like Frankenstein's valise.

"I'm not a diplomat," says Jack.

I nod.

"I'll see you at Easter," I say. "We'll listen to the music."

"Fuck Easter," says Jack. "Take care of the Barber."

Jack goes into his apartment, leaves me standing in the hall.

The atmosphere is as desolate as a stripped and burned-out car.
All right, I think, O.K.

I sit upstairs, drinking a cup of coffee, looking out the window:
my neighbor doesn't show. I stare at the wall. Enid is having a
bad dream.

All right, I think.

I look through my jacket pockets, my hack wear, the old duck-
hunting coat with a game pouch. There's still a little mud on one
sleeve. In the right-hand pocket I find the wallet that was left in
my cab. I open it up and find the credit cards, identification all
snug as a mortuary. The man's name is Lee MacPhail, an insurance middleweight. There's a picture of him on one of the cards.
He's about thirty-five, oozing dread and vodka. I still remember
him from the cab: he looks like he'd be hell on waiters, worse on
dump girls. I sit in the quiet living room and by the light of the
air shaft write, Lee MacPhail, Lee MacPhail. His handwriting
looks as though it had climbed out from under a rock.

I dress in my gray suit, put on a dark tie, and walk up Sixth
Avenue. It's about ten o'clock. There's a thaw in the air, but you
can feel the monster behind it: the cold hasn't gone for good.
There's still a little snow where the sun doesn't shine.

Stargell, my boy, you're cooking again. If they don't catch you,
you can start all over.

A few blocks south of our neighborhood is a warehouse
district, and I go into a phone booth there and write down its
telephone number. The booth isn't much to look at, but I won't
need it for long.

T he bank smells like air-conditioned carcinogens. I can hear
Gregorian chants, see monks moving bales of money around with
hay hooks. I take a seat before the officer. Chrome-and-leather

chairs next to a coffee table. Magazines on it. Enid would love it
here. The magazines are all sailboats and women in bathing suits,
palm trees, golf courses, dinner by candlelight above the moonlit
bay. What things I'd like to do in a cabana after a few drinks
from a glass made out of a pineapple.

The bank officer looks like a shark dressed up in a cheap suit. I
tell him I want to open a checking account. He gives me the
forms and I fill them out.

"Do you have some identification?" he says.

I show him some of MacPhail's cards. The shark looks them
over carefully, checks the signature, gives the cards back to me.
He loves doing the little things that hurt. With him I could make
millions. We could screw the whole neighborhood: parking lots
everywhere.

My shark gives me some temporary checks. I tell him a large
deposit is coming and I want the account clear before that. What
would he need as a minimum deposit?

"Ten dollars," he says.

I give him the ten dollars, shake his hand, walk into the cool,
clear light.

The advertisement reads "Six rooms, two floors, a garden,
fireplace, $1,000." It's in the East Sixties, a part of town that's as
clean as the Sahara. I call the telephone number, talk for a while
to a real estate agent, a man whose voice has the ten percent
fantods. I tell him it sounds good, make an appointment to see
the apartment in twenty minutes. I take the subway, listen to it
crash from side to side, feel it streaming away from me, lifting
into the noise and agitated darkness.

I meet the real estate agent in front of the building. The apartment has a decadent tone and I can feel the presence of ne'er-do-
well sons, the oh-my-God-what-has-happened atmosphere:
they've just swept up all the legal notices. I like the feeling there,
the rise and fall buzz, the sense of things coming to their expos-
ing, messy conclusion: everything bust. The son's in drag on
roller skates, the daughter's in a New Mexican commune that

would make even Jesus tired. I can feel the breeze, the lingering presence of the antique dealer's black wings. I look at closets, bedrooms, a study, dining room, kitchen, maids' rooms. The floors are made of planks with pegs in them, and before the fireplace there are hundreds of small burns, the evidence of decades of fires. The sewing room has an ironing board that folds into its own closet: those were the days, Stargell, no doubt about it.

"I'll take it," I say.

"What?" says the real estate agent. I expect him to be glad, but he seems to be thinking, Now I can get my root canal work done.

"Would you like a deposit?" I say.

"Yes," he says.

I give him one, written on Lee MacPhail's new account. He takes it and puts it in his pocket. I expect him to snap it shut, since it looks like he's feeding a small alligator in his coat.

"I have to measure for my furniture," I say. "I'll need the keys. Can you have the lease ready for signing day after tomorrow?"

"Of course," he says.

I shake his hand.

"The keys," I say.

"Of course," he says, handing it over. "I've got another at the office."

He leaves me alone in the apartment. Wait until the bargain hunters get a load of this place, I think. They'll think they've stumbled into renter's heaven.

At *The New York Times,* in the classified ad section, I write a little notice for the apartment, describe it accurately (better, I think, than the real estate agent), and list it at half price. That'll fetch them, I think. I'll need a baseball bat to keep them away.

I give the number of the telephone booth. The ad says an appointment can be made to see the apartment by calling between 8 A.M. and 9 A.M.

I go into a locksmith's store on Seventh Avenue. The man behind the counter has an imitation eye. One side of the cramped store is covered with photographs of nude women and the other is dull, filled up with broken tools and police locks. The locksmith is embarrassed by the glass eye because it doesn't match the real one, and I want to say to him, Let them see it, let them look at the glass eye. Nothing can match the beauty of your own.

"I need ten copies," I say, sliding across the counter the key to the apartment.

The machine that grinds the blanks makes a sound like someone rubbing a bone on concrete.

"Here," says the locksmith.

The copies are still hot from the cutter.

"Have a good time," says the locksmith.

In front of my building there is a black Mercedes limousine and the chauffeur has on a business suit and his hair is blond. He looks like his idea of a good time is wind sprints and push-ups. On the seat next to him is a small machine gun, one I recognize. In the think tank Jolting Joe showed me a training film for the rifle: it's the latest thing, only a twenty-two, but it can shoot a hundred rounds a second at velocities so high you could pierce a boiler. Jolting Joe says, The sights are a miracle, Stargell. I look at the chauffeur, the automatic rifle on the seat, and then turn into the building. At the door I see the chauffeur's associate, watching the street, the car. The man at the door looks me over and then, without really saying anything, lets me know it's all right to go in. I climb the stairs, hear an odd rumbling in the building. All the doors are open a little and occasionally a Portuguese will stick his head out and look at me. Nice atmosphere: everyone's scared shitless. I climb another story and I can't even hear a TV, a radio, a fight. I see in one apartment a man and a woman eating bread and cheese and drinking wine. Their dark eyes follow me as I move past the door and walk up to the next landing. Stargell, I think, this doesn't look promising. Next to my door there's another one of the death drones with blond hair. He's carrying one of Jolting Joe's favorites and he doesn't even bother to keep it under a coat: it's right out there for everyone to see. Don't shoot, I think, don't shoot. I've still got a couple of days. He looks at me and then raps on the door. It opens and Enid is standing there, wearing her long silk dress. It's wrinkled and she's a little smashed. She hasn't worn the dress for two years, not since the invitations stopped coming from the Fifth Avenue crowd. She stands there now, in her wrinkled dress, smiling at the guard.

"He can come in," she says.

The guard nods.

"Go in, please," he says.

In the apartment, sitting on the love seat (that has the beartrap bed inside), is a man of about forty-five: his features are those of an Eskimo. His dark hair is perfectly groomed and his suit looks like it came from London. Perfect linen. It's so white and smooth it makes my eyes ache. He stands up and puts out his hand. I shake it.

"This is Sonjie," says Enid, "the King of Lampur."

He smiles with an unassuming grace. Enid weaves a little bit, waves her glass of ouzo just a touch. If you didn't know her you wouldn't think she was drunk enough to start puking.

"Your Majesty," she says, "this is my husband."

"Hello," says Sonjie. "It's nice to meet you."

Sonjie is drinking a quart, but Enid has put on the dog, given him a glass. There are saltines on a plate. The Barber's cheese has been presented, too. Sonjie has a bite of cheese, nibbles a saltine, and immediately finds something to talk about. He mentions the think tank.

"I had them come to Lampur," he says.

He looks a little sad when he says this, as though he were saying, I heard recently that my first love hanged herself. Sonjie has a British accent. He doesn't notice, or has the manners not to notice, that Enid is squinting at him: it means she's seeing double.

"I don't work for them anymore," I say.

"Yes," says Sonjie, "Enid told me. You are starting on your own?"

"No," I say. "I got fired."

I explain about the Crab Nebula Daily Double, the moths. This sobers Enid a lot and she gives me a hard look. Sonjie laughs.

"They told me there was no oil in Lampur," he says.

He has a sip of beer and another saltine.

"It would have helped," he says. "My people are quite poor."

He says this with feeling.

"No coal. No natural gas."

I nod. Sonjie looks angry for a moment, but then he smiles again.

"But they gave us an amazing thing," he says. "We have sick people who can't feed themselves. They have nervous disorders. Your company gave us a new spoon and now they can eat. It has a little swivel."

Enid looks at me with one eye.

Sonjie says he's in New York because he thinks someone is trying to poison him. The think tank did some poison work: I tell him that in most cases it's more than one poison and that it will probably come from more than one source. He looks at me for a moment.

"Yes," he says, "I've been pretty sick."

He sips the beer, eats a cracker, and then gets up.

"I'm sorry," he says to Enid, "that I couldn't give you more than twenty minutes notice, but I've got to be careful. Remember me to your father."

He shakes my hand, embraces Enid, and then is out the door. Enid and I stand next to one another.

Enid turns on the television. Sirens wail. Japanese horror movie. Some men in doctors' frocks look alarmed when a building with stomping feet climbs out of a volcano. The Japanese are speaking dubbed English, out of sync.

"I'm beautiful, you know," says Enid.

I take her hand.

"That man from downstairs came to see you," says Enid. "He's so common. What dirty money."

I swallow, control myself. Vegetable choppers come on the television. Enid nods her head slowly, in private agreement with herself.

"I've got to be up early," I say.

"The movie's not over yet," she says.

We watch the last part of the Japanese horror movie. The thing with stomping feet ends up looking like a coffeepot that was left plugged into the wall too long. There are quiet people in the streets of Tokyo, coming out of the ruins into the sunlight.

"It was nice to have the King in," says Enid.

The movie ends, and the national anthem comes on: I see the bluebirds rising into the sky, wings buffeting, the metal rippling from the pressure, the wind. I can feel the seat pressing into my back, can feel the blood drain, can see the dark, buzzing fringeness of unconsciousness. The music dies. A test pattern comes on.

Enid goes into the bedroom, closes the door. I open the bed, take off my suit, brush it off, hang it up. I climb between the sheets. In the dark I can feel the age of the building, the succession of immigrant families who lived here, their strange lust. So it's come to this, Stargell, I think. Here you are, hanging on to the hinges of a beartrap bed, curled up in a ball, waiting for dawn. At least, I think, squeezing the hinges of the beartrap until the bed trembles like something in a cheap motel, at least they're still using the spoon.

There is ice in the gutter, delicate as a membrane: I stoop over it and think of diatoms, of clear, tubular flakes in the ocean. The buildings emerge from the blue-gray dawn, the Druid light. My phone booth is at the end of a block of warehouses. I can see the loading bays, the bent rails, streaked brick. The buildings used to hold party favors, but they're abandoned now. I walk along, thinking of silver and gold hats, streamers, confetti.

Opposite the phone booth, in the last car on the block, is a man, a poisonous-looking old rip. He's drinking coffee and eating a doughnut. I can smell the coffee on the early air. The man is about sixty-five anyway, maybe a little older, and he's bald. His side hair is white and long and falls to his shoulders. The top of his head looks like it's been polished. New-potato nose. John L. Lewis eyebrows.

Dead-cobra telephone: it's hanging by the cable, off the hook.

"It's been ringing for hours," says the man with the coffee. "I couldn't sleep."

I nod: the city has wartime habits. People are up early, queued for everything. I put the phone back on the hook.

I can see in the back seat of the Chevrolet some newspapers, a blanket, a bowling ball bag, eight or nine artificial legs. It looks like someone took a chain saw to a bunch of manikins and threw the leavings in the back of the car. The man in the front seat licks his fingers. The doughnut looks pretty good.

"Where's the apartment?" he says.

"Uptown," I say.

The phone rings. Someone speaks with a conspiratorial voice, a black market inflection: it's as though the man on the other end of the line hasn't tasted butter for a month, beef for six, hasn't seen a woman in nylon stockings for a year. I make an appointment with him to see the apartment. I have a piece of paper before me with times written in for twelve appointments, each one twenty minutes from the previous. I only have ten keys, but I want what the future-planning boys call a "buffer."

"How come you haven't got an office?" says the man in the Chevrolet.

It's a green Chevrolet, or maybe blue, faded and weathered to the color only time can make. There's a round spot on the hood, the size of a pancake, and the paint is peeling away from it. The man in the car has eyes the color of caramel. He puts on a baseball cap.

"I used to have one," I say. "Twenty-eighth floor."

"You get fired?" he says.

"Yes," I say. I'm thinking, Friendly now. The old jackass might start something.

I make another appointment. Lovely voice: it sounded like a cat in a garbage compacter.

"Those people want the place bad," says the man in the Chevrolet. "Housing is a problem. I told them to call back."

"Thanks," I say.

"Yeah," he says. "I thought you'd show up."

I make some appointments. It's about a quarter after eight. The phone stops ringing for a while. I go out and lean against the

fender of the Chevrolet, look through the windshield at the old
rip. He eats another doughnut.

"I got one leg," says the man in the Chevrolet. "In the army. I
go around, one VA hospital and another, and get fitted. What are
you doing with that apartment?"

"Trying to rent it," I say.

In the front seat there are some empty pints and half pints:
cheap labels, unheard-of brands.

"Yeah," he says, "I know that. Something stinks."

I make another appointment. The sun hits the man in the
Chevrolet. He leans back and takes it, stretches, but he's still
watching me. The light is golden now. A few people walk along,
brisk as fresh celery.

"Well?" says the man in the Chevrolet. "You owe me something. I been answering the phone all fucking night."

I make the last appointment.

"Hell," he says, "I'll drive you up there. You aren't too proud
to ride with a man who's only got one leg, are you? I got to move
the car anyway."

I look at the legs in the back seat. He grinds the engine. The
Chevrolet coughs like an old man who's just woken up and put
his bare feet on cold linoleum: with habit and spirit. The blue
light is gone and it's cold, but I can see the sun. I get into the
Chevrolet. The empty pints and half pints clink on the floor of the
passenger's side as the Chevrolet idles.

"You got a name," says the man, "or are you ashamed of it?"

"Stargell," I say.

"Pleased to meet you," he says. "I ain't ashamed of mine either. Just call me Frenchy."

He puts his hand out and I shake it.

"Tell me about this apartment," he says. "Now that I'm the
wheel man."

He laughs. I can hear the artificial limbs gently bouncing one
against the other in the back seat. Frenchy has got a hand clutch.

"I need money," I say.

"Who doesn't?" says Frenchy. "I need it the way a junkie
needs dope. Bad."

The bottles make a cheerful sound, as though they were just

cooking a little, like softly boiling eggs. Stargell, I think, it would
help to have a car. The Chevrolet hums. I tell Frenchy that I
rented the apartment under a false name and with a bad check
and that I'm going to rent that same apartment to ten people in
the next couple of hours.

"Ha," he says. "Ha."

The traffic is getting heavier: brownish smoke, the color of iron
ore, rises over the streets.

"Where is this place," he says, "this apartment that's in such
demand?"

I give him the address.

"You just give me what you think is fair," he says. "Don't you
worry about it. Then after we take care of the real estate we'll
have a drink. I came to town to see a friend. You'll like him. He's
been fired, too."

We start up Third Avenue. There are beautiful women on the
street, fresh from the shower, definite, crisp. I see smooth legs in
clinging material.

"How old do you think I am?" says Frenchy.

Meanness ages pretty well, I think. A nice spiteful bastard can
pass for fifty when he's sixty-five. I look at Frenchy's long side
hair flopping in the breeze. He keeps his large eyes on the traffic,
makes the Chevrolet whine, slaps it into second gear, passes a
truck. I feel the lift, the gyroscopic tug.

"Old," I say.

"You think that?"

Vain, too, but I like to see it. He's saying, Just try to put me in
the dung heap and I'll bust your jaw.

"I'm seventy years old," he says.

He says it as though he were talking about notches on his gun.

He's dying to talk, since he's been on the road for days, and he
gives me a quick accounting of himself. He's driven from Arizona.

We pull into the block where the apartment is. I point it out.

"Look at that," says Frenchy, "a parking spot. I'll wait in the
car."

I wait in the apartment, look out the window. I can see
Frenchy, sitting in the Chevrolet, watching the people walk down

the street: the pedestrians are so precise I think they have scissors for legs. The tenants come and go. I take their checks, each one for five hundred dollars, tell them where to mail their regular rent. One has a large belly, a monument, and he pushes it against the cool plaster of the living room wall. A film producer, a rock star, a trust fund artist: they take their keys and leave.

I look out the window. Half the keys are gone.

Frenchy says he was born in Russia and that he and his brothers, Niki and Abram, walked across Asia Minor in 1917. His brothers were musicians, and I see their stiff gray clothing, their waxed mustaches. They ate roots, whatever food they could beg, insects when things were at their worst. I'm thinking, Asia Minor, musicians. The brothers made it to Yokohama. Those were the days, said Frenchy. Abram found a garage filled with violins and he fixed them up and sold them door to door and he gave five free lessons with each violin. I see unfamiliar fingers on the necks of the instruments, can hear tortured parrot music. Then the brothers got a job in the Yokohama Hotel, in a band. Frenchy played the accordion. I can see the potted palms, the carpets, the quiet waiters. They were fired.

"Fired," said Frenchy, "because Niki played the trombone, and the manager of the Yokohama Hotel couldn't stand the trombone. He heard us in the room where they served tea. That bastard came running in and said, 'Stop playing that trombone. Get out of my hotel.'"

Trombones, potted plants: I look out the window, see helicopters against the sky, the artificial limbs in the back of the Chevrolet.

Some more tenants arrive. I don't even hear myself anymore. They give me checks. I give them keys.

The brothers came to California. Frenchy married a woman. She had dark hair and long fingers, eyes cut from outer space. She was a concert pianist and she died quite young, of a rare untreatable disease: nothing worked for the pain, not even morphine. Some drugs made it worse. Frenchy showed me one of her recordings. There was a picture on the cover, worn almost to invisibility.

"Then," said Frenchy, "I went to Germany and they shot my leg off, but at least I got disability. Look at all these legs."

Frenchy worked for television, designed costumes, spent hours at UCLA watching surgeons perform eye operations.

"They were so delicate," said Frenchy, "better than musicians."

They made mistakes, though, interrupted what Frenchy saw as a perfect score, became awkward sometimes. Frenchy designed a set of instruments for eye surgeons. The patent lawyers showed him what a fool you can be. I see him standing in a courtroom corridor saying, Fuck you. Fuck every one of you. Frenchy wanted to practice eye surgery in California, but they wouldn't let him.

"I been buying and selling cars recently," he said, "until I came to this Chevrolet."

I wait in the apartment for the last appointment.

"I'm a dentist," says the last, "and my office is right around the corner. This will be convenient."

He smiles.

"Good," I say.

The dentist races around the apartment, makes me feel like I'm standing in a large mouth (chopper-white walls, a red carpet). He wants a nice place to impress his friends: he can spend days yanking teeth and bring everyone up here for a good time. I hope he decorates with ivory, makes the apartment look like a happy boneyard, the elephants' final resting place. Ivory knives, forks, spoons, tables, chairs. I see nude, white-skinned women standing in the apartment. Their skin is as pale as the bones around them. They are eating cherries.

I take the last check, give him his keys, walk outside.

Frenchy's sitting in the Chevrolet.

I climb in.

"How much?" he says, looking at the pile of checks in my hand.

"Five thousand," I say.

Frenchy starts the engine, slaps the Chevrolet into gear.

"Arrange the checks, boy," he says. "We got to go to the bank."

We're in luck: three of the checks are drawn on the same bank. That makes eight stops. It's one o'clock now. At least all of them are in Manhattan. The empty bottles rattle in the front seat. The plastic legs bounce in the back. I can see that Frenchy had been looking at his wife's recordings while he waited. We're moving down the street, the Chevrolet buzzing like shot in a twelve-gauge.

"Still got something left," says Frenchy to the car, "ain't you? Ain't you?"

We stop at the light, move downtown a few blocks on Park, pass the large houses, this hemisphere's version of a pyramid. Everything's been turned into a foundation, a library: all the buildings seem to be saying, Who, me? Why, I'm interested in poetry and South American painters, just don't make me pay any taxes. I can see the old women, the survivors, moving from one empty room to another, just wondering, blinking, caught in the question, Why is the house so big and empty now?

We move across town. Frenchy's laughing, feeling the Chevrolet move. We stop in front of a bank.

"I'll wait here," says Frenchy, "you take your time. This is a good place because no one in the bank can see me."

I endorse a check, go directly to an officer, show MacPhail's identification. I'm thinking about Smiling Mary, the legs and pints bouncing in the Chevrolet, California, the pale, killing light. The manager looks at me, sees that I don't give a shit about the check, O.K.'s it. I go out and get into the car.

"Now that's considerate of them," says Frenchy when he sees the money, "isn't it?"

The car is moving again, down Park into the space defined by the green lights. Frenchy chuckles. He's pleased with the Chevrolet. I stop at other banks, cash more checks. We hit traffic. Frenchy sits at the wheel, as frustrated as a benched ballplayer, looking through the windshield at the trucks, taxis, vans, the rising exhaust, the bullet heads sitting at the wheels of other cars. The horns open up as the drivers substitute noise for speed. Frenchy waits at the wheel, then smiles again when we hit an open spot, as we head for Wall Street. The Chevrolet has a solid quarter-mile feeling to it: it will go that far and then the ignition stops. The car coasts and the gasoline moves from the tank into the carburetor, then through the cylinders and into the air behind the Chevrolet. There is a cloud of gas about a hundred yards long. The ignition catches and it almost breaks all the windows out of the buildings on the street. The cloud of gas flashes and bangs behind us. Frenchy laughs, but while the Chevrolet is slowing down he doesn't look too happy, more like a man with a bomb in a paper sack. The Chevrolet jumps forward. The flash can be seen, even in the daytime. We draw some strange looks, some stricken faces, but the rise, the push, is as welcome as a sincere kiss. Sometimes it works the other way, though. We're moving close to Wall Street on Varick, between squat buildings made of brick and glass, as humane as a radio tube, and the ignition stops. Frenchy strains, grimaces, and then there's a slight bang and a hiss. I can see that the pancake-size spot on the hood of the Chevrolet has begun to expand. It opens like a large sea anemone. The edges peel away. Frenchy stops the car.

"Stargell," he says, "will you put out the carburetor? Here."

He takes a piece of cardboard from the back seat and hands it to me.

"Just cover it with that. There isn't any air filter."

I throw the hood open: it's like standing before a dragon. There are flames and smoke, bits of burning soot from the underside of the hood, and in the middle, at the side of the six-cylinder engine, is a flame which is the color of gold. I snuff it out, thinking, Stargell, be careful. You've got to impress the bankers.

I climb back into the front seat. A station wagon is next to us and two clean kids, about nineteen or so, are looking at Frenchy as though he'd just stepped out of a geriatric side show. They giggle, point, laugh. Frenchy picks up an empty pint and throws a strike, smashes the window on the passenger's side of the station wagon. Stargell, I think, Stargell, throw a bottle. I can hear the glass break. The kids seem angry, but Frenchy's got a look on his face that should be in neon lights: If you get out of your car, if you say one word, I'll kill you. I'm just a mean old man now and I won't take any shit from the likes of you.

They wilt.

"Pencil necks," says Frenchy, "nothing but pencil necks."

The station wagon moves off, turns away from us. Frenchy starts the Chevrolet, and we move off toward the Morgan Guaranty Trust Company.

"Thanks, Stargell," he says, "for putting out the fire."

"Sure," I say. "We don't need any trouble."

Frenchy's still hot.

"If you don't want any trouble," he says, "you're with the wrong man."

His white side hair is flapping in the breeze that comes into the Chevrolet. He's heating up, eying the pints, looking for targets. I can still feel the bottle pop: satisfying, distinct. Stargell, I think, maybe it wouldn't be a bad idea if they caught us now, before we do any damage. Nice cool handcuffs. Maybe they'd put them on so I could keep my hands in front, in my lap.

"What the fuck," says Frenchy, throwing a pint back into the pile. "We still got some banking to do, don't we?"

I nod. We've got four left. It's two o'clock now.

"It's going to be a little tight," I say.

Frenchy looks at the smoking, now enlarged pancake on the hood of the Chevrolet.

"The car's getting hot," he says. "I can't guarantee it."

We move over to Broadway, slide along the city's spinal cord, and I can feel it's neural slickness: oily air, flashy bars, and stoplights. There are people on the street who are as gray as brains. The Chevrolet whines, fills the air with a cloud of gas, explodes. Frenchy laughs. I can see he wouldn't have the car any other way. He's pushing it, though. The carburetor catches fire again and I get out and open the hood, stand before the mouth that's belching flames and smoke, and reach into the center. I do it with a matador's quickness since I don't want to get soot on my clothes.

"How do I look?" I say to Frenchy when I get back in the car.

"Good," he says. "No one would know you've been riding around in a heap like this."

We stop in front of the Morgan Guaranty. Frenchy double-parks.

"The carburetor's getting worse," he says as I get out.

"I'll make it short," I say.

"You take your time," says Frenchy, running a finger through his white side hair. "We can't afford to be nervous. I'll drive around the block if I have to."

The horns start honking. Frenchy's cooled down a little, though, since he doesn't reach for any empty pint. He just smiles and picks up the record album, looks at the photographs of his wife. Her hands are beautiful: small wrists, long, slender fingers, delicate veins, probably the color of ivy, beneath the skin.

The Morgan Guaranty Trust Company is deserted. It's like walking into a large flying saucer that has a carpet on the floor. The silence is a thing of wonder, the kind you usually hear right after a bloody-murder scream. It sounds like someone has collected those moments of emptiness that come after coal miners have grunted with a shovel, after accountants have sighed, after surgeons have given a final, terminal diagnosis, and played them into the bank.

Churchy feeling. Thick carpets. The room itself must be fifty feet across and there is nothing in it aside from two solid tables, on which there are calculators and banking slips. The room is circular, and there are places for twenty tellers, but only one is waiting in the cool silence. He watches me as I come across the carpet, as I stop and endorse the check and walk toward him. Stargell, I think, it feels like they're going to shoot you. I look at the teller, who has that fluorescent complexion, and give him the check.

"Hundreds?" he says.

Hundreds, I think, hundreds.

"Hundreds," I say. "Yes."

I listen to the whisper of air that flows from under each bill as it's dropped on the playing field, the small square between the teller and me. I gather the bills together and walk outside, into the healthy noise and light, the hot dog stands and horn honking. I wait for Frenchy to come around the block.

"Some pencil neck tried to give me trouble," says Frenchy.

I look around, but I don't see anyone, any broken glass.

"Don't worry," he says, "I behaved myself, just like I was with quality."

I get in and we begin to move uptown.

"How much time have we got?" says Frenchy.

"Forty-five minutes," I say.

It sounds like the Chevrolet is going to make carrot juice. Stargell, I think, if you live through this you've got to get a nice six-cylinder car. They're the only kind to have. Frenchy is hanging on to the wheel. My head hits the ceiling as we take a bump with the gas pedal on the floor.

"I think it's the fuel pump," says Frenchy. "I don't get much mileage. They haven't made a good fuel pump since 1939."

The Chevrolet stops, starts, makes a small rear explosion, then dies. Frenchy looks as though he were watching a snake eat a rat: curious but not enthusiastic.

"That's new," says Frenchy.

Smoke begins to leak along the sides of the hood. It's thick and black, more like a liquid than a gas. We coast for a while. Pedestrians have stopped to watch. The car comes to a halt at an intersection. There's a pizza parlor there, a florist, a dry cleaner, and a dentist's office. Tall apartment houses. Doormen are wrapped in their winter coats since snow has been forecast.

"Shit," says Frenchy.

We get out of the car. The smoke is now rising straight into the air: it looks like a stationary, floppy tornado.

"Stay back," says Frenchy. "You've got to keep your clothes clean."

The pedestrians are looking, pointing. Frenchy throws open the hood and it's like an Indian making signals: the air is filled with a large rising umbrella of smoke. The flames are blue and green and occasionally there will be a bright one. Frenchy jumps back.

"I think the whole machine is going to go," he says.

We step back on the curb. Frenchy stares at the burning Chevrolet: he looks like a homesteader who's been wiped out by a cyclone. It's a grease fire and the carburetor is burning and the fuel line seems to be dropping gas into a pool beneath the car.

"Stay the fuck away from there," says Frenchy.

I stand back, thinking, Stargell, look at the flames. The old man is jumping around on his leg, trying to kick the Chevrolet. A doorman brings him a fire extinguisher.

"Get the hell out of here," says Frenchy, turning to me, holding the fire extinguisher like a club. The smoke from the car is billowing toward the windshield like black silk.

"Go to the bank," he says. "I'll take care of the Chevrolet."

"Look," I say, "let it burn. . . ."

"Are you crazy?" he says. "Get a cab. Go to the bank. I'll meet you tomorrow. Down by the phone booth. I'll park there."

Frenchy takes a limping step toward the burning car.

"Get the fuck out of here," he says.

I put out my hand and get into a taxi, give the driver the last addresses. We take off up the avenue as Frenchy lets the Chevrolet have it with the CO_2 extinguisher, a cone of white vapor that cuts away at the burning engine. I can see, as we pull away, that the leaking gas has formed a pool around a tire and the rubber has started to burn, too. Frenchy jumps back. After a few more blocks I hear the muffled, distant thump of the explosion. Smoke rises.

The driver is set for life: he has a shrine, mirrors, flags, a framed photograph of a bird that looks like a grouse, pens, pencils, a clock, notebooks, a cold chest, and a Thermos. He's more a tenant than a driver.

"You working long hours?" I say.

"What do you think?" he says.

"Plenty long," I say.

There's a sign on the dashboard that says "Driver Available for Magic Shows and Stag Parties." On our way to the last bank the driver sings, "You are my sunshine, my only sunshine . . . You make me happy when skies are gray . . . Oh, please don't take my sunshine away . . ." and then tells me an obscene joke about a woman and a Hebrew National salami. I cash the last check and get back into the taxi.

"Where to?" says the driver.

"Do you make out-of-town trips?" I say.

"Sure," he says.

I give him the name of the industrial park, and we go through the streets of Queens.

"This is the place," I say to the magician.

He pulls into the parking lot of the industrial park. The burglar alarm factory seems like an old friend. The receptionist looks at me for a moment and then, without my saying a word, she flips a switch on her desk.

"Mr. Rivers," she says, "the man from the Cadillac is here to see you."

This snaps my light. I look at the great old woman with her Frederick's of Hollywood breasts, and I want to say, How's the troublemaker, hmmm? How's the troublemaker? I'll bet you were something, my darling, just a few years ago. What happened to the time, though?

"Send him in," says Rivers. His voice comes through the Japanese box on the receptionist's desk. I can hear the shark's fins whipping water into a frenzy, the teeth closing together with a sound as distinct as someone slamming a door: bam. Nothing left but the stump.

I walk into the display room. The alarms are mounted on the wall like records that have sold a million copies. There's the smell of ozone and milling oil, clean industry. Paneling on the wall. Red carpet on the floor. It's a kind of hunting-lodge burglar alarm showroom.

"Mr. Stargell," says Rivers.

He comes through a door with a one-way mirror, shakes my hand.

"Mr. Rivers," I say.

We meet like old conspirators, veterans of some deep hype the marks are still trying to figure out. Our expressions seem to say, What things we could have done if times had been different. We could have taken the world, could have fleeced everybody.

"How's the Greek?" says Rivers.

"Ari?" I say.

"Yeah," says Rivers, "the old guy with the funny-looking hair."

"Good," I say.

"Glad to hear that," says Rivers with a certain delight. I have the feeling I've told a fox that everything is all right in the henhouse.

"Has he sold all that stuff?" says Rivers.

"He's waiting for a crime wave," I say.

"God knows," says Rivers, "they help. What can I do for you?"

I tell him. He nods, is polite, tells me to wait.

"It'll take a minute," he says.

He walks out of the room. I wander along the wall, from the puny eight-inch bells right up to the Minuteman. I look at the Silent Sentry, and some other stuff, too. Light switches and capacitance alarms. I look into the receptionist's room and see her talking to two men. She's all fertility, wet and humid as preglacial jungles. The men before her are blind, unable to see a thing. They're in the burglar alarm business and they mean it. Safe house, tax advantage, one pop a week with the wife: soon they'll have initials on a black car. There's no place safer, boys, I think, than the grave.

Rivers gives me a large, flat package.

"Here," I say.

I pay him right there. In cash.

"Thanks," says Rivers.

We shake hands. I hold my package.

"Say hello to the Greek for me," says Rivers.

The magician's name is Brock, first initial L. I write it down on a slip of paper. I take his hack number down, too.

"The city," I say.

It rises out of the reddish haze, the urban version of Nile ground fog. The World Trade Center seems to be holding up the sky: it looks like the pillar of a hydrogen bomb. I sit in the back of the humming taxi and think of a machine that makes people. It's like a blender, except the glass thing on top is a big garbage can. I put in Einstein, Mozart, a lobster, and a shark, then push a button and out comes a creature who says, All right, bub, put the jack in my account, look at the universe, feel the beauty of its shape.

Brock stops at the corner where I left Frenchy. The Chevrolet is gone. The sidewalk is a little blackened and the windows in the dentist's office have been blown out. There is a pile of half-burned tire in the street. Brock waits when I get out of the taxi. There's some melted stuff that looks like it came from an artificial limb.

"I don't know a thing," says a doorman. "Car blew up. Everyone's gone."

"What happened to the driver?" I say.

"I don't know," says the doorman. "It was a Chevy that blew up."

You can still smell a little smoke, the burned rubber. The street has the spent, post-riot atmosphere.

"Was anyone hurt?" I say.

"Look," says the doorman, "I didn't see anything but a bunch of smoke. There was a bald old man with a limp. He went up the street."

He points toward Fifth Avenue.

"He looked plenty mad," says the doorman.

I step over the melted plastic in the gutter, get into the cab. Brock sings and tells jokes, drops me at the post office behind the new Garden.

The post office has an institutional glory: it feels as though someone has just been hanged. I put Lee MacPhail's wallet into an envelope and a note in with it. The note says, This wallet was turned in by Mr. L Brock, whose cab number is EN654. He didn't want to ask for a reward but since I'm not asking for myself I think you should send one. He knows a great joke about a woman and a Hebrew National salami. A friend.

I shove it all together, put the right number of stamps on it, and drop it in the slot.

The air is cool and heavy with snow. I walk on the hard, gray sidewalk. Well, Stargell, I think, it's too bad you're going to miss moving day. I think of the ten tenants, each with a moving van filled with furniture, each with a set of keys. They scream and yell, throw wing chairs into the street, knock each other on the head. There must be some mistake, one will say as he sees his vase thrown into the street, and then it will become clear: there wasn't any mistake at all.

In a drugstore I buy a toothbrush, a razor, a comb, and I carry them in an Oklahoma shaving kit: a brown bag. The air is getting cooler. It reminds me of those winter nights when it was so cold I could feel roots vibrate. I lay next to Enid, curled next to her back, feeling the warmth trapped under the blanket.

The Hotel Jax is on the West Side and the lobby has a dirty-sock odor. It's what you'd call an elevator hotel: no one lives here permanently, since they're either on their way up or on their way down. The man at the desk tells me the tenants aren't too friendly now. The day before yesterday a man was murdered in the hotel. Survival's the ticket, I think. Mum's the word. The deskman has no shame. He tells me the guy got popped right in the bathtub. I see an open mouth, under water, screaming bubbles.

My room has a double bed. The sheets on it have been stenciled with the name of a hospital that went out of business in Wisconsin. There's some gum on the baseboard, telephone numbers written on the wall, tips on the horses, women's names, the usual desperation. I can feel the people who have passed through here, can almost hear them rustle: they know where it hurts, all right. I hang up my clothes, take a shower, and get into bed. Stargell, I think, there's no way around it. The place is a fleabag.

Just before I fall asleep, as the bed is embracing me, pulling me down into my own warm and personal slime, I realize how they can catch me. The tenants will go to the police. The police will go to the agent. The agent will give them MacPhail's address. The police will go to MacPhail, who will give them the note I sent from the magician, from Brock. They will give him a description from the tenants and Brock will tell them he took me to the burglar alarm factory. Rivers has my name and address. Or Enid's address, since Ari gave it to the burglar alarm factory as his "North American Office."

All right, I think. All right. After a couple of days I'll stay away from the apartment.

I wake to a face so close to mine I can feel breath on my cheeks. It feels like I'm standing right at the foot of a drive-in movie screen. The face pulls back and I can see it's the maid.

"Just checking," she says.

I slept a little late, but I'm not dead.

"I'm all right," I say.

She goes out the door.

Downstairs the lobby has that fire-sale odor: it's as though they torture rats when I'm not around. Two men are sitting in perfect communion, since neither has a thing to say. I take the key with me, tell the deskman I'll be staying another night. I'm afraid someone will steal my package from the burglar alarm factory, so I take it along, too.

I stand at the end of the block, but I don't see the Chevrolet. I look in every car, but I don't see Frenchy either. There's an early-morning crap game going on under one of the loading bays, and the players are drinking wine out of paper sacks. Sneaky petes. The dice are shot into a clearing in old snow. The wine is the color of red roses. I check all the cars again, stand in the phone booth for a while, check the other streets, but I can't find Frenchy. I wait, feel the emptiness of the warehouses, the absence of party favors, can see, when I stare at the early sky, which looks like white silver, surgeon's hands, moving quickly, holding Frenchy's instruments. A cornea, held gently in an odd pair of tweezers, trembles like a bit of clear jello.

"How are you doing, Sal?" I say.

I stand before his counter, at the edge which has been notched with cigarette burns. On my right there are small racks for potato chips, a shelf for balloon bread (with its strangely festive pack-ages), boxes of candy bars, a few bottles of Pepto-Bismol. There's some beer in a case with a sliding door. The Barber's face looks like an old leather suitcase: creased, but with character. The bumps and scars show where it's been. Smiling Mary has taken her stand by the freezer case that's filled with M-16s. Her arms cradle her breasts and she leans against the porcelain door. Her bruise is almost healed, but she wears clothes that bring out the last yellowish-green outline of a hand.

"I can't complain," says the Barber.

"You were always modest," I say.

"Yeah," says the Barber, "ain't I?"

Smiling Mary has inquisitor's eyes: I can hear the insane laughter of the heretics when she asks with her eyes, when she searches for the facts of the matter. I count out fourteen hundred dollars. The Barber pushes it to his right, toward Smiling Mary. She takes it and puts it under the counter. The Barber lifts an eyebrow. It's as close as he ever gets to giving a warm embrace.

"The fifteen," says the Barber.

"Which fifteen?" I say.

"The fifteen you borrowed before the thousand," says the Barber. His chin is reaching toward his nose. One day the whole thing will roll up like a sleeping bag. Smiling Mary nods.

"That fifteen," I say.

I put the bills on the counter. The Barber pours out another shot for himself and one for me, too. The guest glass, shared by everyone in the neighborhood, is pushed toward me. I drink my portion and smile, even though my eyes are watering.

"Good," I say.

"Yeah," says the Barber. "With this stuff you can tell what you're drinking." The raw booze makes me feel like someone is sanding my brain. Through the windows I can see men and women coasting by, gently stepping over the burned trash in the gutter, the slivers of broken glass.

I ask for a quart of beer. Smiling Mary slides it across the counter, but when I reach for a bill to pay for it, the Barber stops me, tells me it's a present. I thank him.

"Goodbye," I say.

Smiling Mary nods. The Barber has another shot, smashes a bag of chips.

"Not goodbye, pal," says the Barber. "Hasta la vista."

I carry the burglar alarm company's box, the bag from the Barber's. On the corner I can feel the earth tremble, the vibration of the subway. Shiny metal wheels, blue and white sparks, juice that runs underground. I stand beneath the blue sky, feel the vibrant hum, the cold funny bone of death, the slip, the awesome bump. Ah, I think, the speed of light: everything goes dark. The earth shrinks beneath me, contracts, tightens, and I can see the stars, the universe that looks like a mine, light moving on split coal. What distances, I think. I feel the cold hum of the subway.

You've got to pull yourself together, Stargell. You almost popped your window, right on the street.

It's Friday morning. The Portuguese have already left, are hard at work. The hall is filled with the smell of coffee and buttered toast. I climb the stairs and knock on the green door. I still have a key, but I've become a little formal in twenty-four hours.

"Yes?" says Enid, from inside the apartment.

I tap again.

"Oh," she says. "It's you."

She's dressed in her gray robe. Her hair is tangled.

"Is that for me?" she says.

Her small hands take the bag. I follow her into the living room. There are small packages from a Chinese restaurant, empty bottles, fashion magazines spread on the floor.

"I just woke up," she says.

I take her arm, give it a gentle caress.

"Don't touch me," she says. "Your hands are dirty."

I go to the kitchen sink and scrub my hands with the two kinds of soap that are there, dry off with paper towels. We sit opposite one another at the table by the window. The curtains have been drawn.

"I saw that slut across the way," she says.

I give her fifteen hundred dollars.

"Thank you," she says. "It's probably dirty money. But what else can you do?"

I want to tell her about a new invention, a black plastic coat that is tailored to your house. In the wintertime it absorbs heat and makes everything toasty. Everyone runs around naked. In the summertime, you take it off. The house is painted white and keeps the place cool.

Enid smiles, but she has an expression that makes her look like she's giving blood. She knows I'm thinking some crazy stuff and she doesn't want to hear it.

"I went to see my doctor," she says.

That's good, I think. Enid stands before me, makes gestures with her small hands.

"Because of that disease you let my father get," she says.

I can see Ari for a moment, his strange-looking hair.

"I went to my doctor because I thought I might have the disease. I do not have it. My doctor is from Europe and he has practiced there, too. He is the most intelligent man I know."

Here it comes, I think, straight from the source: the gynecologist will tell all. Enid has another pop of beer.

"He says American women are perfectly formed. Their genitals, he means."

Listen to that, Stargell, just listen.

"But he says they are like an American apple. European women are more like apples in Europe. An American apple has no taste. It's perfectly formed, but it doesn't have anything. European apples are smaller and they have more . . ." Enid stops, searches, since she wants to be precise. I wonder what words she's dismissing. Zest? Flavor? Aroma? Bouquet? ". . . tang," she says.

Enid has a so-there expression. I look at her dark hair, her eyes that are as black and shiny as licorice, the lines from sleep.

"So," says Enid, "I'm really better than all these women."

She smiles. I'm about to cry for her.

"Are you going to sleep with younger women?" she says.

Enid's turned into shrink fodder, I think. They'll give her blue pills. What happened to the time, though, the first innocent touches, the crazy itch?

I go into the bedroom and pack a small bag: a few pairs of pants, shirts, socks. I put on a clean white shirt, wear my one gray suit. I pack Barbeau's diary, too. Enid stands at the doorway. She gives me a letter that arrived yesterday.

"I'll give away your other things," she says.

"Good," I say.

I walk into the living room: Enid keeps her distance. I can smell the rotting Chinese food, can see the beautiful women in the magazines around Enid's chair, a pile of murder mysteries she reads.

I take my package from the burglar alarm factory, the small bag, and stand next to the door, in the hall. Enid puts her cheek up. I give her a peck. She pulls back, whispers, "Go away now, my dear one," and then I stand in the hall, before the closed door. The music comes on: I know that Enid stands before the record player, that she begins to undulate, as awkward as a cannibal on a bicycle. She strains after the mysterious beat, the elusive tempo, waves her arms over her head: she can see herself, though, the image of grace and youth, in the center of a dance floor. She is surrounded by men and women who are so intimidated they wouldn't dare speak to her. The tin door vibrates with the music, the time-keeping. I take my package and the small leather bag and descend. The music stops abruptly: I can hear the amplified screech as Enid throws the record player against the wall.

I'll call her regularly. At least I'll be able to keep track of news from California, of my father.

I walk up Sixth Avenue for a while. It's Friday night and the couples on the street have a ten-cent smile. They're going to have a good time whether they want to or not. I walk up Eighth Avenue, look into a Cuban bakery, see men and women drinking coffee as strong as Methedrine. The odor is musky, sharp. I sit at a green counter and have a Cuban sandwich with hot sauce. No one notices me. The sandwich is good: it's on French bread and the crust is hard but the inside is soft, filled with hot pork and ham, a little goat. I drink the coffee and continue walking. At Forty-fifth Street there are hookers cooling their heels, peep shows, men going quietly into a movie theater that is playing *Teenage Lust*. On the East Side there are tall buildings, empty now, but I can feel the eddy left by the day's paper work, can hear the soft, dreadful sound of the fluorescent lights.

In the Hotel Jax I take a shower, shave, clean up my gray suit, then find myself staring at the sheets, the stenciled name of a hospital in Wisconsin. The room is cold: I can see the wispy record of my breathing. Stargell, I think, you're just doing a little time in the penalty box. I see fists pounding the plastic barricade, can hear the roar of the crowd.

I have met many interesting people, my mother's letter says, in the clinic where your father goes for the drugs. We don't make friends. You can understand why. There was a woman whose husband always looked so well and I thought he was getting better. He wore wonderful clothes. He worked for the studios and he went to London and Paris to have his suits made. He really looked wonderful. Your father's clothes don't fit as well as they should. There's something about the disease, more than just loss of weight. So I was always happy to see the man in his wonderful clothes, looking so dapper. He died. They had given him some drugs and there was an extra supply (the drugs are very expensive) so his wife brought them back since she thought someone else in the clinic might be able to use them. I told her I was sorry about her husband.

He always looked so well, I said. I never thought he was losing weight. His clothes were wonderful.

Yes, said his wife, they were.

I'm sorry, I said.

Thank you, said his wife. I'll tell you about the clothes. Every three months he went to his tailors and had another wardrobe made, a size smaller than the last, but still cut from the cloth that was used originally. I'm trying to sell them now. Do you know of anyone who would want to buy the clothes?

No, I said.

The dapper man even fooled us, the people in the waiting room.

Your father is the same. He asks for you. Will you come when I ask? Love, Mother.

I pick up the phone, speak for a moment to the deskman, then hear the distant ringing.

"Hello," says Barbeau.

"Hello," I say.

"Yes?" she says.

"My name is Stargell," I say.

"Yes?" she says.

"We met some time ago," I say.

"Oh," she says. "Yes."

Her voice cools like warm molasses dropped into snow: it becomes hard, brittle.

"I remember," she says.

Her voice has something else in it, too, more than just hardness. It's about to break.

I can see myself clearly, sitting on the bed in a fleabag, my words turning into mist before me: Stargell, I think, what a dirty degenerate you are.

"I wanted to say . . ."

"Why don't you come up for a drink?" she says. There's still that taut quality in her voice. It's as though she were talking through bars, trying to be nice to the jailer who can (if he wants) give her a taste of the cattle prod.

"Yes," I say. "Do you like champagne, oysters?"

She laughs. In a moment that brittle quality is withdrawn: the sound of her quiet laughter relaxes me, makes me feel my crackpot hope. She gives me her address. Uptown, Park Avenue.

"In a half hour," she says.

We hang up. I sit on the sheets from the bankrupt hospital in

Wisconsin, and think, Stargell, it's just like the old days. I haven't been up there since I had prospects, since I was going to be somebody.

"Desk," says the man downstairs when he picks up the phone.

I ask for the time, and think, Stargell, if you don't waste a moment, you can get the oysters. My small bag of clothes doesn't matter, but the box from the burglar alarm factory does: I take it along.

The fish market is still open. I stand before the long, narrow store with the stainless-steel bins, the crawling lobsters that flinch on the ice, still reaching, still wondering, What's out there? People walk along the sidewalk. It's cold and they look like small locomotives, filling the air with puffs of vapor. I hear a tympanic thump, shattering glass, a silence large enough for a saint to walk through. At the corner there are two taxicabs, locked in an automotive embrace. Then the drivers emerge, jump out of sprung doors. They stand before one another, shouting, screeching, pounding a crumpled fender. The passengers get out and talk to one another, too: the lines are clearly drawn. The horns begin to blow.

I buy two dozen oysters. The man behind the counter opens them, puts them on ice, makes a tidy package. I watch the lobsters move. Across the street I buy two bottles of cold dry champagne.

In the street the drivers are pointing. It looks like they are both trying to eat an invisible pizza without using their hands. Everyone is scoring points: lineage defamed, eyesight maligned, intelligence disposed of. One of the drivers weighs three hundred pounds anyway, and the other is almost as large: their bellies are pushed together. The taxis look a little crestfallen, headlights broken, hoods popped open, engines steaming. Oil and water run in the gutter. The heaviest driver smacks the other, right on the kisser. The crowd on the sidewalk bursts into applause. The drivers roll around for a while and then a cop shows up. Everyone goes into Dunkin Donuts for refreshments.

My suit needs a little pressing, but I could be a young banker just off the red-eye flight from Kuwait, Lebanon, Egypt. The money markets are booming, boys, dump your rupees. The doorman checks upstairs, then directs me to the elevator: this is a relief. For a moment I see myself on the A train, eating the oysters, drinking champagne, crying into both. The elevator has a hushed, cushioned ride. The operator looks like a big blue jay with his wings folded: I know him well. He doesn't have any taste, so he's nasty to everyone. What times he must have, though, going up and down, listening to the tail ends of conversations.

Barbeau is as I remember her: about thirty, with dark hair the color of deer in November, green eyes. Trim, small figure. Unsettled hands. They touch mine as she takes the oysters and the champagne. I hold on to the burglar alarm box. She's wearing a white dress with small blue flowers on it. Her dark hair is parted on one side.

I put the box down in the foyer, on a table where there are cut flowers.

"Thank you for coming," she says, in that same taut voice.

No one's going to hurt you, I think.

"There's a fire in here," she says.

We walk into the living room. There are two small sofas there, opposite one another and before a fire. The logs are birch and you can see their paper bark curled in flames. There are bookshelves on the walls, curtains by a window through which you can see the city, punch-card lights against the sky, the avenues where cars move in luminescent bunches.

"Sit down by the fire," she says. "I'll be back."

There's some gaudy crap on the mantel. I watch the fire, settle into a chair, hear the distant clink Barbeau makes in the kitchen. The books look reasonable: middle- to highbrow. Stargell, you've found yourself a culture buff. The walls are light gray, and the sofa is covered with a blue material that has the same tone. The fire is warm and cheerful. There's the whiff of dry ice, though,

Barbeau's dread: the odor, the atmosphere is like that in the
coldbox of a Good Humor truck. She walks quietly in from the
kitchen, carrying a tray on which there are oysters. She puts it
down on the table and goes back to the kitchen. I watch the fire
and then look at an oyster: it is large, and you can see the delicate
gray pool of its flesh. Barbeau brings the champagne and two
glasses. The pop frightens her. The oysters are smooth, with stark
ocean in them. The champagne is as cool and dry as the Arctic in
November. The shells sound as though we were stacking dishes
when we put them down.

The oysters do it for a moment: Barbeau's tautness disappears.
She holds one in her mouth, closes her eyes, savors it. Swallows.
She pushes her lips against the glass, drinks, feels the tingling in
her nose.

"Goddamn it," she says.

She looks up and lets me see her tears.

I know what she wants. She wants to take a baseball bat and
break some windows. We'll make a sound like brittle thunder as
we move down the avenue. Then we'll take a ride.

I sip the champagne.

"I can't stop it," she says.

Her lips are trembling with malaria tempo. She's sobbing.

"It just comes on me," she says. She makes a small sound with
her fingers. "Like that."

I take her hand. She gives me a squeeze, looks away. Maybe it
happens at the dentist, I think. What a scene: a pale, incompetent
man with a metal pick in his hand, saying, Would you like some
gas?

"I'm going to meet my husband," she says. "For the holiday.
In the country."

"What holiday?" I say.

"Easter," she says.

Barbeau starts talking, drinking the champagne, staring into
the fire. She tells me she's leaving her husband (who isn't?). He's
tall and rich and impotent. He has a fish tank filled with sharks,
small ones, miniatures, but they look just like the real thing.

We go into the library, where the tank is. There are kitchen bowls everywhere, too, on the shelves, desk, a table, on the floor, and each one has a fish in it. There is a shark in a martini pitcher.

"They're having some kind of epidemic," says Barbeau.

She smiles, sips her champagne. I eat an oyster and stare at the sharks.

"He's got them isolated so they won't give each other the disease."

Yes, yes, I think. I watch a shark swimming back and forth. Barbeau tells me her husband sits in the room with his calculator, figuring each night his exact worth, depending upon money markets, stocks, estimated values of furniture, antiques, paintings. Barbeau says she stays in their bedroom and she knows when another shark has died because she can hear the toilet flush. I think of the sharks swirling around the bowl, after they sat in a Pyrex roasting pan in the library, where they felt the first symptom, a slight nausea, then the real thing. They turn belly up and die. I see the husband in the dim medicinal light, thinking, What do you think that Queen Anne chair is worth, hmm? He has a calculator in his fist: the markets plunging, sharks dying, wife groaning in the dark. Maybe it would help, I think, if husband made a killing.

We sip champagne, look at the fish.

"He thinks everyone should have a will," says Barbeau. "He likes to say, 'Do you have your will made?' "

She shows me a book.

"Have you seen this?" she says.

I carry it into the living room. We sit before the fire again. The book is filled with photographs of Orientals doing amazing things. They are naked. Her finger moves across a photograph, touches me. I drop the book. We drink champagne. Her lips are full and when she pushes them against the glass you can see the lines in them, the gentle creases in the swollen, delicate flesh. The Orientals are fondling each other. They look a little grim, and that takes some of the snap out of it. Barbeau's eyes pass over the book, then move toward the window, the cars on the avenue, clumped together, damned by computer.

"You're nervous," she says.

I nod, thinking, Yes, yes. I'm not a pimp or a gigolo, not jaded
or bored: just look how awkward we are, how frightened.

We eat the last of the oysters, hold them in our mouths, swallow. The fire takes the chill out of the room. The Orientals are on
the floor. Barbeau turns the page. We go into the bedroom. Barbeau brings the champagne, takes off her clothes. I'm naked, too.
We sit opposite one another. We watch the city. I see the lights in
her eyes, the constricted reflection of distant buildings. The room
has a soothing quality, a reassurance as soft as an aging nanny.
Barbeau is lovely, perfectly cast by the light. She's a little drunk.
On the nightstand there are two photographs of her. One with the
Pope, the other with a big-time swami, one of the hard-cash religion boys. I sit on the edge of the bed, caress her, watch her enjoy
herself. She sighs, as though relieved. Thank God, she seems to be
saying, I'm going to get fucked. She puts the glass of champagne
to the light, then holds it between my legs, pushes the head of my
cock into the glass, the liquid. It's cold: I can feel the vibrant,
almost orgasmic tingling, the arctic fringes, the hard buzzing.
Barbeau lifts the champagne to the window, holds the glass to the
light: I can see the bright bubbles. She is silhouetted against the
window as she drinks the champagne in one draft.

We are polite to one another, ask questions, say, Does it feel
good, does it? Ah, I think, coming. Thank God; thank God.

We lie curled together and finish the champagne.

"We could meet again," she says, "perhaps in a couple of
weeks."

I sit in bed, holding an empty champagne glass while Barbeau
takes a shower. There is a dry, flowery scent on the sheets. Barbeau tells me she has douched.

"Call in the morning," she says, "after ten."

Stargell, I think, that's the Harvard Law. We'll meet when
hubby's in the office, making tax-dodge history.

I dress, collect my package. Barbeau is a little better: the dry-
ice atmosphere has receded. I take my package and think, Yes,
we'll make appointments, meet in respectable hotels with room
service and silence. I'll make a scene in the lobby, will scream,
Stop trying to fuck your husband! I want you all to myself. The

blue jays will resolve around us, flapping their wings, worrying a
gold button.

"I've got to go," she says. She pushes me into the hall.

I stand on the black-and-white tile before the elevator. I carry
my box from the burglar alarm factory, feel the lingering softness,
the wet caress of Barbeau. The mahogany paneling is polished,
dark: I can feel the pressure of the trees, the years it took to make
the wood beautiful.

I go to my room in the Hotel Jax. I've got a pint and I have a
party for myself, a convention of one: I buy myself a lot of drinks.
Barbeau says, I'm not going to leave my husband. That's right, I
think, the sharks aren't so bad. What the hell, I think, there's
always Masters and Johnson. I stare at the sheets from the bankrupt hospital in Wisconsin, get cozy in bed, remember the oysters,
feel the cold air in the room. I can hear the tenants upstairs,
moving the furniture around, arguing, making the bedsprings
work. I toast each one, have the sense of everyone scheming,
planning, organizing their attacks on the financial armies that
confront them. I look for the right mood, one in which the inventions appear, but the pint doesn't do it. I go out for another, and
when I come back I sit in the lobby, on a chair that looks like it's
made out of imitation human skin. Sitting next to me, in a similar
chair, is a man who is reading *El Diario*.

He is about twenty-eight or so, dark. He tells me he is from
Peru, that he and his wife traveled from Lima on a Vespa, that his
name is Vicente. They were sponsored by an oil company.

"I've got a pint," I say. "Would you like a drink?"

He thanks me, calls his wife, and they come to my room. His
wife is called Naomi and she has long, dark hair, a heavy body:
it's difficult to imagine them on a Vespa. They came via Canada
and had a child on the way. The child was born in El Paso and
they mailed it back to their family. It's been twenty-two months
since they left Lima. They came to New York to visit an American friend, a man whom they met when he was in the Peace

Corps in Peru. They didn't think he would be living in the Jax. He probably didn't either, I think, but I don't say anything.

"He was surprised to see us," says Naomi, "embarrassed."

"He has a boyfriend," says Vicente. "They live here. The boyfriend moved out so we could stay."

A Peace Corps diehard, I think, right here in the Jax. Vicente tells me that the oil company cut them off. The original deal was that they would get fifty dollars at every regional Esso station, and Vicente moved the Vespa from pay hole to pay hole; like a metal marble in a pinball machine. The score hit about seven thousand dollars when they got to New York and found that the computer had caught up with them. The deal was off.

"We had about a thousand dollars left," says Vicente.

"A little less," says his wife.

"Yes," he says, "a little less."

Vicente and his wife decided to go back to Lima, but they only made it as far as Pittsburgh, where, through the grace of God, they found a pornographic-film dealer who took nine hundred of their dollars for three films. Vicente thought they'd come back to New York, show the films in a rented loft, clean up, and fly home.

"We embarrassed our friend again," says Vicente. "The boyfriend had to go. I could see he was getting mad. He is black, and he thought that might be the reason. We said it was all right, but Charles insisted. Our friend's name is Charles."

"We come from a Catholic country," says Naomi. "We understand these things."

"Do you know of a loft?" says Vicente.

"No," I say.

We all have another drink.

Vicente tells me it's a little awkward. They want to go back to Peru, but they've got to show the films. Charles, Vicente tells me, has a wife, too, and she is staying with them. She left Charles to work on an Indian reservation in Arizona. Last week, an Indian raped her. She came to New York and found two Peruvians in a fleabag hotel with a black queen stopping by every half hour or so.

Charles used to be a high school teacher, but he's on welfare now.

"Let's see the films," I say.

"Would you like to?" says Vicente.

"Sure," I say.

There's still about a half pint left.

"I bought a cheap projector," says Vicente, "from around the corner."

We go upstairs. I am introduced to Charles, and his wife, Marge. She is a quiet woman with dirty-blond hair and full lips. She shakes my hand. Albert, the black queen, comes in. The movies are as traditional as hymns in a public school. Everyone is wearing masks and phony noses. Albert uses the word "twat." We all sit before the flickering images. Marge is thinking about the Indians, what happened to her. She tells me that she worked in the library and that the Indian asked for a sex manual and that she refused him because he was drunk. I look at her, watch her face in the flickering light, can see the hard set of her jaw.

"Mujeres!" shouts Vicente.

The last movie comes on. Then we go to a restaurant and eat a Chinese meal. All you can hear is the chopsticks moving. The pea pods are green and you can see the peas inside them. Marge is staring over my head, has visions of the desert, of some dry purity that eludes her in Hell's Kitchen. She says she is going back to the reservation tomorrow. Albert looks relieved.

At the Jax, Vicente comes into my room.

"Well," he says, "what do you think?"

It feels like the think tank again: I see "Catholicism" lit up in neon lights. Vicente, Naomi, and I agree that the market is South America. The films will make a fortune in Lima.

"Make a run for it," I say.

Vicente and I go downstairs and look at the Vespa. It's yellow and it's been painted about twenty times. It also looks like a gang of vandals has attacked it with ball-peen hammers. There are names written on it by hand with nail polish, Guatemala, Nicaragua, Peru, and there is a large sign, also made by hand, that says "Esso," but most of it has been scratched off. Vicente and I go back up to my room and figure mileage, the most minimal food, distances.

"Before you get to the border," I say, "tape the cans of film underneath the Vespa."

"Yes," he says.

We do the final tally: Vicente is eighty-four dollars short.

"Here," I say, "take it."

I give him a hundred. Nice and crisp from the bank.

"Where can I send it," he says, "when I am finished?"

"Here."

We sit in my room and I notice that one wall has a two-tone paint job. Someone covered up all the old telephone numbers and tips on the horses with some paint that didn't quite match the rest. Half the wall is shiny, half is flat, and each is covered with telephone numbers and names again.

"Thank you," says Vicente.

He shows his quiet dignity in his eyes, shakes my hand, and goes out the door. I know he'll be all right. I see him on the road, the Vespa straining, rings and pistons gone, compression down to what might be called emphysemic levels, but still running, carrying Vicente and his wife, the pornographic films, through the jungles of Central America. I can see the bright macaws, the slick green foliage, the perfect curve of a banana leaf, the graves at the side of the road. I finish the pint, get into bed.

Someone knocks on the door.

"Yes?" I say, opening it just a little.

Marge stands in the hall.

"Can I come in?" she says.

I nod. I'm wearing a pair of pants, gray slacks from my suit.

"I couldn't stand it anymore," she says. "I just need a place to sleep."

Who doesn't? I think.

It's late now, about two. There's still a little left in the pint. We split it.

"One night I'm going to wake up with the French fits," I say.

She smiles. In her case it would just be better if she cried. We talk for a little. I ask her if she wants to go to the westerns and watch the cavalry shoot the Indians, but she says, No. I just want to sleep. We get into bed, and we both keep our clothes on. She takes my hand and holds it, falls asleep that way, with it just under her chin. Early in the morning, about four, I hear the sound of the Vespa as Vicente turns it over. Marge wakes, grabs me, and says, Oh, my God, oh, my God, what did I do? She holds my hand and shakes her head and says, I'm sorry, I'm sorry. My God. I'm sorry.

I sit there, holding her shoulders.

"I'm sorry," she says, over and over.

Finally she falls asleep again and then I do, too. She still holds on to my hand. She snuggles against me once for warmth. In the morning I wake to the maid's face, again close to mine, again checking to see if I'm alive.

"Your door was open," she says.

I realize that Marge has gone.

"I'm O.K.," I say.

I shower and dress in my gray suit. I have a clean shirt. I check out of the hotel, leave my bag at the desk, take my package from the burglar alarm factory, and go down to the Cuban bakery, where I drink a cup of coffee. There is the smell of freshly ground beans, and the place has a Saturday-morning cheerfulness, young women eating a sweet before going to shop, old men in happy reverie, one looking at another, thinking, I'll have a roll and a cup of coffee and then I'll have a shave and as the blade goes scrape, scrape, scrape, as I feel its tug on my cheek, I'll remember my darling, her smooth ass in silk underwear, her dirty talk and lovely eyes, yes, I'll do that in the barbershop: that's where I'll get my ticket ready for the gates of hell.

I stand outside, on the block where there are empty warehouses, where the party favors used to be. All the cars are jammed together, each backed right against another. I don't see a Chevrolet, and I look in all the cars again. There's no crap game today. I sit on the abandoned loading bay and drink a cup of coffee out of a paper cup. Frenchy isn't in any of the cars. I drink the coffee and watch the deserted street, feel the siesta quality in the cold air. Everyone is either asleep or gone. At the end of the block there is the phone booth, filled with pints of wine in brown paper sacks. The door has been ripped off. The phone is ringing.

Stargell, I think, maybe it's a satisfied renter. Maybe they want to tell me something. There's always the possibility it's the police, my boy, and don't you forget it. And then it could just be a wrong number.

The ringing continues. I go into the phone booth, lift the receiver for a moment and then put it back into its rack. The phone begins to ring again.

It's not a wrong number, I think.

The phone booth smells like a dump, like small-time crime. One of the glass panes has been broken out. Up the street I see a man with a shopping basket, the phone company's scum patrol: he moves from booth to booth, giving each one a little cleaning.

"Hello," I say.

"Where the fuck have you been?" says Frenchy. "I've been letting the phone ring for hours."

"Where are you?" I say.

"I am in the worst place in the world," says Frenchy. "I am in a junkyard in New Jersey."

Frenchy tells me he can see a bulldozer moving a gray wave of trash.

"We were supposed to meet yesterday," I say.

"I thought you had the brains to come back," says Frenchy. "You know, the next day."

I can hear cars going by in the static of the phone.

"How did you get this number?" I say.

"Stargell," he says, "you must be slipping. Out of Thursday's paper. It takes two days to get it to New Jersey."

Frenchy laughs.

"I lost everything," he says. "I'm coming to town. I was looking for a Chevrolet, but they haven't got any. They haven't got a goddamned thing out here. Somebody tried to sell me a fifty-seven Plymouth. That's the kind of assholes there are out here."

We agree to meet on Houston Street at the Bowery. Frenchy's going to take the bus and then we'll meet an old friend of his. Frenchy hangs up. I walk in the morning air and think of

Frenchy, of the exploding Chevrolet, the melting legs, the glass blowing out of the dentist's office. I spend some time in Little Italy, going from butcher shop to butcher shop, smelling the bread in the bakeries, looking at large bunches of spinach, hothouse lettuce. I can smell the dirt on the lettuce. There are some oranges, but it's still too early for any good fruit.

What hurts, says Frenchy, just before hanging up, is that I lost my wife's records. They melted, too, just like the legs.

A taxicab stops at the corner and Frenchy gets out. He's carrying a pint that's almost empty, and I don't think it's his first. I look at his white, long side hair, his bulging eyes, the nose that looks like a new potato.

"That was a good Chevrolet," he says.

"Yeah," I say.

"It had its problems," says Frenchy, "but it was a manageable car."

We walk south. Frenchy tells me he watched it burn, that he saw the red and orange and black flames, that he felt the explosion on his lips. He shakes his head in disbelief. He tells me the story twice, then finishes the pint and throws it in the street.

"Then I cleared out," he says. "I walked right up to Fifth Avenue, limping like a duck with one leg. No one said a word."

Frenchy shakes his head again. I'm thinking, At least it blew up. At least there were some smoke and flames. Sirens.

"I was going to help a friend move," says Frenchy, "I was going to use the Chevrolet for that. But now I'm not worth a shit."

We're limping south. There are men on the sidewalk, leaning against the buildings. You can see they're putting in dead time. They still itch for juice, Stargell, they still want that. We pass stores that sell equipment to restaurants, machines that can make waffles for five hundred people, French fries for a thousand. I can see the waffle eaters, their knives and forks moving like small windmills, just destroying what's on the plates before them. Their faces are sticky with syrup and butter. Good waffles, they think, those are the best waffles I've ever had.

"What's that?" says Frenchy.

He points at my box.

"A present," I say.

"Look," says Frenchy, "you make me a promise. You help this guy move, you hear? I haven't got the Chevrolet anymore."

"Sure," I say.

Frenchy tells me his friend is a waiter. He's blind, though, so he could only work banquets.

"Everything's the same at a banquet," says Frenchy. "They fired his ass because he couldn't pour wine. He had to put his finger in the glass to see if it was full."

We go into a bar. There are men and women sitting on mismatched stools before a piece of plywood on sawhorses. The plywood isn't finished. Most people are drinking a shot with a quart of beer to chase it. Glasses for the shot. Beer comes straight out of the bottle. The bartender is about six four, has a belly like a barrel, a face you could chop down trees with. There is a strange chattering in the room, a mixture of voices that sound like the true religion, the speaking in tongues.

I realize I've started limping, just like Frenchy. When we come in the door, the old women at the bar look us over, then hoist their bottles of beer, suck at the mouths, sigh.

One of the women at the bar begins to dance. She is wearing a green sweater and she pulls one side of it away from herself and uses it as a partner. She hums a little, waltzes along the bar. Over the voices, the old religion hum, I can pick out the tune, "Tales from the Vienna Woods." At the end of the bar there's a man whose features are as sharp as farm equipment and he glances at her and slips into his own reverie, the memory of a dancing woman. The dancer moves along, wraps herself into her sweater. The man just stares at her.

Ask her to dance, I think, you dumb bastard.

I see the old farmer squiring her around the bar, both of them wrecked, beyond humiliation, just waltzing like in the good old days before the walls fell in. The farmer sits there with his bottle and the woman runs out of gas, flops down on her stool like the bundle of rags that she is. All tidy, ready for the trash heap. Maybe she'll dance again, I think, maybe she'll surprise us all. Maybe she'll stand up on the plywood bar and piss right in the bartender's face, right onto the thief who's charging her a king's ransom for a quart of beer and who sells her cigarettes one at a time.

"That's Carew," says Frenchy. "Over there."

He points to a man who's about forty-five. Balding a little. Doughy features and a heavy beard. His eyes are strangely protuberant. The man's short fingers are holding a glass. He's sitting at a table against the wall.

We get something to drink and then join him.

"Frenchy," says Carew, "where you been? I've been waiting for a couple of days."

Frenchy shrugs.

"I brought a friend along," says Frenchy. "This is Stargell."

"Glad to meet you," says Carew. He puts his hand out and I shake it.

Some nails have been driven into the molding above the table and each nail has hung on it a patch of cloth. The patches have names written on them in a festive-looking nail polish: The Georgia Peach, Crash, Specs, Shoe Shine, The Nashville Narcissus, Angel Sleeves, Pep. Each one has a date.

"This place has nice vibes," says Frenchy. "Those patches were cut off guys who died here."

Frenchy is drinking something that would make the Barber flinch: it's as though the tanneries had found a use for the last bit of liquid, the end product of it all. Frenchy is taking it on fast, too: his curtain's getting ready to drop. Carew has a bald spot and he sweeps his hair into an elaborate swirl to cover it.

"I've got a handicap," says Carew.

He blinks in my direction.

"You don't have a handicap," says Frenchy. "You're blind as a bat."

"I can see a little light and shadow," says Carew.

He smiles a little, looks toward the overhead light, the bare bulb.

"Sure," says Frenchy, "sure you can. I know it."

We sit for a while, listen to the sound of the bar, the voices, a collective sucking noise. Through the window I can see the first torn bits of snow, the ragged flecks that look like forlorn confetti.

"Nothing but a goddamned fifty-seven Plymouth," says Frenchy.

You can see that in the center of his head something has gone amiss: his top is running down, about to topple.

"You make me a promise," he says with drunken sincerity. "You help Carew move his stuff."

"Sure," I say.

"Good," says Frenchy.

Carew thanks me. It continues to snow. We wait for it to stop, but it seems to be getting worse. Carew becomes pensive, speaks about his youth, tells me that when he used to go out with friends he always got the ugliest girl. I ask how he knew she was the ugliest.

"My friends told me," he says.

Frenchy looks at him, has another shot, and then silently puts his head on the table and goes to sleep. It looks like someone's cut his string. At the bar everyone has turned to a partner: they seem to be dancing on stools. Faces are pushed close together and everyone is talking and everyone understands because everyone is confused. Stargell, I think, they're running out of trouble to make.

Carew pulls my sleeve.

"It's not far to my place," he says.

It's dark now and it's still snowing.

"Just a couple of blocks," he says.

"All right," I say.

We try to wake Frenchy, but he just groans.

"He does that all the time," says Carew. "It don't mean nothing. We'll have to carry him."

We pick him up and drag him outside. He works with us a little, but then he sags, realizes that we'll pull him along. His shoes make two long tracks in the snow. I have one of his arms and Carew has the other. I'm carrying my package, too.

"It's snowing," says Carew.

I stick out my tongue: there's the taste, the city's own version of perfume and sweat, lipstick and cunt. There is a harshness in the snow, the lingering presence of smoke and soot from a hundred thousand furnaces, from the tall stacks by the river, an acidic reminder of New Jersey, of the oil refineries there. I can feel the sharp, pointed snow itself, those frozen bits in the air, an atmospheric effervescence that reminds me of champagne.

"It feels good," says Carew.

We carry Frenchy.

"Down two blocks," says Carew, "then over one."

Carew tells me he met Frenchy years ago in San Pedro, California. They've stayed in touch through the mail, with postcards, letters. Occasionally they make a phone call.

"Frenchy was a great man," says Carew. "You wouldn't know it now. But he invented things and people listened to him."

I look at the old reprobate with his head hung down, with the snow piling up on his bald head.

"His wife played the piano," says Carew, "but she's dead."

As we walk along I can see that Carew is wearing tennis shoes. He still wears the tops of his socks. The bottom part, the foot part, has worn away beneath the ankle. In the morning he pushes the tops into his shoes, but by evening they've pulled up and you can see a ring of flesh all the way around his ankles. I know in the morning he thinks, I've still got socks. See? You can see I've still got socks.

"Whenever Frenchy came to town we'd go to ball games or tit shows," says Carew. "We always had a good time."

We stop in front of a row house, a brick box that was built with intentions so obvious I'm almost embarrassed. There should be a neon sign in front that flashes on and off: "Let's Fleece the Dumb Immigrants."

We put Frenchy under the staircase on the first floor, and climb four flights. I'm wet, chilled, and I can feel the age of the buildings, the twangy ghosts. I can hear the mills, the slamming and banging of small factories, the insane hum of the sweatshop. I think of a fat woman at her sewing machine. It's winter and she's making bathing suits. She is cold and is wearing a coat that makes her look like a mangy bear. She fondles the smooth fabric, imagines the sun, has chills when she thinks of young, thin women, who are sitting on the beach and feeling the ocean breeze. The old bear comes home to this building. So many bathing suits, she thinks, what happens to them all? Can there really be so many young women?

Carew and I stand on the top landing. Carew discovers a padlock on his door. There isn't any hall light. I drop downstairs, to the front of the building, and root around in the garbage. I bring a piece of pipe back with me.

"What have you got?" says Carew.

His hands touch mine, the pipe.

"Ah," he says.

I give him the package from the burglar alarm factory. I put one end of the pipe underneath the padlock and pull on the other. It looks as though I were holding a long lever that controls a dynamo. The crack, the quick splitting sound, is resonant in the building: I feel like I'd hit my elbow. Cold hum. I know the other tenants are behind their doors, listening, each one thinking, It's that blind bastard, breaking into his own place. I slip the pipe a little farther down, strain again, pry open the door.

Carew's room is simple, asylum spare: one cot, one chair, one table, one sink. There's nothing on the walls except a square piece of chrome about two feet on each side. It looks like four hubcaps in a shiny frame. Carew picks up his suitcase, gives me the chrome, and then we stand in the hall again.

"It brightens the place up a little," says Carew, pointing at the chrome.

We walk down the stairs.

"You know," says Carew. He has a hand out on the rail. The liquor, the moving, have knocked something out of the files. I can almost hear the soft flutter of memory. "I grew up in Holland. During the war we had nothing to eat. My mother burned all the books to keep us warm. We ate sparrow-and-tulip-bulb soup."

I see a bowl filled with bright flowers and birds. Red and yellow blooms. Brown sparrows. Green leaves. It looks like a lush, fertile still life. Carew's small hands are reaching into it and his family take some, too. They're thinking, We'll eat this stuff. We'll eat this shit and when it's all over, we'll still be here. Fuck you, they're saying.

Frenchy's turned his face toward the wall, but he still seems to be breathing.

"He'll be more comfortable there," says Carew. He blinks. "I've got to get a cage for my birds," says Carew, "and get rid of this stuff. We'll be back."

"Birds?" I say.

We walk in the snow.

"Yeah," says Carew. "I'll show you. First we've got to get a cage."

I carry the suitcase. Carew navigates.

"Do you think it's ugly?" says Carew. "The chrome."

"No," I say.

"Frenchy says I've got no taste," says Carew. "He says even seeing wouldn't do me any good."

Stargell, I think, only a friend could be so cruel.

I laugh, shake my head.

"He just thinks he's a snob," I say.

"Yeah," says Carew, limping into the snow. "We always have a good time. Tit shows. Ball games. You name it."

"Here it is," says Carew.

We stand before a building which had a storefront at one time, but it's been boarded up, covered with pieces of plywood. The place has a scarred aspect, the feeling of being more bandaged than closed. There's a chain and lock on the front door: it looks as though the building were wearing a confining watch. The windows have been broken out of the top floors and wood and tin have been put into the frames. A tidy job. Tight as a new drum. There's a trench, a small open hall below the street, a little movement in it.

"Carew," says a voice.

Carew blinks, cocks his head, licks his lips.

"Carew."

Below us I can see a dark bundle of clothes, a woman wearing a skirt, mismatched shoes, a rag bonnet, a cardigan sweater over a couple of skirts. Her face is turned toward us and it's red, as though sunburned. Her hands are on the sidewalk and she stands beneath the stoop.

"This all you got?" she says. She speaks as though she were saying of a boxer, The kid can't hit. He's just somebody who's going to get slapped around.

She looks at the suitcase and the chrome. I can see that on one side of the building she has a shopping cart and it's filled with clothes, bags, scraps of tin and wire, cardboard, shoes, the frail skeletons of umbrellas. I can see why she sneers at Carew. She has a machine, a business. Carew's just another goddamn derelict.

"Yeah," says Carew, a little sadly. "I got to go back for my birds."

The woman looks at my clothes, my wet suit.

"Who's he?" she says.

"Stargell," says Carew.

She's still standing with her nose at the level of the sidewalk. I can see she weighs two hundred pounds if she weighs an ounce. She puts her nose through the bars, pushes it out to give me a sniff. One of my pant legs is taken by her fingers, and I can feel them working, their appraiser's rub.

"Nice clothes," she says, "very nice."

The old bat is a little fresh, but I like her. I want to take her to Brooks Brothers. I'd probably need a baseball bat to keep the undertakers away, but we could go around and have a good feel. We'd touch all the clothes. Maybe she'd take a dive right into the racks of suits. It would be like a bear in the bush: she'd run along, making a rustling swell among the jackets. The undertakers would be hysterical. I'd stand guard with the baseball bat until she was done. Then we'd get a snack and eat it in the park.

"He's helping me move," says Carew. "This is Boileryard."

"That's me," she says.

She puts out her hand through the bars and gives mine a dainty shake. The snow is falling onto her rag bonnet.

"What do you think of my face?" she says.

It's as ugly as a rusty tin can with a jagged lip: pouting, angry, conniving. It would cure medicine men. One look and they'd join the Church of England.

"A miracle," I say.

"Go on," she says. "They don't come much worse. Unless it's those red marks or no noses or kind of saggy like something went wrong in the mold."

She grabs my cuff again, laughs, feels the snow on her face.

"Go on," she says.

She has no shame: she puts her head down and giggles, pulls her bonnet over her face. I taste the snow, listen to her wheezing laughter. Carew blinks. Boileryard stops laughing, but she holds on to the cuff of my pant leg.

"Didn't you have no furniture?" she says to Carew.

"It wasn't mine," says Carew.

"So what?" says Boileryard.

Carew's thinking, I shouldn't be so sentimental. He looks a little crestfallen, embarrassed, as though caught in some slight vice. Let's go back and loot the place, I think. We'll take everything.

"You had a bed, didn't you?" says Boileryard.

"Yeah," says Carew.

"Is the door locked?" says Boileryard.

"No," says Carew. "He broke it open."

He points to me.

"Did you now?" she says. "Did you now, my sweet?"

She gives my pant leg a healthy yank.

"With a pipe," I say. "Bam. Crack. Splinters everywhere."

"Ha!" says Boileryard. "Good for you."

She gives my pant leg another tug.

"Where's the pipe?" she says.

"In front of the building," I say. "There's a pile of junk."

Boileryard turns her face up to me and smiles. She sucks her gums and gives my pant leg another tug. She wants that pipe, all right, and the bed and chair, the door, the knobs, bricks, toilets: I can see her carrying the whole building away, a stick at a time, in her shopping cart.

"What's that?" she says.

She points at Carew's house-trailer sculpture.

"It looks like a bunch of hub caps," she says.

"It's an ornament," says Carew, but he looks like he's getting ready to stomp on Boileryard's fingers. I'm thinking about the woman who should go with it: she'll wear red underwear with a slit in the crotch.

"It's not so bad," I say.

Boileryard looks up at me, shows me her complexion, the skin as red as a radish. She smiles.

"Is that what you think?" she says. "Is it, my darling?"

She gives my pant leg another tug.

"Well, my sweet," she says, "then you can help me carry it."

Boileryard climbs the steps to the street, opens the gate, and comes out to the sidewalk. She's not very tall, about five feet, I'd say, but she's solid, like a barrel filled with Crisco. Carew blinks in her direction, makes a nice smile, but he's turned a little away from her.

"Here I am," she says, "you blind ninny. What happened to Frenchy?"

"He's sleeping it off," says Carew.

"Ha," she says. "That's a life. Taking it on and sleeping it off."

Boileryard picks up the bag with an easy swing, carries it as though it were hung on a hay hook. We follow her into a small alley between the building and the next, Boileryard first, then Carew, then me. There's only an inch or so of snow on the street, but the acoustics have already changed. The street has an amazing softness, a palpable quietness, one that you can feel more than hear. The alley has a Shanghai atmosphere. It's about two feet wide. I'm carrying the chrome. Three boobs in the snow, I think. They should shoot us while we're cornered.

"I need a birdcage," says Carew.

"I ain't giving nothing away," says Boileryard.

"I know," says Carew.

Boileryard stops beneath a second-story window.

"You coming?" she says to me.

I'd follow the old bulldog into the gates of hell and she knows it. She turns sideways in the alley, leans her back against one wall, puts her feet on the other, holds the suitcase in her lap, and begins to ascend, alpine-chimney style. She grunts, strains, blows puffs of white mist into the air, but she goes up as steadily as the water level in a filling tub. Above me, against the red sky, I can see her legs moving under her skirt. What legs, Stargell, what legs. They are the legs of all time, thick as fireplugs, pitted, veined. I'd love to grab them just to see how they feel.

"What are you waiting for, my sweet?" says Boileryard.

I ascend, too, can feel the rough brick through my jacket. One foot moves ahead of another on the opposite wall: it's not half bad, I think. Maybe I won't end up as a busted goon in the alley. Boileryard climbs above me, pushing and stopping, pushing and stopping. It makes me think she's about to have a baby. I carry the shiny chrome in my lap, hear Carew stamping his feet in the snow. I look upward and see her legs again, their glorious size, one rubbing against the other, the pocked, unstoppable flesh. She wears large underwear. I look at those legs and feel the fast-car jolt: the old bat's legs make me think of the great names, Maserati, Ferrari, Ducati, Aston. I watch her strain.

Boileryard stops at a window sill, reaches above her head, and raises the sash. She struggles a little and then she's sitting. A moment more and she disappears: her legs are drawn into the building as though she had been snagged by one of those moving chains you see in car washes.

Carew stamps in the snow.

I hold the chrome in my lap and sit on the window sill. Behind me there is a table and I slide onto it. For a moment I feel like a patient. Boileryard is standing next to me, breathing hard enough to start a fire: I can hear the bellows working. She takes the chrome from me and puts it on the floor next to the suitcase.

"You climb good, my sweet," she says, blowing and snorting. She lights a candle.

We rest for a while. Boileryard tells me the building is owned by some geriatric case in Miami. Every now and then he sends someone around to change the locks, which is a waste of time, since Boileryard doesn't use the door now. But I can see the owner, sitting on a deck chair, feeling the pale, undemanding sunlight, staring at the flat ocean, seeing young people on the beach. He watches their bodies, the healthy sweat on them, and then he dreams of the north, of his building, of Boileryard. He should have married her, I think, the dumb cluck. She would have kept him going. Now he sits down there, getting ripe like a coconut, waiting for the harvest.

By the candle I can see that I'm next to a lathe. The place must have been a shop, alive with the vibration of machines, men standing before them, making perfect curls of metal, comet tails of sparks at the grinder. Now the place is filled, floor to ceiling, with Boileryard's findings: baby carriages, an easel, broken chairs, perfectly baled newspapers, kitchen sinks, spark plugs, a bassinet, plates, a fry-pan, some pressure cookers, boxes of screws, a bottle warmer, nuts, bolts, washers, a roll of linoleum, baby clothes, flowerpots, drawers without their cabinet, a playpen, rags, just big bundles of them that look like Boileryard when she's resting, a high chair, toys, some broken tools, a bathtub, a baby scale. It is as though we are standing in a Pacific Ocean of junk, and one of those swells from a typhoon near Japan has finally reached us, and the wave is about to break. The crest is twenty feet above us, and there, where the wave feathers, I can see the bright, cheerful license plates, Idaho, Texas, Mississippi, Virginia.

We begin looking for the birdcage. The place is alive, too. The stink of rats is everywhere, and you can hear them skittering away, can see the drops of piss. I pick up a piece of pipe and lay one out: bam, a cold hum, a little twitch, the old magic's gone.

"Good for you, my sweet," says Boileryard, throwing the rat out the window.

We prowl among the bales of newspaper, broken chairs, toasters, flat inner tubes.

"I know I've got a birdcage," says Boileryard. She stops and puts one hand on her large hip.

"How did all this stuff get in here?" I say.

"What's it to you?" she says.

We climb to the third floor.

"I brought it in," says Boileryard. "What do you think of that, my darling?"

Another rat comes by, tentative, alert, arrogant as hell. I take a swipe at him but he gets away. Boileryard, I think, I'll take you anyplace you want to go. The Salvation Army store. The Jersey dumps. We continue through the third floor. We're climbing over a short, choppy landscape, one that is made from junk and has been shelled heavily. There are craters everywhere.

"You need a cat," I say.

"Yes, my sweet," says Boileryard. "I need a cat."

The old bear has a tender concern for her findings, her treasures. The Coconut couldn't get rid of her for a million. He's going to cork off soon, Stargell. Just think of the heirs, the inheritance buffs. Death is a scum where lawyers feed, but Boileryard will sit in the building spitting and hissing. She'll tell them to clear off. The shameless stickpennies will have to bring her down with an elephant gun.

There isn't a thing, aside from the lathes and machinery, that is larger than the window. Boileryard's brought everything up alpine-chimney style.

"Here it is," she says.

She holds up a white Victorian birdcage. It's about two feet wide and three feet high. She smiles, holds the candle to it.

"It's a beauty," I say.

"Yes," says Boileryard, "it's a lovely cage."

We go back to the second floor and slide out the table. I go first, bracing myself between the walls. Boileryard is above me, carrying the cage. I see her legs again. Each knee looks like it had escaped from a liverwurst factory.

I drop into the snow. Carew is there, looking like a Christmas-display reject. He brushes the snow off his head.

"Somebody threw a rat at me," says Carew.

Boileryard descends, gives Carew the cage.

"Here," says Boileryard.

His fingers climb over it like small animals.

"How much?" says Carew.

"A dollar," says Boileryard. She takes my sleeve. "Now ain't that a fair price, my sweet, ain't that about right?"

Carew forks over a buck.

Boileryard moves through the snow, kicking it away from her

feet, and climbs down into the space under the stoop. She sits there, as camouflaged as a game bird: her rags blend perfectly with her nest of clothes, newspaper, plastic sheets.

"When you want your suitcase," she says to Carew, "you know where to find me."

Carew and I walk in the snow, each of us moving with a work-camp gait. The light seems to come from a guard tower.

I remember Boileryard, moving through her things, stopping at a rattle, a child's toy, picking it up and making it sound, listening and smiling, then saying, "I don't have my . . . you know, my sweet . . . I can't have children. It's too late for that." She holds the rattle, then drops it, pushes ahead, forcing her way through her possessions, the city's leavings. She stops again, turns to me, picks up a bottle warmer, and says, "No one is ashamed these days. I don't get the monthlies anymore. No kids for me, my sweet." She stands there, with her rag bonnet on her head, her eyes lighted by the candle. "What was it you said about my face?" she says. "A miracle," I say. She giggles, throws the bonnet over her face, doubles over with embarrassment and pleasure. She throws the bottle onto the heap.

"Oh," she says. "Oh."

I think of Boileryard, of a mewling infant: I can see its conception. The genetic strands glisten, coil in deep space, reach light-years for one another, ache for the contact of other genes, each of which is as bright as Times Square, as Las Vegas. The strands embrace, fold softly together, join in galactic spirals. When they touch they make a sound like a trout sucking a fly from the surface of a pool. Stargell, old bean, you're on target again, but you haven't got a fucking place to hang your hat.

I kneel over Frenchy. His lips are blue and he's drooling a little. I give him a shake, but he just groans. I pull him closer to the radiator.

"He looks pretty bad," I say.

"He always does that," says Carew. "He just needs to sleep it off. Come on."

There's a door at the back of the staircase. Carew opens it and we go down into the basement. It's a small room under the front part of the building, cozy, warm as a hothouse. The walls have been painted white, and at the entrance there is a screen door in a screen fence. Four or five bright lights are on.

"Come on," says Carew.

There are some pieces of driftwood hung from the ceiling, and at one side there is a waterfall. The waterfall is running. It's a homemade job. The place is filled with doves, parakeets, finches, and some weird-looking little birds I've never seen before. Carew sits on a bench, in the speckles of shit. He puts the Victorian cage on the floor, reaches for a sack under the bench, and feeds some of the birds. He smiles absently, seems to be feeling at ease, protecting, gentle. The birds move around before him.

"There are zebra finches here," he says. "You see them?"

I look at the small birds with their penpoint bills, bright as an orange, their dark and white markings. The doves make that sound, a *K-k-hoo, K-k-hoo.* I can see cigar boxes on the wall, the birds nesting in them. There are small birds, as fuzzy as dandelions, just snapped from the shell. Carew puts his hands in his lap. Stargell, I think, no wonder they're throwing the blind bastard out: he's got a regular menagerie here. I find myself staring at a bird with blue markings on its wings and back. The colors look like they've been painted on.

"There are rice paddy birds here," says Carew, "from Asia. They only eat hulled rice."

Carew sits in shit, but it doesn't matter. He can't see the droppings.

"Will you catch a couple of birds?" he says. "Zebra finches. They'll breed anywhere."

"Sure," I say.

He tells me how to distinguish the males from the females—the females are a little broader in the hips—and I walk into the center of the aviary. The birds aren't stupid: they can sense the grab-bag atmosphere. I snare one, catch him by the leg. For a moment it's like holding a fan that's having a breakdown: the air washes over my hand in uneven waves. The rest of the birds are spooked. They've got the message now and they make air-show turns and dives. I grab the wings of the one I hold, press them gently against his body, feel the heart beating. It's moving day, Jack, I think.

The room looks like there's been a pillow fight: there are feathers everywhere. A bird takes a Kamikaze exit, dives straight into the waterfall, drowns. Carew stands in the center of the aviary, sniffing and blinking. I catch another bird, shove it in the cage, close the door. Carew stands with his arms outstretched, a blind man in a feather storm, wet, cold, but immersing himself in the fluff, the reminder of the birds he had. Take a good feel, I think. Take it. The feathers are beginning to settle, to cover everything with an imitation snow. Carew, I think, we'll go to the zoo, to the aviary there, and I'll describe all the birds, every one, from flamingos to penguins. Maybe we'll be able to touch an egg, a webbed foot, a beak. How'll that be, Carew?

"Let's go," I say.

"Did you get three?" says Carew.

"Yes," I say.

We walk toward the stairs. Carew is carrying the cage and there is some bird shit on his shoulder.

"I used to sit here in the evenings, drinking a beer and listening to the ball games," says Carew.

Potholders and wicker baskets, Carew, that's the ticket. We'll shame the world into giving you a living. Maybe you could learn to paint pictures with the brush shoved up your ass: still lives are a good bet, you know, the kind of thing that is nice for a breakfast nook.

We stand over Frenchy. He coughs, blinks, looks up at us, then turns toward the wall. Carew gives him another poke, but Frenchy doesn't move.

"This happens all the time," says Carew.

"He doesn't look so good," I say.

"We need a drink," says Carew.

We carry Frenchy along, out under the lights. Carew has his birdcage and I've got my box. The snow touches my face.

We stop at the bar and I prop Frenchy against the wall. Carew puts the birdcage on the table. The people at the bar turn and stare at us and for a moment the place is quiet. Everyone looks as though he'd felt the last beat of his heart, the final pause, the approach of stinging darkness. I'm ready to shout, What the hell do you want? A juggler and a race car driver? Brain surgeons and dynamiters? Bullfighters? Be glad we made it at all, and anyway, you don't look so good yourselves.

I brush us off, but the snow has already begun to melt. I feel like a wet dog. The room is cozy, warmer than outside. I get a couple of shots, one for Frenchy, too. The women at the bar cradle their quarts of beer, tell lies, stories, catalogue outrages, hold trials. The dancer is curled into her green sweater: her gaze is so direct you could hang clothes on it. The farmer is still shy, but every now and then he glances at her. Just one little touch, I think, just one and they'd feel the screw tighten.

Frenchy has his head in a puddle of water.

"Maybe we should take Frenchy someplace where he could stretch out," I say.

"Naw," says Carew. "He'll wake up."

He gives Frenchy a poke.

"There ain't no place to take him," says Carew. "He ain't got a fucking thing. He'll spend the night in a flop, just like me."

We drink our shots. I get another round.

"What about you?" says Carew. "You got a place?"

No, I think, I'm on the lam, too, just another boob in the gin mill, getting ready to storm the patent office. I've been thinking about airplane tires recently, about how they skid on landings. Little windmills on the wheels should make the tires turn, or maybe some engine could be used, you know, with a clutch, so that the speed of the tires would match the ground speed of the plane. No more skidding, no more Firestone chirp on the runways.

"No," I say, "I haven't got any place."

"Too bad about Frenchy's Chevrolet," says Carew. "Let me tell you. He loved that car."

Frenchy is face down on the table, his nose flattened against it, in the center of the melted snow. There is something about his stillness that draws attention, makes him seem monstrous. There seems to be a slight eddy in the air, an odd draft, a hush, as though Frankenstein had just run out of juice. I put my finger against Frenchy's neck, then turn his face toward me. His skin is the color of wet newsprint.

Stargell, the man is dead. No jump, no buzz, no snap.

Carew tells me Frenchy was working in a gas station in Los Angeles. An independent station, says Carew, the old days. He was driving a fifty-eight Pontiac, a wreck he'd bought off a freeway tow truck guy: the front end was smashed so the headlights pointed down, the fuel pump leaked, the carburetor was shot. The Pontiac didn't get more than two or three miles to the gallon. I heard this story enough times to last forever, says Carew.

I look at the woman in the green sweater, the farmer. Someone has put his false teeth on the plywood. Good-looking choppers, I think.

It was a heavy car, says Carew, it had everything. Tinted glass, a compass, leather seats, radio, heater. Frenchy said its transmission was shot, too. If you put it into drive after having backed up, the Pontiac would jump twenty feet, you know. Frenchy said he had whiplash.

Carew stares into the foggy luminescence before him.

So Frenchy started asking everyone who came into the station, Would you like to trade? He wanted something simple, like that Chevrolet he had. He found one, and the guy who owned it was all scarred up something awful. He'd been in an accident in Arizona and he went through the windshield. Broke his jaw, too, and every now and then a bone chip would work its way through his gums. He told Frenchy he wanted to drive a heavier car. Frenchy told him he had just what he needed. The Pontiac was parked so you wouldn't have to back it up. The guy who owned the Chevrolet drove it. Frenchy told him there was a place down on Western where he could get the front end fixed for fifty bucks, but that was just a bunch of Frenchy's shit. It would have cost a thousand.

I touch Frenchy's neck again: there's no mistaking that, Stargell.

Carew is smiling.

So they swapped cars and Frenchy got a hundred bucks, too. They went to the bank and signed the papers. The guy wanted to drive the Pontiac to the bank, and Frenchy thought, What the hell, by the time he backs up, it'll be his. When they pulled out of the parking spot of the bank, the Arizona guy put the car into drive after having had it in reverse. He punched it a little. Nothing happened. Frenchy was already holding his neck, bracing himself. The guy gives it more gas, and then the Pontiac just rises like a jumping swordfish. It was a beautiful flight, says Frenchy. The guy from Arizona looked at Frenchy and Frenchy said, Funny thing, never happened to me.

The bar is filled with voices. The bartender stands behind the plywood, resting his stomach on it. Carew's smile looks as though someone had hooked a finger into the corner of his mouth and lifted it.

The Chevrolet wasn't any prize, though, says Carew. A lot of times it wouldn't start, so Frenchy always parked it on a hill. Sometimes it would die at a stoplight, but Frenchy got so he could jump out and give it a push, jump in, and pop the clutch. That's pretty good for a man with only one leg. The guy from Arizona had to come to the gas station about three times a day to fill his tank, because of the fuel pump and carburetor, and Frenchy's gas station sold the cheapest gas in town. Frenchy would fill him up and say, You liking the Pontiac? I think you took me on this deal.

Carew laughs. Frenchy's light is dying.

One day Frenchy is driving along in the Chevrolet, says Carew, and he looks in the rear-view mirror and sees that a Pontiac is coming after him, and not just any Pontiac either, but a green-and-white one with a smashed-in front end with headlights that point straight down. Frenchy can see that there's a guy driving it and his face is all scarred up. Frenchy said he looked mad as hell, and Frenchy said he had every right to be because that Pontiac was a lemon. Clear and simple. Frenchy thought the guy had gone off his rocker and was going to shoot him.

The teeth are still sitting on the bar: good-looking choppers, I think. I'm shivering in my suit. It feels as though I'm wearing something made from damp newspapers.

So Frenchy's scared, says Carew. He watched the rear-view mirror and saw that scarred face coming closer. Frenchy was thinking of trying to outrun him, but he knew there wasn't a chance against the Pontiac, which (says Carew), although not very much of a long-distance machine (considering how much gas it used), could go fast as hell between gas stations. Frenchy stops at a traffic light and the Pontiac pulls right up behind him. Frenchy is thinking, Jesus Christ, what a way to go: to get shot for selling some asshole a lousy Pontiac. The traffic light changes, and Frenchy was so rattled he stalled the Chevrolet. He jumps out and starts pushing it, trying to get it started, trying to make a getaway before the guy in the Pontiac could do his dirty work. The Pontiac pulled up next to Frenchy, who was hopping along, pushing the Chevrolet. The guy from Arizona reaches over and rolls down the window. Frenchy kept pushing. The guy from Arizona said, Funny thing, that never happened to me, and then takes off, leaving a trail of leaking gas.

Carew laughs.

"What do you think of that?" he says.

Sit up, Frenchy, you piece of scum. Have a drink. Sit up or I'll throw you through the window. I touch his neck again.

Carew laughs again, slaps Frenchy on the back. The birds flutter in their cage: they can feel the absence, the Forest Lawn emptiness.

"Something's wrong," says Carew.

His finger moves over Frenchy's shoulder.

"He's dead," I say.

"No he ain't," says Carew. "He's been drinking with us all night."

The hands go to the cold skin, then jump back. Carew makes one loud, clear cry, one long shriek. No one notices, since the room is perfectly filled with grief.

The bartender has seen so much he's as blind as Carew. I tell him what's happened. The bartender gives me a look you could freeze fish with. I know what the world would be like if he were in charge. There'd be footsteps on the sidewalk, the kind you get in a mail-order how-to-dance course. No mistakes then, Jack.

A short woman who looks like she dyes her hair with something she mixes up in the bathtub says to the woman in green, the dancer, "What do you think it was?"

I stand at the bar, listen to Carew wailing.

"It was his heart," says the dancer.

"The poor guy," says the woman with the dyed hair. "That's terrible."

"I'd say it was his heart," says the dancer.

The birds are still uneasy, rocking back and forth in the middle of the wicker cage. It sits on the table next to Frenchy. Carew looks like a wax version of himself. The woman with the bathtub dye job takes a pair of scissors that hang on a hook next to the bar, then walks with a stumbling ceremony across the room. The farmer comes along, too, and he lifts Frenchy up for a moment. The woman cuts out his back pocket. You can hear the scissors going snip, snip, snip, just like in a barbershop.

Carew feels the movement, hears the sound.

"What's happening?" he says.

He grabs my hand, squeezes it.

"Stargell, Stargell!"

The woman with the stained hair takes the pocket back to the bar, reaches for a bottle on a shelf next to the peg where the scissors hang, and writes the date on Frenchy's patch. The polish looks carnival slick, metallic. The woman comes back to us.

"What was his name?" she says.

"Stanley Bardagaray," says Carew. "They called him Frenchy."

The woman writes "Frenchy" on the patch, gives it to the farmer, his face now looking like something that has a good time in an icehouse. He takes a hammer and a nail and fastens the patch to the molding above Carew's head.

Carew's still holding my hand, and I can feel him flinch at each stroke of the hammer.

"I'm O.K.," he says.

The blackbirds arrive. The police come through the door in their dark slickers, their caps with the short, shiny bills. The ambulance arrives, too, with its light flashing as though someone were trying to hypnotize us all. Frenchy is taken off.

"He didn't have nobody," says Carew.

The police ask where he lived.

"In his Chevrolet," says Carew, "or in a flop."

One of the cops writes something on a slip of paper.

"Somebody's got to make arrangements," they say.

They mean we've got to plant the poor bastard. I can feel the cold ground stir. The cops leave. No one looks at Carew or me. The place where Frenchy sat is so empty you could put a water buffalo there.

Carew carries the birdcage. I've got my box from the burglar alarm factory. The air is filled with snow and it makes me feel like I'm walking through a cold sandstorm.

"You know a place?" I say.

"Yeah," says Carew.

The birds fluff themselves up.

"How long were we carrying him," says Carew, "when he was . . . you know . . ."

"He was O.K. at the bar," I say.

Carew's socks have pulled out of his shoes and I can see a white band of skin at his ankles.

"This guy is cheap," says Carew.

Carew begins to cry. I touch his shoulder but he shakes me off.

I want to tell him that grief is a flower that only blooms in the best gardens.

"Maybe we won't have enough money," says Carew.

"Don't worry," I say. I've got the death spore right in my pocket.

The whole street has a forlorn aspect, except for one sign: "Hraboski's Funeral Parlor." It's in a deep purple neon, a color that looks like one you'd see on a color television that's out of whack. There's another sign, too, in white neon, and it says: "Service To The Community Twenty-Four Hours."

Carew seems mesmerized by the blinking neon. The birds are shivering. The cadence of the blinking sign is unmistakable: fuck you, fuck you, fuck you.

"This is Hraboski's," says Carew.

It's a brownstone building and it has an awning over the steps and the sidewalk. The cover for it (that has "Hraboski" written on both sides) is made out of frayed canvas: it looks like the cheap mortician's flag it is. Enid's map to paradise, the lot number, would come in handy now.

Beneath the stoop there is another sign, which says "Office." Carew takes his birds and we descend. I ring the bell there, brush the snow off my suit. The door is opened by a young man, twenty-two or -three years old (at the most: I think he'd have trouble buying a bottle of booze). He's dressed in a dark suit, one that's made of material as fine as burlap. It looks like he's waiting to grow into it. Beyond the door I can hear music, something by Tito Puente. The man who opened the door looks at me, Carew, and the birds.

"Ah," he says.

He is as smooth as a worn shovel handle.

"Excuse me," he says.

He closes the door and then the music dies. What the hell, I think, there's no need to be so grim. What's wrong with Tito? His shit stinks, too, you know. We're not the only people with a corpse to plant.

The door opens again.

"Mr. Hraboski?" I say.

"No," says the man. "My name is Concepcion."

I nod. This one's tougher than his years, Stargell. Just wait until you talk turkey.

"Come in," he says.

We walk into the hall of the cellar. Carew continues blinking and his birds are rustling around. The walls are covered with veneer paneling, a variety of the hunting lodge look (which I last saw in the burglar alarm showroom). The carpet is green, nice and fertile. We come to the middle of the hall and turn into an office, in which there are two desks. There's a divider, a plastic bamboo curtain, that can be drawn through the middle of the room in case there's some land-office business. Concepcion sits down, puts the tips of his fingers together.

"What can I do for you?" he says.

Stargell, I think, maybe this is the answer: the boy looks like he's just raking it in. And there's a sucker being born every minute. I'll bet the boy's a Catholic. Maybe I could make a bundle and Enid would fall in love with me again. I look at Concepcion and I want to say, What do you think, Jack, we came to get our fortunes read?

"A friend died," I say.

"Ah," says Concepcion.

Across from him, on the opposite wall, there are photographs of his daughter. Each one is dated a year after the previous, and there are five altogether. I can see all seventy of them, those taken when the girl with the dark smiling face and faintly crossed eyes has turned into a strange beauty, all itchy and wet, when she has fatted up and is obviously a great screamer, when she has aged and when her face has suddenly been perked up by those dentures she always wanted and finally bought on credit, when she is ready for something her father could have gotten for her wholesale. The blank walls must make the girl crazy with anticipation.

"A good friend," says Carew.

"Where is he?" says Concepcion.

"The police have him," I say.

Carew pushes the slip of paper across the table. It seems that

Frenchy is finally dead, as though the magic didn't stop in the stinking gin mill, but right here as the paper is picked up and caressed by Concepcion's long, delicate, and cool fingers. Concepcion has short hair, a thin nose, eyes that look like the pupils are made of frozen oil.

"When?" says Concepcion.

Just listen, Stargell, listen to the way he talks. He's kissing each word goodbye, as though each one were a twenty-dollar chip he slapped down in one of those casinos in Europe where everyone's in evening clothes and no one's supposed to give a flying fuck about money. I like the greasy bastard.

"He died in a bar," I say. "His heart."

"Ah," says Concepcion.

I want to say, Let's talk turkey, my boy, let's get down to the heart of the matter.

Carew starts sobbing.

I put my hand on his shoulder and he stops.

"Go on," he says.

"I imagine that cost is an issue," Concepcion says.

I want to scream, No, no, it doesn't mean a thing, I want all the extras. A jazz band and naked girls and the best champagne. And I want Johnny Carson to give the eulogy and I want a machine put into Frenchy so he can sit up and drink gin and grab the girls.

"Regrettably," I say, "it is."

"Of course," says Concepcion.

Carew says he wants something with a little dignity.

"Is there a family?" says Concepcion.

"No," says Carew.

"Would you like a viewing, a reposing?" says Concepcion.

"Where?" I say.

"We could have it here," he says, "or we could rent a neighborhood chapel."

"Let's see what it looks like here," I say.

"Of course," says Concepcion. "This way."

I get up out of my chair. Concepcion leads the way, into the hall. I look at the photographs of his little girl, the pile of tapes of Tito Puente, the picture of a knowledgeable, trusting sort who looks like he's devoted a life to the horses. Underneath it there's a small, cheap plaque that says, Albert Hraboski. Carew stops me as I'm about to leave.

"Stargell," he says, "I want it to look right."

"I know," I say.

We climb the stairs and walk into a small, stuffy room. It seems like a hotel lobby. There's a couple of chairs, a sofa, some potted plants, an imitation fireplace. I can feel the men and women who have passed through here, their heads filled with visions, of sons and daughters, appointments not kept, checkbooks unbalanced, of the grizzly work of sawbones, of trembling space that awaits them. There's the smell of dirty socks, the definite odor of shit.

"Look," I say, "let's talk."

Concepcion turns to me and gives me a look that makes him seem as though he'd escaped from an Arab bazaar: his face broadens, smiles. You old dope peddler, I think, you old slick-handed money king, I can talk to you, all right. Where's your camel, your desert horse, and your long silver rifle? He says, "Ah," and it makes me think of a time-lapse flower, a slow and beautiful thing.

"Of course," says Concepcion.

I sniff the air. Next to the reposing room, the cheap hotel lobby, there's a long line of wooden seats. It's the chapel, I think, that's what it is. I walk into the reposing room and sit down on one of the greenish chairs. The color is perfect, probably absorbs salty water the best. Plastic covers would be better, but they sweat. Concepcion sits opposite me. I sniff the air again.

"We usually spray."

I want to grab Concepcion by his heels, want to shake him until he tells me what he needs. He's in control, Stargell. I feel like I'm in a nuclear submarine where the coffee is made by computer. Mildew, mold, shit. It stinks in here. I can hear the generations weeping, moaning, can see the blank faces staring at the lights above them, can see, too, the gladness, the life-race winners thinking, Well, there's another I outlived, there's another weak bastard who doesn't measure up.

I'd like to go to a send-off myself, would like to grab the stiff, the dead body, and say, You miserable scum, you got your ticket punched. What are you going to do now?

Lamb chops, I think.

"Let's talk," I say.

Concepcion smiles. I hold my cardboard box on my lap. Concepcion sits down opposite me.

"About what?" he says.

The smile is still there. He seems to have been waiting for me all his life, as though he knew I was going to show up here with a blind man and a cage filled with birds, that I'd come around in my wrinkled suit, holding my cardboard box and say, Let's talk.

"How much?" I say.

"Money?" says Concepcion.

His thin fingers almost, but not quite, begin to rub one against the other.

I nod.

"Well," says Concepcion, "there's removal of the remains, a casket, reposing, flowers, chapel, minister, a plot . . ."

Real estate, I think. Those boys never give up.

"What about a plot?" I say.

"They're going for next to nothing in Jersey," he says. "Three hundred dollars."

Now we're getting down to cases, I think. I can see the New Jersey ash pits, those waves of burning garbage pushed by gray machines, the gray gulls moving in the sky that's as thick as a dust-bowl windstorm. Three hundred bucks! I think of Carew's sculpture, and then I know he wouldn't see the beauty there, out by the airport. No, Stargell, that'll never do. We're in the Astroturf league, all right.

"Jersey won't do," I say.

Concepcion raises an eyebrow: it looks like a cat taking a stretch.

"Carew may be blind," I say, "but he can still smell."

"Ah," says Concepcion. "Of course."

His eyes are miracles in themselves. I feel as surly as an Indian with magic over the bullet. Concepcion, I think, you're not dealing with some death hick. I've got the juju, Jack, and don't you forget it. I know Concepcion's thinking, Maybe we could do something to the blink, fuck up his nose and bury his friend right in the stink belt.

"Look here," I say. "How about a thousand dollars? One box, one plot, one limousine."

Concepcion looks at me for a moment, then sadly shakes his head. It doesn't seem that he's sad about the money, but that I could consider such a cheap outrage. It is an insult not only to him, but on his house. In Concepcion's eyes you can see generations of angry desert people, turning slowly in their graves.

"Fifteen hundred," he says, "and I'm doing your friend a favor."

"I thank you for it," I say. I can hear the bazaar around us, the braying camels, can smell the fragrant silks, the musk of beautiful women, the rustling of spices, the odor of honey, the dust of ancient carpets. "But I can't pay more than a thousand."

Concepcion flinches a little.

"My people have always been generous," he says. "Twelve fifty."

"Nope," I say.

I shake my head, hold my package in my lap.

"Maybe," says Concepcion, "we can come to some accommodation."

He puts the tips of his fingers together. I sit opposite him, feel the presence of the people who have passed through this room, their whispered, airy trace, the composite shit stink of them, the beauty of their desires: all of them say, I want a piece of chocolate cake, that beautiful woman (do you see the way the silk clings to her thighs?), one more sunrise, one more milk shake, the end of God's sidereal distance. Wouldn't they have liked to sit around when the will was read? The chairs, the walls, the imitation fireplace, have a solid quality, if only because they've been around for so many farewells. Concepcion and I sit in the odor and stare at one another. I'm squeezing my juju so hard it squeaks.

Concepcion sighs, shrugs his shoulders, and says, "There's always cremation."

"Yes," I say.

Concepcion cocks his head.

"What about ashes?" I say.

"Put them in an urn," he says, "or spread them."

I nod.

"How much?" I say.

He waits, inhales, smells the others who have already made the trip, gives me the double-barrel glance.

"You're a hard case," says Concepcion.

"How much?"

I can hear him thinking: it's as though someone were rattling ball bearings around in a cigar box. There's a transient atmosphere in the room, one that would be recognized by any traveling salesman. These are humble beginnings, I think, but beginnings nevertheless. Maybe Concepcion has big plans, maybe one day he'll quick-freeze millionaires and shoot them at the sun in a rocket, and all the bodyguards and mistresses and wives and sycophants will have to go along for the ride. People from the desert understand such matters.

Concepcion sighs.

"Check?" he says.

"Cash," I say. "Tens and twenties."

This cheers him up. As a matter of fact, he smiles again. The grief racket wasn't looking so good for a moment, I think, but he's coming around now.

"What would you say," he says, "to seven hundred and fifty dollars?"

He says "dollars" like "sons." I have five hundred sons.

"You've got yourself a deal," I say.

He doesn't blink. We rise from the reposing room and walk downstairs. Concepcion is careful to turn out every light: the darkness makes the stink worse. We glide down the stairs. Concepcion moves before me, leads me down to the hall, the fluorescent light, the imitation paneling. I see Carew sitting before the desk, holding his birds. He blinks in the light, waits, is wet from the snow and still a little drunk, but he's braced up, and is holding the cage rigidly in his lap. He hears us when we come in, looks up with an expectant, proud glance.

"It doesn't look so good," I say.

Concepcion stiffens.

"No?" says Carew.

"No," I say.

"This is, you know," says Carew, "a cheap place."

Concepcion shows his stuff, his proud lineage, his tolerance for such insults. His head moves back with one quick, aristocratic twitch, which makes me think someone had maligned the lineage of his horse.

"I know," I say.

"What are we going to do?" says Carew.

The birds rock back and forth. Carew looks in my direction.

"Cremation," I say.

"Oh," says Carew.

We sit for a while. Concepcion explains that it can be done quickly.

"Beggars can't be choosers," says Carew.

Carew's hanging on, too. I can feel the city now, cool and distant. I want to talk to Barbeau, want to say, I love you, I love you. The next day I won't believe a word of it. Stargell, my boy, she won't either. But we'll feel the desire again, the need for one another, and we'll know that it's as elusive as perfection. What trouble we'll make before Concepcion and the boys get their slick hands on us.

"Can they, Stargell?" says Carew.

No, Carew, they can't. But we'll get around it. We'll spring Frenchy from the morgue, take a cab to Central Park, and I'll get a shovel and we'll plant him right there in a softball field.

"What about the ashes?" says Concepcion.

"Stargell?" says Carew.

"You want an urn," I say.

"What the hell am I going to do with an urn?" says Carew.

It's decided. The ashes will be scattered. I take the envelope from my pocket and count out seven hundred and fifty dollars. Concepcion looks as happy as a Cadillac taking on gas.

Well, Frenchy, I think, here's your share.

"It'll be done on Monday," says Concepcion. "Over the ocean."

"From a plane?" says Carew.

"Yes," says Concepcion.

Carew hesitates for a moment. I look at the paneling, the pictures of Concepcion's little girl, the pile of business cards.

"I want to go along," says Carew, "in the airplane."

Concepcion shows his desert blood, the desire to maintain propriety, the business-as-usual slickness. But I can see Carew, sitting in the airplane with a small package in his lap, feeling the speed, the takeoff sprint as the plane rises into the air. The blue Atlantic will creep over the horizon, will push against the city, and right there, at that point, when the city can still be seen, when it is just an ugly smear, something that looks like lichen on the smooth blue stone, the pilot, a man wearing dark glasses who has a nose like a hawk's, will say, Do it here. The engine will make that steady drone, one with gentle undulations, and the light will come off the wing like a sword: quick and sharp. The pilot will open a small window and the wind will come into the cockpit. I can see the second set of controls moving as though the plane were being piloted by a ghost. The light will be so bright, so piercing, that Carew will be able to see a pale luminescence, like the first few moments of foggy dawn. Then he will pick up the package, will untie the string, and find the small canister there. The pilot will bank, will stare impassively through his dark lenses, dreaming of the squirm, the quick, grasping movement of a beautiful woman, whose lips are as soft as the clouds, and then Carew will lean forward, into the cold wind, will feel his arm buffeted as he reaches into it with the canister, bracing himself against the speed and turning the canister with its mouth toward the tail of the plane. One quick puff, and that's all. The pilot and Carew will fly back to the city, feeling a little dust in the cockpit. Carew will sit with his hands in his lap, blinking in the light, listening to the gentle undulations in the pitch of the engine.

I look at Concepcion, give him the high sign, but he ignores me, intent on the desert's way of doing things.

"That was not in the agreement," he says.

"I want to go in the airplane," says Carew.

He squeezes his hands together when he says this, and I'm thinking, Don't worry, Carew, we're not going to let this filthy camel dealer screw you out of your rights. The birds tip back and

forth on their perch. Concepcion looks at me and shows me his
bazaar smile, his you-stepped-in-the-shit grin.

All right, I think.

"We did not agree," says Concepcion.

I hold up my fingers, a five and then an O. Concepcion doesn't
even see me. His eyes are set on the shimmering heat of the
desert, on the moving, quicksilver air.

"I want to go," says Carew. His hands are clinched and he
looks as determined as a junkyard.

I hold one finger and two zeros. Concepcion blinks a little,
pretends he sees some minor distraction on the horizon. He is a
cool bastard, no doubt about it, Stargell. I don't know whether I
should shake his hand or break his jaw. Maybe both.

All right, you white slaver, I think, you flesh merchant.

I flash up two fingers and two zeros.

I can hear the camels grunt and snort, can smell the haze of
hashish, the fragrance of cloth on the bolt. Concepcion doesn't
even look at me. He just puts out his hand and I count out the
two hundred dollars and drop them in. He doesn't count it, but
he knows it's right. Finally he puts it away and smiles at me
again.

"It can be arranged," he says.

"Glad to hear it," I say.

Carew looks relieved. Concepcion smiles broadly now: everyone's ancestors have been appeased.

"Come here on Monday," says Concepcion. "I will have the
remains."

Concepcion says this with a certain amount of desert pride. It's
his end of the bargain.

"How's he going to get to the airport?" I say.

Concepcion bristles a little.

"I will drive him," he says.

"Ah," I say. "What kind of car have you got?"

He looks as though he'd been slapped in the face, as though he
felt the first squeak of an earthquake. Yes, I think, you smug
money grubber, that's where you live, all right.

"A late-model Plymouth," he says.

"Is that good enough?" I say to Carew.

He blinks, holds on to the cage.

"Sure," says Carew.

"Good," I say to Concepcion. He has recovered, but you can see he's thinking about buying a new car. What about a Maserati, I think, a Ferrari? Which does Allah prefer his servants to drive?

I pick up my package. I can still smell the odor from upstairs, the lingering fragrance of the send-off. I shake Concepcion's hand: I'm not squeamish. I give it a good squeeze. See there, I think, I'm not afraid of you. We are men of honor.

"Monday then," I say, "at noon."

Concepcion nods. I look into his split-coal eyes. His nostrils flare and he stands as sternly as a young sheik who's just been slapped. He knows I'm thinking, Look here, you rotten thief, you handmaiden of sorrow, you salaried scum, just let one thing go wrong with this deal and I'll come back and feed you to the neighborhood's hungry dogs.

"You can trust me," says Concepcion.

"I know it," I say.

We're still looking at one another.

"Come on," I say to Carew. "It's time to go."

Concepcion nods.

"You can trust me," he says.

I believe the young desert rat. What the hell, I think, we speak the same language. I feel as though I've been in the desert all my life, where I watched the dunes and sky and cleaned the tin plates with sand. Carew and I walk down the hall, pass the panels of imitation wood, the fluorescent lights, another portrait of Hraboski, the patron saint of Yonkers Raceway. Concepcion walks us to the door.

"Until Monday," he says.

I want to give him Allah's blessing, but I don't. Carew and I are left in the cold air beneath the neon sign. After the door closes, the music begins again.

I carry my box and Carew is holding his birdcage.

"Let's look for a flop," says Carew.

Stargell, I think, one more good pop on the head and the secret of the universe will be yours: soon I'll be able to inhale the shit stink, will be able to wrap myself in the dirty sheets of a concentration camp hospital and listen to Mozart, will tremble and rock and shed tears, will feel the lightning strike: the convulsion will take me and through its ravaging knocking, its pins-and-needles roar, through the vomit and clinging dread, I will say, Fantastic. So that's it.

"I know a cheap flop," says Carew.

The money's about gone. Seven hundred and fifty left.

I feel like getting down on my hands and knees in the snow and moaning, praying out loud, I don't care what you do with me, Lord, but just don't turn me into another crackpot mystic with a beard. I want a house-trailer beauty and raw liquor and we'll fuck in front of the color TV.

We pass windows filled with oversize cooking utensils, ovens and stoves, spatulas you could row a boat with.

"It don't cost hardly nothing," says Carew.

We stand underneath a bright, flashing sign that says "Sunshine, Sunshine, Sunshine." The entrance is a double door. On the left is a boarded-up storefront. On the right is a bar. We walk straight through the doors and down a long hall which has, at the end, a desk, a man in a cage. It's warmer inside, but it still hurts to walk. The birds look like balls of fluff. The man in the cage is about fifty-five and he has a bald head, white side hair, a hearing aid: he seems to be white rather than flesh colored, so pale that he'd disappear if he stood in the snow. He looks up, turns on his hearing aid, squeezes his battery to get a little more juice. He puts down his copy of *Guns and Ammo*.

"How are you, Carew?" he says.

"All right," says Carew.

"Glad to hear that," says the man. He looks at me.

"This is Stargell," says Carew. Then he points at the man in the cage. "That's Gentle Willie."

"Hello," says Gentle Willie. "I heard you had an apartment, Carew."

"Yeah," says Carew. "I did."

"Well," says Gentle Willie, "that's too bad. But there's always room for you here."

Gentle Willie turns his white face on me, then on Carew's birds.

"We don't allow pets, Carew," he says.

Carew holds on to his cage.

"They can't make much more of a mess than the people who stay here," says Carew. "I'll pay a full share."

Gentle Willie begins to chuckle.

"Well," says Gentle Willie, "just for tonight."

There's a clock above Gentle Willie's head: 3 A.M.

"You got beds?" says Carew.

"No," says Gentle Willie. "You'll have to take a wait."

"O.K.," says Carew.

We each slide fifty cents across. There really isn't a lobby, because the cage is set back into the end of the hall. There's not even a chair. The fluorescence makes everything look a little buzzy, as though the whole place were traveling in time and was almost, but not quite, stopped. Gentle Willie goes back to his copy of *Guns and Ammo*. We walk into the staircase, up steps covered with linoleum the color of fresh spinach.

"I heard Frenchy bought the ranch," says Gentle Willie.

"Yeah," says Carew.

Carew walks with a comfortable, familiar step. The birds are in their cage, shaking, warming up. We climb one flight and come to the landing, a large room, one that's about twenty-five feet square. There are four iron posts in the floor and from each post to a wall on the other side of the room there is a rope. The ropes are held taut by a ratchet on the top of each post. There isn't much light in the room, but I can see that twelve or so men are sleeping there: it looks like a bunch of clothes have been hung from the ropes to dry. Most men have a jacket or a piece of cloth to use as a pillow. I stand before them, feel the dreams flitting about the room, as strangely affecting as fish in dark water, the little ones that just brush your legs. Occasionally I can feel a monster stirring, something from the blind depths. The snoring is ragged, blubbery. By the dim light, through the rank steamy air, it seems as though the men have already been through Concepcion's hands, that this is the last stage in some old Egyptian process.

Carew and I find an almost empty length of rope. I hang up his birdcage for him, and then Carew pops off like a cork out of a bottle. Both his arms hang over the rope and his jacket has been pulled up for a pillow.

"Good night, Stargell," he says.

I stare into the darkness, listen to the sleeping men. I can see their dreams, the Technicolor epics, stinging landscapes, a bridge that sways in a blue-green marsh. There are space men, too, and they have landed in the Hudson River. The dreamers row out in boats and look into the clear water and see the creatures, men in glassine globes, their arms cut off at the elbow so they look like paddles: the atmosphere in the globes is one of half-burned newspapers and deformity. I look around the room, see split bald heads, long, gray, and greasy hair, smashed noses: everyone is breathing through a gimpy horn. They're still alive, Stargell, they're still making trouble. I see the Hudson, the rowboats, the creatures in the globes, and then the western lands, the fields that are open and ready for the first seeds. Everything is ticking. The trees are watching the length of the days and soon they will erupt, will chop into the air, the oaks and ash being so coolly concerned with the length of the days. The fertilizer is harsh and it burns your eyes and throat, and it seems as vile as the shit stink of Concepcion's but the farmers spread it, each saying to himself, There will be no late frost this year. It doesn't take long: I'm in Paris, walking up the steps of a house I know there, the two-story building with the yellow walls, with the trees over the garden. I am greeted by a woman with auburn hair. We sit in the living room and I say, My God, I've missed you. She's smiling, even though she's been miserable, is able to smile even though the misery is still there, and then I see she's crying and I say, My darling, my darling. She's glad I've come to see her. My darling, I say. It's been bad for me, too. I know just how you feel.

The ratchets are released with a sound like someone throwing a handful of ball bearings down a drainpipe. I wake, flying through the air, just find the time to put out my hands.

"Happy Easter, boys," says Gentle Willie.

Stargell, I think, it's a good thing they don't let you sleep all day around here. Carew twitches and flops next to me: he's been dreaming of fish. I put out my hand and he stops. Gentle Willie moves to the other posts, releases the ratchets. The men hit the floor. Everyone is grumbling. In some places there is a pile of groggy, coughing, and snorting men: they were stunned even before they woke up. They squirm, try to sort themselves out. I hear one man say to another, in a voice that sounds as though it were made with old beer cans, "You're standing on my hernia, you dumb cocksucker." They're already kicking, surly as hell, and I'm thinking, Let everyone know you're pissed off. It only comes to a little pushing and shoving. I give Carew his birds, pick up my package. We walk to the rear of the room, where there's a bathtub: everyone pisses into it and then goes downstairs.

"Everybody out," says Gentle Willie.

He turns off his hearing aid.

The sky is A-bomb bright. The other men tromp in the snow, join in ragged formation. Somebody's got a line on Sunday-morning booze, or a little sweet wine, an eye-opener.

Carew and I stand in front of the hotel.

"You coming on Monday?" says Carew.

"Yes," I say.

"It's a beautiful sky," says Carew.

I'm squinting like an Eskimo: the light is enough to knock me into the seeing eye dog market.

"I'll be there on Monday," I say.

"Stargell," says Carew. "I want to take this occasion to offer my thanks."

He walks down the street, into the snow that's as crunchy as old cake frosting. He passes the institutional fry-pans, carries the birds. The cage swings from his arm. Beyond him I can see the twin towers, the World Trade Center, rigid as Samurai, cold, filled with secrets. Carew recedes, walking carefully, trying to avoid the fireplugs. He just disappears, is absorbed by the light, the brightness that's as hard as polished steel.

I stop at the Hotel Jax, pick up my bag, go to the Port Authority bus station and shave in the bathroom. I can smell the buses. The bathroom is as big as a factory, one that does assembly line surgery. I brush off my coat, straighten my tie, brush my teeth.

Well, Stargell, I think, you look like hell.

The atmosphere isn't the best: it feels like they give cheap electroshock here.

I take the subway downtown: everyone is dressed to please. Easter bonnets. The kids are carrying chocolate rabbits and the rabbits are beginning to melt.

I climb the stairs and knock on a door. Jack the Ripper opens it.

"Stargell," he says. "I didn't think you were going to make it."

"Happy Easter," I say.

"The same to you."

It seems Jack has gotten bigger over the last few days, and it's certain he's gotten uglier. Zipper marks on his hands and face. He's wearing a purple suit and a green tie.

"Come in," he says.

I walk into the living room and sit down.

"Your suit could use a little pressing, Stargell," he says.

I sit in a chair opposite the equipment, the chrome cases in which there are twitchy needles and knobs and various sliding scales. The speakers look like the black part of a target you can shoot at from two hundred yards.

Jack looks at my package.

"What's that?" he says.

"A present," I say, "for you."

This cheers him up. I don't think Jack gets presents. He goes into the kitchen and takes a bottle out of the icebox. Sparkling

Burgundy. Jack, I think, you've outdone yourself. I can't wait for a glass of that pink rot. Jack opens the bottle, fills two strange-looking glasses, and hands one to me. Jack puts the record on. We toast one another.

"Here," I say.

The music hasn't started yet: a touch of the finger will do that. Jack picks up the box, shakes it a little. He has a theatrical approach to presents. He's saying, I wonder what this could be. Maybe, I think, I'll check into a motel in the middle of the New Jersey ash pits and watch color TV.

Jack drops the cardboard, the gray waffle packing.

"Stargell," he says. "A Minuteman bell!"

I nod, sip the wine.

"It'll fit right into my system," he says.

What could be better? I think.

"Thanks, Stargell," he says. "I didn't think you could get one. I thought the Arabs were leaving us all the shit."

Jack holds the bell up to the light. The metal has been polished: the disk itself is twenty-three inches across. I wish I had had it engraved, but I didn't have the time. I hold the sparkling Burgundy to my ear, listen to the seafoam pop. Jack the Ripper hits the button and we sail right into the Longines Symphonette Society's great moments in music. He slaps the volume right up there in the police-alert range, but I don't think anyone in the building cares. Down the block they're not so kind. Over there, they're thinking, That big ugly wop is playing that shit again. But not me. I sit back in a white plastic chair that looks like a huge egg and let the music break over me. The trembling takes me right in the middle of Tchaikovsky's First Piano Concerto.

"What's the matter, Stargell?" says Jack the Ripper. "You paid the fucking money. They ain't going to hurt you."

I watch the dials, feel the electricity flow.

"What are you crying for, Stargell?" says Jack.

"It's the music," I say.

"Yeah," says Jack. "I know what you mean."

By the time we get to Chopin, I'm chattering like a toaster that's gone amok, and at Beethoven I'm crying and laughing. Jack the Ripper is as stern as a piece of pipe. He takes his pleasures a little more seriously than I do. Stargell, I think, you've got to keep running, or the fucking desert people will get you. I see them loping over the sands on the camels, their silver rifles shimmering in the heat. The Ninth comes to an end.

Someone is knocking at the door. Jack opens it and I see Enid standing in the hall: she looks as crazy as a fifty-cent whore.

"I knew you'd be here," she says. She's holding Western Union's envelope by a corner. "This came for you."

She drops it into my hands and goes upstairs. Enid ignores Jack the Ripper, and that's a good trick. I can hear her upstairs, stomping around and moving the furniture. It sounds like she's having a barroom brawl. You'll get it to look right, I think, and when you do, start praying.

I open the envelope.

Come soon, it says.

I stand in the cool, time-travel air of the terminal. The women at the counter stare at me as though I were a hijacker. Stargell, my boy, they have every right to be suspicious. I can hear the cheers of the plastic surgeons and real estate brokers when I look at the ticket women: each one has been fixed, each has paid a little something for a piece of East Hampton, you know, down by the beach. I haven't got a reservation. We haggle. They don't like the desperation in my voice since it doesn't match the nothing-ever-goes-wrong atmosphere of the airport. Everyone seems to be thinking, We're all on TV. What's wrong with you? But I stare them down. As I look at the perfect woman who is touching the keys of the computer terminal, I think, I'm the wreck who makes you beautiful. Without me you'd look like a screwy bug.

They give me a ticket, and I walk through the crowded tunnels, feel the processed air, the wonderful awkwardness of people saying goodbye. I sit for a moment in a white chair, something that looks like a pedestal from Houston, Texas. I run my fingers along its smooth surface, and I think of a job I did in New Jersey. An injection-molding factory (one that made rubber dolls) had turned out ten thousand baby manikins that looked like thalidomide cases. The Slasher told me to take a look. When I arrived, the parking lot was half filled with the little monsters, all knobby on the arms and legs. Look at all those sick dolls, I thought, just look at them. I got in touch with an injection-molding whiz (he was another *Hunk* man, a correspondent who was as screwy as Jolting Joe: every couple of months the whiz would order a new Japanese bride) and the problem was solved. Our polymer man showed the factory's polymer man where he was making a mistake. Too much viscosity for the machines. As I walked away from the factory, through the factory, and past the pile of dolls, I saw a man who was about forty years old and who had large ears and sideburns and a six-day beard, and who wore a coat lined with a blanket, a cap with flaps, glasses with one arm held to the frame by a paper clip. He was next to the pile of dolls and he was shoving them into a shopping bag. When I passed he said, "Shit, this will really make Christmas at my house."

Opposite me, on a Houston pedestal just like mine, there is a short woman. She sits with her legs dangling, her hands neatly folded over a small make-up box. I think of Enid, of a day I spent in a Groucho Marx crouch, trying to keep my eyes at the same height as hers.

"What are you doing?" said Enid, looking at me suspiciously.

"I want to see how things look to you," I said.

"Oh, oh," said Enid. "I love you."

The fact of the matter is that things seemed a little more imposing from Enid's angle. The icebox looked big enough to have football players come running out, and the back of every shelf was mysterious.

"Now you can see what it's like to drink that shitty powdered milk," said Enid.

I smell the thanatoid odor of the airplane's cabin, climb aboard, strap myself in. Maybe, Stargell, I think, this time you'll get to use the oxygen they're always promising. Then we'd feel that incandescence, all of us sucking at the yellow mask, staring at one another, our eyes popping with expectation, waiting for the blast of arctic air, the fun-house spin. You'd feel the blood jump then, Jack. That's when you'd know your skin was filled with magic.

In Los Angeles I take a taxi to the house, and we drive through the smooth streets, pass oil pumps that are humping the ground, drawing the black, clotted blood from the earth.

My father is lying on the sofa, touching himself under the blanket that will no longer keep him warm. When he sees me he nods lazily. The old man is watching the sun as though it were the news. When he looks at me I feel like I'm expanding and contracting, growing young, growing old. The TV blats. I sit next to him, realize that through his underwater haze, through the drugs, he's still straining, still shaking his head. He drifts for a moment, but then picks up where he left off. We sit together for ten minutes or so, the old man coming and going like a pendulum, always arriving at the same defiant point, where he trembles, grimaces, almost breaks into the silk-dress smile.

It's a mild, pleasant night, and my father wakes from his nap.

"I'd like to go outside," he says.

My mother and I help him into the backyard, where he sits in the hydrocarbon, caressing air, smelling the eucalyptus. Down below and in the distance you can see a studio's back lot. Some work is being done tonight, and it looks like there is a pile of flares in the middle of the sets.

"I wonder what they're making," says my mother.

"I don't know," I say.

"A western," says my father. His words slur. "That's what they make."

My father rubs his side.

"I've been over there," he says.

He shifts a shoulder toward the back lot.

"Everything's built back to back," he says.

I can feel his inconstant, drifting presence. He thinks of the sets, a western town on one side, a side street of New York on another, igloos and ice against the back of an English country home. The old man seems to swing from Paris to Pittsburgh, from the deck of an aircraft carrier to an African village. Thatched huts, dirt floors, clear skies overhead.

Later, inside, my father sips a little tea. My mother and I sit at a table and eat our food. My father gets into bed.

During the days I sit with him on the sofa, feel him push into the light when (in the morning) it strikes the room. He dozes, sleeps, snores. That's right, I think, rattle the screws right out of their hinges.

After he's been awake for a while his head begins to tilt slowly backward, a little bit at a time, as though it were on a ratchet, or jack, dropping, then catching when he comes to. My father wakes and looks at me and he knows I'm asking, Do you want me to stop it? I'll do that for you. I'll go out to the garage and get something heavy like a piece of pipe and I'll stop it. I'll do it right: you'll just think someone slammed the door. Bang! And then, when it's over, when he's loosy-goosy dead, I'll wrap him in his blanket and say, Do you see this? Do you? This was my father and he was a good man. But he looks at me with eyes that are white in the pupil, almost completely drug bleached now, and he's saying, No, I don't want that. I'm alone now, he says, and what I'm doing has nothing to do with you or anyone else. Stay here, boy, and keep your hands out where I can see them.

Yes, Stargell, that's it. We'll sit in the sunlight and the last thing we'll say is, Fuck you. Being alive is like praying.

So we sit together and I can feel his trembling in the sofa. We spend days before the insane blatting of the television.

In the evening my mother says to me, in the kitchen, over our cold meal, "He never liked to have someone say no to him. It made him mad."

Our silver makes an empty, rattling sound in the house, a grating, blackboard screech.

My mother says, "What's wrong?"

"I just don't feel right," my father says. "Take me to the hospital."

He speaks clearly, but I know he sees the buzzing edge, the light that seems to come from a neon lamp that isn't working very well.

"They'll know what to do," he says.

He puts on his jacket, a pair of slacks. I can see his swollen ankles when he gets into the car. My mother drives. I wait in the house.

It happens quickly: he dies staring at a white ceiling. The body is taken from the hospital and burned.

My mother comes home and we have a quiet party and both of us get a little smashed. I drink cold beer, look out the window, see the lights of the valley.

"We had wonderful times," says my mother.

She takes a picture out of her pocketbook, shows it to me: there's the old man, standing in the buff in some banana trees.

"That was taken in Mexico," she says.

Ah, I think, at least they didn't grow old gracefully. The two of them were running around in the banana trees, eating and drinking, doing the best they could.

In the morning I get up early and drive to the beach, take off my clothes, and swim. The Pacific is cool, rough. I swim out through the breakers, feel the sand moving so quickly it cuts my legs. The iodine smell, the seaweed odor, the salt, are bracing. The water turns white where the wave breaks, where I swim like hell and catch one: I keep kicking, hold my chest and belly out of the clear, soft water. The speed is amazing. I move across the wave, kicking, always staying in the rising, clear water, feeling the cold spray, hearing the wave tear itself apart. I turn, allow myself to be pulled into the white water, the layer of foam that's three feet thick. The bubbles snap, break around my eyes, on my skin. I turn and swim beyond the waves, float for a moment, feel the beasts in the water beneath me, beyond me, at the horizon. I remember seeing whales there when I was a child. I wait for the long, rising wave, hear the crackling roar (so much like brush fire), feel the quick fall, the foam. The wave washes me up on the beach. I sit on a towel. There's no one around. I stare at the Pacific, the swells that have come all the way from Japan. The water dries on my skin, leaves it salty, taut. I dress and drive up the coast a ways and stop at a bar. It's one of those places where you can look out at the ocean. I have a beer and when I drink it I can hear the snap of the Pacific. I think of the speed of the wave, the acceleration, the sound it made, and I think, too, of Enid's poor fears, Barbeau, of my father, his orchids, plants, his hands, of the restaurant where he smiled at a woman, of how much he enjoyed being alive: his ashes were scattered over the Pacific. I feel my taut, salty skin. Maybe that's a little of the old bastard right there, I think, rubbing some of the white residue between my fingers. Maybe that's him.

I pay for the beer, drive home. The house is filled with friends, relatives: everyone looks like he's escaped from someplace. I smile, have a snack with them, realize I'm not needed. I say goodbye to my mother, pack my bag, take a cab to the airport.

From a phone booth on the street in New York I call Enid.

"Hello," she says.

"Hello," I say. "How are things?"

"Good," she says.

We listen to the noise the telephone company makes.

"There's a letter for you," she says, "from my father. Why don't you pick it up?"

I walk the few blocks to the apartment. The afternoon is smoky, trapped in skim-milk light, dusty air: it needs a breeze, kite-hard, you know, one that cleans the city and makes all things seem possible again.

"How are things in California?" says Enid.

"Over," I say.

"Oh," says Enid.

I stand at the threshold that's as familiar as old clothes. Enid speaks through a crack in the door.

"I never liked your father," says Enid.

"I know," I say.

He'd come to New York and we'd had dinner together. He asked Enid if she was going to finish her food and that made her mad.

"I want to tell you something, Stargell," says Enid.

"Can I come in?" I say.

"No," says Enid. "If you come in you'll just bother me. I don't trust you. But I wanted to tell you that I forgive you."

I can see that she's wearing high-heeled shoes and stockings with her robe.

"I'm going to get a job," she says. "I saw an advertisement. I will work for a film producer. We will make decisions about films.

Failing that, I will become a pilot. I have called about taking flying lessons."

Over her shoulder I can see the apartment is almost filled with the small boxes that Chinese food comes in. There is a path from the bathroom to the bedroom. There are also a number of dead soldiers, empty bottles. Enid pokes a letter out the door, holds it with the tips of her fingers, as though it were possible to catch Ari's dose from the paper. I take the envelope from her and put it into my pocket. Enid closes the door and I can hear the water running in the kitchen sink as Enid washes her hands. She stares into the mirror over the sink and sings, Baby, baby, I love you.

Downstairs I push against the building's doors: they open as easily as an old whore's legs, and they seem to have the same spirit, too. I'm glad to be here, they seem to say, and look at that, would you. I move as easily as a rocking chair. There are two young policemen on the sidewalk and their car is parked in front of the fire hydrant. The Barber is sitting in his store, staring out the window, making some sign: he is holding one hand in the air, and two of its fingers are hanging toward the counter. The Barber is making them move back and forth and he is mouthing one word over and over again. Well, Stargell, I think, Smiling Mary's finally taken her well-earned revenge. She's knocked the filthy brute's brains out, and now he's just sitting in his store, waggling his fingers and crying for help. The breeze picks up and I can smell New Jersey. Smiling Mary is standing behind the Barber, and she's looking at me with her most severe flinch: one eye is closed and the other's brow is raised so high her forehead is furrowed. She just stares at me while the Barber spends his time acting like an idiot. I want to say, Where did you hit him, my darling? Smiling Mary holds her hand up, too, and begins to make that same strange, two-fingered waggling. How about that, I think, both of them have short-circuited. Smiling Mary mouths one word, once, the same as the Barber's, and since it's the only thing she's ever said to me I watch her carefully. She's saying, "Run."

One of the cops holds up his fingers and makes the same running motion, and the other looks at me as though he had paid fifty cents for the peep. Well, Stargell, I think, you're all grown up now. Even these two property drones are younger than you. Not by much, though.

"Is your name Stargell?" says the peep show cop.

"That depends . . ." I say.

"That's him," says the other.

Up the street, in the milky light, there's a man sitting on a chrome chair that has a green plastic-marble seat. The chair is tipped back and the man who's sitting on it weighs three hundred and fifty pounds. He's eating an orange and his stomach is so large he can put the peels on it, as though he had a little shelf. Look at him, Stargell, just look. I think for a moment of making a run for it, of dashing down the street while the soft bullets flatten against the brick, of sprinting right past the huge fellow on the chrome chair.

"No you don't," says Peep Show.

The small ratchets in the handcuffs click, and then I feel like I'm all shoulders since my hands are behind my back. They advise me (it's sound advice, really, be careful what you say, that's my motto), shove me into the back seat, close the door. Peep Show gets in with me. The other cop drives. He starts the engine and I can hear its deep and throaty sound.

"Hey," I say to Peep Show. "Will you do me a favor?"

"Sure," says Peep Show.

"There's a letter in my pocket," I say. "Will you open it?"

"Is that all right?" he says to the driver.

"What?" says the driver.

"Can I open his letter?"

"Sure," says the driver. "Open it up for him."

Peep Show picks the envelope out of my pocket, knocks the contents to one side, rips open the end. He blows into the ragged tear, makes the paper flap. Peep Show peers inside, and I know he's thinking, What kind of mail does the prisoner get? Hmmm? Nice letters from the little lady?

"There isn't any letter in here," he says.

He sounds disappointed.

I lean next to him and nod my head at the envelope.

"What's that?" I say.

Peep Show sticks his fingers into the envelope and pulls out a newspaper clipping. It's about two feet long and a foot wide, and it's printed with type that's as thick as a ruler. The headline is in Greek, and Peep Show stares at it.

"Do you know Russian?" he says.

"No," I say.

He holds it up and at the bottom I can see the translation written in Ari's meticulous (but excited) hand: CRIME WAVE SWEEPS ATHENS. HA!

"What's that say?" says Peep Show.

"Can you turn on the light," I say to the driver, "and go a little faster?"

The car is a nice new one, but it already has that asylum stench. The driver smiles for a moment, as though he's flirted with a few hundred horses himself: Stargell, my boy, I think, he knows what you want.

"Sure," says the driver, with that same sly smile.

The car takes off and I can feel the drag-strip jump, the sucking embrace of the seat. The siren begins to wail. Give it the gas, I think, put it right to the floor.